Rave Reviews for *Picket Fence*

"Cates weaves a tantalizing and emotional tale that strums the heartstrings and keeps the reader spellbound until the joyful, gratifying ending."
—*Booklist*

"Forgiveness and acceptance are key elements in this outstanding new family drama, which offers the deep insight into the human soul and the touching story that are hallmarks of a Cates novel. 4 ½ stars."
—*Romantic Times BOOKclub*

"Kimberly Cates provides a discerning look at love offering its healing power if only the lead trio would take a chance."
—Harriet Klausner

More Praise for Kimberly Cates

"One of the brightest stars of the romance genre."
—*New York Times* bestselling author Iris Johansen

"Kimberly Cates is an extraordinary storyteller."
—Jill Barnett, author of *Sentimental Journey*

"A truly gifted storyteller."
—*Romantic Times BOOKclub*

"Kimberly Cates takes readers on a heartwarming journey of secrets, emotional upheaval, and the meaning of unconditional love."
—*Romantic Times BOOKclub* on
The Mother's Day Garden

Also from Kimberly Cates and HQN Books
Picket Fence

KIMBERLY CATES

THE GAZEBO

H
HQN™

ISBN 0-373-77051-0

THE GAZEBO

www.HQNBooks.com

Printed in U.S.A.

To my daughter Kate, the most beautiful bride ever, and to Kevin, the son I always dreamed of.
Here's to Happily Ever After!

CHAPTER 1

THE SMALL WHITE HOUSE at the end of Linden Lane didn't look like the kind of place where secrets lived. But no one in the river town of Whitewater, Illinois, knew better than Deirdre McDaniel that appearances could be deceiving.

The lawn was manicured with military precision. No dandelion had dared invade from behind enemy lines—the yard of the neighbor, whose lackadaisical attitude toward weed control had been the bane of Deirdre's father's existence.

She wasn't sure which would have hurt worse—seeing her childhood home down at the heels, the way vacant properties often were, or witnessing her older brother's valiant attempt to keep the place ready for their father's inspection when the hard truth was Captain Martin McDaniel was never coming home.

Deirdre shifted the white van into park and killed the engine. Catching the inside of her full lower lip between her teeth, a nervous tick no one else could see, she stepped out of the car, her grip tightening on the keys in her hand.

Breezes tugged chin-length wisps of unruly mahogany

hair about a face too sharply drawn, with its pointed chin and high cheekbones. Eyes so intensely blue they seemed a breath away from catching fire stared at the red-painted front door. She wished there was a key somewhere among the cluster in her hand she could use to lock away her memories, but it was too late. They flooded through her, the past far more vivid than the glorious late-September day.

She could remember crushing wrinkles into her mother's crisp cotton Easter dress as she gave Emmaline McDaniel a chocolate-bunny-smeared hug. She could smell the wood shavings on her father's callused hands and hear herself wheedling her big brother, Cade, into letting her join the "boys only" club that had the coolest tree fort in the neighborhood.

She could see Spot, the ragged coal-black mutt she'd rescued, racing down the lane howling, the neighbor cat's claws dug into his back, triumphant glee on its feline face. Deirdre's father with his military bearing and loathing of weakness glowering in disgust.

If that dog was a marine we would've shot it by now.

But you couldn't shoot your daughter. Not even if she did the unforgivable.

Merry Christmas everyone. I'm pregnant... That was one Christmas no McDaniel would ever forget. Seventeen years had passed since Deirdre had made that announcement, and her stomach still turned inside out whenever she thought of it. The only small mercy in the whole ordeal: her mother hadn't been alive to hear what she'd done.

Emmaline, always the quintessential lady, would have burned with shame to see the telltale bulge of Deirdre's belly and hear the whole town buzzing that the wild McDaniel girl had gotten what was coming to her. Maybe they were right.

Deirdre quelled the old hurt welling up inside her and walked up to the familiar front door. Her hand shook so badly it took three tries to fit the key into the lock.

You don't have to do this. Cade's voice echoed in her memory as she stepped inside the house. The living room stood empty except for brighter patches of paint where pictures had hung and divots in the carpet where furniture legs had left their mark. A few boxes and some rolls of bubble wrap stood neatly in a corner, Cade's always-efficient handiwork. He would have spared her this last task, too, if Deirdre had been willing to let him.

You've got nothing to prove, he'd insisted with a hug.

But how could the family golden boy ever understand? She *did* have something to prove. To herself. And she was running out of time.

The house was for sale. She might never have another chance to make peace with the home she'd grown up in. To say goodbye to the maple tree she'd climbed down to sneak out at night, her father's workbench, her mother's petal-pink bedroom—a sanctuary Deirdre had rarely entered because *it* was tucked under the eaves. Illustrating just how big a failure Deirdre was when it came to being Emmaline McDaniel's daughter.

It was such a simple thing to hold so much pain, just an old-fashioned cedar chest with dollops of copper trim.

"This is your hope chest," Emmaline explained when Deirdre was still too young to be a disappointment. "My mother gave it to me, and her mother gave it to her. Someday you'll give it to your little girl."

"What is it hoping for?" Deirdre had asked, clambering up on top of it, the buckle on her shoe cutting a raw white scratch in the wood. Her mother's lips had tightened in a way that would grow all too familiar as she hauled Deirdre down.

"A hope chest is a place to store dreams for when you grow up," Emmaline had explained.

Deirdre remembered running grubby fingers over the smooth orange-streaked wood as she tried to imagine what dreams looked like. Would they pour out like the glitter she'd put on the cookie dough star she'd made for the Christmas tree? Would they float out, shimmering, and sprinkle her all over like fairy dust?

She'd been five years old when she was finally strong enough to wrestle the trunk's lid open and saw what was in the chest.

Every object was fitted like pieces in a giant puzzle. Old-fashioned aprons and dainty white napkins with handmade lace were painstakingly starched in neat squares. A fluffy white veil and wedding dress, every fold stuffed with tissue paper so it wouldn't crease. Silverware marched across one end of the chest in felt sleeves, and crystal vases like the ones her mother put roses in all over the house sparkled in nests of cotton batting.

Undaunted, Deirdre figured the treasure must be hidden somewhere amid all that worthless junk, like the lamp in the Aladdin story Cade had read her. If she could just find a way to unleash its magic...

One bright summer morning while her mother was tending her roses, Deirdre sneaked one of the vases from the wooden chest so she could try to pour the dream out of it. The dream she could see sparkling inside it, just out of her reach. She'd climbed up on the rocking chair by the window and stretched up on tiptoe, holding the vase as close to the sunbeam as she could, hoping to see the dream more clearly.

She could still feel the sickening sensation of wavering, losing her balance, hear the horrid smashing sound as the vase fell, striking mama's table full of delicate ladies on the way down. Shattering crystal and china released not glistening dreams, but the hard, ugly truth that made Deirdre bleed inside the way her fingers bled when she tried to scrape up the broken glass, hide it before her mother could see.

There was no point in giving a girl like Deirdre McDaniel a hope chest. She was hope*less* and not even her mother's magic chest could change her.

"Mom? Hey, Mom?"

Deirdre nearly jumped out of her skin as her own daughter's call yanked her back from memories imbedded like the slivers of crystal even her father hadn't been able to remove. They would work out from beneath her skin's surface on their own when they were good and ready, he'd promised. When it came to ignoring pain, Captain Martin McDaniel was an expert.

Deirdre braced herself as sixteen-year-old Emma burst through the door, her thick black curls tumbling halfway down her back, her heart-shaped face aglow. Love still punched Deirdre in the chest every time she looked into Emma's dark eyes, terrifying her, amazing her. It was dangerous to love anyone so much. But Deirdre had never been able to help herself.

"How in the world did you find me here?" she asked, trying not to sound as relieved as she felt not to be alone.

"I ran across the garden to Uncle Cade's. He guessed there was a chance you might be here at Grandpa's house."

"My brother the psychic." Deirdre grimaced. "I specifically told him I was coming here and I didn't need anyone to hold my hand. In fact, I seem to remember threatening to murder him if he came within a hundred yards of this old place. I'm afraid I'm going to have to kill him."

Emma groaned. "Not again. Couldn't you at least come up with something more original?"

Deirdre's chin bumped up a notch along with her aggravation. "It's not funny. I can do this. Alone." Maybe so, but she couldn't deny how grateful she was to see Emma's earnest face. *Methinks the lady doth protest too much…* What was it about having a daughter in Miss Wittich's drama class that set Shakespeare rattling around Deirdre's head? "I'm hardly going to fall apart," she asserted stubbornly.

Emma sobered. "Maybe you'd feel better if you did."

"That's your aunt Finn talking. She's always so sure she knows me better than anyone else."

"She's wrong about that." Emma regarded Deirdre with old-soul eyes so shadowed with worry that guilt twisted in Deirdre's chest. "Nobody knows you better than I do."

That's exactly what Deirdre was afraid of. It kept her up late at night, pacing through the white elephant of a house she and her sister-in-law had turned into a thriving business.

March Winds…where the past comes alive.

Finn had even incorporated the Civil War–era mansion's resident ghost into the B&B's logo—a sketch of the distinctive tower window framing the silhouette of a little girl, a candle in her hand. A brilliant marketing tool, if only Deirdre could look at it without being carried back to when Emma was ten and so terribly alone that the ghost had been the child's only friend. How could any mother ever forgive herself for that?

"Mom, for once this McDaniel-style mutiny isn't anyone's fault but mine. I have to head in to work in less than an hour and I couldn't stand to wait until the library closed to tell you the news from school."

It still blew Deirdre's mind that the news from school

was always good where Emma was concerned. For years the McDaniels had been Whitewater High's personal Bad News Bears.

"Mom, you'll never guess what Miss Wittich picked for the senior play."

The drama teacher had kept her selection under wraps for weeks, leaving her students on tenterhooks—perfect leverage to keep restless seniors from going bonkers in class. Of course, it had also put Emma through the tortures of the damned. The girl couldn't help but hope the fact she was the best actress Whitewater High had ever seen would win her the lead. But the rest of the students made no secret that homecoming queen, cheer-leader and Emma's longtime nemesis Brandi Bates was a shoo-in for top billing. Considering small-town politics, Deirdre was sure they were right.

"Don't tell me. *Sound of Music? Oklahoma?*"

Emma had been dreading some lightweight musical ever since last year's performance of *Bye Bye Birdie*. "Nope. Not a singing nun in sight."

"If it were up to me I'd have your class do *The Crucible*," Deirdre said, still stinging from the jabs Brandi and her crowd had dealt Emma over the years. "Explore the dangers of a pack of nasty girls gossiping in a small town. It might make some of those little bi—uh, *witches* stop and think."

Emma gave her a quick hug. "I quit caring what they thought about me years ago."

If only Deirdre could believe it. She could remember all too well how it felt to be different, an outsider looking in. "You know, not one of those girls is even half as wonder-ful as you."

"Yeah, well, you're not exactly an impartial judge. But Miss Wittich is and— You're getting me all off track! I'm trying to tell you about the play. We're doing the most brilliant, most wonderful, most amazing play ever written." Emma paused for dramatic effect. *"Romeo and Juliet!"*

"Romeo and Juliet?" Deirdre gave a snort of disgust. "Is your teacher out of her mind? Stuffing hormone-crazed kids' heads with romantic nonsense—glorifying sex, defying one's parents and committing suicide. Teenagers generally screwing up their lives. That play should come with a warning from the surgeon general."

"My mother, the last of the great romantics." Emma rolled her eyes. "When was the last time you went on a date?"

"When was the last time Mel Gibson was in town? Oops, he's married. Guess I'm out of luck. Besides, one die-hard romantic in the family is enough. You got your uncle Cade married off. Be happy with that."

Happy? She'd never believed it possible for a McDaniel to be that happy. With his adoring wife, five-year-old twins and another baby on the way, Cade's life was damned near perfect. At least until the patient from hell had moved into the spare bedroom. Their seventy-six-year-old father who'd broken his hip tackling some kid who'd snatched a teenage girl's purse.

Damned embarrassing, the Captain had grumbled, to find out the kids involved were brother and sister, just horsing around. Deirdre almost managed to smile at the memory of the crotchety old buzzard blushing to the roots of his thick, iron-gray hair. And yet she couldn't stop the ache in her chest. His injury had changed everything.

"Mom, don't you ever get lonely?" Emma asked.

"With you around? Never."

"But I won't be around forever. After Christmas—"

Emma had been hovering over the mailbox for weeks now, waiting to see if she'd won early admission to the drama school she'd dreamed of since she'd gone to theater camp there last year. Truth was, Deirdre dreaded Emma leaving, yet was anxious to get her out of this dead-end town. High school and its dangers had terrified Deirdre, but Emma had a good head on her shoulders. She was way too smart to get trapped the way her mother had.

That said, maybe it *still* wasn't such a bad thing that Brandi would be the one to do the whole balcony gig. "The nurse is a great character part," Deirdre said, trying to sound sympathetic. "You'll be brilliant."

"I'll be brilliant all right. But not as the nurse." Emma shone and Deirdre's heart tripped. "Miss Wittich says I'm the most perfect Juliet she's seen in thirty years of teaching!"

Oh, God. A perfect Juliet? That's exactly what Deirdre was afraid of. Emma glowed with innocent passion, stubbornly determined to race into the world with open arms, not knowing how badly life could hurt her.

"Aren't you going to say something? Like congratulations?"

"I'm just...I thought Brandi...everyone was so sure she was going to get the lead."

Emma grinned with pardonable triumph, considering all the times Brandi had lorded it over the less popular kids. "Man, is she ticked. Her boyfriend, Drew Lawson, is Romeo. And I get to kiss him on stage!"

Deirdre's nerves tightened. "A little less enthusiasm, please."

"Oh, Mom, it's just acting. But he *is* gorgeous in a soulful, Orlando Bloom kind of way."

"That's just great." Couldn't Wittich have done something revolutionary? Like cast some shy, pimpled computer geek who wouldn't make Emma's cheeks turn pink with anticipation?

"Uncle Cade said it's too bad Grandma isn't around to hear my news. He says *Romeo and Juliet* was her very favorite play in the whole world. Is that true?"

Deirdre stifled a frown. "That sounds about right."

Their mother had loved all that star-crossed lover junk, sobbing her way through movies like *West Side Story* time after time as if the tragic endings sneaked up on her totally unexpectedly to bite her in the butt.

"Mom, what was Grandma like?"

"Perfect." The word slipped out before she could stop it. Emma shot her a puzzled frown. "I mean, she was one of those women who gardened in a house dress long after other moms had changed to jeans. She liked more…old-fashioned things. Like floppy straw hats and china teacups and frilly dresses on little girls."

Deirdre remembered the look of horror on her mother's face when Deirdre mutinied against Emmaline's dress code. Deirdre had taken her mother's sewing shears and dragged out a pair of Cade's old jeans. Hacking the legs off so the frayed hem hit below her knee, Deirdre had threaded one of the Captain's neckties through the belt loops, then tied it tight around her far-narrower waist. After all, she couldn't climb up to the tree house in a stupid dress.

"Do you think Grandma Emmaline would like me?" Emma asked, a wistful light in her eyes.

"Absolutely." Deirdre tried to ignore the twist of pain in her chest. "She would have adored having someone to share teacups and poetry with." Maybe the fact that Deirdre had produced such a granddaughter would have redeemed her a little in her mother's eyes.

Deirdre felt a jab of envy, reluctant to share any of Emma's love, even in her imagination.

"Am I like her?"

"No," Deirdre said flatly. Then more softly, "Yes. In some ways. But you're stronger than my mother was. She always seemed as if she were waiting for something bad to happen."

"I wish I'd gotten a chance to know her. I asked the Captain about her. His face got all stiff and sad when I mentioned her, just like yours does. But Uncle Cade said everything there is to know about Grandma is in that wooden box upstairs. There's even a copy of *Romeo and Juliet* she kept from when she played Juliet in tenth grade. Uncle Cade used to read it to cheer her up when she was sad."

She'd been sad a lot. Even boisterous Deirdre had longed to be able to comfort her. But when the melancholy had stolen over Emmaline McDaniel's face, the last thing she wanted was Deirdre racketing around.

Can't you ever sit still? her mother would mourn. *You're just like your father.*

Not that the Captain had approved of her wild side, either.

"I'm just dying to get my hands on that play," Emma pleaded. "Can I come with you and look for it?"

Deirdre's jaw clenched. Score another point for Cade. He'd not only made certain Emma would check on her in the house, he'd guaranteed the kid would shadow her every step of the way to the cedar chest.

"Emma, I'd..."

Rather not let you see how much it hurts me to sort through Mom's things, see how badly everything in the chest suits me. What a disappointment I was to a mother I never really knew...

There had been an ocean of secrets between Deirdre and her mother. Deirdre had almost lost Emma's trust, as well. She'd deserved to. Jesus, God, how she'd deserved to. But she'd fought to mend the wounds between

17

them, swore she would never hide things from Emma again, never keep secrets that would fester, destroy.

She'd be the worst kind of hypocrite to change the rules now.

She forced herself to smile. "If you really want to come upstairs with me, it's fine."

Emma gave a skip of delight. "You're the best mom in the whole world!"

Deirdre flinched inwardly. She knew better.

Emma grabbed Deirdre's hand the way she had every Christmas morning before they headed downstairs to see what Santa Claus had left, never disappointed even those times when the man in the red hat had to scrape the very bottom of his sack for presents.

Half dragging Deirdre, Emma rushed up the stairs to the soft pink room that had been Emmaline's own. Not that Deirdre had entered it willingly after shattering the china ladies. The afternoon sunlight showed the dust on the top of the chest, smeared with finger marks, as if Cade hadn't been able to resist touching it. *He* should take the blasted thing, Deirdre thought. For him there would be warm memories as well as pinching ones.

"Oh, Mom!" Emma enthused. "Do you know how many times I wanted to open this thing? But the Captain would never let me."

One thing Deirdre and her father had shared was a desperate need to forget. Deirdre knelt beside the chest, sucking in a steadying breath.

"How about we open it on three?" Emma said, curling her own fingers around the edge of the wooden lid. "One, two, *three*."

The hinges creaked, the sweet smell of cedar filling Deirdre's nose as she set the length of brass into place, to hold the trunk lid open. But the scent was the only thing familiar. Deirdre frowned, puzzled. Instead of precisely folded linens and silver lined up like soldiers on parade, the trunk's contents were a jumble as if someone had dug frantically through the contents. Atop it all lay a worn copy of *Romeo and Juliet*, bits of its blue cardboard cover flaking off, a smear of blue dye staining the bridal veil beneath as if it had gotten wet somehow during the years.

Emma cried out, snatching the script up, clutching it to her chest as zealously as Juliet had clutched the dagger. But it was Deirdre who felt the piercing of old pain, old grief.

"I just...I can't believe I'm actually holding a play she loved as much as...as I love it."

Deirdre's throat felt so tight it hurt to squeeze words through it, but she wouldn't have spoiled Emma's pleasure for anything in the world. The child was far too intuitive as it was, always picking up on the hurts and secret sorrows of everyone around her. "Then keep it."

"Uncle Cade says Grandma's stuff is all yours. You don't have to give this to me."

"I want you to have it." Maybe Emmaline McDaniel was looking down from heaven, delighted, too. Her beloved play script was going to someone who wouldn't regard it with cynical distaste.

Reverently Emma cradled it in her hands. "Listen! I'll read the part I used for the audition!" She started to open the script, but it fell open in the middle, a yellowed envelope seeming to mark a place. "What's this?" Emma said, slipping the envelope free. Deirdre recognized her mother's elegantly swirled handwriting.

"It must be a letter your grandmother wrote to somebody."

"But it's stamped 'return to sender.' I wonder why she kept it. It must have been important. This is the place she kept all her most precious stuff. Maybe it's something wonderful! Mysterious! Like something in an old Nancy Drew book."

"Or maybe she was reading the play and had to stop to cook dinner or answer the phone so she just stuffed a stray letter in to mark her place. Go ahead and open it. I can see the suspense is killing you. Just don't be disappointed when it turns out to be no big deal."

Emma folded herself down to the floor, crosslegged, and pillowed the script on her lap, carefully loosening the flap of the letter. She withdrew folded sheets of stationery embossed with a graceful bunch of lilies of the valley.

She cleared her throat, beginning in her most theatrical way.

"Dear Jimmy,
    After so many years, I hardly know how to begin. Three nights ago there was a horrible accident. My daughter, Deirdre, fell off the wing of a plane in the local hangar, damaging her kidneys. She nearly died, and the doctor says it's so serious she may need an organ donor."

"That's why you've got those scars on your back, right?" Emma glanced up at Deirdre through her lashes.

"Not one of my finer moments. I was climbing around on the plane, trying to get your uncle's attention and— well, it was a really bad idea." Bad? How about catastrophic? The guilt had all but destroyed Cade. She'd come out of the anesthetic to find that the bright, laughing older brother she'd adored had vanished forever.

She'd tried to prove to him she wasn't worth all the misery in his eyes. She was so wild, so reckless, it was no one's fault but her own when life steamrolled her.

But what the heck was Mom writing to this Jimmy guy about the accident for? One of the few things Deirdre could remember from the fog of pain that had engulfed her as she drifted in and out of consciousness was the Captain's gruff voice, telling the doctor to cut him open right then and there, give his daughter his kidney, hell, his goddamned *heart* if the girl needed it.

She'd felt so loved for that short space of time. Her mother's tear-streaked face desperate, her father so fierce, as if he could hold back death. And Cade...he'd looked as if the sky had fallen on his head. But there had never been any question her big brother loved her. She'd never doubted it for a moment, even years later when she'd gambled everything on his love, taken advantage of his generous heart.

The memory still brought tears to Deirdre's eyes. Why hadn't her family been able to hold on to that far-too-brief closeness? How could it have slipped away?

Emma cleared her throat, began reading.

"They tested my husband and me to see if either of us is a suitable donor. The tests showed the un-thinkable. My husband can't help my baby girl. Neither can I. There is only one person who can. Her real..."

Emma stumbled to a halt, hurt welling up as she raised her gaze to Deirdre. "I thought we told each other every-thing. Why didn't you tell me you were adopted?"

"What are you talking about? I'm not." Deirdre took the letter out of Emma's hands, scanned to where her daughter had stopped reading. *Her real father...*

Deirdre reeled, struggling to grasp the unthinkable. "I didn't know..." she breathed, her knees starting to shake.

Deirdre began to scan the writing silently, but Emma put a pleading hand on her arm.

"Read it out loud. Don't...shut me out."

If there was any place on God's earth Deirdre understood the pain of being shut out, it was here. Swallowing hard, she started over in a wavering voice.

"I knew in my heart God would find a way to punish me for loving you."

Loving who? This stranger? This Jimmy?

"What happened between us fifteen years ago was wrong. My husband will never forgive me. And my son—oh, God, Jimmy, he knows all about us."

Deirdre fought to breathe. Her mother...her mother had cheated on the Captain, gotten pregnant...

No! Icy hooks tore at Deirdre's stomach. She wished she could shove the letter back into the chest and burn it. Wished she'd never seen the envelope tucked in the play script. Wished Emma were anywhere on earth but here, peering at her with dark, stricken eyes.

Deirdre pressed her hand to her mouth. This was impossible. She couldn't believe it. But suddenly a lifetime's worth of pain and rejection made horrible sense.

They'd known she wasn't a McDaniel at all! Her mother and the Captain and Cade. Did they talk about the dirty little secret when she wasn't around? Shake their heads and say it was no wonder she'd been such a disaster as a kid? She'd been a mistake from the moment she'd been born.

She closed her eyes, remembering every time she'd found the three of them around the dinner table, whispering, going silent when she walked in the room. And yet, her parents had hurt her before, hadn't they? It was Cade who stunned her now. Cade's silence that cut the deepest.

"Mama?" Emma hadn't called Deirdre that since she was so tiny Deirdre could pick her up in her arms. Deirdre struggled to control her own reaction, felt as if she were about to shatter. "Did Grandma have an *affair?*"

Deirdre's head swam with betrayal. She'd been born out of some sleazy affair. No wonder the Captain couldn't be in the same room with her for five minutes without exploding. No wonder Cade had run away to the air force and tried to leave her behind. She was the living evidence of how his mother had betrayed him. Of all the McDaniels' secrets, Deirdre's mere existence was the dirtiest, the ugliest.

"I'm sorry," Emma quavered, tears streaming down her cheeks. "I didn't mean to…"

Dig up the rotten truth after so many lies? Emma blamed herself. Deirdre could see it in her daughter's anguished face.

Deirdre tried to keep her voice calm, even. "You didn't write that letter, Emma. You didn't lie or cheat or bury things so deep I never understood…until I thought…"

There was something horrific about me, some flaw so ugly, so unforgivable neither of my parents could love me the way they loved Cade.

Deirdre unfastened the brace and closed the lid of the trunk, the edge of the letter crushed in her hand. "Emma, you head on in to work. Okay, honey? I need a little time alone." Wasn't that what she'd told Cade what seemed a lifetime ago? Why the hell hadn't he listened? Was that why the stuff in the trunk was a mess? Had he been looking for that letter? Anything that could sully the image of his precious, perfect mother?

"Time for what?" Emma asked, as Deirdre scooped up her keys. "Where are you going?"

"To find out the truth. The Captain and Cade owe me that much at least." Deirdre started down the stairs.

"But, Mom...I want to come with you. I—"

"No!" Deirdre snapped. Emma flinched back, tears spilling over her dark lashes. "No." Deirdre repeated more softly. She cupped Emma's cheek in her hand. "You head on over to the library. They're expecting you to show up for work, and you're going to need time off for play practice starting next week."

"I want to stay with you."

"Please. Just...go. Try to understand." She felt flayed wide-open inside, bleeding. Didn't want her baby to see her like this.

"What's going to happen now?" Tears ran down Emma's face. "You're all upset with Grandpa and Uncle Cade. I just got my family back. I'm scared everything will be all ugly like it was before. Mom, promise me...you won't..."

Run away again? Turn her back on Cade and the Captain? Pretend away her pain? It had been six years since Deirdre felt such an urge to leave Whitewater behind her.

"Promise me you won't let this change everything."

Oh, God. Emma was so young. So innocent. She couldn't possibly know that the letter already had.

"I swear I won't let it change anything between us, baby. You and me. Nothing could change how much I love you."

"But—"

"I'll be all right, angel girl," Deirdre assured her, but she could see disbelief in her daughter's eyes. Emma knew she was lying. Hiding. But her family—they'd cornered her. What else could Deirdre do?

Plenty. Starting with getting straight answers for the first time in her life. Deirdre hugged Emma fiercely, then stalked out to the van. She backed out of the driveway, glimpsing Emma, shoulders drooping, cheeks wet with tears, one last victim trapped by the house and its secrets.

Damn them—damn them all. Her mother, the Captain, the brother she'd trusted more than God himself. She'd sworn she'd never let the misery of her own childhood touch her little girl. Now Emma was caught in the cross fire.

Deirdre's fingers clenched the steering wheel, pain, betrayal cutting so deep she couldn't breathe. No, she vowed. She wouldn't let them hurt her anymore. Wouldn't let them hurt her little girl.

She morphed pain into something harder, more familiar, easier to endure. White-hot McDaniel rage.

CHAPTER 2

TOYS SCATTERED THE PLAY yard fronting Cade's log cabin, his beloved view of the Mississippi obscured by a fence designed to keep his five-year-old twins from tumbling into the river. But as Deirdre strode toward the gate, an escape attempt was well underway. Sturdy, dark-haired Will struggled to balance a tower made of furniture from the playhouse, while Amy perched on top with the grace of a fairy and the tenacity of a pit bull, attempting to unravel the mystery of the childproof latch.

A hot stab of grief shot through Deirdre, their intrepid innocence reminding her poignantly of her own childhood rebellions, how she'd chafed at any boundaries her parents set. *It was for your own good.* How many times had she heard that refrain? No doubt she was about to hear it again. An excuse for years of secrets and silence.

We were only trying to keep you safe....

But there was no such thing as "safe," Deirdre thought grimly. Cade might try to convince himself his fence would protect his family, but Will and Amy would grow. The lock would eventually open. And the danger would still be waiting, inevitable as the letter Emmaline McDaniel tucked in her copy of *Romeo and Juliet* so many years ago.

"Freeze, you two!" Deirdre ordered.

The startled twins tumbled to a heap on the ground. Undaunted, they grinned up at her, sure that she adored them.

"Aunt Dodo!" Will called out. "My best plane flied right over the fence." He jabbed a finger complete with bright orange bandage toward a rosebush Finn had planted last year. Deirdre's heart twisted as she retrieved the killer paper airplane so obviously Cade's work. He'd built Deirdre dozens when she'd been Will and Amy's age. She could still see her brother's long fingers folding the sheet of paper so precisely, as if making that plane for her was the most important thing in the world.

"You ever try to stage another jail break and I'll make sure you never fly again! Got it?" They clambered to their feet and saluted the way the Captain and Emma had taught them—an almost fail-safe trick to get them out of trouble. Deirdre unfastened the gate and edged past the stack of child-size table and chairs.

"We never would'a tried to 'scape," Amy explained as Deirdre returned the plane to its miniature pilot. "But they're having big trouble screwing in there."

"Screwing?" Considering the fact that Finn's pregnant stomach was roughly the shape of her VW Beetle, the logistics of the R-rated definition boggled the mind.

"The crib," Will explained. "Daddy's been trying to put it together all morning and he keeps screwing it wrong."

Her brother, Mr. Magic Hands, who made his living restoring antique airplanes, was stumbling over putting together something as simple as a crib? Deirdre refastened the gate and started toward the French doors that stood open to the breezes.

"Want me to show you where they are?" Will offered.

"She'll be able to find 'em all by herself," Amy said. "Just follow the bad words."

The kid was right as usual. Deirdre could hear Cade and the Captain arguing in the freshly painted nursery long before she could see them. Finn, garbed in overalls and one of Cade's T-shirts, was doing her best to smooth ruffled feathers. But her smile didn't hide the lines of strain crinkling around her eyes and digging deep around her mouth.

She looked exhausted, this pregnancy taking far more out of her than when she'd carried the twins—or maybe it was the hopeless task of trying to keep the peace with so many McDaniels under one roof.

"The baby isn't coming for three more months," Finn soothed. "There's no reason why we have to put the crib together today."

"The twins were six weeks early," Cade said, and Deirdre caught a glimpse of his face. He had the expression of a man walking barefoot across hot coals. "I'm not taking any chances."

"If your husband would quit being stubborn and give me the goddamn screwdriver—" the Captain grumbled.

"Yelling at each other isn't going to help," Finn said. "I don't blame either one of you for being distracted. But Deirdre's stronger than you think."

Deirdre ached at her best friend's vote of confidence. Finn had had faith in her from the moment they'd met, when Deirdre had been a heartbeat away from surrendering the only thing in her life that really mattered.

Her daughter...

Deirdre hated the thought of Finn being caught in the middle of the impending storm, but she'd married into the McDaniel family with her eyes wide-open. What else could she expect?

"Besides," Finn said, "Emma's with her."

The memory of Emma's stricken face slammed into Deirdre like a fist to the solar plexus, shattering any consideration Finn's condition warranted. Anger flared anew. "As a matter of fact, Emma *was* with me," Deirdre snarled, charging into the room. "Thank you all so much for that little treat."

"Deirdre!" Finn wheeled toward her, Irish green eyes asking more than Deirdre could ever give her.

"Thank God you're here, girl!" the Captain grumbled. "You put this damned thing together! Your brother can't tell a nut from a bolt today! I can't figure out what the hell's wrong with him."

"That's easy enough to explain. Nothing like a guilty conscience to screw up your concentration, is there, big brother? You sent Emma to the house."

"That's right. I told the kid where you were." Cade tossed his screwdriver to the thick blue carpet and levered himself to his feet, his chin jutting at a belligerent angle that accented the faint scar he'd gotten hauling their father out of a fight years ago. "Go ahead and string me up. You wouldn't let me come with you, and I didn't think you should be alone."

"I didn't hold your hand when you were sorting through that box with your old comic books in it. Why shouldn't I be alone to look through my own stuff?"

"You know damned well why." Cade raked his dark hair back from his forehead and glared down at her with eyes as blue and blazing with defiance as her own. "That chest might as well have been stuffed with dynamite the way you blew up whenever you went near it."

"And to think that was *before* I knew what was inside. You should have dug a little deeper when you went pawing through it the other day, Cade."

"What do you mean when I pawed through it? The chest is yours. I never even opened it."

"So you drove the Captain over for one last attempt at search and destroy?"

The Captain scowled. "If I could climb the stairs to that second floor, missy, I'd be in my own house where I belong instead of dragging my sorry self around here, getting in the goddamn way."

"Captain, we're glad to have you—" Finn started, but Deirdre plunged on.

"I found what you were looking for, Cade," Deirdre said, her gaze locking with his. "It was there all the time."

He gritted his teeth, struggling for patience, an expression painfully familiar. And yet there was something brittle about him, his blue eyes burning, intense. "How could I be looking for *it* when I don't even know what *it* is?"

Deirdre drew the letter out of her pocket, betrayal burning through her anew. "Don't even try to lie your way out of this, either one of you." Deirdre brandished the envelope at her brother and father. "All this time you knew—"

"Knew what?" the Captain asked, looking bewildered. "There was nothing but frills and nonsense in that cedar chest. Get hold of yourself right now, girl, and act like a McDaniel."

Deirdre gave a harsh laugh. "I wonder how many millions of times I heard that one? 'Act like a McDaniel, Deirdre. McDaniels don't cry. McDaniels never quit. McDaniels don't run away.' I stunk at being a McDaniel, didn't I? I just never knew the reason why. But you did. You and Mom and...Cade." Her voice broke. She hated herself for showing weakness, reached deep inside to quell her tears. "This is a letter Mom wrote when I fell off that stupid plane."

"Sonofabitch!" Cade paled. He grabbed the letter.

"Go ahead and take it," Deirdre said. "I've already read it."

Finn slanted a worried glance at the Captain, then hustled over to Deirdre, slipping one arm around her. "Why don't you and Cade go into the kitchen. The two of you can talk—" Empathy and regret softened Finn's face, her eyes far too easy to read.

"Oh my God, Finn!" Deirdre said, the truth jolting her. "You know it, too."

"Know what? What the hell are the three of you talking about?" Martin McDaniel complained. "Quit acting like I'm not even here! I'm old, not stupid. And I have no idea what you're all so upset about."

Deirdre glared back at him in disbelief. "Don't you get it? The game's over. The secret's out. But I've got to admit, you were damn good at covering it all up, Dad." She all but spat the word.

"Deirdre, wait, he didn't—" Cade started to intervene, but Deirdre didn't even stop to draw breath.

"This whole pack of lies was just an earlier version of 'don't ask, don't tell,' right, Captain? I've got to hand it to you, though, you handled it like an officer and a gentleman."

"Deirdre, don't," Finn pleaded. "You'll regret—" But Deirdre plunged on.

"Must have galled the hell out of you, having to pretend I was your daughter."

"Pretend?" the Captain echoed.

"Having to look at me every day and know that Mom crawled into bed with some other man."

Despite his injury, the Captain pulled himself ramrod straight. "Don't you dare say such a thing about your mother!"

"Why not? We both know it's true. My real father is some guy named Jimmy Rivermont. No wonder you couldn't be in a room with me for ten minutes without losing your temper."

"You're not making any sense!" the Captain blustered. "Your mother was a perfect lady! She would never have…"

"Stop it, for God's sake," Deirdre raged. "If I hear what a perfect lady Mom was one more time I'm going to throw up! Don't you get it? The game is over. I know the whole sordid story. It's all in the letter Mom wrote to the guy she was screwing while you were off God-knows-where playing hero."

Martin McDaniel staggered back a step, so damned confused Deirdre's heart hurt. She had to fight to hold on to her outrage as he took the letter from Cade's fingers, opened it, read it. He didn't make a sound. Stood there, so still, as if he'd been turned to stone.

"What did you do?" Deirdre asked, like a kid poking at a sore tooth. "Sit at the table and shake your heads? 'The girl is a mess, but what can you expect? It's not as if she's a McDaniel.' I spent my whole life tearing myself apart wondering why I didn't fit in with my own family. Why you and Mom loved Cade better. At least now I know the truth. It wouldn't have mattered how hard I tried to be what you wanted me to be. I'd still be Emmaline McDaniel's dirty little secret. No wonder you couldn't love me."

She dared her father to deny it was true, wanted him to insist that knowing she wasn't his by blood hadn't made any difference. She was his daughter in every way that counted. She needed her father to close the space between them, put his arms around her. But he didn't.

The Captain turned to Cade, eyes once eagle sharp now pleading. "You knew about this? That your mother…your sister…"

Finn moved to her husband, slipped her arm around him. And for a heartbeat Deirdre wondered what that felt like—to have someone support you when the roof caved in. A soul mate who would walk through fire to shield you.

Cade drew strength from his wife, faced the rest of his family.

"Yeah. I knew."

The Captain let the letter fall from his fingers. Deirdre could almost see his once-formidable strength drain away, his body suddenly frail, terrifyingly old. She wanted to reach out to him but couldn't. He'd just proved the greatest terror of her childhood to be true. He didn't love her. He couldn't even look at her.

Cade laid a hand on Martin McDaniel's arm as gently as if the craggy old man were one of his twins. "Dad, wait."

Deirdre flinched at the unexpected word. *Dad.* Cade said it so tenderly, closing the distance the whole family had kept by addressing the Captain by his rank all these years.

But Martin McDaniel didn't seem to notice. He turned, shuffling out the door.

Cade looked as if he wanted to follow, but he was enough like his father to know it would be futile. McDaniels hid their weaknesses, burrowing in somewhere to lick their wounds like savage animals.

Silence fell, so thick Deirdre couldn't breathe.

"I've been dreading this day since I was sixteen," Cade said. "Scared that the truth would come out somehow. But I thought…hoped the secret died with Mom. God, Dee, haven't you suffered enough? And the Captain, hell, what could the truth do but hurt him? Dad didn't know about this any more than you did."

"But that doesn't make any sense," Deirdre stammered.

"I was never supposed to know, either. I accidentally overheard Mom talking to the doctor at the hospital. They were afraid you might need a kidney. When they tested for a compatible donor, the truth came out. Your blood work and the Captain's proved you couldn't be father and daughter."

"My God." Deirdre sagged into Finn's rocking chair. "That's why Mom changed once I got home from the hospital."

Cade nodded. "It killed her just to look at me, knowing I knew her secret. Sometimes I think she was so afraid you and Dad would find out the truth that she wanted to die. Yes, she had an affair with some musician—"

"A musician?" Deirdre echoed. "Like me?"

"It doesn't matter what the guy did for a living," Cade said, but Deirdre could tell that he knew it did; it mattered to her in ways he'd understood far too long. "Mom stayed with us," Cade insisted. "She tried to make things work. She loved all of us."

"Don't even go there, Cade." A lifetime's bitterness spilled through Deirdre. "She loved *you*. That's why she stayed. She never loved me. At least now I know why."

"Deirdre, you don't know that," Finn said. "People make mistakes. Do things they regret. You disappeared from Emma's life for nine months, but that didn't mean you'd stopped loving her. How do you know your mother—"

"Nice, Finn," Deirdre said. "Real nice. Throw that up in my face."

Tears welled in Finn's eyes. "You're my best friend. The sister I never had. I don't want to hurt you, but I love you enough to tell you the truth."

"The truth..." Deirdre echoed, Finn's words lancing

through her. "Yeah. Maybe it is time I faced the truth. My mother and I never could be anything like you. You're so damned easy to love I could almost hate you for it. You even got three hardcases like the McDaniels to adore you. I mean, two McDaniels," she corrected. "The Captain and…and Cade."

Cade glowered. "Deirdre, none of this changes the fact that you're my sister."

"Don't even try to tell me you felt the same way about me after you heard the truth!" Deirdre exclaimed. "You could hardly look at me after I came home from the hospital. It was like…like someone ripped all the joy right out of you. You were a stranger."

"Dee, it was my fault you got hurt! I felt guilty as hell. Mom told me you came to the hangar because you missed me. All I did was yell at you, try to drag you off that plane. All I cared about was my damned job and the flying lessons it bought me. You almost died! And then to find out about Mom and— Hell, yes, it shook me up! But I didn't stop loving you! I was just a kid myself, hurting, mixed up…"

"Deirdre," Finn interrupted, desperate, "I wish you could have heard Cade when he told me how much he regretted the distance between you. It tore him apart."

"No wonder he thought I wasn't a fit mother for Emma," Deirdre said. "I was the product of some sleazy affair."

"You abandoned the kid on my goddamned doorstep without a word of explanation! I didn't know where you were for nine months! It had nothing to do with who the hell your father is!"

"Tell yourself that, if it makes you feel better," Deirdre said, drawing in a shuddering breath.

"Okay, you want the truth? I would have given my

right arm to keep you from finding that letter. To keep you and the Captain from finding out about a piece of ancient history that could only hurt you. But when it comes right down to it, you're still my kid sister. The Captain's still your father. That letter doesn't change a damn thing."

"You're wrong," Deirdre said, her chin bumping up a notch. "It changes everything."

"Don't go off half-cocked and do something we're all going to regret. I know you've got a hell of a mad on, but the truth is you're hurt. Hurting people back isn't going to make you feel any better."

"Maybe not. But finding my real father might."

"The Captain is your real father," Cade roared in exasperation. "He's the one who taught you how to throw a baseball, who ran all over town looking for orange pop when you were sick!"

"Yeah, well, the military trained him to fall on a grenade if necessary," Deirdre said. "Duty, honor, country and all that crap. When it comes right down to it, we should all be relieved! None of us have to pretend to be a big happy family anymore."

She snatched the letter. Cade swore. He grabbed for her arm.

She wheeled on him, flames all but shooting from her eyes. "Leave me the hell *alone!*" she roared.

"Damn it, Dee, I'm sorry. Tell me…tell me what to do. How to fix things."

Fix things…that's what Cade had always been good at. But all the magic in the world couldn't erase the letter's contents from Deirdre's mind.

"You want to know what hurts most of all?" Deirdre said. "You lied to me, all this time. Cade, I trusted you." Tears pushed against her lashes. She turned, fled.

She could hear Cade start after her, heard Finn's insistent voice. "Let her go. She needs time to sort this through."

Finn probably thought once Deirdre calmed down everything would be all right. Finn and Cade would try to put the broken pieces of the family together again. They didn't know it would never work.

The hurt of a lifetime finally made sense. She wasn't a McDaniel. It was time to find out exactly who she was.

She raced across the garden that separated Cade's cabin from March Winds, slipped around to the back door to avoid the newlyweds mooning over each other in the porch swing. She rushed into the private living quarters she and Emma called home and stumbled to the small office that was her haven, a room devoid of the antiques and Victorian furbelows that gave the rest of the old house its old-world aura.

Deirdre slammed the door and leaned against it as if a wolf were chasing a few feet behind her. She sucked in a deep breath, the tears finally falling free. Disgusted with herself, she scrubbed them from her cheeks with the back of her hand. She wasn't going to waste any time crying. She was going to do something. But what?

How was she supposed to find this Jimmy Rivermont so many years later? Considering the letter was returned to sender it was obvious her mother hadn't been able to find the man. And at least she'd known who she was looking for.

Deirdre didn't have a clue how to begin. How did you find someone who'd disappeared?

She closed her eyes, her memory suddenly filling with a tall man in a long outback-style coat, a black cowboy hat on his head, his steel-gray gaze dangerous, ruthless. Six years had passed since she'd opened the door to find Jake Stone on the other side—the private investigator tracking down the small fortune Finn's ne'er-do-well father had stolen. Obliterating the inheritance Finn had believed was proof her father had loved her enough to provide her with the home he'd never given her as a child.

Stone had shattered Finn's illusions, all but destroyed Cade and Finn's chance at happiness, then gone, leaving ugly scars in his wake. Finn had made peace with it as best as she could, she and Cade working hard to repay every penny, but her father's betrayal still haunted her. Deirdre could sense it when no one else was looking.

She hated Stone for what he'd done. Let him know she thought he was lower than pond scum. What else could he be, digging into people's lives, destroying them for a fee?

She recoiled inwardly from the man, what he did for a living. The ruthlessness in his eyes. He was a son of a bitch. But he was a talented son of a bitch. If anyone could find her real father, he could.

Deirdre grabbed the phone book from its perch on her desk, leafed through it and found the entry. "Jake Stone, P.I. By appointment only…"

Ripping the page out, she grabbed her purse and keys and headed out the back door. Forget making an appointment. It had been loathing at first sight between her and Stone. Face-to-face it would be harder for him to turn her down.

Considering what he'd done to Finn, it was obvious the man was willing to do anything for the almighty dollar. She'd pay him what he wanted. She wasn't going to take no for an answer.

CHAPTER 3

DEIRDRE DID A DOUBLE TAKE as she pulled up to Stone's office. She'd expected an anonymous-looking brick building where people could slink in to ask Stone to unravel secrets. Something from an old detective movie, not the immaculately kept Arts-and-Crafts-style bungalow, its fresh coat of café au lait paint with splashes of hunter green and deep red trim gleaming amid other, more down-at-the-heels houses nearby.

But if Stone's office defied her expectations, the trio of Harley-Davidson motorcycles blocking the driveway fit the clientele she'd imagined Stone would associate with. Skulls and crossbones decked two of the machines, the other inscribed with the motto, "Born To Raise Hell," amid an elaborate design of flames.

Stone's clients? Or informants stopping by to ruin someone's life? She didn't have time to care.

She parked, climbed out of the van. Squaring her shoulders, she marched up to the porch. The door stood ajar, and from the sound of things, whoever was inside wasn't happy. Good. She had wished Stone nothing but misery over the past six years as she'd watched her brother and sister-in-law struggle to pay back the remainder of a debt that wasn't theirs.

The thought of Cade and Finn knifed Deirdre in the chest, their betrayal of her, and the anguish on their faces as she'd stormed away flooding through her. She shoved the image down, hard.

Angry masculine voices rang out from inside Stone's office. A wiser person might have headed back to the car to wait until whoever was ruining Stone's day stormed back out to their bikes. But the opportunity to see Stone under fire was too sweet to miss, and she couldn't risk him locking the door behind these guys once the fun was over. Adrenaline kicked her pulse into high gear, as she slipped, unnoticed, through the dark green door, gauging the scene in a heartbeat.

Apparently Stone was having a *very* bad day.

Three men roughly the size of gorillas had Stone cornered between a mission-style desk, two Stickley-esque armchairs and a wall of glass-covered bookcases, but the P.I. didn't seem to have the brains to realize he was about to get the stuffing kicked out of him.

He lounged against a sliver of wall like a model in some sexy blue jeans ad, all hard muscle, testosterone and mystery, his long black hair caught back from sharp cheekbones, a bored expression on his darkly handsome face. "…and here your momma thought you couldn't read," he said.

The gorilla with the shaved head and a swastika tattooed on his skull sneered. "I had plenty of time to work it out. You were front-page news for months. Got me all excited, thinking I'd get to see you out in the prison exercise yard."

Prison? Deirdre puzzled.

Stone shrugged one broad shoulder, his black T-shirt clinging to muscles an Olympic athlete would have envied. "Life is full of disappointments."

"Yeah, but you never can tell what fun might be waitin' just around the corner."

The other two men chuckled.

"There we were, Stone, on our way to Colorado, when we stop to suck down a cold brew. And plastered right there on the wall by the bar is a blow-up of the article about you getting thrown off the force."

Deirdre caught her lower lip between her teeth. She had wondered what made Stone become a private investigator. Being thrown off the police force just might do it. But didn't a cop have to do something pretty serious for that to happen? Stone didn't even look ruffled.

"I wanted to do my Al Capone imitation for the camera that day," he said, "but some people just can't take a joke."

Swastika scowled. "When I told the bartender you were the one who busted me, he was happy to give us your address."

"Yeah, well, they say everybody needs a hobby. I happen to be his."

"He said it was your fault his old lady left him."

Stone grimaced. "I confess. I did it. I shoved his hands down that other woman's pants."

Rage fired in Swastika's eyes. "Still acting so high-and-mighty! You're no better than the rest of us cons! Any other poor son of a bitch would have had their ass thrown in prison for what you did! Fucking cold-blooded murder! But your father-in-law, the police chief, couldn't stomach throwing the force's golden boy to the animals."

Deirdre waited for the explosion. Stone should be furious—the lowlife was accusing him of murder, for God's sake! Cade would have broken the gorilla's nose by now, and, Deirdre admitted, probably would be getting pulverized by Moe and Curly, there. But Stone examined a piece of lint on his black T-shirt as if it were the most pressing thing he had to deal with at the moment. He flicked the speck off his bunched biceps. "Due process is a beautiful thing. Gotta love truth, justice and the American way."

A chill ran down Deirdre's spine. Stone was all but admitting he'd killed someone. *Murdered* them, if Swastika's accusation was to be believed. And Stone wasn't denying it. For an instant she thought about quietly backing out of the door, but she dug in, stubborn. She didn't know where else to go.

"Don't talk to me about justice, Stone," Swastika fumed. "You send me to prison for breakin' someone's neck in a bar fight, but you can gun down an unarmed man and your badge gives you a get-out-of-jail-free card?"

"Not free." An edge crept into Stone's voice, his tone even softer. "Never free." Deirdre saw his eyes flash, then go flat again, emotionless. She wondered what darkness Stone's words had betrayed.

"Face it," Stone drawled. "I got dealt the lucky hand this game. Better cut your losses and walk away. Think about how you can play your cards better next time you end up in front of the docket. I might even be able to give you a few pointers."

"Hell, you hear that?" Swastika's fuzzy haired crony grumbled. "He doesn't even have the brains to deny he got special treatment!"

"You owe me, Stone!" Swastika snarled. "And I'm not leavin' here until I get some of my own back!"

Deirdre swallowed hard. She could understand where King Kong was coming from. If she'd been his size six years ago she might have been tempted to take a swing at Stone herself. Once again she was the queen of rotten timing.

Stone couldn't have gotten the crap beat out of him the hundred other times she'd wished him ill. No, he had to wait until she actually needed him standing upright with his brain functioning to take on three house-size cons at once.

"Ten years," Swastika griped. "I spent ten years in the joint."

"And I've spent eight off the force. Let's call it even."

"Just tell me how much it cost, Stone," Swastika demanded. "To make your murder rap go away."

"Hedron, I know how it is for you," Stone said, quietly persuasive. "You go and get yourself all drunked up and crazy, and there's my ugly mug staring at you from Conlan's wall. So he stokes you up and sends you over here looking for a fight. Why not? Conlan's got nothing to lose. But you, Hedron, you're gonna lose plenty, breaking parole. All you're gonna get here is another aggravated assault charge and a few broken bones in the bargain."

Two of the cons looked downright edgy, Deirdre marveled. But the ink the tattoo artist squirted into Hedron's skull must have pickled the part of his brain that dealt with impulse control. He didn't look daunted in the least.

"Hell, man, I'm not worth it," Stone said.

He meant it, Deirdre thought astonished, wondering at the shadows that suddenly stormed in his remarkable eyes.

Stone spoke so quietly, so evenly, as if he were trying to talk someone down off a ledge. "Just get the hell out of here, climb on your bikes and head for the nearest bar," Stone urged. "We'll forget this whole thing."

Swastika's eyes narrowed, as if he could sense a chink in Stone's armor, was trying to sniff out the best place to draw blood. "You know, I remember that pretty little wife of yours." Stone was married? Deirdre glanced at his left hand—no ring in sight.

"Police chief's baby girl, wasn't she?" Hedron taunted. "Did she go crying to daddy to save your ass?"

A muscle in Stone's jaw twitched. "That's none of your damn business."

"Oh, I think it is. Tell me, Stone. Why did I spend ten years with only my hand and Miss November while you spent it screwing a real-live woman's brains out? Come on, Stone. Explain it to me."

Something shifted in Stone's face, hardening the planes and angles, turning his gray gaze flinty. "Sorry. I only use reason on animals that are at least in throwing distance from me on the evolutionary scale. My dog, for instance."

Hedron's lips snaked over teeth whose repair would have paid for a dentist's summer home. "You still think you're untouchable, don't you, you arrogant son of a bitch. I'm not leaving until I prove that you bleed red just like the rest of us."

Stone's eyes narrowed, his powerful body taut, ready. No, Deirdre realized—not just ready—eager to fight. "I bleed plenty red," Stone said. "But today I'm all out of Band-Aids."

"Stop it!" Deirdre cried out. All four men nearly jumped out of their skin, heads jerking around to look at her, but only Stone's gaze pierced deep, stark recognition registered on his face.

"What the hell? Deirdre?"

He recognized her, remembered her after six years, Deirdre realized, stunned. Cornered as he was, Stone lunged, trying to bulldoze his way between Swastika and

Curly in an effort to put his body between her and the other men. But she'd obviously shattered his concentration. He didn't even see Swastika as the giant man's fist drove into his midsection. Air whooshed out of Stone's lungs, and Deirdre expected him to go down, out cold, but he stayed on his feet, bellowing warning.

"Get out of here!"

Good advice, Deirdre realized. But instinct kept the soles of her shoes glued to the floor. It wasn't a fair fight. McDaniels never deserted— Pain shot through her, the letter and its ugly truth surging into her mind.

So what if she wasn't a McDaniel. She couldn't leave Stone to get pulverized. The man wasn't going to do her any good in the hospital.

"Lookit Stone's face," Swastika gloated. "We've got his girlfriend."

Stone sucked in a painful breath. "She's not...my girl-friend."

Deirdre met the bikers' gaze with a fearless one of her own. Well, almost fearless. "I wouldn't date Jake Stone if he was the last man on earth."

"Then how about giving me a test drive, sweet thing, and we'll call it even? It's been a long time since I had me a woman."

The con turned toward Deirdre, the stench of cheap whiskey rolling over her in suffocating waves as Swastika closed in on her.

Stone lunged, lightning fast, just as Moe swung some kind of club—a blackjack, Deirdre realized from fights in the nightclubs she'd sung in so long ago. Stone dodged, the blur of black leather glancing off his jaw instead of breaking it.

Deirdre cried out, her voice drowned by Stone's bellow as he fought to keep his feet under him. Deirdre grabbed Stone's arm, tried to steady him, but the P.I. tore away from her.

"Get the hell out of here!" he yelled. But Swastika's arm snaked around her ribs, yanking her back hard against him. The stench of cheap liquor made Deirdre's stomach churn, panic welling through her. Helpless. She felt so helpless. No. She'd sworn she'd never be helpless again.

Deirdre drove the sharp edge of her heel hard against the ex-con's instep, just like the Captain had taught her. Swastika howled as she yanked free.

"Run!" Stone yelled, plunging between her and the raging men. She had a straight shot to the door. But the blows had dulled Stone's reflexes, slowed his speed. Even if she could reach her cell phone, Stone would be toast before anyone could get here.

She didn't owe Stone any kind of loyalty. He was the last person she should be defending. And yet... She stared, suddenly frozen, as a thin stream of blood trickled from the corner of the P.I.'s mouth.

"It's red," she cried, inanely.

All four men looked like she was insane. "What the hell?" Swastika snarled.

"His blood," she insisted. "It's red!" Her cheeks flamed. "You've proved he bleeds, now why...why don't you all leave." She thought longingly of her cell phone, wished she'd had the brains to call before she'd barged into the office. But then, Moe, Curly and Swastika didn't know she hadn't. She drew herself up as if she were a six-foot Amazon instead of a five-foot-three midget the three stooges there could snap with one hand. "I called the police from my cell phone before I came in here," Deirdre said.

Swastika chortled. "Sure you did, lady."

Deirdre glared right into Swastika's mud-colored eyes. "The dispatcher said they'd be right here. Her name was Joan."

"Joanie?" Stone feigned recognition. "She's a hell of a looker, that one. Too bad you won't have a chance to romance her, Hedron. She doesn't like men in orange jumpsuits."

Swastika's buddies glanced uneasily toward the door.

Swastika sneered, pacing toward Stone. "He's laughing his ass off at you," he told Moe and Curly, taking a menacing step toward the P.I. "You two can be cowards if you want. I'll beat the shit out of him myself."

In a split second Stone coiled like a whip, sprang into action. Whatever grogginess he'd felt from the blows evaporated. Deirdre watched, stunned as Stone hurtled his body through space, fists cracking bone, long powerful legs executing rib-crushing kicks to Swastika's midsection in such fast succession he drove the man across the room.

Moe and Curly gaped as if they'd fallen into a *Lethal Weapon* movie. Moe dropped his blackjack. Curly fumbled for something in his pocket—a knife. But he was shaking so hard he struggled to open it. Dee grabbed a bronze statue of lady justice from Stone's desk, slamming it down toward the con's head. Curly ducked, the heavy base grazing his temple, exactly the kind of blow the Captain always said only made combatants madder than hell.

Only strike if you've got a clear shot, the old man had drilled her. *Hit to kill. A woman's got only one chance to surprise an attacker.* She'd already used that up when she'd stomped Swastika's instep flat. But Curly wasn't coming back for more. He and Moe cowered like whipped dogs as Stone kicked Swastika square in the face. The con doubled over, blood spurting from his nose. Stone bounced lightly on the balls of his feet, his whole body ready to fly into action as he turned toward the other two men. "Who's next?" he dared them. "Any more takers?" But Swastika's streaming nose was as effective as a flag of surrender. The three cons bolted out the door.

Deirdre braced her trembling body against a chair, trying to remember how to breathe, as she heard the bikes' engines fire up, roar down the street. But before she could get oxygen into her straining lungs, a hard hand gripped her shoulder. Stone whipped her around to face him. He crushed her against him for a heartbeat, his big body hard and overwhelmingly male. Then, as abruptly as he'd grabbed her, he let her go.

Deirdre stared, momentarily struck dumb. Mr. Cool was mad as hell. Not roaring mad—roaring mad she could handle. Quiet, nuclear-meltdown kind of mad— eye-of-the-hurricane kind of mad. Tornado-warning, head-to-the-basement-before-you-get-blasted-to-smither- eens kind of mad. Deirdre pulled away from his grip, un- consciously tried to take a step back. Her bottom collided with the chair.

Stone swiped the blood from his bottom lip with the back of his hand. A strange flutter awoke in Deirdre's middle. She had seen just how lethal a weapon those hands could be moments before. Skilled and powerful— his eyes alive with rage. She stared at his mouth, lips knee-meltingly sexy, as if he could drive a woman's common sense right out of her body if he kissed her. She wondered if he knew she was immune to all that animal magnetism.

The last thing she wanted in her life was a man— someone who thought he could tell her what to do, someone to report in to, someone who might slip past her guard to find things she had to keep buried.

"What in the hell did you think you were doing barging into the middle of a fight like that?" Stone pinned her with his glare. Deirdre met his gaze, determined not to let him see how much the encounter had shaken her.

She clenched her fists to keep her hands from trembling. Story of her life. Deirdre McDaniel—great in a crisis, but once it was over, she'd start shaking like a scared puppy.

"I was trying to hire a private investigator," she said, with as much cool as she could muster. "Preferably one who wasn't in traction. I still need to, by the way. Hire you, I mean."

Stone scowled. "What the hell do you need a P.I. for—never mind," he said, sounding so damn certain, Deirdre wanted to deck him. "I'm all booked up."

After everything she'd gone through in this hideous day, she wasn't about to back down. Stone might be an arrogant bastard. He might even have killed someone, just like Swastika had said. But he hadn't been thrown in jail for it. And somehow, the instant she'd seen his name in the phone book, she'd felt in her gut that he could help her. She'd learned from hard experience how bad it could be when she ignored her instinct. But he didn't look like a man who would easily change his mind. He'd said no. Case closed. But Deirdre doubted he'd ever met anyone as stubborn as she could be.

"I'll pay double what you usually get," Deirdre said boldly.

"A thousand dollars an hour?"

Deirdre faltered. Maybe the man didn't have his office in some sleazy low-rent building, but this wasn't the Taj Mahal, either. Surely that sum was ridiculous. No one could possibly...then she glimpsed the edgy humor in his eyes. He was just trying to pull her chain. "Damn you, very funny. I'll pay you whatever you're worth."

Stone arched one thick black eyebrow. "About as much as pond scum. At least, that's what you seemed to think last time I saw you. You hated my guts on sight."

He remembered that? She'd only seen the man a few times. She'd been front and center when he'd told Finn the life-shattering news about her father. And she'd been around a few more times when he'd come to organize a payment schedule with the newlyweds. Hell of a way to start out a marriage—a hundred thousand dollars in debt. Cade had sold the antique plane that had been his most cherished possession to save Finn's dreams for the old house she'd loved. And Deirdre had told Stone off with true McDaniel flare. Back when she'd still believed she had fighting blood in her veins.

"Why the hell should I help you?" Stone challenged.

"Because I..." It was harder than she'd imagined, telling the horrible truth to a stranger. Or was it something about this man that made her throat feel too choked to let the words squeeze past? "I need to find someone."

"Who?"

"My father."

Stone frowned. "Your father went missing? From the background check I did on all of you before I contacted Ms. O'Grady, Captain McDaniel is a capable, crusty old son of a...gentleman. He's probably out hunting rattle-snakes or wrestling alligators. He'll turn up when he feels like it."

Deirdre's cheeks burned. "I'm not looking for the Captain...I mean, I'm searching for my real one. Uh, my birth father. A man named Jimmy Rivermont."

"You're adopted?" One brow arched in astonishment. "I never would have guessed it."

"I'm not." Deirdre drew in a deep breath, saying the words she'd practiced a dozen times on her drive to

Stone's office. Practice hadn't made it any easier. "My mother slept with this guy when the Captain was out of the country on some mission. I found this."

She withdrew the yellowing envelope from the purse she'd abandoned when she'd tussled with the Three Stooges. She held the thing out to Stone. He took it, scanned the envelope, then the letter inside, his gray eyes so fierce, so intent, Deirdre felt some of the crushing misery in her chest lift.

She'd been right to come here, she thought, watching him absorb the letter's contents. With Stone's razor-sharp intelligence, street smarts and tenacity, he'd get to the bottom of all this in a hurry. He'd find the truth and tell it to her, no matter how harsh it was or who got hurt in the process. He'd proved that when he'd told Finn about her father.

Deirdre winced, remembering the way her sister-in-law adored the Captain, how many times she'd said how lucky Deirdre and Cade were...

Deirdre ripped her thoughts away from her best friend and the hundred small kindnesses the Captain had done to make Finn feel a part of the family. If only he'd reached out the same way today, when Deirdre's heart lay trampled, bleeding. Suddenly Deirdre felt something almost tangible touch her face. Stone. He was leveling that terrifyingly sharp gaze at her.

She felt as if he were unscrewing the top of her head, trying to get a look inside. Deirdre met his gaze, defying him to see past defenses she'd had up forever. A force field nobody had been able to penetrate since she was an awkward teenager, so hungry to be loved. Sometimes it made her sad to know that now no man ever would. She'd been alone too long.

After a moment Stone took her hand, folded her

fingers around the letter with unexpected gentleness. "Here's a bit of free advice. You've got a real nice family back home, from what I remember. Digging around after some guy who might have made a sperm donation— well, I don't advise it. I mean, I wouldn't advise it even if I was willing to take your case, which I'm not."

His hand engulfed her smaller one, long fingers so strong, an artist's hands. Who would have guessed Jake Stone would be capable of tenderness. "Go home, Deirdre. Forget you ever saw this letter."

"I can't. I need to know where I belong."

"Go home to your father and your brother and that sweet Finn O'Grady. Go home to your little girl. Emma."

He even remembered Emma's name? Some part of her marveled before disappointment washed over Deirdre, followed by desperation. "It's not up to you to make that decision. Help me. Please."

Stone would never know how much that plea cost her. She looked into those stormy gray eyes, the irises ringed with a thin line of blue, the black lashes so thick and rich Emma's high school friends would have envied them. But there was nothing soft about the emotions roiling beyond those lashes. Stone's gaze, full of power, full of heat, full of fight. Traits Deirdre would do anything to have him use on her behalf at the moment.

Anything? A voice whispered in her head. Her gaze flicked, unbidden, to Stone's mouth. A James Bond kind of mouth that kissed women senseless in secret fantasies all over America, and then vanished once the danger was over to seduce someone else. The kind of mouth Deirdre would never let within kissing distance of her own.

The phone rang. Deirdre jumped, startled, expecting him to ignore it. Stone glanced down at the caller ID. A faint smile played about his lips, something that irritated Deirdre driving shadows out of the investigator's eyes.

He palmed the receiver and held it to his ear. "Trula Devine," he said in a voice so rich it could probably unsnap a woman's bra without so much as a touch. Of course, Deirdre doubted anyone with an outlandish name like that would put up much of a fight. "Hey, baby, you finally decide to put me out of my misery and call? Damn it, woman, you've been making me crazy!"

Stone hovering over the phone waiting for a woman to call? It just didn't seem in character. But then, if she'd learned one thing on the road with the band all those years it was that most men didn't have much restraint when their libidos were involved. Stone wouldn't be the first man who'd turned idiot over a woman.

"What about the money?" Stone asked, a smile quirking his mouth—the slightly swollen place at the corner of his lips making him look all the more maddeningly sexy—as if he'd just come up for air after one soul-sucking kiss. "Hell, yes, sugar. I'll pay. Whatever you want."

Deirdre could hear a murmur from the other end of the phone. Stone laughed, and for an instant Deirdre felt a stab of envy, wondering what it would be like if he ever turned that thousand-watt smile onto her.

"What's that?" he asked. "Yeah, Trula. You've still got the best legs in Vegas. With that body of yours you could bleed a man dry and he'd be smiling all the way to the bank to empty his accounts for you."

Deirdre clamped her mouth shut, some of the grudging respect she had for Stone melting away. It was nauseating, the way Stone was talking. It irritated the blazes out of her—on principle of course. She didn't want his mind on some other woman's legs. She wanted it on the case she was hiring him to solve.

Stone turned away, tension evident in his shoulders, his voice suddenly stern. "Fine. I'll pay whatever you want. But no more games, Trula...you heard me. When you wouldn't pick up the phone I even stopped over. You weren't there. I didn't know where you were..."

Controlling bastard! He expected this Trula woman to check in with him before she stepped out of the house? The thought made Deirdre's temper burn.

Breathe, Deirdre, she thought, trying to keep the lid on. *Long, deep breaths. You can't lose your temper. It doesn't matter if Stone is a pig to his girlfriend. You need this man...even if he is a first rate son of a— Count backward from one hundred. One hundred, ninety-nine, ninety-eight...*

Stone chuckled, the sound raking at Deirdre's nerves, startling her, scaring her. Making her wonder for an instant if he'd seen... No, Deirdre told herself. That laugh was for Trula Devine. Piercing as Stone's eyes might be, he couldn't read Deirdre's mind.

"Do I love you?" he asked in that low, rough-edged voice that made Deirdre feel as if he'd run his hand over her skin. "What do you think, woman? You better have your dancing shoes on next time I knock on that door, and be ready to tango. That's an order."

He hung up the phone, glanced at Deirdre from beneath hooded lids. What was he trying to do? Hide the fact that he was aroused from talking to his sex kitten? Or exploit the fact that the conversation had made Deirdre uncomfortable?

"You're still here?" Stone asked, feigning surprise. "I thought I made it clear my caseload is too heavy to take you on."

"An army of men like you couldn't take me on!" Deirdre fumed. "Maybe you're used to ordering women around like they're—they're slaves or something, but—"

"Oh, honey, believe me, there's nothing, er, involuntary about the way Trula serves me."

"You did everything but order her to wrap herself up in cellophane so you could run right over."

Stone grinned. "I *did* tell you I was busy. Of course, I can't wait to pass on your suggestion. Believe me, Trula will love it."

"You know what? If I'd had any idea how you treat women, I would have hit you over the head with that statue and let the Three Stooges use you for a punching bag."

"The Three Stooges?" Stone chuckled, then his face drew back into unyielding lines. "Lucky for me you didn't find out what a male chauvinist jerk I was until it was too late."

Deirdre fought back tears of exhaustion, exasperation. She'd despised Stone for years. Hated him. And yet... she'd been so sure he would untangle this mess. She'd never even considered he might say no. What was she going to do now?

Well, she sure wasn't going to lie down and quit, she thought grimly. She'd fought her way through plenty of trouble before with no help from anyone.

"Know what?" she said, with a wave of her hand. "Forget I ever came here. I'll find Jimmy Rivermont myself."

She should have turned and walked out, chin high, shoulders squared—in what the Captain had always called her "Queen Elizabeth walking the plank" imitation. But for once she couldn't carry it off. Why did it matter so much that Jake Stone was turning her away? Because she didn't know what else to do. Couldn't imagine where to begin. Because finding that letter had shaken everything she'd been sure of for thirty-two years. And she'd needed someone on her side.

Her memory filled with Finn's gaze—full of empathy and love. Cade's fierce blue one, angry, sad, for once not knowing what to do. And the Captain…it wasn't his eyes she'd never forget. It was the sight of his back as he turned and walked away.

She looked straight into Stone's eyes and fought to keep her voice from breaking. "You're a real son of a bitch."

Stone's grin faded, his gaze holding hers, dark with secrets of his own. "I thought you had that figured out a long time ago."

CHAPTER 4

JAKE PRESSED THE ICE PACK to his swelling jaw, hoping the ache would distract him. But even the *memory* of Deirdre McDaniel would be damned before it cooperated with him.

He closed his eyes, arched his head back, trying to blot out the feline angles of her face, the defiance in her I-dare-you eyes and the taunting softness of lips that had haunted his dreams more times in the past six years than he would admit even to himself.

She was still every bit as wild and beautiful as the mustang mare he'd rescued from the glue factory as a kid back in Nevada. He'd been determined to get past the horse's defenses, teach her to trust. He'd gotten a broken collarbone and three cracked ribs before his grandmother had drawn the line. She'd told him some creatures were broken inside, too deep for anyone to fix. Sometimes the kindest thing to do was leave them alone.

Where Deirdre McDaniel was concerned, Jake had sure the hell tried to do just that. Stay as far away from the lady as possible.

And yet, down in Jake's gut where instinct lived, he'd always known she'd walk back into his life someday. And that she'd hate him.

Jake stalked through the open door joining his office to the private part of his house and turned to glare down at the occupant of a giant-size cedar pillow on the floor near the heating vent. The mass of wrinkles around the bloodhound's droopy face made her look as if she had melted into the Black Watch plaid fabric.

"I could have used some help in there," Jake complained, nudging a hindquarter gently with the toe of his boot. The dog opened an eye and thumped her tail once on the pillow as if to say, *I knew you had it covered, boss.*

"Oh, yeah. I had it covered all right," Jake murmured irritably. Three cons he could handle. What he couldn't handle was five feet three inches of woman with a giant-size chip on her shoulder. What a kick in the gut it had been when he'd seen Deirdre standing there. All that fire still in her eyes.

Hell, any red-blooded man alive would wonder if she was as hot in bed as that mouth of hers promised. It had been lust at first sight. Her skin creamy smooth, touched with roses, her chin-length hair tousled as if mussed by a lover's hands, her eyes so blue a man could swim in them if he had the guts. Because, in spite of her petite size and the feminine curves of her body, there were dangerous waters running deep in Deirdre McDaniel, monsters under the surface she didn't let anyone see.

And what had he done? Blurted out her name like some idiot. It was damned embarrassing remembering the stunned expression on her face. He'd made it plain he hadn't been able to get her out of his mind all these years, and put her in even more danger when Hedron and his boys got the crazy idea that he'd had his hands all over her. Yeah, right. In his dreams.

"So I remember her name. So what? I'm just a kick-ass detective, right, Ellie May? It's my job to remember details. And the woman *did* slam my foot in her door the first time we met."

Deirdre had been as fierce as a lioness that day, defending Finn, a woman she'd known only a few days. God, she'd been magnificent—all righteous indignation, so damned loving and brave. She'd made him want her from that first moment. Want her beneath him, want to bury himself in her heat, see if he could make all that fiery passion break free and warm the cold places inside him no one else could ever touch. He got hard even now, just thinking about—

Yeah, that kind of thinking could land a man in big trouble.

It was a damned good thing Trula had called, just the sound of her voice bringing him back to his senses. Because when he'd been standing there, looking into Deirdre McDaniel's eyes, listening to a woman so proud, pleading for him to help her...he'd been on the brink of making one spectacularly stupid move.

But then, he'd always had a hard time saying no to damsels in distress. Not that Deirdre was his usual type. He liked his women leggy and gorgeous and feminine, adoring him, making him feel invincible. The way Jessica had before a smoking gun had destroyed their future.

Ellie May pawed at his leg, sensing his dark thoughts. She gazed up at him soulfully, as if to say he didn't need any other woman but her. *She* loved him. Adored him.

The dog rolled over, exposing her belly. Her pink tongue lolled out the side of her mouth, the animal certain that looking ridiculous would make scratching her belly irresistible to Jake.

"You're pathetic." He hunkered down, running his fingernails lightly over Ellie's sleek chest. "No wonder the K-9 squad washed you out." Ellie wriggled in delight.

"I know, I know. Masters who live in glass houses shouldn't throw bones. You're right. This is crazy. I just need to forget this whole deal. I told Deirdre I wouldn't take the case, didn't I? I'll be damned if I'm going to help her destroy her life, hurt her family. I've had a bellyful of that, especially where the McDaniels are concerned."

He remembered the brother—Cade—and his pretty wife solemnly handing over the first check to repay the money Ms. O'Grady's father had stolen. The two had moved heaven and earth to make good on Patrick O'Grady's debt. They'd surprised Jake, made him realize just how jaded he'd become, how little he believed in people anymore. Honest people. Decent people. People who did what was right even when they could just turn and walk away. But then, cynicism was an occupational hazard when you made a career out of exposing people's dirty laundry.

Deirdre McDaniel should get down on her knees every night and thank God she had the family she did. Burn the letter and forget she had any father but that irascible character, Martin McDaniel.

That would happen when Ellie May had a face-lift, Jake thought grimly. Deirdre McDaniel would never let this thing go. She'd worry it until there was nothing left of her.

And she'd lose. Lose big. There were plenty of people who would rake the past up for the right price and wouldn't give a damn...

Well, too damned bad. He'd warned her, hadn't he? If she was too stubborn to listen, fine. Let her have at it. She wasn't his responsibility. He'd seen too many people disillusioned. He didn't want to see her that way. He wanted to keep her in his memory the way she'd been that first day, all fight and fire and fierce, bright love.

Except that now he'd spend forever wondering what she'd uncovered, how it had changed her. Wondering if she'd let anyone catch her when she fell.

Jake paced to the sink, let the ice pack fall. Gingerly he touched the swelling where the blackjack had grazed him. Deirdre would be fine. She was far from helpless, he reminded himself.

She was a fighter.

After all, an hour ago the woman had even fought for him.

What had she been thinking jumping in like that? Irritation burned through him afresh. She could have been hurt. Hell, once things turned ugly, she could have been killed. One of the cons had tried to pull a knife. Hedron hadn't come into the office bent on murder. He'd just been juiced up by Conlan, and aching for a fistfight to teach Stone a lesson. But if that knife had driven home, all three cons would have been desperate to cover their tracks, keep out of jail. They might not be the brightest crayons in the box, but they'd have to be cretins to trust Deirdre to keep her mouth shut. And the only way they could be sure of her silence was a permanent solution.

But now Hedron wouldn't be back. Thank God he was basically a coward, not evil the way some of the lowlifes Jake had to deal with were. Still, there was plenty of scum out there.

How could Jake know for sure that this Jimmy Rivermont wasn't one of them? A leech or a con man or worse still, some sociopath ready to suck Deirdre dry? Destroy her family? He remembered her little girl, Emma. All big, dark eyes, a face too tender for the real world. What if Deirdre was unwittingly bringing a monster into her daughter's life?

He heard the lazy click of Ellie May's nails on the slate floor, glanced down to see her gazing up at him as if he were some kind of hero. One who would never leave Deirdre and Emma McDaniel to the wolves.

"Quit looking at me like that!" he told the dog. "She's not my problem."

Ellie May licked his hand. He shot her the glare that made grown men back down. She wasn't impressed.

"Fine," he snarled. "Have it your way. I'll be damage control for the woman, if nothing else. I've never met any woman more likely to get herself in trouble."

Ellie tipped her head. He'd never seen a more eloquent expression saying the canine equivalent of "yeah, right." He could almost hear the dog laughing her wrinkles off.

She eyed the jar of dog treats on the counter longingly. Now she wanted him to reward her for being a world-class nag? Not in this lifetime.

"Know what, Ellie?" he grumbled. "You're a real bitch." Then he threw her a goddamn Milk-Bone.

DEIRDRE HAD BEEN DREADING the slam of the screen door for hours. She pulled the covers up higher over her pajamas and glanced at the clock on her bedside table, knowing Emma was home. The girl was more reliable than Old Faithful. Always on time or calling to check in if something earth-shattering was making her late. It made Deirdre a little sad, knowing how careful her daughter had become in the years since Deirdre had left her with Cade for those nine long months. It was as if some part of Emma were still afraid Deirdre might leave her again if the going got rough.

And in the near future things around here were bound to get rough indeed. Because Jake Stone or no Jake Stone, Deirdre wasn't about to give up on finding her real father. A musician, just like she was, she thought with a tingle of anticipation. She wanted to see him, wanted to know how she looked like him, how they were alike. Wanted to see unreserved approval in a parent's eyes and know…know that someone believed her perfect, just the way she was.

There is no guarantee he'll feel that way, her subconscious warned in a voice annoyingly like Jake Stone's.

But she had to believe Jimmy Rivermont would understand how it felt to make mistakes, and fear you could never make things right. After all, he'd had an affair with a married woman, gotten her pregnant. Had he known he'd fathered a child? The letter made it sound as if her mother had never told him.

"Mom?" Emma called softly, knocking on the bedroom door.

Deirdre's heart squeezed. "I've told you a jillion times you can just come in."

Emma carefully opened the door and peered inside, her face far too pale, too sad, too young. Deirdre's heart ached for her. This was supposed to be Emma's big day— getting the part she'd worked so hard for, defying the high school pecking order and earning the chance to prove to everyone that she was the finest actress White-water High had ever seen.

"Come in already," Deirdre urged with tender impatience. "What are you waiting for?"

"I keep hoping someday I'll knock and you'll surprise me." Emma gave a wan smile. "You'll get all embarrassed and say, 'Just a minute, sweetheart, let Mel Gibson here get on his clothes.'"

"Emmaline!"

"I can't help it. I won't be around forever, Mom. I…worry about you."

Deirdre surrendered any effort to keep her game face on. "Children aren't supposed to worry about their parents. It's meant to be the other way around."

"Tell that to Uncle Cade."

"That's exactly what I mean. I'm an adult. I'll be fine."

"I don't think so. Especially after...well, after today. That letter." Emma fretted her lower lip. "You looked like—like it was the end of the world when you read it. I called Uncle Cade on my break, to warn him, you know...about what you read. So he could fix it."

"Oh, Emma!"

"You should have heard him, Mom. He said you'd already been there. He sounded like... I hadn't heard him sound like that since the morning when I was ten and we woke up and you were gone."

Deirdre tensed. Imagining that morning had become the stuff of her worst nightmares. "The information in the letter wasn't exactly news to your uncle," Deirdre said, feeling defensive.

"It was to Grandpa. He's really upset, Mom."

Deirdre's heart sank. Sometimes she almost felt jealous over the relationship between her daughter and Martin McDaniel. Envied their easy camaraderie. Who ever would have believed two people as night-and-day different from each other as Emma and her grandfather could understand each other perfectly? "You saw the Captain?" Deirdre said, already guessing the answer.

"I took off a little early." Emma blushed—and no wonder, Deirdre thought. She'd broken McDaniel rule number 563—never take off work unless you're in the hospital, a car accident or dead.

"Miss Madison said I looked sick." Emma's eyes turned pleading. "It wasn't a lie. I felt like I was going to throw up."

"Oh, sweetheart." Deirdre threw back part of the covers and opened her arms. Emma crossed to the bed and climbed stiffly in beside her. It had been too long since Emma had done this, Deirdre thought with a tug of regret.

Once this had been an every-night treat, Emma snuggling up in her mother's bed before she'd toddled off to her own. Emma had talked and talked in her adorable, oh-so-serious way, confident her mother could explain all the mysteries of the universe. But once she'd turned thirteen, Emma had guarded her new dignity so fiercely the nighttime ritual had all but vanished.

Deirdre wished that she could just relax and enjoy this night and the closeness she'd once taken for granted, Emma warm beside her, baring the secrets of her heart. But what had happened today had changed everything. There was no going back. Even Emma would have to understand that.

"Mom, everybody's a mess over at the cabin," Emma confided. "Aunt Finn's been crying until her eyes are all swollen. And Uncle Cade's gritting his teeth so hard his jaw looks like it's going to crack. And the Captain, he wouldn't even let me talk to him about—well, about the letter. But I wouldn't go away. I cornered him and I told him not to worry. You always told me it didn't matter who my father was. What mattered was who *I* was."

Deirdre flinched, Emma's words digging deep. She cuddled Emma close, burying her nose in the crown of her head. A sweet, fruity scent filled Deirdre's nose—no simple baby shampoo for Emma anymore. She'd changed to something that promised to tame the wild curl in her hair. Thank God it hadn't really worked.

Deirdre closed her eyes, thinking about how many times she had told her baby how wonderful she was, had said her father didn't matter. Deirdre had tried to shield Emma, protect her, give her armor against inevitable gossip, even though she knew plenty of nasty jabs would slip through. Everyone in Whitewater was aware that Emma had never known her father. And she never would.

Deirdre started, realizing Emma had kept on talking, certain her mother was hanging on every word. "That's why I had to see Grandpa and tell him that as soon as you cooled off, you'd know it doesn't matter who your birth father is, either. Because that's what you told me."

"Oh, Emma."

"I hate that tone of voice. It's your 'poor little Emma can't understand something so grown-up' voice. But nobody in the whole world understands better than I do about this. Wondering who your father is. Wondering if he'd love you or if he'd turn away, trying to pretend you didn't know each other."

Deirdre swallowed hard, tried to grasp the least painful way to tell her daughter the truth. "Emma, I know this is hard."

"Yeah, well, hard is starting over at new schools so often you don't even bother trying to make friends anymore. Hard is getting stuck in fifth grade with kids who'd known each other since kindergarten. It's not like I don't know what 'hard' means."

Deirdre's eyes stung. "Emma, you're a smart girl. You have to know things have never been great between the Captain and me."

"It's because you're too much alike. You just keep butting heads and no one will say they're sorry, even when you both are."

"This is my decision. Can you understand that? Trust me to know—know what I need to do?"

"You can do whatever you want. But I'm keeping the family I've got. I'm not calling anyone but the Captain Grandpa. It would break his heart."

And I always thought he was more concerned about his pride. Deirdre bit her lip until it stung to keep from saying the words aloud. Her daughter didn't need to hear them.

"What are you going to do?" Emma asked. "How are you going to...well, how does a person look for their father if they don't know him?"

"I'm not sure," she said, thinking of Jake Stone, a knot of helplessness and frustration balling up under her ribs. "But I intend to find out."

"Mom?" Emma hung on to Deirdre, tight.

"What, angel girl?"

"I'm scared."

"I am, too. But we'll...we'll get through this together, okay? Nothing can come between the two of us, right?"

Emma gazed up at her, doubtful.

"Enough of all this gloom and doom. I want to hear about you. Tell me about the play. About rehearsals and running lines and all those things you love."

A shadow of a smile curved Emma's lips, and Deirdre burned at the injustice that the disastrous letter and Emma's triumph had surfaced on the same day.

"Mom, we can talk about all that later. I know you don't feel like—"

"Hearing how my baby turned the whole drama department on its ear? Oh, yes, I do. Come on," Deirdre encouraged, forcing a smile of her own. "You must be excited."

"Yeah. Most of the time. But sometimes, well, it's scary, too."

"You've never had stage fright in your life!" Deirdre said, surprised.

"All the popular kids in school want me to fall flat on my face," Emma confided. "They say Juliet was Brandi's part. She was so sure she was going to get it that her mom volunteered to donate costumes for the play. She had this place in the Quad Cities sew a velvet Juliet gown to die for."

"I'm sure it will look wonderful on you."

"I suppose. But it's a lot of pressure, you know? I'm going to have to practice real hard. And at school, well, it's going to be awful tense with everybody hoping I'll screw up."

The little jerks, Deirdre thought, wishing she could spank every one of the spoiled, undertalented brats.

"Anyway, I was thinking, well, I wanted to ask you if you'd mind…"

"Mind what?" Deirdre said, knowing she'd do anything in her power to drive the self-doubt from her precious daughter's face.

"If Drew and I practiced here after school sometimes. Away from all the craziness." Emma's gaze flitted like a butterfly, landing anywhere but her mother's face. "We could use the gazebo."

Deirdre closed her eyes. She was always thrilled when Emma had friends over; her daughter's close little crowd had always been a delight. But right now, with her insides churning, her mind racing, trying to think how to begin this search—for once, Deirdre just wanted to be alone.

"You're not going to let little witches like Brandi Bates ruin this for you, are you?" she hedged, trying to sort things through.

"Of course not. I just…she's acting so weird. All jealous. It's ridiculous. She's gorgeous and I'm…well…I'm me. It isn't like she has any reason to think I could steal her boyfriend even if I wanted to."

Deirdre's heart skipped a beat. "But you don't want to."

"Mom!" Emma drew out the word in the age-old voice

of teenage disgust. Deirdre tried not to worry that Emma wasn't looking her straight in the eye. "I know things are crazy right now, but Drew and I won't get in the way. I promise. You won't even know we're here."

"All right," Deirdre said, giving Emma one last hug. The whole *Romeo and Juliet* thing made her nerves twitch. But if Emma was going to be making big eyes at this Drew person, better Deirdre should be around to keep an eye on things instead of some brain-dead teacher who obviously thought all this teenage romance stuff was exquisite drama.

Deirdre knew better. She'd found out the truth the night her daughter was conceived.

DEIRDRE WOKE WITH A JOLT, a bright ray of sun squeezing between cracks in the plantation shutters sending frissons of panic racing through her. She glanced at the alarm clock, but the ringer was off. Did she forget to set it last night? Finn was going to kill her. The giant oak table in the dining room should be full of guests expecting one of March Winds' famous breakfasts of fresh-baked muffins and spinach omelets and there wouldn't be a crumb in sight. Why hadn't Finn wakened her when she came over to help serve?

Deirdre scrambled into jeans and a T-shirt, raked a brush through her unruly hair, swiped a toothbrush across her teeth and ran for the kitchen. She was halfway down the stairs when it hit her—the cold, clear memory of the day before. Deirdre stumbled to a halt, loss, betrayal and anger washing over her as if they were brand-new.

Her stomach turned over, and for an instant she wished it was yesterday morning again. She and Finn preparing breakfast together, laughing over one of the twins' latest escapades.

Deirdre had never had a friend like Finn before, someone she felt completely safe with, trusted enough to let glimpse her softer side. Someone she trusted—who had been lying to her the whole time.

How long had Finn known the whole sordid story? How much of Finn's friendship was based on plain, ugly pity?

Poor Deirdre...not her fault... She could just imagine the scene at the cabin, even without Emma's description the night before.

Thank God no one else in Whitewater knew the truth. Only Emma and Cade and Finn and the Captain. More humiliating still was her encounter with Jake Stone. She squirmed inwardly. Never before in her life had she begged anyone for anything. But she'd begged him to help her. Probably given him something to laugh about with Miss Great Legs, Trula Devine.

Deirdre's cheeks burned. She wished she could turn around and run back to her bedroom, lock the whole world out until...

Until she was in control again. Control of her feelings, her life, her past...but then, anyone in town could have told her a long time ago that she was out of control.

Still, dodging breakfast duty wouldn't change any of that. She'd have to face Finn sometime. Better get it over with now.

Deirdre opened the kitchen door, but instead of chaos, an amazing serenity reigned, the kitchen smelling of cinnamon apple muffins, the antique china Finn cherished neatly rinsed, stacked and waiting to be loaded into one of the dishwashers. Finn leaned over her very pregnant stomach, settling teacups in the top rack.

"It was supposed to be your day off kitchen duty," Deirdre said.

Finn shot her a searching look, then shrugged. "I told Emma to shut your alarm off before she went to bed."

Was that why Emma had slipped into bed with her last night? Because she was on some subversive mission from the enemy? Deirdre wanted to be aggravated, but it was so like Finn to think about her, do something kind. Deirdre's throat ached.

"What did you think? If I took a nap like a good girl I'd get over the crazy notion of trying to find my real father?"

"No. I thought you might be tired." Finn poured a mug of coffee and pressed it into Deirdre's hands. "You aren't a morning person on the best of days."

And she never would be, Deirdre thought. All those years of singing in clubs had thrown her body clock completely out of whack. One more way Deirdre had been out of sync with the early-bird McDaniels. But maybe Jimmy Rivermont would understand. Musician to musician.

Not that she was a musician anymore, she told herself firmly. She'd hadn't sung anything besides "Happy Birthday" in six years.

"Finn, listen, I appreciate you coming over and playing back-up. But I'm here now, and I'm in a real barn burner of a mood, so if you have to hover over somebody, hover over Cade and the—"

A sharp knock on the door cut Deirdre off midsentence. Please, God, she thought, exhausted, don't make this one of those "speaking of the devil" deals. Facing Finn was one thing. Cade and the Captain? That was one confrontation she just wasn't ready for.

"The Captain and Cade have the old Porsche in pieces all over the garage. With Amy and Will 'helping,' they may never get it back together again," Finn supplied, able to read her thoughts as usual.

Deirdre should have guessed what her brother would

be up to. It was vintage Cade McDaniel, trying to fix the nearest engine the way he could never mend his family.

Deirdre started toward the door, but Finn cut her off. "I'll answer it. You'll scare the guests away glaring like that."

Finn opened the door, but her "Welcome to March Winds" speech died on her lips. Deirdre's heart jumped, wondering what was wrong. "M-Mr. Stone?" Finn's voice quavered. "Did something happen to Mrs. Aronson?"

Deirdre quelled the butterflies fluttering in her stomach. Trust Finn to inquire after the woman she and Cade had written all those checks to over the years.

"No, ma'am," Stone said, so respectfully Finn might have been the Queen Mum. "Mrs. Aronson is just fine. I've come to see Deirdre."

"Deirdre?"

"She visited my office last night regarding a private matter."

"Oh. Oh, I see." Finn shot a searching look Deirdre's way. Finn was white as March Winds' ghost. And what was this "I see" garbage? Why didn't she just say, "How could you hire this man who reminds me that my father was a thief?"

Stone stepped inside. He wore black jeans, another black T-shirt and a black Stetson. Who'd he think he was? Johnny Cash? Stone removed the Stetson, cradling it in one strong hand. His gaze dipped to Finn's impressive stomach. "You look wonderful, Mrs. McDaniel. Happy. I'm glad."

Yeah, Deirdre thought. Her sister-in-law was so happy at the moment Deirdre would be lucky if Finn didn't deck her later.

"Stone," Deirdre said, trying not to hope he'd changed his mind about helping her. But then, why else would he be here? To try to talk her out of pursuing the whole thing? Deirdre grimaced—she'd just tell him to get in line.

He turned toward her, and Deirdre found herself staring smack in the middle of all that imposing male chest. "I've been considering your case. Talked it over with someone and decided I might have time to take it after all."

Deirdre tracked her gaze up his corded neck, past his square, chiseled jaw and hawklike nose so she could glare right into his eyes. "Let me guess. Ms. Great Legs Trula Devine needed more cash than you had on hand?"

Finn looked as if she'd swallowed a teacup.

"Actually, another lady friend of mine convinced me to come. She's a real looker, too, with sensational red hair. And she's definitely less expensive than Trula. All this lady wants is a meal."

Great. He had two cheap bimbos on the string. Jake Stone could be the poster boy for why Deirdre had sworn off men.

Stone fingered the brim of his hat. "I was hoping I could get some information from you. Interview anyone who might give me a place to start."

"My brother. He's the only one our mother ever spoke to about—well, about my father. He's at the cabin."

Finn started to object, stopped. Deirdre figured she knew better. "I could go to the cabin and send him over here." Finn offered. "That way no one else needs to know." She looked more McDaniel-like than ever before—dead stubborn— and Deirdre knew who she was trying to protect. The crotchety old man whose heart Emma feared might break.

Finn dodged out the kitchen door as quickly as her advanced pregnancy would allow. Deirdre could almost see her, hurrying through the garden, disappearing beyond the white picket gate as she headed home.

Deirdre should have been glad she was gone, taking her reproachful eyes with her. But the kitchen seemed to shrink with Stone's big body in it, the intensity of the P.I. sucking all the oxygen from the room. It was too easy to remember how he'd felt those few moments when he'd held her after the fight. Powerful, dangerous. Fierce and forbidden. Hot and hard and blatantly male. He'd towered over her, making her want...

Want what? Total disaster? Jake Stone was a prime example of Mother Nature's cunning, ready to trick an intelligent woman into spinning completely out of control. Surrendering independence to taste physical pleasure. No question Stone was temptation incarnate. Let Trula Devine and his gorgeous redhead play with Stone's brand of fire. Deirdre wasn't about to get burned by any man.

Again.

The word echoed through Deirdre's mind. She started, suddenly aware of Stone's cool, assessing gaze on her face. She could almost hear the gears in his head spinning, trying to figure her out. Her cheeks burned, an instinctive need to flee racing through her veins. She needed a few moments alone to compose herself, put herself back together. So she could face her brother, she told herself firmly.

Deirdre made her excuses, and went to fetch the letter from her room. If anything had the power to drain some of Stone's undeniable magnetism it was the prospect of seeing her brother.

She fought down a surge of guilt. Old habits die hard, she told herself. For once, a mess wasn't her fault. Cade was the one who'd had choices all these years. She had every right to be furious with him. All she was trying to do was find out the truth.

By the time she got back to the kitchen, Cade was

standing two steps inside the door, arms crossed over his chest as he told Stone exactly what a rotten idea he thought this search was.

Deirdre cut him off. "Either tell him what you know, Cade, or don't. It's up to you. I intend to get to the bottom of this with or without your help."

"I'm sure you'll run it down to the bitter end no matter who gets caught in the cross fire," Cade said.

"The Captain knows I'm not his daughter. So does Emma, thanks to your sending her over to the house to babysit me when I opened the hope chest yesterday. And Mom's dead. There's no one left to protect."

"There's a sick old man over at the cabin and he's tearing himself up inside over this—"

"Over Mom's affair. His sullied honor." Deirdre kept her gaze carefully away from Stone. "Truth to tell, he's probably relieved to know he doesn't have to take any responsibility for my screw-ups anymore. He's got the perfect out—"

"You don't believe that," Cade insisted.

"Don't I?" She struggled to push down a lifetime of insecurity, hide her raw, secret places from Stone. But the words spilled out, in spite of her efforts. "If the Captain loves me so much, why didn't he tell me so? Right then and there, in front of you and Finn? Why didn't he say the stuff in that letter didn't change anything?"

"God, Dee, you should have seen your face! If you had, you'd know why he acted the way he did!"

"What would you have done, Cade? If you had found out something horrendous like this about Amy or Will?"

Cade scowled. "How would I know?"

"You'd do the same thing you did when Finn was trying to be noble and call off your wedding. You'd dig in your heels and wouldn't leave until you'd pounded the fact that you loved them into their heads. You'd tell them to hell with what that letter said. You're their father."

"The Captain is your father. That's what I've been trying to tell you, damn it."

"That's right," Deirdre said, excruciatingly aware of Stone watching them, weighing them, unraveling far more than the words should have revealed. "That's what *you've* been trying to tell me. The Captain just turned and walked away."

Cade looked like she'd punched him in the gut. She could see him scramble for excuses. "Dee, Dad is an old man. A proud one. And, damn it, he's in so much pain he can't even walk up the stairs to go to the bathroom. He's feeling weaker than he's ever been in his life. And you hit him with the fact that even when he was at his strongest, his most invincible, it was all an illusion."

"Guess even Superman had to deal with kryptonite." She tried so hard to sound flippant. Instead she sounded cruel. And hated it. But she'd hate breaking down in tears far more, especially with Stone's laser beam attention focused on her. Was he trying to judge what she'd say? she wondered. Or trying to figure out what she couldn't put into words.

"Mom lied to Dad, Dee. Can you imagine how much that must hurt?"

"As a matter of fact, yes. I don't have to imagine anything at all when it comes to being lied to by the person you trusted most in the whole world." She glared at Cade, saw his face twist with pain. Direct hit. Score one for her side.

Cade's voice roughened. "Mom carried another man's child. And you're practically rolling out a banner to announce Dad's humiliation to the whole world?"

"That's right! I'm supposed to be interviewed on the news at noon."

"Damn it, you don't think this is a joke, no matter what you're saying. You know how painful this is, and how damaging. Not only do you throw the past in Dad's face, but you outright reject him right there in front of Finn and me."

"*I* rejected *him*?" Deirdre snorted, incredulous. "In case you failed to notice, I'm not the one who walked out of that room yesterday."

"Hell, no. You didn't have to. It was perfectly clear you had already made up your mind to track down this other guy before you set foot in the cabin."

"Mr. McDaniel," Stone cut in smoothly, "arguing about what happened yesterday isn't going to get us anywhere. Deirdre's made it clear she intends to pursue this matter. Perhaps we can agree the least painful way to settle things for all concerned is to get to the bottom of this as expediently as possible. With time—"

"My father is seventy-six and can't even walk up stairs," Cade snapped. "Just how much time do you think he has?"

Something like empathy sparked for a fleeting moment in Stone's hooded eyes. "Whatever time is left, we're wasting it right now."

Cade paced across to the sink, leaned against the white porcelain, glaring intently out the window. Deirdre stared at his profile, catching sight of a glint of moisture at the corner of her brother's eye. "What do you want from me?"

"Deirdre says you're the only person Mrs. McDaniel spoke to about her relationship with the birth father. Is that true?"

"As far as I know. I hardly think she discussed it with the wives down at the officers' club."

"It's not something I'd imagine you'd discuss with your son, either," Stone observed. "So how did you come to know about Deirdre's parentage?"

Cade's features darkened. "There was an accident.

77

The doctors thought Deirdre might need a kidney transplant. I overheard the doctor telling Mom that our father was not a compatible donor. It was biologically impossible that Deirdre was his child."

"Your father wasn't there to get the doctor's report?" Stone didn't manage to mask disapproval.

"No. He was gone."

Deirdre figured Cade must have sensed some kind of censure in Stone. Cade's temper sparked. "Dad was feeding Dee's dog. Dad and Spot had this kind of love/hate relationship. But the old man knew the first thing out of Dee's mouth when she regained consciousness would be asking after that damned dog. He wanted to show her he hadn't forgotten."

Deirdre winced.

Cade turned to Deirdre, gaze fiercely intense. "Don't you call *that* love, Dee? He was worried sick, wanted to stay at the hospital, hear the first word when the doc reported in. But he knew what mattered most to you. He tried to—to put your mind at ease."

She didn't dare show the effect his words had had on her, or Cade would hammer her forever, hoping he could make her call this whole search off. She could handle Cade furious. But pleading, sorrowful, hurting…those were a more dangerous approach.

Deirdre tossed her head. "It's more likely he just couldn't stand to deviate from the schedule," she said. "Feed dog at 0800 hours."

Cade swore.

Stone cleared his throat and continued. "So you and your mother were alone in the waiting room, Mr. McDaniel. The doctor walks in and reveals something this explosive in front of you?"

"They both thought I was asleep. Even so, the doctor

asked Mom to step out of the waiting room into the hall. But I could tell from the man's voice something had gone horribly wrong. I...thought my sister was dead."

Deirdre had to clench her hands into fists to keep from reaching out to Cade, touching him. The breach yawned between them, so painful it hurt to breathe. She could see Cade there, at the hospital, his body not yet filled out with a man's muscles, his face still boyish, the scar on his chin still new. He must have been devastated, feeling responsible for anything that went wrong in the family, the way he always did. She could almost hear the litany of self-blame running through his head.

I should have foreseen she was going to fall, stopped her from being so reckless.

I should have hurled myself on the open toolbox so she wouldn't have hit the sharp metal edges when she fell.

He'd thought she was dead. He must have been going through hell. It should have been over once the doctor said she'd live, but he'd only exchanged one level of hell for an even deeper one.

Cade blew out a steadying breath. "Mom begged the doctor not to tell our father unless it was a question of saving Deirdre's life. She prayed Deirdre would recover without needing that kidney. Deirdre did. Mom made me promise I would never tell. I never did."

"So, that's the Cliff's Notes version," Stone said. "Think you can add anything more?"

"Cade, for God's sake! I know you're doing this under duress, okay? Your objection has been duly noted and thrown in the circular file. Now tell the man something useful or stop wasting his time."

"This isn't easy, Dee. I don't want my family hurt."

"Oh, yeah, and I'm just loving this. It's so much fun," Deirdre snapped.

"Mom said she'd had an affair with a man named Jimmy Rivermont. He was selling band instruments in the area, or something. She would leave me with another army wife while she…" Cade shrugged. "I don't know the woman's name. She lived next door to our parents."

"In military housing?"

"Yes."

"Where were they stationed?" Stone asked.

"Fort Benning, Georgia. Must have been, what? Thirty-three years ago."

"Did this friend of your mother's have a name?" Stone probed.

"I sure as hell never asked what it was."

Deirdre tried to sound confident. "The Captain would know who Mom's friends on base were, wouldn't he?"

"You can't ask him that!" Cade raged. "For God's sake, Dee!"

"We'll try other avenues first," Stone said. "I promise you, Mr. McDaniel, I'll try to make this inquiry as painless as possible for you and your family."

"I'd be…grateful. Anyway, I'm out of here. I've told you all I know." Cade's jaw tipped up at that angle that always made Deirdre want to take a swing at it. "Except that Deirdre already has a father who loves her."

"Damn it, Cade!"

"I know," Stone said. "I mentioned that myself."

Cade stalked to the door. Stopped. "I just have to say this one last time, then I'll keep my mouth shut."

"Yeah, right!" Deirdre scoffed, turning her back on him and bracing herself against the counter.

"Don't do this, Dee."

"It's already done."

CHAPTER 5

CADE SLAMMED THE SCREEN on his way out. The sound reverberated through the roomy kitchen of March Winds. Deirdre and Stone stood in silence a long time. She rubbed her eyes, disgusted that she was close to tears. Damn, she wasn't going to cry.

"So," she said, fighting to keep her voice steady. "Is that enough to start on?" She grabbed her purse from the counter, started digging in what Emma called "theworld's smallest landfill." "How much do I owe you for a retainer?"

She didn't expect Stone to cross the room, circle her wrist with his warm fingers. Deirdre tried to keep from shaking. But Stone wasn't buying her tough act. He slid the purse out of her reach, then stunned her by tugging her gently until her back flattened against the hard wall of his chest. He wrapped his arms around her.

Oh, God, Deirdre thought, breathing in the scent of him, exotic, dangerous, deliciously male. He felt so solid, so big, as if he could hold back crumbling mountains, or crumbling lives.

For a heartbeat she wanted to stay there, safe. Protected. Not alone.

He leaned his cheek against her. "It's all right," he breathed against her temple, stroking her hair. "Cry if you need to."

Damn the man! What did he think? She was going to fall apart right in front of his eyes? But then, between Trula and the redhead, he was probably inundated with feminine tears.

Indignation sizzled through Deirdre. She tried to wriggle free, but he held her, determined to what? Comfort her? She stomped hard on his foot.

Stone yelped, yanked away, glaring at her. "What did you do that for?"

"Because I—" *Because it felt too good. Because you smelled heavenly. Because I was afraid part of me would be weak enough to like it. Like being held, even by a jerk like you.*

"Mom?" Emma's voice dashed like cold water over Deirdre. She wheeled to see her daughter staring wide-eyed at Stone. Did she remember him? Deirdre wondered, recalling the tumultuous period when the P.I. had first charged into the McDaniels' lives. But if Emma had any idea Stone was a private investigator she'd be doing her finest Snow Queen imitation instead of standing there grinning like a cat who'd just swallowed Tweety Bird whole.

No. Emma didn't have a clue who Stone was, nor why he was at March Winds. The flabbergasted expression on the girl's face was just plain astonishment because she'd never once seen her mother in a man's arms.

For an instant Deirdre considered blurting out the whole truth. But Emma's world had been so badly shaken in the past twenty-four hours that the thought of wiping a genuine smile off her daughter's face was just too miserable to handle at the moment. Defying Cade and Finn and the Captain was difficult enough. Knowing Emma would take their side hurt more than Deirdre could bear. The thought of any rift between her and her daughter terrified her, carrying her back to the wall that had separated Deirdre from her own mother for so long.

Deirdre had sworn she'd never let anything get between her and Emma again. She'd come close enough to losing her daughter six years ago.

Yet, during that upheaval, Deirdre had managed to shield Emma from Jake Stone and his business with the McDaniel family. She'd do the same thing now. Until she could find a way to make Emma understand.

As if her daughter would ever be able to understand doing anything that might hurt her beloved grandpa.

"Yo, Mom, guess you took that advice I gave you last night after all. Talk about fast work!" She might as well have broken into a chorus of "It's Raining Men, Alleluia." Deirdre swept to the far side of the room, cheeks burning.

"This isn't what you think," Deirdre cautioned. "Mr. Stone is a professional...in restoration."

Stone regarded her silently. It wasn't a lie, Deirdre insisted to herself. The man restored things. Like sanity to lovesick idiots, and the money he'd gotten Finn and Cade to pay. He'd restored it to the person Finn's father had stolen it from.

Whatever Stone's thoughts on her evasion, he took his cue from her. "Your mother and I are working together on an historical project of sorts," he said.

Emma flashed Stone her brightest smile. "So then we'll be seeing a lot of you? I mean, if you're working on March Winds' ballroom. Aunt Finn has been saying for months she wants to expand something besides her waistline, Mr.—?"

"Stone. Jake Stone." He extended his hand. Emma intentionally misunderstood and took both his hands to shake instead of the one. Deirdre died of embarrassment as her daughter none too subtly inspected the ring finger of Stone's left hand.

Emma fluttered her lashes at him. "Awesome name. You should be an actor. And you've got a great face. All rugged and rough, like you've lived real hard. Not too pretty, know what I mean? Nothing more boring than a pretty man, right, Mom?"

Deirdre made a garbled sound that might be assent as she considered ways to throttle her daughter.

Stone ate the praise up. "Thank you," he said. "You must be Emma. I've heard a lot about you."

Emma beamed. "Mom's been talking about me again, huh? I promise she gets off the subject of how wonderful I am eventually. Then she's a real crack-up."

Stone raised one silky black eyebrow. "I'll bet."

"Hey! That is way cool!" Emma enthused. "That thing you do with your eyebrow. Can you teach me how? It would be great for character parts. Not that I intend to do many of those. I'm an actress. I just got the part of Juliet. But that's just high school stuff. Mom sent me to camp last summer at the coolest drama school in the world. And my teachers offered me early enrollment. If everything works out right, I'll take early graduation and be in New York by spring."

Stone whistled. "New York is a long way from home. What's your mom think about that?" The P.I. looked as if he really cared.

"She's happier about it than I am!" Emma wrinkled her nose. "She doesn't want me to get stuck in this little town. Like I would, ever!"

Deirdre wondered if her daughter had any idea how many times Deirdre herself had vowed the same thing.

But life was tricky, dangerous. And what was that saying Cade quoted so often? If you want to make God laugh, tell him your plans.

"I know you're loving this scintillating conversation with Mr. Stone, Emma, but he's a busy man. I'm sure he has business to take care of." Deirdre shot Stone a glance of dismissal impossible to misunderstand.

But Stone was regarding her with infuriating innocence. "Actually, my morning is free. And I'd love a chance to talk theater with someone who really understands quality performing. I saw a lot of it when I was growing up."

Oh, yeah, that line of baloney fit the Stone she loved to hate. Mr. Broadway. He'd probably had front-row seats at striptease clubs and burlesque shows.

Damn the man! Couldn't he see she was trying to get him out of here?

Deirdre wished she could demand to know what the real story of this little performance was. But she couldn't do that without tipping her own hand—something she couldn't risk doing in front of her daughter.

But if Deirdre could see right through Stone, Emma was blinded by his action-hero looks and lethal charm. No wonder Stone was such a successful private investigator. He could wrap women around those powerful, long fingers of his and make them want to thank him for it. A dangerous skill, and an unforgivable flaw where Deirdre was concerned. But Emma was utterly enchanted.

The teenager laughed, looking so adorable Deirdre doubted Attila the Hun could deny her anything she asked. "Mom and I have this tradition that when I get a new part," she confided, "we go out for breakfast at this really cool place called Lagomarcino's. It's like an old-fashioned soda fountain from a jillion years ago."

"More like a hundred," Deirdre grudgingly corrected.

"Whatever," Emma conceded breezily. "Want to come along, Mr. Stone?"

Duct tape, Deirdre thought inanely. Duct tape was the only solution. If she could just tear off a strip and plaster it across Emma's mouth, she could put an end to this whole situation once and for all. But that would be child abuse, unless, of course, she got a jury stacked with mothers of teenage girls.

A rogue ex-cop who'd done something so bad he'd lost his badge wouldn't be the kind of company Deirdre would want her daughter around, period. The danger of Emma discovering exactly what Deirdre had hired Stone to "restore" made the invitation even more alarming.

"Emma, Mr. Stone is a very busy man," Deirdre began.

"Everybody has to eat. Please, Mr. Stone!" Emma didn't bother trying to wheedle her mother into it. She turned the Big Eyes directly at Stone. "This town is the cultural armpit of the world. Sometimes I feel like I'm *starving* for news of the big wide world out there." The girl all but pressed the back of her hand to her forehead, playing out her best death scene. "It would be heaven to talk to somebody who really knows theater. Besides, Mom and I never get the chance to be escorted by a dark, mysterious stranger around here. We'll have the whole town talking. Think what fun that would be."

"Being the subject of town gossip is highly overrated," Deirdre said.

She felt Stone's gaze rivet on her, knew that something in the tone of her voice had intrigued him, impelled him to try to chip away at secrets. Panic fluttered under her breastbone. She crushed it. Let him dig away. Deirdre figured before the end of this case he was bound to find out that she'd been number one on Whitewater's Most Talked About List often enough.

Deirdre started to make excuses, but Stone either jumped at another chance to irritate her or had fallen under Emma's spell.

He crooked Emma that killer smile. "Who could pass up an opportunity to get the whole town buzzing? And enjoy the company of two such beautiful ladies in the bargain?"

What in the name of heaven was the man thinking? Stone was one of the most calculating people Deirdre had ever known, with a reason for everything. Why on God's green earth would he want to spend the next hour eating pancakes at some quaint little restaurant with a woman he didn't much like and a star-crazed sixteen-year-old who would obviously talk until his ear shriveled up and fell off?

He had to know she was concealing things from Emma. They couldn't say a word about the case. What possible reason could a man like Stone have for wasting his morning this way?

Deirdre groped for some way, any way, to send the man packing. "Two's company, four's a crowd," Deirdre warned. "Don't you think Trula and your redheaded lady friend would object? Or aren't they the jealous type?"

The corners of Stone's eyes crinkled, his sexy laugh setting alarm bells jangling up and down Deirdre's spine. "Oh, my ladies are plenty jealous, but I'll charm my way out of trouble. I can be irresistible when I want to be."

"I'll bet." Emma laughed, softening the lines of strain etched in her face from the night before. "Come on, Mom. This'll be great. No offense, Mr. Stone, but with just the two of us at the table, conversation gets a little dull sometimes."

Deirdre forced a smile. "It won't be boring next time, Emmaline Kate. I promise you that."

Ignoring the warning in grand style, Emma slid her arm into Stone's and grinned. "My mom is really, really picky about men. She wouldn't go out with just anybody, you know. This is your lucky day."

THE KID WAS DEFINITELY on the make—for her mother, that is. And if they gave Oscars for performances designed to get Mom a date, Emma McDaniel would be giving a hell of an acceptance speech come next year.

That is, if she survived her mother's wrath in the hours to come. Steam might as well have been rolling out of Deirdre's ears, the woman twitchy as hell. But then, Deirdre was usually so blunt, Stone supposed it was tough for her, trying to keep the lid on the reason he'd been hired. The more time he spent with Emma, the more likely the kid would figure out she'd been duped. And in Stone's experience royalty objected to being made to look a fool.

Her Royal Highness deftly maneuvered them to her "lucky" table, set up for three, where she was able to manipulate her mother into sitting next to Jake on a crowded bench. Emma made her move with such cunning there was no way out of the predicament unless Deirdre was willing to be completely rude.

He figured Deirdre could be plenty rude on occasion, but to do so now would reveal to Emma that something was rotten in the state of Denmark. And once that happened, Stone wagered Emma would latch on to the mystery and never let go.

Besides, Stone figured he owed the teenager big-time. He was devil enough to enjoy Deirdre's discomfiture and man enough to savor the pleasure of being close enough to touch the woman who'd been prickly toward him for so long.

He could have been a gentleman and squashed himself against the wall so he wouldn't touch her, but what fun would that be?

He let his big body take up all the space it needed. His thigh touched Deirdre's, his elbow brushing her arm whenever he moved. She was so near he could smell scents that had haunted him for so long—something exotic like bergamot or oranges alerting every one of his senses that this wasn't your average woman—something so spicy and defiant it barely seemed possible so much emotion could be contained in such a small woman, a wild inner freedom that wouldn't buckle to any man.

He wondered if Deirdre knew that such obvious reluctance on her part was the most addictive aphrodisiac of all. Could she guess how many questions she awoke in a man because of the boundaries she'd drawn so clearly?

She made it easy for Stone to understand why his ancestors had raided proud highland villages in ages past, so they could fill their beds with such strong, defiant beauties and have their sons carry the women's fighting blood in their veins.

An all-too-vivid imagination flashed a scene from *The Quiet Man* in his head—but instead of Maureen O'Hara, it was Deirdre who struggled in Stone's arms as he carried her into a thatched cottage, dead set on making love to her.

Stone yanked himself up short. Get a grip, he told himself. Stick to basics. The reasons you took this case. You're here because you're attracted to the woman. And because somehow she slipped past your guard to where your guilty conscience hides.

Remember who you are: a hard-nosed private investigator who can't afford to feel emotions like these. Hell, he hadn't even realized he still had it in him, thought he'd left them behind with the badge that had been taken away.

The cop he'd been back then had seemed like a stranger for years. An idealistic fool too damned young, too involved, too emotional, who cared too much even when he damned well knew throwing himself into a case that way was going to bite him in the ass and leave him bleeding.

When he'd walked away from the force, he'd thought he was done playing Sir Galahad. From that moment on he'd see the world with all its hard edges, people taking whatever they could get, even the best ones looking for ways to wriggle out of nasty situations.

And damned if it hadn't worked until he'd crashed into the McDaniel clan, a family more stubbornly honorable than anyone he'd known since he'd crossed swords with Sergeant Tony Manoletti at twelve years old.

Stone fought to quell the memories of that dark Italian face, and the uncomfortable emotions Deirdre and her family loosed in him.

Concentrate on the entertainment value, he told himself. Here he was, sitting close enough to kiss a woman he figured would never so much as stay in the same room once he'd entered it. Yeah, it was big fun, Stone told himself cynically, except it only made him wonder what she'd taste like. Deirdre was so small, he'd have to bend way over, gather her up against him and—

"...and Hugh Jackman in *The Boy from Oz* played this gay singer who— Mr. Stone, you're not listening," Emma accused.

Stone actually felt the back of his neck get hot.

"Whatever you're thinking about, it sure isn't theater," the girl scolded. "I expect you to tell me right—oh!"

Saved by the bell. Literally. The old-fashioned brass

bell above Lagomarcino's door jangled. Emma's eyes widened, her face turning a shade pinker than the moment before as a tall kid of about seventeen entered the diner, his sun-streaked blond hair and angular, windburned face giving him a kind of Ralph Lauren, preppie outdoorsman look. For a heartbeat, Stone could see the incredible woman Emma would grow into. Then, between one moment and the next, she transformed back into a fluttery teenage girl.

"Ohmigod," she breathed. Her mother's gaze pinned her.

"Emma? Are you all right?"

"Mom, cut it out!" Emma hissed under her breath, one hand sweeping up in an effort to smooth her flyaway hair. Wasted effort, Stone wanted to tell her. Like her mother's unruly locks, Emma's hair looked best a little tousled.

Of course, on Emma it looked cute. On Deirdre it looked like a man had just buried his hands in the silky locks. Unless, Stone figured, the guy looking at the two McDaniel women was seventeen. There was no missing the appreciation lighting the boy's hazel eyes. Trula would have called them bedroom eyes. Stone figured they were closer to a golden retriever's—and not one that had honored the humane society's mandate for neutering.

Ignoring her daughter's stammered plea not to embarrass her, Deirdre glanced over her shoulder to see what held her daughter's attention. She needn't have bothered. The boy nabbed a can of Dr Pepper from the pop machine, then headed straight for them.

The kid smiled at Emma, something about him so damned shiny and new it made Stone feel a hundred years old.

"Hey, Juliet," the kid said, shoving one hand into the pocket of jeans his mom had obviously pressed.

"Hey, Romeo."

So this must be the kid cast opposite Emma in the play. "Romeo" had that soulful, romantic look that would give all the impressionable girls watching the performance something to dream about for months.

So why did the look on Deirdre's face make Stone wonder if the kid would be giving *her* nightmares?

Romeo turned respectfully to Deirdre. "You're Emma's mom, aren't you? I'm Drew Lawson."

"Hello, Drew," Deirdre replied. Stone knew that tone. It was the icy one she'd used on him so often. Stone had to credit the kid for guts as Drew awkwardly offered the Ice Queen his hand. Deirdre glanced at his fingers, then away, a pointed rejection that astonished Stone. Why didn't she just kick that poor puppy and be done with it?

Drew tugged at the open collar of a purple-and-green-striped rugby shirt. It looked like the kid registered Deirdre's chilly reception loud and clear. Even so, the kid didn't beat feet for the door. He stood there, nervous but determined. "I just want to tell you how glad I am Emma got the lead," Drew said. "Her audition had half the teachers bawling."

Drew slid Emma another glance. "I'm looking forward to working with her."

Yeah, kid, I'll bet you are, Stone thought. Wasn't there a kissing scene or two in the play? And it didn't look like Emma would object to rehearsing it with this particular Romeo. So why was Deirdre giving the kid a glare that could be aimed at barbarian hordes bent on pillage?

The kid wasn't wearing a Marilyn Manson shirt or sporting enough body-piercing to fill Jake's grandmother's pincushion. And he could hardly have offended Deirdre. Drew had just introduced himself.

Besides, Emma was sixteen—and a real looker, like her mother. Even if, by some miracle, Emma hadn't been kissed yet, it was going to happen and soon. Wasn't this clean-cut, all-American type kid every mother's dream boyfriend for her daughter?

"Emma is very talented," Deirdre said firmly. "But I can't say Juliet is a part I think she's suited for."

"Really?" Drew asked, incredulous.

"Emma's got far too good a head on her shoulders to be sucked into that whole star-crossed-lover bit—she's going to have to work hard to make it believable. I mean, the whole thing—the poison, the suicide, the whole parents-being-evil bit just isn't her style."

Emma grimaced. "*That's* why they call it acting, Mom."

"I *knew* there had to be a reason." Deirdre smiled at her daughter. "I'm glad Emma got the part, and I know she'll be phenomenal, but the role of Juliet seems a better fit for your girlfriend."

"Huh?" Drew glanced from mother to daughter in genuine puzzlement.

Emma kicked under the table, missing her intended target and slamming square into Stone's shin instead.

"Yeow!" Stone exclaimed as pain shot up his leg. He felt the press of three pairs of eyes on his face, both McDaniel females and this Drew character looking at him as if he'd gone crazy. "Y'all know, I, uh, really need some coffee," he improvised, signaling the waitress, a high school girl with bottle-blond hair and inch-thick makeup who seemed to be studiously ignoring them.

Was Stone imagining it, or did the waitress really give Emma a nasty look from above the edge of her order pad? Drew looked over his shoulder. "Hey, Chris," he called, the girl unable to ignore his summons. "They'd like to order over here."

"Be right there," the girl said sourly, turning to fiddle with a tray of water glasses. Stone wondered what the story was.

But Emma was too busy trying to do damage control to notice. "I was telling my mom that everybody assumed Brandi Bates would get the part and that the two of you were going out."

"People assume a lot of things," Drew said, his gaze holding Emma's a little too intently. "That doesn't mean they're true."

Emma blushed. "Listen, about rehearsing— Mom said we could use the gazebo out in the garden at March Winds."

Deirdre's eyes flashed. "You know, I'm not so sure that's such a good idea. The guests love the gazebo and—"

"The guests will understand," Stone interrupted, figuring he could lend Emma and Romeo a hand. "What mom could resist looking out her kitchen window to watch the whole process of her daughter developing her lead performance? It's a once-in-a-lifetime chance."

Emma didn't look pleased about the setup he'd described, but Deirdre seemed to reconsider. "I don't know," she mused grudgingly.

"Emma's dad will be jealous as hell." Stone told himself he wasn't fishing for information. He was just trying to make the deal irresistible. From what he'd seen of broken marriages, nothing delighted an ex-spouse more than sticking the knife in and breaking it off. But the flash of something in Deirdre's all-too-expressive eyes made the back of his neck prickle.

"Emma's father isn't—"

"He vanished before I was born and never cared about seeing me again. And that's fine with me. I never needed a dad, anyway." Emma gave her mother a pointed glance. "I have Uncle Cade and the Captain."

Drew looked even more uncomfortable than he'd been moments before. If Deirdre's obvious disapproval hadn't chased him off, the tension thickening the air this time seemed to make him look for an exit line.

"Actually, I'd better get going," he said. "I was heading home to work on learning my lines now."

"Oh." Emma wasn't quite a good enough actress to hide her disappointment. "Yeah, sure."

Drew hung in there a moment longer in spite of The Mother from Hell. "Some of the language in this play... well, it's not like normal dialogue, you know? It doesn't exactly roll real easy off my tongue."

"It can't be too difficult," Deirdre said. "People have been performing it for five hundred years."

"It's brilliant," Drew said, brave enough to risk the evil eye in defense of the Bard. "I love listening to it, reading it, seeing it performed. I just feel a little dorky doing it alone. My kid brother and I share a room, and he's a real pain in the a—neck when I try to practice lines. You know how brothers are."

"No, I don't," Emma said. Was that wistfulness Stone detected in her voice? "It's just Mom and me at home."

Drew almost looked envious. "Wow. That must be awesome when you're trying to practice."

Maybe it was great at times like that, Stone mused, the hint of loneliness in Emma's dark eyes echoing memories of his own childhood. It was the rest of the time that stunk.

"Well, I'd better head out and get busy humiliating myself in front of my brother," Drew tried damned hard to get Emma to smile. "I'm not as good at memorizing lines as you are." Drew turned to Stone. "You should see Emma. She's a shoo-in for the drama department Hall of Fame.

She's got like this photographic memory. No one learns lines as well as she does."

"Actually," Emma said, "I just came out to breakfast with Mom and Mr. Stone because Mom made me. You know, that whole quality family time deal."

Deirdre made a strangled sound in her throat, but, to her credit, didn't say what she was thinking. Stone figured she didn't have to. Emma already knew.

Emma gave her mother her most irresistible smile. "I know I said I'd come with you, but running lines is more important than breakfast. And it's not like you don't have company."

Deirdre's eyes widened, and Stone knew just what she thought about the company Emma had tricked her into keeping.

Emma turned back to Drew. "Mr. Stone is helping with the restoration of March Winds' ballroom."

"That's great. You know, people used to say the house was haunted." Drew looked as if he found the possibility fascinating.

"March Winds haunted?" Emma echoed. "Really?" But there was something just off-key in her astonishment that made Stone sense some hidden joke. Didn't these McDaniels ever just say what they meant, straight-out?

"Mom, you don't mind if I go off with Drew, do you?"

Bad question, Stone thought, watching Deirdre grind her tooth enamel to dust.

"To work on the play," Emma added, as if she'd read his thoughts. "You know how seriously I take my work. I want to be rehearsing off-script as soon as possible, and working with Drew, I'll pick up my cues a lot faster."

"I should make you sit right here and eat pancakes with the rest of us," Deirdre threatened.

"I know you should." Emma's grin blazed as she slid gracefully out of the booth. "But you won't."

If the boy hadn't been standing there, Stone would bet Emma would've dropped a kiss on her mom's head. She leaned close to Deirdre, and Stone had to strain to decipher her whisper.

"I was planning to ditch you somehow, anyway," Emma said, devilment lighting her animated features. "So you and Mr. Stone could be alone. Have fun. You can kill me later."

Emma flipped them both a wave and breezed out of the diner, Drew Lawson a few steps behind her.

Deirdre all but dove off the end of the bench, and slid into the one Emma had vacated. Hell, she didn't have to look so relieved about it. It wasn't as if he was planning to bite her. At least not in any way that hurt. Now, making her moan because she liked it so damned much, that was another possibility altogether. Heat stole through him as he imagined skimming her lightly with his teeth, wondered where she'd like it best.

"I'm going to have to ground her for the rest of her life. Maybe the witch had the right idea with Rapunzel. Lock her in a tower and be done with it."

Stone chuckled.

"It's not funny!" Deirdre objected, her cheeks turning a pretty shade of pink. "She did this on purpose. Tried to…well…"

"Set us up?" He let his voice drop low, husky. He knew damned well the effect it had on most women. "I had that figured out in the first five minutes."

"Then you shouldn't have come along in the first place!"

He glanced at the curve of her throat, wondering if teething *that* spot would make her scream.

She looked all the more flustered, and she didn't even know his virtual lovemaking had dropped a few inches lower to where he could just make out the top edge of her bra through her white shirt. "What were you thinking?" she demanded.

Stone's gaze dropped to the full curves of her lips. What would she say if he told her the truth? That he'd wanted her from the moment he'd met her. Tried to convince himself he'd just played right into that undeniable male pitfall of wanting what he couldn't have. But seeing her again, he'd had to face the truth: that purely physical hunger hadn't abated.

It bit deeper than ever, setting his nerves on edge, making his body harden and his logic desert him. What he wanted was a hellaciously sexy one-night stand so he could get Deirdre McDaniel out of his system. But one night wouldn't be nearly enough for what he wanted to do to her.

He crossed one leg over the other, trying to mask a reaction that would embarrass a green kid like Drew Lawson, let alone a grown man who should be able to control his reaction to a woman, hot as she might be.

What the hell was the matter with him? Deirdre McDaniel was just another woman. And this was just another case, Stone tried to tell himself. *Yeah, and the* Titanic *was just another boat.*

The woman and everyone around her were dangerous as all get-out. Because she made him cross lines he'd sworn never to cross again. Feel things like guilt, responsibility. Hell, he got paid for digging up secrets, exploding bombs in people's lives. He'd gotten used to it, cynical as it sounded, mastered a cool detachment that meant survival. But something about the McDaniel family stripped all that away.

They'd forced him to see they were different. Paying back not only stolen money that had been left as a supposed legacy by Finn O'Grady's father, but a hundred thousand dollars her old man had gambled away, money they'd never seen.

What was he doing here? Stone could barely admit it even to himself: he was trying to make things right.

He stiffened, feeling Deirdre's angry gaze boring into him, knowing she was waiting for an answer. Damned if he could tell her the truth. He groped for something that would give him cover.

"Actually, watching you in action here has been a big relief," he drawled. "I thought it was just something about me that got your Irish up, but it looks like you hate the whole male race. You could have given that poor kid a break. From what I could see, he was a mom's dream come true."

"Not this mom's." Bitterness curled Deirdre's lips. "In my experience I've found out that if something looks perfect, it's usually too good to be true."

Stone watched old pain flicker in Deirdre's eyes, found himself wondering if a man had put it there.

"God, you make me so furious!" she snapped. "What were you thinking, coming here in the first place?"

"How much fun it would be to tick you off."

"Next time don't bother to go to so much effort. You pretty much tick me off every time you open your mouth."

"Yeah, well, I have problems with your mouth, too." *Every time I see it I want to put my tongue in it.*

He groped for some way to defuse the heat Deirdre McDaniel had stirred up in him without even trying. Hell, what would happen if the woman ever gave him the green light? Spontaneous combustion?

Never happen, buddy, a voice inside him echoed. Not in a million years. But she was here right now, trapped in this booth with him. A week ago he wouldn't have thought that possible, either, would he? Still, he sensed if he let her know what she did to him, she'd ditch him faster than Emma had ditched breakfast for Drew Lawson.

Think, Stone, think. Don't let the woman know she makes you sweat....

He should have fired off some edgy quip, something to irritate or distract, or make her laugh.

Instead he said the thing he least expected—the truth.

"You know, you've got a great kid. Even if she is anything but subtle."

Deirdre's chin bumped up. "Yeah. Emma's terrific. You'll forgive me for being honest. But you're not exactly the kind of company I want her around."

"Because I have a Y chromosome?"

"Because you apparently killed someone."

Stone went still. "Did I?"

"That convict said you did, and—and you admitted yourself that you lost your badge. You must have done something terrible enough to deserve it."

"Just ask my ex-wife."

"As for the—the details—"

"Oh, it's all there. A matter of public record. Check at the library in the old newspapers, March 11, eight years ago." Anger, frustration from another lifetime surged through Stone. Hell, he'd thought he was done with all that burning up inside over things he could never change. But Deirdre's condemnation ate at him as if the whole thing had happened yesterday—the stifling courtroom, reporters thronging the courthouse steps, the death of the man he'd resolved to be when Tony had taken a rebellious punk and turned him into the son he'd never had. For an instant he hated Deirdre for dragging all that garbage through his memory again. As if he could ever really forget. He took aim at her most vulnerable spot, fighting dirty, the only way he knew now.

"You want all the gory details, sweet thing, have Emma help you do a search at the library. What she turns up ought to scare the kid shitless of me. But then, wait. That won't work. Emma thinks I'm some kind of fancy home repair guy, doesn't she?"

Deirdre swallowed hard. "Don't try to turn this around on me."

"There's no *trying* involved when it comes to hitting such an easy target. You want to judge me, lady? Just remember, you're no straight shooter yourself."

"Emma...the situation is complicated."

"When I mentioned her dad, Emma made it crystal clear how she feels about this search of yours. Cases like this can get messy. Result in collateral damage you never expect. You may not think it's fair, but the truth is, this isn't just about you, Deirdre, just like the case I got hung for wasn't just about me. Other people might get hurt. Like Emma."

For an instant he glimpsed a vulnerability in Deirdre he'd never seen before, was glad he'd gotten back some of his own. But her face hardened, leaving her more determined than ever. "You let me worry about my daughter," she said. "You worry about what I'm paying you for."

Whatever you're paying, lady, Stone thought, it won't be enough.

"So let's get on with it. What's your next move?"

"Finding the woman your brother told me about— this friend of your mother's who watched Cade while your mother went out to meet her lover."

Why didn't he just say meet "your father" and be done with it? Stone wondered. That was obviously the way Deirdre was determined to think of this total stranger. But Jake couldn't do it, because even six years later he could still picture Martin McDaniel, that craggy old man with eyes like a hawk and a "take no prisoners" scowl when his family was threatened.

And Stone had threatened the McDaniel family's happiness before, set loose a disaster that had almost cost Cade McDaniel his wife.

"I'm going with you," Deirdre insisted.

"You just had a major meltdown because I came to eat a few pancakes in your presence. Now you want to tie yourself around my neck like a damned millstone while I do my job? That's the most idiotic idea I've ever heard of."

"Then it's a good thing I'm not asking for your opinion."

He wanted to stay angry, wanted to blast the woman for cutting him to the quick. *With a weapon she didn't even know she had?* a voice whispered inside him. *Be fair, Stone. Hell, if you had a daughter like Emma, you wouldn't want her hanging around a bad cop, either.*

The fight seemed to have gone out of Deirdre, as well, but not that tough-as-nails determination. "This is about me, Stone. *Me*," she said, her beautiful, brave eyes revealing for just a heartbeat that haunting pain he hadn't been able to forget. "I've heard nothing but lies my whole life. Now, I intend to hear the truth."

But whose truth? Stone wondered. Her mother's? Her father's? Did she have any idea how different from each other they could be? Hell, all she had to do was look at the mess Finn's father had made—not only tearing up the life of the woman he'd stolen from, but his own daughter's life and the life of the man who loved her.

He'd left them with a fight that wasn't theirs, guilt they didn't deserve, while they made choices so tough Stone had hardly believed honor like that still existed. Or love…

Hell, if he'd known the whole truth, Stone wondered if he would have just turned and walked away. Never told them…

But hadn't he learned the hard way that sometimes the truth doesn't matter? In the O'Grady case he'd done what he'd been paid to do. And Cade McDaniel and his pretty wife had suffered the consequences.

This case would be different, Stone promised himself. He'd make damned sure Deirdre McDaniel's story had a better ending.

One that wouldn't stalk him on nights he couldn't sleep.

CHAPTER 6

MAYBE A WEEK hadn't done anything to improve Jake Stone's attitude, Deirdre thought as she glanced across his pick-up truck's interior at the sexy-as-all-get-out P.I., but then, she hadn't hired him for his charming personality. It was results she'd wanted, and her instincts about his skill had been dead-on.

He'd found her mother's friend four days after what Emma called "The Great Lagomarcinos Caper," and, miracle of miracles, the woman now lived three hours away from Whitewater. Driving distance, Stone had said on the phone, but still six hours in a car and God knew how long for the interview itself. There was no sense in Deirdre throwing away her whole day, especially since she'd been so all-fired mad when Emma had trapped her into spending half an hour with him at the diner.

Deirdre still ground her teeth when she thought of how skillfully Stone had tried to play her: the P.I. attempting to convince her he was doing her a favor by trying to keep her away from the one person who might be able to throw some light on the questions that had been tearing Deirdre up inside.

She'd told him where he could put his "favor" in no uncertain terms. There was no way she was going to learn about her birth father secondhand. She had questions of her own to ask. And there were others Norma Davenport wouldn't be able to answer in words. Deirdre would only learn some truths by looking into the woman's eyes. If being trapped in a car with Stone for six hours was the price she had to pay, so be it.

There was only one glitch in that line of reasoning, Deirdre thought wryly. It was a whole lot easier to *say* being this close to Stone was worth it than to actually *do* it.

From the moment she'd slid into the passenger seat, she'd felt claustrophobic, as if Stone's attitude took up even more room than his six-foot-four body.

He'd looked like Mr. Professional for the first hour of the drive, his white dress shirt starched, his long, sleek hair caught back with some sort of fastener with a silver Celtic design. And as for coming up with conversation, that was one problem she didn't have to worry about at all. Stone was so preoccupied with his cell phone from the moment they pulled away from March Winds that he might as well have been alone.

Deirdre used the hours to focus on the meeting ahead, writing down in a spiral notebook every question she might have for this woman so she wouldn't forget. And yet, as the landscape whizzed by, her own agitation built along with Stone's, the truck's cab seeming to shrink around them until there wasn't enough oxygen for either.

She slanted a glance at Stone, the deep stress lines carved into his rugged face making him look even more ruthless, his hard tone making her wonder just how far he'd go if someone crossed him. Or had he already proved that eight years ago with his gun? Stone left yet another terse message, demanding someone call him, then turned his head to glare at Deirdre.

"What did you tell Emma?"

The question jolted Deirdre like a live wire, coming out of the blue. Damn the man, it was none of his business. "I didn't tell her anything. She'll be at school while we're gone."

Stone grimaced. "She's a smart kid. Sooner or later she's going to suspect something is up."

Stone's warning only fed Deirdre's growing dread. If Emma's keen instincts where her mother was concerned weren't enough to put the fear of discovery in Deirdre, there was the distinct possibility that Cade or Finn would spill the truth, however inadvertently. What was that World War II maxim Deirdre could remember her mother saying to the Captain when she wanted to stop something explosive from falling out of the old man's mouth? "Loose lips sink ships." But McDaniel mouths were experts at tripping up and landing people in trouble, and Cade and Finn were no exception.

Deirdre pressed her hand against her stomach, trying to push back the feeling of impending doom that had never quite left her since the moment she'd lied to her daughter. She couldn't let that change the course she'd set. Much as she loved Emma, and loath as she was to hurt or disappoint her, Deirdre wouldn't knuckle under to guilt.

"People pay me to give them the hard truth," Stone said, big hands flexing on the steering wheel. "Every day you let pass without leveling with the kid, you're digging yourself a deeper hole."

As if Deirdre hadn't figured that out for herself. She winced, remembering when Stone called last night. Of course Emma had dived for the phone, the delighted sixteen-year-old chattering to Stone for five minutes before she handed the receiver over to Deirdre.

And the girl who would bemoan her lack of privacy whenever Deirdre stayed in the room during Emma's phone calls hung over Deirdre's shoulder as if Stone were reading off the numbers of a winning lottery ticket.

How much longer could she keep Stone's profession a secret?

Stone scooped up the cell phone again, fumbled with it until he pressed some kind of speed dial. Deirdre took the gift of his distraction, hoping to use it to her advantage, staring out the window in hopes the man would lapse back into a silence as hard as his name.

But whatever hold Stone had kept on his temper seemed to snap. Deirdre jumped, startled as Stone nearly slammed the phone into one of the cup holders on the dashboard. Hooking his long fingers into the knot of his tie, he yanked it down as if it had been strangling him. Tearing the loop over his head, he threw the tie into the back seat. He swore under his breath as he unfastened the first two buttons of his collar, revealing the tanned hollow of his throat and beneath it, a dusting of dark hair.

"Problem?" Deirdre asked.

"Hell, no. This day is turning into a fucking joy ride." Stone growled, and attacked his cuffs, unbuttoning them one at a time and rolling the sleeves up until they skimmed just below the crook of his elbow, exposing sinewy, tanned forearms. His jaw was set so fiercely Deirdre almost felt sorry for whoever had ticked him off.

Almost. Part of her was glad the jerk who was so good at pushing her buttons was having a few of his own buttons stomped on, hard.

He should have looked like hell, or at least disheveled,

the way he was decimating those Mr. Cool clothes. Instead, the man oozed sensuality, reminding Deirdre of a tiger on a branch, seeming distracted, but ready in a split second to leap on its prey. His gaze burned so hot through the window, it seemed the glass should melt, his shoulders felt broader with suppressed anger, the hard muscles she'd felt when he'd pulled her against him knotted with tension.

Would he bring that kind of intensity to everything? Burn a woman up with passion if he ever let loose the emotions so tightly coiled under all that tanned skin?

Her imagination flashed to an image of Stone's big body covering hers....

Desire and alarm warred inside her. Deirdre bit the inside of her lip, and looked out the passenger window, trying to blot out the overwhelming presence of the man beside her by thinking of the interview and the tangled past she'd come from. But she could smell the blatantly masculine scent of him, feel the primitive power in him, sense the kind of passion that could turn in a heartbeat from anger to something far more dangerous.

"It's showtime," Stone bit out as he pulled to a stop before a row of lovely condominiums, their perfectly trimmed yards almost *Twilight Zone* identical, the house numbers so tastefully small she wondered how Stone could be sure he had the right place.

Deirdre sucked in a steadying breath, filled with a sudden reluctance, absurd considering how far she had come.

Had her mother kept in touch with this woman? Sent Christmas cards? What would her mother's friend think of her? Deirdre wondered. Did the woman know... It didn't matter what this woman knew about Deirdre's rocky relationship with Emmaline McDaniel. Deirdre was the one whose questions mattered today.

Please, Mom, Deirdre stunned herself by praying, almost as if for forgiveness. *I have to know...who I am.*

She started in surprise as Stone yanked open her door, and she realized she hadn't even noticed him climb out from behind the wheel or round the vehicle to her side.

"You're not going to change your mind now?" Stone taunted.

Deirdre climbed out of the car, smoothing the sage-green tunic she'd worn over black slacks. Showtime, Stone had said, as naturally as Emma might. Deirdre had to wonder just how this meeting would play out— High drama? Tragedy? Or farce?

NORMA DAVENPORT FANNED a handful of old pictures out on the white marble coffee table next to a tray of coffee and store-bought cookies she'd arranged on a plate. Her face, tanned as old leather, provided a stark contrast to the wispy, silver-blond hair coiffed to perfection. "After we spoke on Tuesday, I went through my old photo albums and found these," the older woman said, perching on the edge of an oyster satin wing chair. "Emmaline was such a shy little thing, almost a baby herself, with that darling little boy of hers and that big, handsome husband. She reminded me of a lost bird. Whenever there were parties at the officers' club I swear she'd try to melt right into the wallpaper."

Deirdre shifted on the rose-colored couch and picked up the photo closest to her, peered at the image of her mother looking stiff and unhappy as she stood beside a much-younger Norma at a cocktail party.

Emmaline's brown hair curled around a delicate, pale face, a far-off look in eyes too big. Deirdre could almost hear her singing those haunting old jazz ballads that were the only lullaby Deirdre had ever known, songs full of yearning and pain and love gone wrong.

But once Deirdre had grown old enough to understand the words and recognize the genuine sadness they brought to her mother's soft eyes, the songs hadn't soothed anymore. The ballads had left Deirdre longing to be like Cade, able to comfort her, draw their mother back from those dark waters.

"She never did like getting her picture taken," Deirdre said. She and Emma had gone through a box in the attic once, at Linden Lane, sorted through a long succession of holidays, Christmas trees, turkey dinners, sledding parties and Easter egg hunts, that showed just Deirdre and Cade and the Captain, as if Emmaline McDaniel had already been a ghost.

But looking at Norma's photos, it seemed that Emmaline had always had that haunted quality about her. It hadn't appeared later, the way Deirdre had so often thought, after Emmaline was saddled with such a disappointing daughter.

"She looks so sad here," Deirdre said softly, running her thumb across the picture's slick edge.

Stone leaned toward Norma, an absurdly fragile coffee cup cradled in his big hands. "Did Mrs. McDaniel give you any reason why she was unhappy?"

Norma shrugged, her shoulders bird-thin beneath a tangerine-colored golf shirt. "Yes, she shared some of what she was feeling, just the way all women do. She said she was weary from being dragged from place to place, missing her mother. They were very close, you know, Emmaline and her mother."

Deirdre's heart stung. She gulped a burning hot swig of coffee, then set her own cup abruptly down. She felt Stone's gaze shift to her, could almost hear the wheels whirring in his head. God above, did the man ever miss a nuance, a flash of emotion?

In an instant the hint of concern she'd thought she'd seen vanished, probably little more than her imagination.

"So," Stone said, "it sounds like there was trouble from the beginning."

"The army can be hard on a marriage. Even the strongest ones. And Captain McDaniel was as gung-ho as men come. He loved the danger, the challenge, pushing himself."

Deirdre grimaced. The old buzzard hadn't changed much. It was just a little harder to find danger and excitement in Whitewater, Illinois. But those rare times there was some kind of mayhem he usually ended up in the middle of it, to the amusement of the Whitewater police force.

Norma sipped her own coffee, staring for a moment into the rich dark depths as if she were peering back in time. "Emmaline hated the fact that Captain McDaniel was gone so much. He'd volunteered for hazardous duty, and would disappear for months at a time. My Paul was with him." Norma's eyes softened with grief and worry ages old.

"That must have been hard for you," Stone said, so gently it surprised Deirdre.

"Both of our husbands had cut their combat teeth in Vietnam, long before your father met your mother, Deirdre. Some of the things Paul told me about their tour of duty…" Norma shuddered. "Well, it helped me understand the demons that drove him. But I don't think Emmaline wanted to hear about the ugliness. Or maybe Martin didn't want that world to touch his wife."

"The Captain still doesn't talk about it," Deirdre said.

"Most vets don't," Stone said as if he knew. "Unless they talk to each other. "

"You know about combat vets, then, don't you, Mr. Stone?"

"The brotherhood of cops is the same. Your husband must have trusted you deeply."

Stone's comment made the old woman glow with soft pride. "Paul was twenty when he first arrived in Saigon. But Martin was even younger when he fought there. Did you know that, Deirdre? He was on the front lines when he was just eighteen."

"He never told me," Deirdre said. But then, why would he? He'd certainly never trusted her, deeply or otherwise. And they'd never shared the broken pieces of their lives. They'd just pretended vulnerable places didn't exist. Still, she could hardly get her mind around the concept that the Captain had only been two years older than Emma was when he'd been dropped into hell, faced that brutal world.

An ache settled in her chest. She didn't want to hurt for the Captain. She wanted to feel she'd been justified in keeping silent the past week, reminding herself that he'd shut her out of vital parts of his life, too.

"And after Vietnam?" Stone set the cup down and picked up another picture, this one of a far younger Martin McDaniel and a buddy displaying bulging biceps with matching tattoos.

"After the war was over, Paul and Martin stayed in the Special Forces," Norma said. "Sometimes I think it was almost worse, not even knowing what continent they were on. It was terrifying, watching them pack up and walk away to whatever mission they were sent on."

"There was plenty going on in the world then," Stone said, with a meditative frown. "The Cold War, unstable governments all over Asia and South America. All of it covert."

"They made me so proud, our husbands. I'd look at them and think how fine they were, how lucky we were that they were keeping America safe. And yet...every time you kissed them goodbye, you knew it might be the last."

"That must have been hard," Deirdre said.

"It came to a head three weeks before Christmas one year. That knock on the door. Opening it. Seeing the company chaplain in dress uniform. I was at Deirdre's *Norma* making spaghetti sauce when he came. His eyes... I'll never forget the chaplain's eyes as he told us the operation had gone sour. The helicopter that was supposed to extract them from wherever they were had crashed. All men missing."

"Mom never...never told me," Deirdre breathed, thinking how little she'd known the woman who'd given birth to her, raised her.

"We didn't even know what country they were in," Norma continued. "And odds were we never would. The one thing we did know for certain was that when a mission went wrong, the men were on their own. Our government would claim they'd turned rogue. No one in the military would ever acknowledge they were following orders."

Stone nodded, his eyes suddenly dark, still, with an empathy Deirdre would never have suspected him capable of. A shadow touched his mouth, like something bittersweet. "It must have been hideous," Jake said. "Thinking they'd given their lives for their country. Fearing they'd be branded as traitors because it was convenient for the high command."

Deirdre tried to imagine her fragile mother in that situation, so far from anyone she was close to, believing the

Captain was dead or maybe being tortured in some hellhole in the darkest corner of the world.

"The little boy...Kincaid," Norma said, pausing to remember his name. "Why, he made it even harder for Emmaline. All he'd talk about was his daddy. Two years old, and he'd wear the hat from his father's dress uniform, and practice his salute in the mirror. Insisted on kissing Martin's picture every night before she tucked him in. Insisted Emmaline kiss the picture, too. Kiss Martin's picture, wondering if he was dead, or how she'd ever tell that child."

Tears burned Deirdre's eyes. She blinked them away.

"The wives of the missing men, we all celebrated the holidays together, trying for just one day to hold back our grief for the sake of our children. Your brother was playing Christmas Day with a toy gun Captain McDaniel had bought him the day before he deployed, yelling the way boys do. It was the only time I saw Emmaline break down."

Deirdre wished she could reach out, touch Norma's wrist in that gentle way Finn had of comforting even a stranger. But she wasn't Finn, and she couldn't even comfort herself.

Stone surprised her, laying a gentle hand on Norma's arm. "It must have been torture, not knowing."

Norma nodded, her face twisting, making the pain of that grim Christmas seem fresh as yesterday. "When the men arrived back on base, Emmaline told the Captain she couldn't bear the army life any longer, waiting to hear if he was dead. His tour of duty was almost over. She didn't care what he did, as long as people weren't shooting at him and she wasn't left alone. She wasn't going to tell that boy his daddy was never coming home."

"What happened?" Jake asked quietly.

"Captain McDaniel came home roaring drunk three days later. He'd re-upped without telling her."

"That sounds like something he would do. He's so hard-headed." Deirdre winced inwardly, wanting to kick her father for steamrolling her mother with the pain of that near-fatal miss still so new. And yet, shouldn't her mother have known better than to forbid the Captain to do anything? The instant someone laid down the law to Martin McDaniel, he felt honor bound to break it. "He always did have to have things his own way."

"Why, what else was he supposed to do with his life?" Norma asked, astonished. "Sell shoes? Teach school? Deliver mail? He was a soldier, the best of the best. He was the one who brought all those other men home when they'd gone missing. Paul told me Martin outsmarted the enemy, gathered his shattered team together, got them through a jungle, God knows where."

Deirdre's heart ached, but she couldn't get past the bitterness, imagining Cade waiting for a father who might never come.

"Yeah, my dad, the hero," Deirdre sniped, trying to hide the raw feeling in her heart, Norma's description of Cade jabbing at a far newer wound—Cade's heartbreakingly familiar face stark with pleading as he tried to shield the Captain, tried to explain his own betrayal.

"The Captain still has this obsession with trying to save the world. And damned the cost," Deirdre said. "His last little performance left him with a broken hip."

"Oh, dear," Norma said. "I'm so sorry to hear that."

"Not as sorry as my brother," Deirdre muttered. "The Captain's staying with Cade at the moment." God only knew where Martin McDaniel would end up. Sure, he was staying with Cade for the time being, but despite all Cade's good intentions, a restless, independent warrior like Martin McDaniel wouldn't stay a guest in his son's house for long.

"Mrs. Davenport," Stone cut in smoothly, "is there anything else you can tell us that might help us understand how this whole deal went down?"

"Deal?" Norma echoed.

"What brought the marriage to the breaking point," Stone explained.

Norma turned toward Deirdre. "After Captain McDaniel re-upped, things between your mother and Martin went from bad to worse. She cried all the time, and he started staying away from the house as much as possible. Army housing is cramped, the walls were thin. I could hear them fighting. Everyone could. Their little boy, he got quieter, too, like he was always watching, waiting for the next explosion."

Sometimes Deirdre was sure Cade was still keeping watch the same way.

"It's not easy, being married to a man in uniform," Norma said gently. "Just doing their job demands more of them than most men would ever be capable of giving.

"Being a soldier isn't what they do. It's who they are. Emmaline didn't understand what she was asking when she wanted him to go civilian. She was asking Martin to change everything that mattered to him—a lifestyle, a code of honor. She might as well have asked him to change his blood and bone."

"In other words," Deirdre said, "you're telling me that he'd chosen to have a family, then refused to do what was best for them."

"Did he?" Norma asked.

"What do you mean by that, Mrs. Davenport?" Stone watched her, intent.

"I know what Captain McDaniel did might seem hard,

unfeeling to you. But Emmaline knew what she was getting into when she married him. She'd signed on to be an army wife. When a man is as good at his job as the Captain is, he's bound to love it. And frankly, his country needed him. It's hard for a man to turn his back on that kind of responsibility, especially when his superiors are telling him he's the only one who can lead a team deep enough into enemy territory, smart enough to get whatever documents or drugs or military secrets are buried in the middle of some jungle and get them into American hands."

"At least he's consistent," Deirdre said. "He still thinks he's the only one who can do things right when it counts. He does the cops' jobs for 'em, the sheriff's job, and if the courts would let him, he'd be happy to be the judge and jury, too. He would have made a great dictator of some no-name country out there. I'm not sure how great a husband he was, though. Did Mr. Stone tell you why we came here today? To ask…"

Deirdre hesitated. Why was the truth so hard to say?

"He said you had questions about the time Emmaline and I were on base together at Fort Benning. It does my heart good knowing you love your mother so much you want to talk about her, even now when she's gone."

Deirdre's cheeks burned. She glanced at Stone. Hadn't he told the woman that this wasn't some benign trip down memory lane? Or had he been afraid Norma Davenport would refuse to see them if she knew the truth?

"Actually," Stone said, obviously sensing Deirdre's unease, "there's a little more to it than that. Hearing about life on the base, I mean. Deirdre recently discovered a letter that proves her mother had an affair during the time you and Emmaline McDaniel were friends."

Dismay flooded Norma's features. If Deirdre had had

any doubts this was the friend her mother had relied on during the affair, just looking at Norma's reaction would have set them to rest. "I...why, I can't break a confidence..." Norma stammered. For the first time Deirdre realized why Stone had been so careful, lulling the woman into a false sense of security, getting her to reveal how close she and Emmaline had been until it would be impossible to escape.

But Norma Davenport didn't have to tell them anything, Deirdre realized with a start. She could politely show them to the door and take Emmaline's secrets to the grave.

Quiet desperation filled Deirdre. "My mother is dead, ma'am," she said. "And the Captain knows about the affair, same as I do. Somewhere out there is my real father, my birth father. And I intend to find him."

Norma's fingers fluttered to her throat. "Oh, dear. But how can you be sure..."

"There was an accident," Stone explained. "The blood tests proved Deirdre isn't Captain McDaniel's biological daughter. Mrs. McDaniel managed to keep the truth from her husband, but left this letter where she was sure someday Deirdre would find it and learn the truth."

Stone handed Norma the letter. The old woman groped for a pair of frameless glasses hanging on a gold chain around her neck and slipped them on, reading the anguished lines her friend had written.

"Why would my mother keep this unless she wanted me to find my way back to this man, whoever he is?" Deirdre pressed.

"I don't know," Norma said, waffling.

"My brother, Cade, heard the story straight from Mom's mouth years ago. There's no denying the affair happened, or that I'm the daughter of some man I've never seen."

"But even if that's true, it doesn't mean I know anything about this."

"Cade demanded to know what Mom had done with him while she—she was sleeping with this man. Mom said he stayed with her best friend."

Norma pressed her hand to her throat in dismay. "I wouldn't want Captain McDaniel to know that I...well, had anything to do with—"

Why should that matter? Deirdre wondered. It was obvious her mother had told this woman plenty when it came to what the Captain had done to wreck the marriage. But obviously Norma Davenport cared very much what Martin McDaniel thought.

"Mrs. Davenport, this is a private inquiry," Stone tried to reassure the woman. "There's no reason Captain McDaniel needs to know you've even spoken to us if that would make it easier for you to tell what you know."

"I know you must think I'm being a silly old woman, trying to keep secrets no one should care about anymore. But Martin McDaniel saved my husband's life and...I've always thought of the thirty years of marriage we shared after that mission as a kind of gift from him. One I treasure. To be the one to throw Emmaline's infidelity in his face—"

"He doesn't know anything about you." Stone cut in, his tone soothing, as if trying to lure a jumper down off a ledge. "We're only here because all the research I did pointed to you as Emmaline McDaniel's closest friend at the time in question."

"Mrs. Davenport," Deirdre pleaded. "I'm begging you. Please."

Norma looked from Deirdre to Stone, obviously torn about what to do. Stone stepped into her line of vision, giving her that penetrating look that always made Deirdre feel as if he were a superhero with X-ray vision and if she wanted to keep her secrets she'd better dive behind a solid lead wall.

Deirdre could almost feel Stone melting the woman's resistance, getting Norma Davenport to somehow trust him.

After a long moment, Norma spoke. "All right, then. Yes. There was…a man. Emmaline was still distraught over what Captain McDaniel had done. Then the squad was deployed again, before they could work things out."

"You mean, before the Captain could bully her into seeing things his way?" Deirdre asked grimly.

"She loved music. We went to a jazz club called The Rat Pack, and there…there was this man onstage playing saxophone."

"Do you remember his name? What he looked like?"

"Jimmy…something. He was beautiful to look at—so different from our men. Tall and slender, with these big, dark eyes that looked as if they'd seen too much of life. And when he held that saxophone, it was as if every woman in the place could feel his hands on her and wanted to take his pain away."

Deirdre remembered her mother's songs, the haunting sadness inside her that the Captain had never understood. But this Jimmy must have understood the gentle, fragile places in Emmaline McDaniel, places bruised when her husband had discounted her fears, thrown her back into that terror of uncertainty after she'd begged him not to.

"Jimmy promised to take her home after the club closed," Norma continued. "I told her it was crazy, but…I think the Captain's betrayal hurt her so much she wanted to hurt him back." Norma raised eyes filled with empathy to Deirdre. "It may not be noble to do something like that, dear, but it's very, very human."

"She began to see this musician after that?" Stone asked.

Norma nodded. "Emmaline slipped away every night, just to hear the music, she said, but I knew better. She left Kincaid to stay with me all night, claiming it was unfair to wake him to take him home. Then she'd steal out to the car, dressed up in something soft and pretty. For the first time since I'd met her, her eyes—her eyes, they just sparkled. She'd laugh and smile and looked so young. That sad young wife I'd first met transforming before my eyes. It made me understand what made Captain McDaniel fall in love with her."

Deirdre tried to picture her mother glowing and adventurous, breaking all the rules. Happy in a way Deirdre had never seen her. Had she been insane? Cheating on the Captain so close to the base, where anybody might see her? Or by that time was she just too hurt to care?

"It's too dangerous, I'd warn her," Norma said, "but she'd just toss her hair and say her own husband loved danger more than he loved her, so why shouldn't she taste some of it herself? Maybe she'd finally understand what he found so irresistible."

"So she was trying to get even with the Captain?" Stone asked. "Then why keep it secret for thirty-some years?"

"Only Emmaline could tell you that. I can tell you this—that her world came crashing in. The Captain got caught in a cross fire and was airlifted back to the States two weeks later, badly wounded. Emmaline rushed to his bedside. They must have worked something out because I never heard her mention her jazz musician again."

"Revenge. Nice," Deirdre said bitterly. "I was conceived to get back at the Captain. Guess that worked, and then some. Nothing like a hell-born kid like me to punish someone."

"What about the musician," Stone probed. "After the McDaniels left the base, did you ever hear about him?"

"He sold band instruments during the day at a place called Lelands near Fort Benning. It closed four years later when the building burned to the ground. I'm afraid if you're looking for records, you'll find a dead end. People drift in and out of an army town, you know. There have been so many new families in and out of the base since Emmaline and I were there that it wouldn't even seem like the same place. From the little Emmaline said about her musician, he'd moved even more often than she had."

And would have continued moving from town to town, stage to stage, Deirdre figured, remembering her own years of singing for her supper. Another stage, another crowd, another chance to be discovered.

"Deirdre." Mrs. Davenport laid her hand on Deirdre's arm. "Even if this turns out to be a dead end, there is something you need to know. Your mother was a good person."

"Yeah, just ask my father. She was perfect. Except for the part where she slept with some guy who wasn't her husband, and then passed me off as the Captain's kid."

Norma winced at her bluntness. "I don't think life was easy for her. Especially during the time Captain McDaniel was in the army. She didn't fit in with the other wives, hated bridge and golf and tennis. And shy—lord, she was shy. And the soldiers, well, they brought the rowdy out in each other. Drinking and playing poker and pool. Staying up all night. And the Captain, he was such an adrenaline junkie, a workaholic. So consumed, he didn't even see how much she hated it all...."

The older woman seemed lost in memories. She twisted the thin gold wedding band around one gnarled finger. "You know, it wasn't long after the Captain was injured that her mother died. I was glad when I heard Emmaline had a daughter of her own, someone to love, share all the things she and her own mother had."

Deirdre swallowed hard, couldn't manage a reply through a throat thick with emotion. Maybe her mother had been happy, those first months after she'd been born. Been able to dress Deirdre up in frilly clothes, put ribbons in her hair, imagine giving her pearls and teaching her to do all those needlework things Emmaline had always loved. And if Emmaline had longed to recapture the closeness she'd had with her own mother, she must have been even more disappointed in the daughter she had than Deirdre had imagined.

Norma reached up, took Deirdre's chin between her fingers, lifting her face to the light. "Strange. I never would have guessed you were Emmaline's daughter. It's hard to see any hint of her in your face, Deirdre—do you know that?"

"Yeah. We, uh, never looked much alike." She wanted to get out of here. Needed some air. The past was winding too tight around her chest, making it hard to breathe. "If you don't know anything else, maybe we should go," Deirdre said. "Not, uh, take up any more of your time."

She dreaded that the older woman might see a crack in her armor, couldn't bear the humiliation of anyone trying to comfort her, reassure her, attempt to convince her that what she knew was wrong. That her mother hadn't seen her as one giant mistake.

But Norma still seemed puzzled, her brow wrinkling despite an obvious face-lift. "Well, isn't life just full of surprises," she mused. "You're nothing like I expected you'd be when Mr. Stone here told me I was going to get to meet my dear friend Emmaline's daughter."

"I wasn't the daughter my mother expected, either," Deirdre confessed, old wounds twisting inside her. *Or the daughter she wanted,* a voice whispered in Deirdre's head. "Goodbye, Mrs. Davenport. And thank you."

Stone was still giving the woman his card when Deirdre walked out the door.

CHAPTER 7

DEIRDRE SLID INTO THE TRUCK, dreading Stone's approach, figuring the P.I. was probably going to comment on how rude she'd been or make one of those obnoxious jibes he liked so much, just to raise her blood pressure. Worse still, what if he leveled one of those stares on her that made her feel like that Visible Woman model Emma had made for the sixth-grade science fair, every nerve revealed through clear plastic skin.

For a wild moment she wondered what a shock it would be to the jerk if she burst into tears. No, better to slug him in the arm so hard he'd be sore for a week.

But Stone just slid into the driver's side, looking relieved the interview was over. "We got all the information she had to give."

"You think?" Deirdre snapped. "You've done your job. Now I don't want to talk about it."

"Fine with me." He switched on the CD player, and Cole Porter poured into the cab of the truck. She wished she could turn it off, but another part of her ached to listen, hearing it in her mother's untrained voice, knowing for the first time where the soulful, haunted quality in Emmaline's music had come from.

Stone grabbed the cell phone that hadn't been out of his hand for ten minutes at a time during the drive to Norma's.

He punched the buttons, held it to his ear.

"Don't tell me. You missed a call from Sherlock Holmes," Deirdre sniped.

Stone scowled at her and backed out of the drive. "No, the CIA's calling me for advice."

Obviously, more of Stone's bullshit. Maybe the state of the nation wasn't in danger, but the state of Stone's sanity was. He was edgy as all get-out, his temper ready to snap.

Twenty minutes later Deirdre couldn't stand the tension another moment.

"It's a car, not a phone booth," Deirdre complained as Stone hit automatic dial on the cell phone for the fifth time since they'd left Norma's. Stone swore.

"The answering machine again!"

"Is there a problem?"

Stone glared at her. "Damn it, Trula," he snarled into the receiver. "Pick up the damned phone! I know you're there!"

"Lovers' quarrel?" Deirdre asked so sweetly Stone looked like he wanted to kill her.

Stone slammed the heel of his hand against the steering wheel in frustration. "She knows it makes me crazy when she does this."

"Does what? Refuses to be at your beck and call? If you were yelling at me over the phone like that I'd change my phone number."

"Just as long as she doesn't change the locks. We're going to have to make a quick stop on the way home," he growled.

"Oh, no," Deirdre objected. "I'm not being dragged over to some dramatic scene with your girlfriend. Emma and Drew are supposed to come over after school, and—"

"God forbid the poor kid sneaks a kiss in before you get home," Stone steered onto the highway at a speed that would've gotten him pulled over if a cop had been in sight. "It won't be the end of the world."

"Jake Stone, the great expert on kids. Exactly how many do you have?"

"None. I'm an expert on teenage boys, though. That kid has it bad for your daughter."

Deirdre's heart lurched. "Damn it, Stone, turn this car around. I mean it."

Stone tried to jam his fingers back through his hair, cursed as he yanked on the silver band. He ripped the tie free and threw it into the back seat along with the necktie he'd shed earlier. Thick black hair fell to his shoulders, making him even more dangerous looking and sexy than he had moments before. He looked like a pirate or an outlaw or a highwayman in one of those romance novels Finn was always leaving around, hoping Deirdre might read one.

If gradually disrobing was Stone's way of handling frustration no wonder he had so many girlfriends. Pretty soon he'd be buck naked. The image wasn't one Deirdre wanted to deal with at the moment. At the moment? Ever.

"Stone, I mean it. You take me home this instant or—"

"You can either stay in the car while I do what I have to do and end up home an hour late or you can get out and walk, in which case you'll get back to Whitewater sometime next Tuesday. It's immaterial to me."

"You're a bastard."

"Finally something we agree on. What's it going to be?

Do I pull over at the nearest gas station?" Stone wrestled with his cell phone again.

Deirdre clenched her fists, hating the fury, the fear, feelings of utter helplessness flooding through her. He was right, the jerk. She was trapped like a rat.

Thank God he looked every bit as miserable as she was—Mr. Cool was one seething lump of masculine outrage and worry. Was it possible he actually loved a woman named Trula Devine? Enough to warrant the scowl on his rugged face, the granite set to his jaw, the flash in those hunting tiger eyes.

What would it be like to have a man as hard-edged as Jake Stone care so much about you that he'd tip his hand, let a virtual stranger see the kind of power a woman had to tear him apart?

Deirdre felt a tingle of something that couldn't be envy. So Stone had it bad for a woman. And no man had ever felt that fiercely about Deirdre. She didn't want that in her life. Had made damn sure no man would take the place of the music she'd once loved, distract her from making up to Emma the months her mother had been gone.

Hide behind Emma, she could almost hear Stone jeer. *God forbid you let yourself be a woman.*

Her stomach soured. In anger, she assured herself. Not from any sense of loss because Emma would leave soon, too soon, and she'd face the rest of her life alone. And no matter how much that broke Deirdre's heart, she'd be glad. Glad when Emma was out of Whitewater. Glad when Emma was safe...where the bright lights and energy on Broadway would remind her every day of dreams she didn't want to lose.

But Emma wasn't out of town yet. And Drew Lawson would be coming home from school with her, going out to the gazebo that had become a favorite trysting place for lovers during the past six years, "a realm of magic" one guest had written in the B&B's memory book, "a rose-covered haven where no one could help but fall in love." Enchanting as all that sounded, at least to people whose brains were stuffed with all that "happily ever after" propaganda, Deirdre knew for a fact the gazebo had sheltered far earthier interludes than a few stolen kisses and vows of eternal love.

She still winced at the memory of Finn's glow the day she'd told her she knew the very night she'd gotten pregnant with the twins. On their anniversary Cade had taken her to the most romantic place in the world…out to the gazebo where they'd been married and…

More information than she needed to know, Deirdre thought again, but a flutter of panic sprang up in her afresh. If a grown woman didn't have better sense than to succumb to the gazebo's aura of romance, what chance did a teenage girl playing Juliet have?

Deirdre dug in her purse for her cell phone and started her own frantic dialing. Maybe she couldn't wrestle Stone for the steering wheel and make him head back home. But she could get ahold of Finn and beg her to keep an eye on Emma.

Come on, Finn, be home, Deirdre pleaded silently. *God, let somebody be home.* Deirdre hadn't spoken to the Captain for a week, but even if he answered, she'd swallow her pride, ask him… To what? Drag himself across the garden between the two houses with his broken hip? The terrifying thing was he was just stubborn enough to try it and somewhere on the uneven path fall and break whatever other bone hit the flagstone first.

But Emma…

Deirdre's heart sank as Will's self-important little voice came on the phone. *This is the McDaniel res-ee-dence.* Amy chimed in, *We got things to do, so leave a message after it beeps,* then softer, the twins clamoring, *Did we do it right this time, Daddy?*

The answering machine buzzed. "Finn, this is Dee. I'm going to be later than I thought, so could you or Cade…" Deirdre thought of the Captain. He only answered the phone when he felt like it and could be listening. If he were, he'd set out across those flagstones. Deirdre had enough guilt. She didn't need to add to it.

"Just call me on my cell phone as soon as one of you gets back." A jolt of memory shot through her, Finn's most recent complaint about Will and Amy, the enterprising twins figuring out how to delete messages after their pre-school teacher threatened to call because Will had gotten in a fight when another kid had peeked under Amy's dress.

"Hey, kids, don't delete this message before your mom or dad hears it, and I swear I'll take you to the Whippy—" the beep alerted Deirdre the tape had shut off, but she had to finish anyway "—Dip."

Stone snorted in disgust. "And you griped about *my* expertise with kids. You're bribing them over the phone, not to mention lying to your daughter when you damned well *know* you're going to get caught."

"Drop it, Stone."

"Oh, yeah. All this because that poor kid might actually kiss the princess in the tower. But you're not worried at all that Emma's heading for New York in a few months. What do you think, that drama school has an army of nuns guarding the girls' doors? There'll be whole dorms full of boys trying to kiss your daughter, and you'd better get used to it. You'll be half a country away."

"Emma will have her work. She's far too serious about acting to—"

"To what? Be curious about what goes on between a man and a woman? Get real, lady. She's growing up and there's nothing you can do to stop it. If that kid steals a kiss it won't be the end of the world."

"Maybe not for the boy," Deirdre snapped bitterly. "But for a girl—" She bit off the last words. No. She wasn't going to tell Stone, wasn't going to let him see…beyond her defenses, into her fears, past Emma to the girl Deirdre had been before….

But the words plunged relentlessly on in her mind, the silence only serving to make them more terrifying.

For a girl a kiss could change everything. Trick her into believing…what? That she was beautiful, that he loved her. Get her to trust…

In one fatal night, to risk all her dreams.

The way Stone talked, he'd probably help the kid carve Emma's notch on his bedpost.

No. Not *her* little girl. She wasn't going to let Emma get hurt….

The way you did? a voice whispered in her heart. *Your mother would have been thrilled with Drew Lawson.* Deirdre winced, remembering the brief time she'd actually had her own mother's approval.

The day when a tall, clean-cut high school senior had started hanging around the house on Linden Lane. And for a few precious weeks before Emmaline McDaniel had died, Deirdre staked everything on the blind hope that finally, she just might belong.

PINK. THE HOUSE WAS PINK. Deirdre stared, aghast, as Stone whipped into a narrow driveway. Stone's "best legs in Las Vegas" showgirl must've used one of her feather boas in designing this disaster. The modest little ranch-style house was as pink as an Easter bunny's behind, with lime-green shutters and—Lord save us!—sunflower-yellow window boxes with a psychedelic nightmare of flowers rioting everywhere while a vintage Halloween-orange muscle car sat up on blocks outside the garage.

In spite of how furious she was with Stone, Deirdre couldn't suppress a smirk.

"Whoa, I can see why you were so worried," Deirdre jibed. "God knows what Trula Devine would paint next."

"If she's playing one of her games, by God, I'm going to kill her." Stone pinned Deirdre with a savage glare. "Stay in the car, damn it. I mean it." He levered his big body out of the driver's seat and slammed the door so hard it almost jumped right off its hinges.

Deirdre choked out a laugh, then made a face at his back as he stalked around the corner. Not that she could blame him. God knew, if her lover lived in a house like this, Deirdre figured she'd be too embarrassed to go in the front door, too.

But when it came to obeying orders, she wasn't much better than the Captain. And who could resist seeing a woman named Trula Devine who lived in a pink house, anyway? Talk about a once-in-a-lifetime chance! Not to mention the opportunity to stick it to Mr. Are-You-Walking-Home Jake Stone.

Deirdre slipped out the door, shut it quietly—no sense sneaking up on the guy if she was going to give him any warning. She traced his steps around the corner, heard Stone's swearing drowned out by a feminine squeal of delight.

What had the woman done? Met him at the door wearing some of that new colored Saran wrap? Something in a tasteful purple with pink polka dots?

"Jacob, what a lovely surprise! Why, I had no idea you were stopping by!"

"Damn it, Trula, why didn't you pick up the phone! Do you know what you do to me? God, woman, you scared the hell out of me—"

"I must have been taking a bubble bath," that Bette Davis husky voice said, so breezily it was obvious Stone's temper didn't faze her.

If she'd been soaking in the tub since they'd left Whitewater, Deirdre figured even the best legs in Vegas must be shriveled into two hot dog-length prunes.

"You're the sweetest boy in the whole world, worrying about me that way!"

Deirdre crept to the door Stone had left open, peeped inside.

She gasped. Maybe Trula Devine was obscured by Stone's big body, but her arms twined joyously around Stone's neck, a fluff of black ostrich feathers around her wrists, while her fire-engine-red lipstick smeared the man's cheek. Whoa, Deirdre was tempted to say, get a room. But Stone *had* told her to stay in the car.

Suddenly the woman peeled herself off Stone, her eyes lighting up as she gave Deirdre the shock of her life. The tall, still-voluptuous woman had to be sixtysomething years old! A well-preserved sixtysomething, but *still*—

"*You* are Stone's girlfriend?" Deirdre's jaw all but hit the floor.

Trula's hand fluttered up to the most spectacularly dyed red hair Deirdre had ever seen. "Why, bless you for thinking so! Jacob, why didn't you tell me you brought a friend?"

"A client, Trula. A client," Stone said. Good God, Deirdre marveled. Was Mr. Tough Guy blushing? "I thought I told you to stay in the car."

"Shame on you!" Trula said, smacking Stone on the arm. "All those years backstage in Vegas, I would've thought you'd learned how to treat a lady!"

"Aw, Trula—"

"I'm Jacob's grandmother."

"His *grandmother?* What were you? Twelve when you gave birth to his...well, whichever of his parents?"

"His mother," Trula supplied. "Oh, my. I really *do* like this girl, Jacob! I'm seventy years old. And this is the real me, without a single plastic surgery. The love of a good man, that's what my secret is. Well, several good men, actually."

Stone winced. "She outlived them all. Hell, she'll probably outlive me."

"Yes, well, Jacob's the only one left." Trula tsked, her expression suddenly fraught with the tender resignation of mothers and grandmothers everywhere. "He's a good boy, really. But he's got far too many more important things to do than sit down for a visit."

"I do have a job, you know," Jake grumbled.

"Well, if you were bringing company, the least you could have done is said so on the answering machine."

"What answering machine? I thought you didn't hear it."

"Well, maybe I did. But if I'd answered it, you wouldn't be here, would you? And you wouldn't have brought this lovely young lady along. Ms.—?"

"Ah, Deirdre McDaniel," Deirdre supplied, offering the older woman her hand. Trula ignored it, sweeping her into a big hug. She smelled of Chanel No. 5. Deirdre remembered when her own mother had opened a bottle at Christmas. She'd never worn it. And she'd never hugged like Trula did, freely, openly. No, Emmaline McDaniel's hugs had been careful ones, as if she were afraid not to hold something back.

"Pleased to meet you, Deirdre." Trula released her, flashing a smile. "Jacob doesn't bring his friends over nearly often enough. Except that darling Tank Rizzo and his wife. Why, when the boys were on the police force together they'd stop here for lunch at least once a week."

"I'm not on the force anymore."

"I know that, dear, but I can't help remembering how lovely it was when you were." For the first time, a soft grief touched the old woman's face.

Deirdre wondered what this woman had thought when she heard the awful truth that her grandson had shot an unarmed man.

"Jacob, why don't you hurry into the kitchen and set another place at the table. I've got your favorite chicken and homemade dumplings on the stove, and Twinkies for dessert. Who would look at this big strapping man and guess he was a Twinkie addict?"

Trula hustled them through a wide open door where Deirdre could see a small table, carefully set for two. "Looks like you were expecting Stone," Deirdre couldn't resist observing.

"All I have to do is ignore the phone and sure enough, he'll show up on my doorstep."

"Because I think you've fallen down the steps, you crazy old woman!" Stone ran his hand through his hair in exasperation, but his eyes betrayed just how much the possibility had frightened him.

"Bah. He thinks I'm old! Why, I still feel like I'm twenty. My, Deirdre, dear, you should have seen me then!" She did a few dance moves in her slippered feet, and for an instant, Deirdre could picture her turning men's heads as she sparkled with sequins.

"You should meet my father." The words slipped out before Deirdre could alter them. Father? She didn't even know how to *think* about the Captain anymore after all Norma Davenport had revealed. But Trula was obviously waiting for Deirdre to finish her thought. "The feeling-twenty thing. He's the same way."

"Oh, well, I've still got it, don't I?" Trula finished her dance demonstration with a flourish, her bright pink fingernails striking a picture frame on what looked to be a desk. The frame tipped over. Miraculously the vast assortment of other photographs and trophies teetered but didn't fall.

"Oh, dear! I almost wiped out my Jacob shrine!" Trula pressed her hand to her breast. "Just look at what a handsome boy he was!"

"Trula, for cripe's sake!" Stone moaned. "Deirdre doesn't want to look at a bunch of idiotic pictures."

"Oh, Jacob, you're so wrong," Deirdre said so sweetly Stone shot her his blackest "you'll pay for that later" glare, but Deirdre was having way too much fun to heed it. She could hear his nerves crackle as she picked up the nearest frame. "I'm dying to see— My God, Stone. *You're in tights!*"

"Perfect. Just perfect. Thanks a lot, Trula!" Stone arched his head back, closed his eyes. He looked as if he wanted to slink behind Trula's Technicolor drapes.

"There's nothing wrong with a man who can dance!" Trula said. "And my Jacob is a wonderful dancer. The girls just flocked to my dance classes when they knew he'd be there to partner them."

"I'll bet," Deirdre said, giving Stone no quarter.

"He'd race over to class as soon as his karate lessons or football practices were over and take every class he could."

"Who would have guessed?" Deirdre said.

"Nobody, I hoped," Stone muttered.

"Jacob would never tell you this himself, but my dance school was struggling. A few parents found out I'd danced in Vegas and thought I'd been a prostitute."

"Trula, you can't go around saying that!"

"Well, it's the truth, isn't it?" his grandmother demanded, with wide-eyed innocence. "Deirdre's too intelligent to think that a dancer and prostitute are the same thing."

Deirdre hoped Trula didn't have her grandson's gift for peering into people's heads. She didn't want the woman to know all the nasty things she'd been thinking about "the greatest legs in Vegas" when she'd thought they belonged to Stone's bimbo girlfriend.

"Anyway, my dance school was struggling, and Lord above, girl, I loved to dance! It was the only way I could keep doing what I loved when Tony—my second husband—dragged Jacob and me to the middle of Illinois."

"That's a tired old story Deirdre doesn't want to hear." Stone looked as though he wanted to borrow the duct tape Deirdre had wanted to use on Emma the morning they went to Lagomarcinos.

"No, I'm fascinated, Stone. It's showing me a whole new side of you."

"Jacob knew how much I loved that silly little school. He'd hung up his tap shoes when he started on the football team. But once he knew the school was in trouble, he told all the girls he was taking class. Why, those girls were so crazy about my grandson, they were lining up to take dance from me, their parents' objections be damned."

"They must have been disappointed when Football Jake didn't show," Deirdre couldn't resist ribbing him.

"Oh, he showed all right. He'd run all the way from practice. Didn't even stop to take a shower. Just put on his tap shoes and hit the floor, still dripping sweat. The girls didn't mind," Trula said with a mischievous twinkle in her eye. "They just wanted to see Jacob in his tights."

"You know what, Trula? Next time I think I'll leave you at the bottom of the stairs," Stone grumbled.

"Of course you will, dear," Trula said, patting him on the arm. "Deirdre, do you dance?"

"Nope." Deirdre picked up another frame, this one holding a montage of scenes from various high school musicals, starring none other than her least-favorite P.I. "I've got three left feet." She really did try not to laugh at a much younger, but still rivetingly sexy, Stone playing the lead in *Joseph and the Amazing Technicolor Dreamcoat*.

"Ah, Joseph," Trula sighed at the memory. "The dungeon scene where Jacob was dressed in a loincloth drove all those tittering little cheerleaders to swoons."

Stone choked, and Trula pounded him on the back. Deirdre almost felt sorry for him.

"My daughter Emma dances fairly well. She hasn't taken any lessons, but she's a theater kid and picks choreography up pretty quick. She may be leaving for drama school in New York at New Year's."

"But she hasn't had dance class?" Trula made it sound like Deirdre had let the kid bungee jump without a safety harness or something. "Why, if your Emma wants to succeed in theater, she needs to be a triple threat."

"Isn't that some kind of baseball term?" Deirdre asked, perplexed.

Trula laughed. "Theater people use it, too. Tell her what it means, Jacob."

"A triple threat can act, dance and sing," Stone looked for all the world like a surly kid reciting multiplication tables. "It makes them the strongest contenders when it comes to getting cast."

"Your Emma must have dance lessons!" Trula enthused. "Why, I could teach her!"

"Bad idea," Stone objected. "It's a three-hour drive from Whitewater. Besides, you're not as steady on your feet as you once were. I don't like the idea of you sliding around in tap shoes."

Trula gave him a black look. "I was giving Ginger Rogers competition before you were even a twinkle in your father's eye, young man. And I dance. I don't slide."

"Emma would probably love it," Deirdre said, suddenly wondering if Trula was some sort of gift from God. The perfect antidote to keep Emma from getting too lost in either the role of Juliet or the Orlando Bloom look in Drew Lawson's eyes. "She has school and play rehearsal, and works part-time at the library. But you might be just the thing she needs to keep her eyes on her dreams."

"Emma's playing Juliet, and Romeo's hot for her."

Deirdre's eyes widened. She couldn't believe even Stone would talk to his grandmother that way.

But Trula was as earthy as she was warm, and terms like *hot for her* had probably been a staple of the diet backstage in Las Vegas.

"Oh, my, young love!" Trula said, scrawling her phone number on a scrap of paper and handing it to Deirdre. "You have your Emma call me," the older woman insisted. "Just hearing about her carries me back. I remember when I played Juliet. What magic! I lost my virginity closing night."

"Trula!" Stone looked ready to die.

"What?" Trula raised thin, heavily penciled brows, honestly bewildered. She turned to Deirdre. "Between you and me, I always thought Romeo was a twit. And anyway, in this performance Mercutio was at least six inches taller and had a body to die for."

"Why the hell didn't you just stay in the car," Stone accused Deirdre.

"If you're going to turn into a prude at this late date, Jacob, you can go sit in the car yourself while Deirdre and I have a lovely lunch."

But Trula's tale of losing her virginity to Shakespearean magic had jolted Deirdre back to her greatest fear. She glanced at her watch, trying to gauge whether or not she could get back to March Winds before the star-crossed lovers got home from school.

"I'm sorry, I can't stay. I've got to get home. Emma... well, she and this boy are going to rehearse and I need to be there."

Stone wasn't one to take all her jibes lying down. "She's afraid the kid might cop a feel."

"I certainly hope so!" Trula said. "Life should imitate art. Surely Deirdre remembers when she was sixteen!"

That was the problem, Deirdre thought, fear leaving a bitter taste in her mouth. Deirdre pocketed Trula's phone number and said a hasty goodbye as Trula dumped the soup into a Tupperware bowl, and shoved it into Stone's hands.

"Do you have enough money?" Stone asked his grandmother quietly, obviously trying not to let Deirdre hear him. "You got the check I sent you?"

"The mortgage is all paid. Tony's retirement check must've gotten lost in the mail. I'll pay you back—"

"Keep it. Buy yourself some new sequins."

Trula blinked eyes heavy with mascara, then smeared the rest of her lipstick across Stone's other cheek in a kiss so warm and filled with love Deirdre's heart felt sore. Damn Stone, anyway, the man set the bowl down so he could give his grandmother a rib-crusher of a hug, showing the world how precious the old woman was to him.

"Don't you ever scare me like that again," Stone warned.

Trula stretched up on tip toe so she could look into her grandson's eyes. "I love you, too, Sugar Bear," she said.

Deirdre slipped out the door, not wanting Stone to see that Trula had managed to choke her up, made her want something she couldn't have—a mother or grandmother to hug her that way. Someone to pour out her pain to, all the anguish she'd felt since she'd opened that cursed hope chest. Or maybe long before that, when she'd found herself pregnant with a baby of her own.

CHAPTER 8

DEIRDRE CLIMBED INTO STONE'S truck, and concentrated on banishing the vulnerability from her face. *Sugar Bear.* She forced herself not to think of the sweetness and love behind the endearment, grabbed on to the tease factor of having the name applied to six foot four inches worth of muscle-bound man.

Stone strode around the side of the house and opened the car door, settling the soup and a box of Twinkies on the floor of the back seat, before he slid behind the wheel.

"Sugar Bear?" Deirdre echoed.

Her emotional fake-out worked. He glared at her, looking like Cade just itching for a fight. "Yeah. She's my grandma and she calls me Sugar Bear. Want to make something of it?"

"No, I...I love it, Stone. Really."

"Fine," Stone said, pulling out of the drive. "Just laugh and get it over with."

"Maybe I'll cut you a break. Restrain my impulse to buy space on a billboard and tell the whole world who you really are. *Sugar Bear Stone, Private Eye.*"

"You really should audition for a spot on *Letterman*," Stone said, hitting the gas. "You're hysterical."

"Only when someone is sweet enough to give me such great material. Speaking of hysterical, you must have been laughing plenty yourself in your office that first day, letting me believe Trula was some kind of floozy. You did that on purpose."

"Yeah, well, I hoped I'd disgust you so much you'd find some other P.I. stupid enough to take the case."

"You could have said no. In fact, you *did* say no. So why change your mind and show up at March Winds the next morning? And don't give me some hard-assed line this time. How about the truth? Or I could ask your grandma." Deirdre chuckled. "Who would've guessed a guy like you would have a grandma?"

"What? You think I crawled out from under a rock?"

"Yeah." Deirdre grinned. "I just didn't know you were dressed in tights."

Stone glared. "Ha, ha, ha."

"I've got to admit, you're full of surprises. First you turn into Karate Man and kick those convicts' butts, then I find out you're a triple threat."

"One talent led to the other. If you want to teach a boy how to fight, put him in tap shoes."

Damn, if Stone's honesty didn't make her like him at least a little. "You might as well can the whole tough-guy act with me now, Stone. Even the Terminator wouldn't look threatening if you'd seen him in tap shoes."

Deirdre wanted to hang on to humor. But suddenly she remembered Trula's hug. She didn't feel like laughing. "She's amazing. Trula, I mean. You're lucky to have her."

"Tell me about it," Stone said, so tenderly Deirdre's throat ached.

"Did you really grow up backstage in Vegas?" She

couldn't resist asking. She didn't expect Stone to elaborate. He wasn't any better at giving away pieces of himself than she was. But something between them had changed in Trula's pink living room. Deirdre knew she'd never see Stone quite the same way again. The P.I. rolled his shoulders, settling deeper into the driver's seat.

"My parents died in a fire when I was two. Trula took me in."

"I'm sorry."

"Yeah, well, I don't remember them much. Don't remember anything until I landed in Vegas. I loved all the excitement, watching Trula transform into this—this magical creature. God, she was so beautiful, and when she danced she was so happy she just glowed. Every man in the joint was crazy about her."

Deirdre could picture it so clearly—Trula, the queen of the stage with dozens of bedazzled men buzzing around her.

"It was like a family when I was there. The showgirls were like—well, it was like having thirty big sisters."

"At three, maybe. But once you were older..."

Stone laughed. "I was the envy of every twelve-year-old boy in the world, surrounded by gorgeous women. But a lot more things than my voice changed that year. That's when Tony Manoletti started arresting Trula every chance he got."

"Arresting her? But she said she wasn't a...well, a prostitute." Deirdre's cheeks burned. And people thought *she* was blunt. She could take lessons in it from Trula.

"She wasn't, but that didn't mean she didn't have gentlemen friends. There was this Mafia boss who made her his mistress. Showered both of us with stuff—if I'd had a license he probably would have bought me a car."

"An orange muscle car like the one up on blocks?"

"Nah. That's Trula's baby. Tony gave it to her for her fiftieth birthday. She can't drive it anymore because her eyesight's not so great, but, man, oh, man, did she love to go fast!"

"So what happened to the Mafia version of Santa Claus? I mean, you were a cop. His influence doesn't seem to have stuck."

"It turned out he wasn't a Santa Claus. More like the bloody-horse-head-at-the-end-of-the-bed kind of guy if anybody dared to cross him." Stone's mouth set, grim. "That last year in Vegas was a hell of a show, and I don't mean on stage. Giancomo stalking Trula, coercing her into staying with him by threatening to hurt me if she didn't. Tony arresting her and me…feeling so goddamned helpless. The first time I saw Giancomo actually take a swing at Trula I went after him with my baseball bat."

"God, Stone! You're lucky he didn't kill you."

"He laughed his ass off and gave me a little souvenir." Stone touched the corner of his right eye and Deirdre could see a two-inch scar there, a thin white line where a man's fist had connected. "Told Trula if she didn't do what he wanted, he'd start taking things out on me. Then he left. Trula had a show to do, then afterward, a party for the high rollers. Said as soon as they were over…she'd make sure Giancomo could never hurt anybody again."

"Didn't Giancomo ever hear that mother grizzly analogy? He should've been shaking in his shoes."

"Trula was a hell of a woman, but she was no match for a mob boss. I knew that even as a kid. I was the man of the family," Stone said. "I was supposed to protect her."

"At twelve?"

"I headed out to the street swearing next time I faced off with Giancomo things would be different. I hadn't exactly had a Dr. Seuss kind of childhood, you know? I'd heard enough from the men around the casino that I had some idea what to do. I sold all the stuff Giancomo had given me—the television and stereo and God knows what else. When I had enough money, I bought a gun off some other street punk."

Was that when Stone had realized he had the strength to pull the trigger? When he was just twelve years old? Deirdre wondered. Had it made it easier to shoot the man who'd cost him his badge?

"Tony nabbed me about two minutes after I bought the thing. He'd watched the whole deal go down. The guy grabbed me by the scruff of the neck and yelled me half-deaf, telling me I shouldn't be worrying my grandmother. Then he saw my eye—turned into a hell of a shiner. I started to cry."

Stone's voice dropped low. "He was this giant of an Italian, barrel-chested with hands big as hams. He should've dragged me straight to juvie hall. Instead he took me to this little diner—a lot like the one you and Emma took me to—and he bought me a chocolate milk shake. He told me he wouldn't take me to the station if I told him what happened to my eye. The truth. So I told him."

Stone fell quiet, just driving, his mind God knew how many years and miles away.

But Deirdre couldn't let him brood, had to know the rest. "What happened then?" she asked.

"I'd never seen Tony so quiet. He was always blustery and swearing and laughing. Took me back to the place Giancomo had rented for us. This high-class apartment. The doorman didn't even want to let him in. But Tony pulled out his badge. Trula had the place torn apart, packing things for the two of us, ready to run. Tony sat across the table from Trula—God, she looked so ashamed.

She'd let a monster like Giancomo get close enough to threaten her grandson."

Stone kneaded the back of his neck with one hand, the other deftly handling the steering wheel.

"I think Trula was afraid Tony would call child welfare, that they'd take me away from her." Stone chuckled softly. "Who could have guessed that Sergeant Manoletti would tell Trula that he'd spent the last year scared to death for her. He knew how dangerous Giancomo was, but what could a plain man like Tony offer her in the bastard's place? He'd done the only thing he could think of to keep her safe. Figured if she was in court she'd be so high-profile Giancomo would have to know Tony was watching him, would have to think twice about hurting her. Or me. I remember Trula asking why Tony should care. There was no way out of a relationship like this for an over-the-hill showgirl who had a boy to support.

"Tony...he turned bright red. Stared down at the table and said there *was* a way out. He said...he loved both of us. Wanted to marry us. *Us.* Not just Trula." Stone still sounded surprised.

"But a guy like Giancomo wouldn't just let the three of you disappear into the sunset, would he?" Deirdre asked, fascinated by the story in spite of herself.

"Tony had been working for months to get the goods on Giancomo's son. Said he'd keep it under wraps if Giancomo left us alone. It's the only time he ever crossed the line in fifty years he wore the badge. Tony said he was never sorry. They got married in an Elvis chapel, then he packed Trula and me up in his car and moved us to Illinois. And that was the end of my career as a juvenile delinquent."

"He must have been proud of you, trying to defend your grandmother that way."

Something haunting stole into Stone's eyes. "He lived just long enough to see me graduate at the head of my class from the police academy. I'm glad the old man can't see me now."

A muscle in Stone's jaw twitched. Deirdre had fought for distance from old pain often enough herself to know what Stone was doing. Silence stretched, filled with things Stone couldn't say. It was hell just *thinking* sometimes, being alone in your own head. Empathy filled her, and she wanted to give him a hand. Drive back the shadows in his face in the way both she and Stone seemed to know best.

Laugh…try to make him laugh….

"So that's how you ended up in Illinois, huh? Bet you had plenty of stories to tell the kids about feather fans that slipped. Still, it was a big change from Vegas. Especially for a twelve-year-old boy."

Stone took the gift she offered. His mouth crooked in a smile. "It was a real bummer. Getting kicked out of the dressing room about the time I figured out what all those beautiful breasts were for."

"What a letdown."

Stone surprised her by the seriousness in his reply. "It *was* a letdown, but not the way you think. I missed it. Really. Missed *them*. Being in the middle of all that woman stuff. The smells, the 'soft' of them, the way they'd all stop to kiss me good-night. When I was little, Trula would set up a cot in the dressing room, and I'd sleep until the show was over."

Deirdre winced at a bittersweet memory, a much-smaller Emma sound asleep, curled in a nest of blankets in the back room of a nightclub, a book clutched like a teddy bear in her arms.

Shame warmed Deirdre's face. She fiddled with one of the softly feathered strands, wishing it was long so she could hide behind a silky curtain of curls like Emma and Finn sometimes did. But all her fidgeting accomplished was drawing attention to her burning cheeks. She surprised herself by confessing. "When I was on the road singing with the band, I did that to Emma sometimes. A little girl, sleeping in places she never should have set foot in. I wonder if she'll ever forgive me for that. Or if I'll forgive myself."

Stone's eyes suddenly gentled. "Are you sure you need her to? Maybe all that mattered to her was that you were there to tuck her in."

"I wasn't exactly a Super Mom. She...she deserved better. I hope I've managed to give it to her the past six years. But it's still hard. I...I abandoned her for almost a year, left her with Cade."

What was she trying to do? Make sure Stone saw her for what she was? Damaged. A failure...a woman who'd run away. Not once, but twice in her life. She couldn't look at Stone, didn't want to see the disgust in his eyes.

Stone surprised her, reaching across the console to gently squeeze her hand. "You'd just come back for Emma when I came to see your sister-in-law that day."

"You...knew?" Deirdre didn't pull away, needed the warmth, the strength of someone's touch. Who would have guessed she'd find that in Stone? "I can just imagine what went through your mind when I came to your office that day. What a hypocrite. She wants to dump on her family now and run off looking for some stranger? She's lucky they took her back the first time after what she did. No wonder you didn't want to take my case."

"Is that what you think?" They were passing a deserted park, Stone pulled in, ground to a stop in the shelter of a copse of trees. He killed the engine and turned to look square in her eyes. His face was so rugged, so handsome, so unexpectedly kind, Deirdre had to look away.

He curved his fingers under her chin, forcing her to meet his gaze. "What happened with Emma didn't have a damned thing to do with why I tried to send you away. Truth to tell, I admired you for coming back. It's not easy to admit you've made a mistake."

Deirdre didn't want to cry, felt her eyes burn, his touch so warm, so gentle. Who would have believed Jake Stone could be gentle?

Stone shrugged, grimaced. "I figured you hated me, Deirdre. You made it pretty plain."

Deirdre knew she should pull away. "I...I hated what you did to Finn and Cade."

Stone's thumb swept her cheek. "I hated what I did to them, too. Hell, if I'd known what good people they were maybe I'd have walked away without ever telling them." He gave her a shadow of his killer smile. "Some tough guy, huh? Six years later and I still think about them."

Stone's eyes darkened, dipped to her mouth. The brush of his gaze set her lips tingling. His voice dropped low. "I still think about *you*."

Deirdre swallowed hard. "Me?"

"About you and me together. About how you'd taste with all that fire in your eyes...about...aw, hell. I didn't trust myself in a room with you because I figured you'd laugh in my face if I was ever stupid enough to..." His eyes were burning her up.

"But you didn't stay away."

"No. I told myself I could fix things for your family. Some kind of...of penance, maybe. I could make sure nothing more hurt you and *then* walk away. I swore I wouldn't kiss you, wouldn't touch you. Hell, I'm a professional asshole, aren't I? You told me that yourself."

"Ruthless. I said something about ruthless."

"I am, damn it. I want sex, Deirdre. With you. Hot, sweaty, pounding-myself-into-you-until-neither-one-of-us-can-walk kind of sex. That's all. I don't want any of this."

"Don't want what?" Deirdre's pulse thudded hard in her throat.

"What your brother has. What Tank Rizzo has. What Trula and Tony had. No offense to you, it's just that I'm not cut out for anything permanent. Hell, just ask my ex-wife. What I did…when I pulled that trigger…it'll follow me the rest of my life."

"Some things do," Deirdre said bleakly. All the years she'd loved Emma, cared for her, couldn't change the nine months that Deirdre had left her little girl alone.

"A good man would've stayed away from you. But you were right about me. I'm not a good man. I'm just a selfish bastard who wants you."

Alarm bells jangled in Deirdre's head. No, this was crazy. Her tongue swept out, moistened her lips.

Stone closed the space between them. His mouth capturing hers in a kiss so fierce her head spun, her body flamed. She didn't want to kiss him back. Didn't want her fingers to curl into the shoulder-length waves of hair, but they did, instinctively savoring the contrast between that dark silkiness and hot skin.

A hungry sound rumbled in Stone's throat, and he deepened the kiss, his tongue insistent and male and masterful as it parted her lips. He was inside her, tasting of sex and surrender and risks Deirdre didn't have the courage to take.

He dragged her against him, not giving a damn about the console between them, his big hands rough with need, showing her how much he wanted her. For sex. Just sex.

No! Panic iced through Deirdre, and she struggled in his arms. Stone resisted, long moments that seemed an eternity. She bit whatever part of his mouth her teeth could reach.

Stone cursed, yanked away, pressing the back of his hand against his bottom lip. Deirdre groped for defiance, gathered the shreds of her pride around her, prayed he couldn't smell the fear on her or the confusion.

He stared at her, breath rasping in his throat, that tiger-like hunger in his face.

"Deirdre, what the hell?" he said, bewildered.

"You wouldn't let me go. I'm not—not interested in sex."

"Could have fooled me, lady. The way you were looking at me with those eyes of yours. Your tongue on your lips, making them wet for me. Oh, you want it, all right. But a simple no would have been enough. You didn't have to draw blood!"

Hadn't she cried no? She thought she had. But he looked so bewildered. Of course, a man who looked like Stone wouldn't hear no very often. In fact, there were moments when he was right, she *had* wanted it.

Stone naked, slick with sweat. Stone hungry, his hands all over her, inside her. Stone shattering the icy walls she'd never been able to break through...

Heart hammering in her chest, Deirdre pushed herself against the truck door, as far away from him as she could get. "I have a sixteen-year-old daughter waiting for me at home, doing God knows what with Romeo." She battled to keep her voice from shaking. "If I expect her to show self-control, don't you think I ought to show a little myself?"

"Damn it, I—"

"It's not about *you*, Stone. I mean, my saying no. I'm sure you're not used to rejection, but…well, maybe that redhead who convinced you to take my case will be happy with just sex."

"I think there's a law against that. The redhead is my dog. Deirdre, listen—"

"No, you just shut up and drive. I need to get home."

Home…away from feelings she couldn't have, fantasies she couldn't fulfill, risks she couldn't take. Where she could forget the power of a man's hands and the damage they could do. Where she could bury all the wanting in her that she'd thought was dead.

Stone's jaw set, hard, a tiny cut from her teeth on his lip. He threw the car into gear. At least there was no way Stone would ever want to kiss her again, Deirdre thought, trying to be glad.

She'd made sure of that.

CHAPTER 9

DAMNED IF HE'D LET HER SEE HIM touch the place where she'd bit him, Stone thought, even though his lip throbbed and his pride stung and some other emotion he didn't dare name made him feel hollowed-out inside. And as he swung his truck along the road leading from small-town Whitewater to Jubilee Point, he wondered what the hell had gone wrong.

He sneaked a look at Deirdre, sitting so still, so silent a mere foot away, yet as walled off from him as if she'd laid down brick and mortar. Maybe he should have expected that. He already knew her well enough to figure she'd try her damnedest to shut down emotionally in a crisis, not let anyone see how badly recent events had shaken her.

The interview with Norma Davenport had been hell for Deirdre; but then, Stone had known it would be. Hearing about your mother's affair wouldn't be labeled fun on anyone's list, and in the past few hours Deirdre McDaniel had suffered enough shock for anyone.

Hadn't he warned her not to come along? But even if he admitted that hearing the gory details about her parents' rocky marriage might have been a necessary evil where Deirdre McDaniel was concerned, it was what happened afterward that had made him do the unforgivable. He'd crossed the line.

Hell, he'd told her things he hadn't even told his exwife. Let Deirdre get under his skin far deeper than he'd ever have believed any woman could. Deirdre, with her flashing eyes, her inner strength, that haunting touch of sorrow that crept past her guard sometimes, leaving her even more beautiful than before.

Watching Deirdre with Trula had shifted everything he knew about the McDaniel woman again, like shifting the colors of a kaleidoscope, leaving her even more intriguing than before. Deirdre accepting Trula with such open delight had astonished Stone, got around all his hard edges. Deirdre McDaniel seeing past the godawful paint on Trula's house and Trula's face, past the outlandishness Trula used to say "screw the world"—who would've thought it? Or maybe he should have known the two women would connect. Deirdre had defied convention herself until six long years ago.

Deirdre genuinely envied him his eccentric grandmother, the wistfulness shining in those incredible blue eyes making part of Stone wish he could draw her in...into the pink house filled with Twinkies and photographs so embarrassing they made him want to hide. Into Trula's world of age-awkward dance steps that had once been flashy and sharp, into hugs and laughter and people who loved you so much they'd scheme just to get you through the door.

Oh, Deirdre had teased him plenty...hell, a saint couldn't have resisted after Trula called him that hideous nickname of hers. And yet...Deirdre had cared, really cared about the old woman.

Cared about *him* enough to ask…about who he'd been, how he'd grown, what had made him become the man he was.

The *bastard* he was. Stone glanced over at her, remembering her mouth under his, her sweet lips parting, letting him in, the taste of her driving him wild as he swept into her with his tongue. She'd been as hungry for it as he was those first soul-stealing moments. He could *feel* her wanting…

And he was arrogant enough to admit he was a damn fine kisser. She should have been as mindless as he was when he pulled her against him.

What the hell had gone wrong? Whatever it was, he was going to get it straight before he left March Winds. Once Deirdre saw that Drew Lawson wasn't having his way with Emma in broad daylight in the gazebo with the guests at the B&B giving them pointers, she'd settle down enough to talk.

She'd have to, Stone told himself. He wasn't going anywhere until he got to the bottom of this.

Stone pulled into the driveway of March Winds, parked under the chestnut tree. Deirdre got out, closed the door. Hell, she didn't even say goodbye.

But that was fine, Stone figured. He wasn't leaving anyway. Deirdre hugged herself as she hurried around the side of the house. This time Stone was the one who followed. The scent of late-blooming roses wafted around Stone, and he remembered the last time he'd been here, the garden still wildly overgrown, the restorations to the Civil War–era mansion unfinished, Deirdre's future with her daughter still hanging in the balance.

She'd been singing in clubs, Deirdre had said. Chasing dreams on stages of her own. What had it cost her to turn her back on all that? The passion that had consumed her so completely that she'd even considered giving up the child she obviously loved more than life? Where had Deirdre McDaniel put that woman when she'd walked off the stage the last time?

Stone had grown up around dancers, musicians, performers of all kinds. It was passion that drove them, a thirst that made them dive deep into life. What had made Deirdre pull herself out of those creative waters and shut away not only the passion in her music, but in her life?

My mom's real picky about guys, Emma had said the day she'd lured him to the diner. Had there been any men around since Deirdre had come home? Stone ran his tongue over his sore lip. If biting any man who tried to kiss her was her evasion technique, it was no wonder anybody with a Y chromosome had run the other way.

Unfortunately, curiosity was Stone's fatal flaw. He damned well needed to know what was going on inside the woman's head.

Stone had almost caught up with Deirdre when he saw her slam to a halt. She was angled so he could see enough of her face to register it had turned white. Stone followed her horrified gaze to the gazebo with its lacing of green vines and the teenagers inside it.

Whoa, baby! Stone thought. Mom wasn't the only one who'd gotten the daylights kissed out of her!

Emma McDaniel reclined across one of the benches, one hand, palm up, draped above her head, while Drew lay partly across her body, his mouth exploring hers, one hand in Emma's hair, the other skimming over her hip. Both teenagers seeming so desperate for each other, as if they were trying to squeeze a lifetime's worth of lovemaking into these few moments.

In a split second Deirdre's horrified freeze shattered. She stormed toward the kids. "Emma!"

The kids leapt apart, Emma struggling upright, flushed with surprise and undeniable guilt. Yeah, the kid had been into that kiss big-time. Like her mother had been at first...

"Mom!" Emma pressed her fingers to her reddened lips.

"Mrs. McDaniel," Drew stammered. The kid looked scared to death. Stone couldn't blame him, considering the expression on Deirdre's face. "We were rehearsing..." Drew stammered. "I couldn't get it right."

Deirdre mounted the gazebo steps like a fury. "I thought learning the lines was your problem. It's pretty hard to speak in Elizabethan dialogue when you have your tongue in my daughter's mouth."

Emma went bright red. "Mom, he didn't—"

"I think you've rehearsed enough," Deirdre said briskly. "Drew, it's time for you to leave."

"Mom, we weren't doing anything wrong. It was the wedding night scene...we just couldn't make it look real." Emma's gaze lit on Stone, and she blushed even deeper. The poor kid. Her utter humiliation wasn't bad enough without a virtual stranger watching. But cutting out on the kid now would only make things worse.

"Hi, Emma," Stone said with a forced smile. "Hey... Drew, isn't it? We met at the diner."

The boy straightened his shirt. "Yeah, I mean...yeah, we were talking about the play."

Time to lighten things up, Stone figured. "Well, from what I've seen, you've got that whole reality kink worked out. Just look at Emma's mom's face." Stone forced himself to chuckle.

"This isn't funny, Stone," Deirdre said between gritted teeth.

"Maybe not on your end," Stone observed. "Finding

your kid in an, er, compromising position has to be a real jolt—even if it is *just* acting."

Deirdre glared at him in patent disbelief. Not that he could blame her. It looked like Emma had her mom's talent for sending the male of the species into spontaneous combustion.

"Maybe you guys should take a break," Stone pushed on hastily. "My grandmother was in theater most of her life and she always said overrehearsing a performance was every bit as bad as not rehearsing enough." Stone pulled a ten out of his back pocket. "Why don't you two go grab some ice cream or something? We could all use some cooling off."

"Emma's not going anywhere but up to her room." Deirdre turned to her daughter. "You and I need to talk."

Drew's Adam's apple bobbed in his throat. Stone had to admire him for not racing out of there as fast as his Nikes could carry him. "Mrs. McDaniel, nothing happened that—well, that wasn't in the play," Drew tried to reason.

"That's what I'm afraid of. Just say your goodbyes and let's get back to the real world." Deirdre stepped back giving the kids a modicum of privacy. Stone had to give her that. What Deirdre really looked like was the witch ready to build Rapunzel's tower a few miles higher.

"Better rein it in a few notches," Stone murmured in Deirdre's ear. "You're making a big mistake."

She drove her elbow back, but he was too quick for her, the blow just grazing his ribs.

"Emma," Drew said, looking miserable. "I guess I'll see you at school. And we're still on for Friday?"

Emma managed a smile. "I can't wait."

Deirdre was right about one thing. This particular

Romeo and Juliet had moved beyond acting. Emma McDaniel was knee-deep in puppy love. Stone felt a tug in his midsection, remembering the rush of feelings, that awakening of sexuality, feeling your body shift from a family station wagon to a Maserati, even though you didn't have the skills to drive it.

And as if the thrill wasn't addictive enough, there was the tunnel vision of youth, believing pure infatuation was really the happily-ever-after kind of love. Adolescence. What a hell of a ride it was.

Drew started to offer his hand to Deirdre, then thought better of it. Stone shook the kid's hand instead. "See you," Stone said.

The second Drew was out of sight Emma wheeled on Deirdre and glared from her mother to Stone and back. "Mom, how could you?" Emma demanded, her cheeks hot spots of color.

"Emma, how could *you?* This is a public place, with paying guests and you're—you're all over some boy—"

"We *weren't* all over each other," Emma asserted, looking as stubborn as her mom. "We were rehearsing the scene."

"Well, if you play it that way at school, your drama teacher's going to have to give the performance an R rating."

"More like PG-13," Stone said, trying to get one of them to crack—to see how off the charts they were getting. But he wasn't sure either McDaniel woman even heard him.

"Miss Wittich is the one who told us to try the scene out when we were alone. It felt so weird with other people watching I couldn't concentrate! But I guess Drew and I should've stayed in the auditorium with the whole cheerleading squad glaring because they hate me! It would have been better than having my mother sneak up on us and start going crazy over nothing."

"I didn't sneak up on you! And this certainly isn't 'nothing,' Emmaline Kate! I trusted you, and—"

"No, you didn't. You didn't even listen to me, didn't even wait to hear what I had to say. I've *never* been so *embarrassed* in my *life!* I'll be lucky if he ever wants to be seen with me again!"

"Highly dramatic. But hard to pull off since he's playing opposite you in the performance."

"He's doing a lot more than that!" Emma exclaimed, defiant. "He's taking me on a date."

"A what?"

"A date, Mother. You know, like all the other girls my age go on. Where a guy you like takes you to dinner and a movie and—"

Was that real fear Stone detected in Deirdre's face?

"You said you thought dating was stupid," Deirdre said. "Boys would just get in the way of your acting."

Emma raised her chin and glowered. "Maybe I've changed my mind."

Stone saw Deirdre hesitate, as if suddenly realizing she'd crossed the line, lost control. What was the deal? Deirdre looked downright sick. If possible, Emma looked even worse. The kid was asking to go on a simple date. She wasn't asking for an X-rated negligee and the latest form of birth control.

Deirdre sucked in a deep breath. "Emma, honey, I'm sorry if you think I've overreacted—"

"If *I* think it?"

"I just...don't want you to get hurt."

"You should've thought about that before you blew my whole family apart! You're the one hurting me. And everybody else I love! Uncle Cade and Aunt Finn. And the

Captain..." Emma's voice broke. "My family's falling apart because of you, and now you go postal at me over one lousy little kiss?"

Stone could feel Deirdre struggle to keep her voice low. But pain and fear throbbed just under the surface. "It's not the kiss I'm worried about," Deirdre said. "It's...God, Emma. I just want to keep you from making a mistake. Screwing up your life the way I did."

"You mean by having *me?*"

Deirdre flinched as if Emma had slapped her. Hell, a slap would've been more merciful than having to watch the kid's face contort in anguish, see Emma's tears fall free.

"Oh, baby—" Deirdre reached for her, shattered. But Emma yanked away.

"Don't 'Oh, baby' me. *I'm* the mistake you're talking about, aren't I, Mom? *I'm* the reason you're so scared I'll start sleeping around."

"Emma, don't twist this around on me. I only—"

"It was *just* a *kiss,* Mom. You don't have to worry. I'm *nothing* like you." Emma spun away, ran not toward March Winds, but in the other direction, across the garden to the cabin Stone knew lay beyond the picket fence.

To her uncle, Cade McDaniel, and his wife. Stone's heart ached for Deirdre. He'd heard the insecurity in Deirdre's voice when she'd talked about the time they'd been apart, knew how much she worried that somehow she'd scarred her little girl.

How much did it hurt Deirdre to stand there, watching Emma's flight to the cabin where her daughter had spent those nine months without her?

Deirdre sank down onto the gazebo bench, buried her face in her hands. For a moment Stone thought about getting the hell out of Dodge. There wasn't a man alive who liked emotional scenes. And Deirdre sure wouldn't be thrilled he'd hung around to see this little gem between her and her daughter. And yet, Emma would have that nice Finn O'Grady's shoulder to cry on. With the strain in the family, the anger over Deirdre's insistence on searching for Jimmy Rivermont, who would be around to comfort Deirdre?

Oh, yeah, Stone, a voice mocked him. You're the next fucking Oprah—

He hesitated for a moment, then sat down across from Deirdre, his knees spaced apart, his elbows resting on them as he stared at his loosely clasped hands. "That was pretty spectacular," Stone ventured after a moment.

"Why are you still here?" Deirdre's voice shook but, damn, the woman still had a mean glare.

"I suppose telling you that you handled that all wrong would be a bad idea."

"Not if you have a death wish."

Stone shrugged. "Well, wouldn't be the first time someone's accused me of that. Don't you think it seems pretty harsh to come down on them so hard when just a few hours ago you and I were doing the same thing? Uh, at least until you bit me."

Deirdre's eyes flooded with a mixture of confusion and regret. "Did Emma look like she was going to come to her senses? I don't think so."

"So that's what happened. You came to your senses. Because kissing me was so terrible?"

"Damn it, Stone, I have standards—"

"And kissing pond scum like me is below them, huh? Even if you were the one who hired me."

"When I did, I didn't know kissing the client was part of the contract."

With you I'd consider making it one, if you could learn not to draw blood. Put those teeth of yours to more pleasurable use....

Hell, he couldn't say that to her. At least, not right now with her knotting everything up, making him sound unethical somehow. Hell, it *was* unethical to get sexually involved with a client. He'd sure never kissed one before. He'd just recorded images of other people lit up with passions so strong they risked everything...and often lost it.

Stone, get your mind out of your own bed and get back to the real crisis—an innocent kid who's just been blasted.

Stone searched for the right words, wondered if anyone could find them. "Listen, I know you love your daughter. And for whatever reason, you're afraid for her. Maybe...well, from what Emma said because you..."

"Because I was an unwed mother? Seventeen and pregnant to the gills? Oh, yeah, that was big fun. Walking through the halls with my belly like a basketball while all the kids said what a slut I was. That's just the kind of party I want to set up for my daughter."

Stone didn't want to feel the cut of all those eyes following proud Deirdre McDaniel down the school halls, didn't want to imagine the acid of all those jibes she must have heard. He could see her, head held high, determined not to let anyone see they'd left her bleeding. No wonder she was terrified for her kid. And yet, nailing Emma in a barrel and not letting her out until she was thirty was hardly an option. Even if Deirdre thought it was for her own safety.

Stone steepled his fingers, looked at the boards under his feet. "So that's the story. You got pregnant in high school."

"Yeah, Stone. That's the story. I got knocked up because I was stupid and careless and all those dreams I had of singing on stages across the country died. A slow death, I'll admit, because I was so stubborn, but that just made it hurt even worse. Emma deserves more in her life. I won't—won't let her—"

Stone took a chance, slid next to Deirdre on the bench. "You know, I'm no parent, but—"

"People who don't have any kids are always *so* eager to give advice."

"I'm pretty sure this advice is on target. Don't do this...." Stone waved his hand to where the two kids had been kissing. "Don't turn this into some big drama. There's not a teenager in the world who hasn't seen that play and pictured themselves desperately in love, their parents the evil villains keeping them apart. Don't force Emma to play Juliet for real, Deirdre. She'll be far too good at it if you do."

Deirdre didn't say anything. Damn, he wanted to hold her, but sensed if he was fool enough to touch her now, she'd make that cut on his lip seem like no big deal.

"If you just back off," Stone said, "odds are the relationship will burn itself out."

"After he gets what he wants from her, and maybe ruins her life."

Stone wanted to make her tell him who'd ruined *her* life, put the pain and wariness in her eyes. Stone wanted to find the asshole's address and rearrange the guy's dental work.

Instead Stone watched as she pushed herself to her feet. She cast one long, heartbreaking look across the space that separated her from Cade McDaniel's cabin, the place where her daughter had gone.

And Stone thought how easy it would have been for her to follow if she had never opened the hope chest, never found the letter.

"Goodbye, Stone," she said. He watched, helpless as she vanished into March Winds, alone.

"G-GRANDPA?" EMMA RAN through the cabin door, calling his name, wanting his strong arms around her.

"In here!"

She followed the sound of Martin McDaniel's voice, found him in the long hallway, half collapsed against the wall, his hair sweat soaked, his fingers white as he tried to haul himself upright again with his walker, fury and shame on his gray face.

Fear stabbed Emma, seeing him look suddenly so old.

She rushed to his side. "Let me help you. Where are you trying to go?"

"Up and down this goddamned hall until I get my strength back. When I do, I'm going to run over this fluffy contraption with my Jeep." He slammed the heel of his hand against the walker's metal bar. "What I wouldn't give to be able to swing a sledgehammer."

Emma's need to confide in her grandfather faded in the light of the old man's pain.

"Damn it, girl, I *hate* having you see me like this!"

"It's okay, Grandpa. Maybe your hip's broken, but the rest of you is stronger than anyone I know."

"Not anymore, sweetheart. Your grandpa used to be strong as a bull, but now...hell, just look at me."

Emma's throat hurt. She took him by the arm. "You're going to get better soon. You've got to teach the twins how to fight. A few death shots, remember? Like you showed me?"

The Captain grunted but let her help him regain his balance between the walker's metal supports. He grabbed the rubber grips as if he were trying to strangle them.

"Could we go back to your room?" Emma asked. "You could sit in your big chair and we could talk, just like we used to."

"Why the hell not. It's obvious I'd end up flat on my face

if I tried walking that hall anymore. But tomorrow—humph. This hip doesn't know who it's f— I mean, fooling with."

"Nice save," Emma said. "You almost had to put a dollar in Aunt Finn's swearing box."

Finn had instituted the box when the twins had started picking up colorful language. When it was full, Finn was going to tally up the twin who'd sworn the least and let them get a toy with the cash.

Emma wanted to make her grandfather smile. Anything to distract him from the pain twisting his beloved features.

She got the Captain to the room Aunt Finn had made for him, trying to recreate the living room back at Linden Lane as much as possible. The Captain eased himself into his big armchair, and Emma wished she was still small enough to curl up on his lap, and that he was still strong enough to let her. Eagle sharp eyes took in her face—and Emma knew she must be all blotchy from crying.

"Now, why don't you tell me why you're here?" the Captain asked.

"I missed you. And Mom—Mom's just being hateful." Emma sniffed, hard. She'd never disgrace herself by crying in front of the Captain. McDaniels didn't cry, he'd say. They fought back with everything they had.

The Captain's mouth hardened, and Emma waited for him to let loose his own temper at the upheaval her mom had caused. That was the Captain's way—blast pain right out of the water. But Martin McDaniel asked stiffly, "How is your mom?"

"She's being impossible. Says she wants to—to find that man…" Emma faltered, not knowing what to say, not wanting to humiliate her grandfather or hurt him by calling "that man" by the name *father*. "And it's making her crazy. She just—just blew up at me in front of Drew Lawson while this restoration guy was watching. I thought if she had a date once in a while she might let up on me."

"Your mom's seeing a man?"

"This guy named Jake Stone. He's real hot, Grandpa, but now, well, I hope she never sees him again...."

"Hold on there, soldier." The Captain stopped her, his eyes sought hers, and Emma thought she'd never seen them so sad. "Emma, you're not a little girl anymore. You're almost a lady. A beautiful, intelligent lady with a heart as big as your smile."

Emma caught the inside of her lip between her teeth, hating the inevitable, that the more of a lady she became, the more the Captain's strength would fade. She curled up on the floor next to him, leaning her face carefully on his good leg. "I wish everything could just go back to the way it was before. When I was little and you were in your own house where you belong."

The Captain smoothed his hand over her hair. "Looks like even I can't stop time, sweetheart. Growing up means you have to hear hard things sometimes. And do what's right, even if you want to kick the whole world in the teeth."

"I'd feel a whole lot better right now if I could. Starting with that dumb kid who stole his sister's purse. If you hadn't thought it was a real mugging, Captain, you wouldn't have chased after him. You wouldn't have hurt yourself. You were trying to take care of that girl. I wish I could take care of you."

"Maybe there is something you could do for your old grandpa. Something important."

Emma looked up, saw the plea in the Captain's eyes, almost a desperation. "I'd do anything for you, Captain.

Cross my heart." They'd sealed a hundred conspiracies just that way in years past, always partners in crime.

"All right, then." Her grandfather seemed to brace himself. "Emma, Jake Stone isn't restoring any house over there. He's the man who broke up your aunt and uncle's engagement six years ago by proving Aunt Finn's father had stolen all that money he left her."

"Wh-what?" Betrayal and disillusionment swirled through Emma. "Mom said—"

"I know what your mom said. Your uncle told me all about it. That she didn't want you to know the truth. But it's plain and simple. Jake Stone is a private investigator."

"He's the one— She's gone and done it? Actually hired someone to—" Emma pushed to her feet, a sob too hard to control. "She lied to me! She promised she'd always tell me the truth! She said I didn't have to worry. She'd never lie again the way she did when she promised she'd still be at Uncle Cade's when I woke up. When she left me—"

Panic washed through her, and she felt ten years old again, terrified, abandoned with an uncle she didn't know, desperately wanting her mother.

"Emma, I told you this was hard. I wouldn't have told you at all except that you're the only one I can trust to help me."

"H-help you with what? Oh, Grandpa..." She tried to scrub her tears away with her fist. "I...I'm sorry.... I'm crying...."

"Don't tell anyone else—I'll deny it to the death—but sometimes your grandpa cries, too. Come here, little girl." He held out his hand. Emma crossed to him, took it. His hand felt all work roughened and bruised. In spite of his broken hip he'd managed to ding himself up, and one of the twins' SpongeBob bandages was on his thumb.

"First, Emma, you can't let your mom know that I've

blown her secret out of the water. She'll tell you all about it in her own good time."

"That's not fair! Grandpa—"

"It's what I need you to do. Swear you won't tell your mom you know who Jake Stone is. It would only make things worse between your mom and me. I don't think I could bear that."

"It's her fault things are all messed up! If she hadn't gone poking around in that stupid hope chest..."

"I went through that chest myself years ago, wanting to make sure it was safe for your mom. It was like something inside of me knew it might hurt her...instinct, you know? The kind that kept me from stepping on land mines in Nam." The Captain grimaced. "Whenever your mom and that cedar trunk got mixed together, there's always been nothing but trouble. Since she was just a little girl, climbing around on it, breaking things."

But this time she's breaking your heart, Emma thought. "I wish she'd never opened it."

"I do, too. But she did. There's no changing that now. Just like there's no changing the fact that I didn't leaf through that damned play script when I had the chance. It just felt too...tender, Emma. That play was everything about your grandmother that I couldn't understand. I felt like my Emmaline deserved her privacy. Silly, wasn't it? With her so long dead."

"No, Grandpa. It just shows how much you loved her."

"Maybe I loved her long, but I didn't love her well. And now—" he swallowed hard "—now your mom and you are paying the price. It's too late to turn back, honey. We're already on the beachhead, and the drop boat's ten miles out to sea. And here I sit, stuck in this goddamned house, with my hip in pieces."

Martin rubbed at his eyes. Emma's cheeks burned, and

she looked away, determined not to let him know she'd seen the moisture clinging to his lashes. "God, I *hate* having to depend on other people. It makes me want to smash something."

Emma squeezed his other hand. "It's not other people, Grandpa. It's just me."

"So it is, my Emma. So it is." He kissed her fingertips, hard, the scruff on his cheeks scratching just a little. Emma leaned against him, drawing in the faint scent of tobacco and Pepsi and engine oil. He smelled like love.

"Emma," he said gravely. "Honey, this is what I need you to do. Kind of a covert mission, you know? Don't let on that you've got this Jake Stone's number. But keep your eyes and ears open. You're a smart girl. You'll be able to figure out what's going on."

"You mean, like, spy on Mom?"

"Somebody's got to keep me informed of the situation. You're my only hope. God knows, the girl will never talk to me about what's going on."

"Grandpa, I..."

"You have to help me, Emma. Promise to tell me the instant your mother finds her—" he winced, then plunged on "—this blood father of hers."

"But...but Grandpa..."

"I mean it, Emma," he said grimly. "I don't care what your mother or your uncle or aunt say. They think they have to protect me. Protect *me.* Hell, I was on the front lines in Vietnam before they could even suck on their thumbs. I'm not going to sit here like a toad and let this jerk hurt my little girl."

His fierce eyes pinned Emma. "Promise me, Emma. I need you."

"I promise," Emma said softly.

He crushed her hand as if he'd never let it go.

CHAPTER 10

WHAT HAD HAPPENED TO HER BABY, the Emma she'd known and loved and laughed with for sixteen years? Deirdre wondered, heartsick as she watched her sullen daughter stir a bowl of melting ice cream.

For a week since the disaster in the gazebo, Deirdre had done her best to mend fences. They both should have cooled off enough to talk reasonably by now, but Emma just got surlier and more silent by the day until the weekly family night the two had shared since Deirdre returned to Whitewater was a torture worthy of the Spanish Inquisition.

And there wasn't any chance to call in reinforcements. Cade's cabin sat dark and empty, her brother, Finn, the twins and Martin McDaniel having traveled to Montana for two weeks at Jett Davis's ranch. Cade's best friend and Hollywood A-list actor hoped the trip would take some of the pressure off Cade and lift Martin McDaniel's spirits. But Deirdre figured it was Finn who needed a break. She looked more worn-out every day and so distressed over the breach in the family Deirdre felt almost relieved she was gone.

Except that Deirdre was desperate to talk about Emma. Then Deirdre realized how alone she really was. Oh, she had a few friends—acquaintances, really. But she had always held her deepest emotions close to the chest. She wasn't about to let those women poke around in vulnerabilities Deirdre tried her best to pretend weren't there. She didn't trust easily. She never had. And since God had brought her brother's warm, openhearted wife to Deirdre's doorstep, she figured her closeness with Finn was enough.

They'd shared everything these past six years—their joys, their heartaches, the business they'd built together at March Winds. Finn had even insisted Deirdre be in the birthing room when the twins had been delivered. Deirdre had sworn nothing would ever separate her from the people she loved most in the world again. It wasn't the first time she'd been wrong. But after the precious years of belonging so completely, this isolation hurt worse than anything she could imagine.

She figured she must be losing her mind because three times in the past week she'd picked up the phone and almost dialed Jake Stone. Just to see how the case was going, she'd tell herself. What she really wanted was to hear his voice, let him make her laugh or else just pick a fight with him. Stone wouldn't give her the silent treatment or just level her with Finn's weapon of choice, the big, sad eyes.

Jake could probably even crack through Emma's wall of silence with his irreverent sense of humor. Deirdre stole another glance at her daughter. Emma had to be madder than Deirdre had ever seen her. Nothing short of a nuclear meltdown could make her chatterbox daughter so silent, so grave.

"Emma, I'm sorry you're upset with me," Deirdre said,

her own ice cream tasting like dust. "I've said it a hundred times. Can't we at least talk about this?"

"Why bother? You'll just lie."

Guilt soured Deirdre's stomach. She'd meant to straighten things out with Emma, tell her the truth about Jake Stone and his business at March Winds. But things around the house were bad enough without drop-kicking that nest of hornets.

"How will I lie? Tell me." Deirdre hedged, not wanting to get caught outright if somehow the truth had slipped out. Finn and Cade had sworn secrecy. The Captain didn't know. When Deirdre had pushed Cade about it he'd taken her head off, saying their dad was in rough enough shape, physically and emotionally after the bomb Deirdre had dropped on him. Hell if Cade would be the one to pile more misery on the old man.

She could hear her brother's voice reasoning in her head, clear from Montana. Maybe Deirdre should stop and think…why didn't she want Emma or the Captain to know about the private investigator? Was Deirdre's conscience bothering her? Maybe she should just call the whole thing off.

But was it such a terrible thing to want to know where she'd come from? To long for a father who understood who she was? Or, more accurate, who she'd *wanted* to be with her music?

Yet Emma was paying a price. This whole *Romeo and Juliet* gig she was playing with Drew Lawson was turning dangerous, too. Emma wouldn't even tell Deirdre what she was so angry about. And the anguish and rage in Emma's eyes cut Deirdre to the core.

"Emma, please. How did I lie to you?" Deirdre prodded.

Emma jabbed at the ice cream with her spoon. Oh, God,

it was so hard tiptoeing around her daughter when for so long a hug, a joke, a heart-to-heart talk in Deirdre's big bed had been able to solve all the problems in Emma's world.

Not all the problems, a voice whispered inside her. How many months had it taken to heal Emma when Deirdre had finally come home six years ago? Had Emma really healed at all?

Deirdre had spent countless hours watching her daughter, looking for any cracks in their relationship, terrified that someday the dam would break and all Emma's anger and betrayal and bitterness would pour out, all her roiling emotions toward the mother who had abandoned her. Was that what was happening now? Payment for the nine months she'd left her little girl behind?

"May I leave now?" Emma demanded. "I spent two hours here. It's stupid to sit here and not talk."

Deirdre forced back irritation. Emma had played her "twenty questions from hell" game a few times in the past, making Deirdre dig for whatever was bothering her. As if to make Deirdre prove she really cared. But the game had never felt so serious, so dangerous or for such terrible odds.

"You're right. It is stupid to sit here in silence. So let's talk. If you won't tell me what's wrong…"

"I told you." Emma's eyes blazed. "You promised you'd never lie again. But you did. Just like the night you dumped me with Uncle Cade. You promised you'd still be there when I woke up."

Just stick a dagger in my heart and be done with it.… If only Emma could know how much that lie had haunted her. For years and years and years.

"I did lie to you then. I…" *I was falling apart, on the verge of a nervous breakdown. I was desperate and alone and wanted you to have things I couldn't give you...a real home, not a rented room for a couple months before we moved on. I didn't think I was good enough to be your mother but I knew your uncle Cade.... He'd take care of you better than I ever could....*

She'd believed with all her heart she'd done the right thing in leaving Emma with her brother, until she'd met Finn at a dark little club.

What Emma needs is her mother....

"I'll regret what I did every day of my life."

Emma's eyes teared up, her lips trembled. Deirdre held her breath, praying for a breakthrough. "Then how—how could you..." Emma ducked her head, climbed to her feet and crossed the kitchen, dumping the bowl into the sink. "No," she mumbled tightly. "Promised..."

"How could I what?" Deirdre urged gently.

But whatever the child had almost said was gone. Instead she said tightly, "You lied when you said that you trusted me."

But I did trust you—before Drew Lawson kissed you in the gazebo. When your heart was set on reaching your dreams, and you swore you'd never let anything get in the way.... When I wasn't so afraid...didn't know how helpless I could feel, no matter how hard I tried to reach you....

"There. I told you how you lied. Now, can I go out? Some of the cast was meeting at Staci's."

Deirdre almost bent the family night rules. She thought what a relief it might be to have the house empty of Emma's quiet fury for a little while. Time when Deirdre could catch her breath. And yet, "some of the cast" no doubt meant Drew Lawson. The date last Friday had been a disaster as far as Deirdre was concerned. Emma had spent hours getting ready—her door firmly shut against her mother.

Deirdre had spent the four hours the teenagers had been at dinner and a movie pacing the floor. After Emma's return, her daughter hadn't said a word to her about the night, but hectic color stained Emma's cheeks, and she looked a little rumpled, a lot breathless. Worst of all, Emma had spent the days leading up to the "Great Montana Escape" babbling to Finn about it until the woman should be half-deaf. But the instant Deirdre had walked into the room, Emma had lapsed to stony silence.

Of course, it was a wonder Emma wasn't hoarse, considering the amount of time the girl was spending on the phone. Drew had called every night the past week at nine o'clock and Emma had locked herself in her room, the murmur of her voice audible long after Deirdre went to bed. Not that going to bed had anything to do with sleep anymore.

Deirdre would lie awake, her thoughts bouncing like crazed ping-pong balls from Emma to the affair, from the Captain to Jimmy Rivermont, from the perfect Drew Lawson to another boy...and maybe, most disturbing of all, to a man with tiger's eyes who had kissed Deirdre in the deserted park, awakened things she was sure she could never feel again.

"Emma, you know, the rule is that we spend family night together. No going off to do something with other people. Otherwise all you'd do is spend what time we have together looking at your watch."

"Fine. I'll go to bed. Family night is stupid anyway. We don't even have a family anymore since you found that letter."

"Don't exaggerate. Things are strained right now, but—"

"Strained?" Emma gave a bitter laugh. "We used to go over to Uncle Cade's all the time, or they'd all come over here. You barely talk to anyone anymore. Even Aunt Finn. And the Captain..."

"I've talked to the Captain." A few awkward sentences. Terribly polite. The most miserable conversations Deirdre had ever had, except for the recent ones with her daughter. Or listening to Jake Stone on the answering machine.

I've got some leads I'm following. I'll call you when I have news. Damn it, Deirdre, pick up the phone. I want to know how Emma is. How you are…

Deirdre didn't dare call him back. She wanted to hear his voice far too badly.

"Well, if that's talking to Grandpa, I've talked enough for three weeks tonight to you. I'm going to bed."

"Fine. Go." Deirdre hated the sharpness in her voice. She hesitated, watching her daughter's retreating back, wishing she could call out, the way she had before, so easily, so naturally, taking it all for granted— *Hold it right there, little girl…where's my good-night kiss?*

But Deirdre couldn't bear the idea of Emma giving her a kiss filled with resentment. Deirdre swallowed hard and called after her baby.

"I love you."

For two hours, Deirdre couldn't settle. She did the paperwork for March Winds. Tidied up both the public areas and the private ones she and Emma shared in the big empty house. Deirdre crossed to the parlor where she'd insisted Cade set the hope chest under a window.

Her placement of the chest still drove Finn a little crazy—an heirloom where the main hustle and bustle of guests took place. But Deirdre didn't need the symbol of all her childhood failures and self-doubt to be in her bedroom, the last thing she saw at night. All the hope chest stood for haunted her sleepless hours too much as it was.

Finn had acquiesced to Deirdre's decision at last and

slipped some pillows on top of the cedar chest so guests could curl up there and gaze at the garden, never dreaming they were sitting on a bomb that had exploded. God knew what else was in the thing. Deirdre was afraid to look.

And yet, she couldn't help wishing she could go cry all this out to her own mom, the mother she'd wished Emmaline McDaniel had been.

Deirdre knelt before the chest, opened the lid, the pillows sliding backward. She ran her fingertips over linens, lifting a pile of them out, digging deeper. She froze as light spilled across a bundle of what looked like dish towels held together by one of Deirdre's old hair ribbons.

Deirdre lifted the bundle out, her throat suddenly tight. The top towel was labeled Sunday in red embroidered lettering. But it was the image stitched above it that touched her heart—a frolicking puppy running off with a Sunday bonnet. The puppy, all black like the stray Deirdre had adored as a child, its collar stitched in blue… Spot.

Deirdre untied the ribbon, carefully lifting one towel after another and fanning them across the floor, one towel for each day of the week, each one sporting the black puppy in different kinds of mischief. A sudsy Spot in a washtub for Monday, delving through a shopping basket, carrying a pair of torn overalls to lay beside a sewing basket. The last, Saturday, showed the black dog in the arms of a little girl—a simple line drawing traced in colored stitches, and yet, the hair was Deirdre's own, the dress on the iron-on decal scrubbed until its blue outline had almost vanished, a pair of freehand jeans stitched on in its place.

Her mother had stitched these, Deirdre knew. Emmaline had always had some bit of needlework in her hand. And Deirdre had never noticed. She could see her mother tucking them into the chest as a surprise, maybe hoping someday her restless daughter might pause long enough to think about the time spent creating them, the tenderness in portraying Deirdre and her beloved dog.

Mama, why didn't you ever show these to me? Deirdre whispered, wishing her mother could hear. Deirdre could still remember the scorn she'd felt toward her mother, how she'd curled her lip in distaste. But then, a plain old boring mother, a wife, was all Emmaline McDaniel had ever been. Deirdre had been so sure of that until she'd read the letter to a lover she'd never have guessed her mother bold enough to take.

Knowing she still couldn't sleep, Deirdre carried the towels with her to her favorite chair and popped in a movie. But the night wasn't the same without Emma.

Better get used to it, Deirdre told herself. *Come January, Emma will be in New York, and you're going to have to learn how to live alone....*

Alone? At least as alone as a woman could be, running a bed and breakfast. And yet, she *would* be alone in a house full of strangers.

Why did she wonder what Stone would think of this movie? Imagine his lightning-quick wit, his humor, his heat—the way he could fill up any space he occupied with nothing but his cocky attitude.

Deirdre wondered what it would be like to have what Finn and Cade had. Sharing a bed, a breakfast table, fighting over the remote control and making up long afterward in bed?

For sixteen years Emma had been all she needed. Filled up her heart, her time, her worries. Even the time a single mom got to herself was precious. Deirdre liked her own company. She had never realized that she wouldn't like being alone; that loneliness could seep through all the cracks in her heart; that a future of occasional phone calls as Emma hopped around the globe chasing the stars would leave too much empty space in her life.

Deirdre leaned back her head for just a moment, closed her eyes. She didn't even know the moment she fell asleep.

The grandfather clock chimed two, startling Deirdre awake. She rubbed the stiffness in her neck. No wonder her whole body ached, tense as she was and sleeping in that godawful chair. Deirdre pushed herself to her feet, surprised as the towels fluttered to the floor. She picked them up, hugged them for a moment, then laid them carefully aside. Maybe she could show them to Emma in the morning, Deirdre thought. Maybe Emmaline McDaniel's handwork would give them something to talk about, really talk about for the first time in a week.

Deirdre snapped off the television, turned off the lights and headed upstairs. The house was quiet, so peaceful time might have spun backward to the days before Deirdre had opened the hope chest and the letter had changed everything.

If it was *then*, Deirdre would have opened Emma's door, quietly slipped into her room. She would have tucked the covers over her sleeping baby girl, and watched her dream of angels. She would have bent over Emma and, oh, so whisper soft, kissed her little girl's cheek.

If it was *before*.

Deirdre started to move away, stopped. God, what was she doing? Emma was leaving home come January. Time would slip by so fast. She couldn't afford to waste even one more night. So what if Emma was too old to be tucked in anymore? Deirdre needed to see that she was safe, sleeping, maybe more now than ever before.

Flattening her palm on Emma's door, she pushed, easing it open on creaky hinges. By the soft moonlight filtering through the curtains, Deirdre padded across the room to Emma's white iron bed.

Deirdre's heart twisted with love. Emma was huddled all the way under her blankets tonight as if to shut out the world.

It's the law, Mommy. Emma had explained at six. *Nothing bad can get you if you're underneath the covers. You can't let even your baby toe peek out or* bam! *a monster might bite it right off.*

It had been far easier to keep monsters away back then. Tonight, so many were out stalking. Deirdre almost left Emma in peace. But after a moment she took the coverlet between her fingers, eased the blankets back and—

Pillows. Nothing but pillows filled the place Emma should have been. Deirdre's heart flipped. She hurried into the hall, switched on the bathroom light.

Empty. Deirdre rushed back to Emma's bedroom, turned on the bedside lamp. Emma's nightgown lay in a puddle on the floor. The window above the porch was wide-open, the trellis easy access to the ground, the driveway visible beyond. The *empty* driveway. The van was gone.

Anger and worry raged through Deirdre. She went to the phone, dialed Staci's number, trying to forget that the kid's father was a football jock from Deirdre's own high school days. A groggy male voice answered. "'Lo?"

"This is Deirdre McDaniel. May I speak to Emma?"

"Emma?"

"She came to the get-together Staci was having with the rest of the cast."

"Hey, Dee. Sorry to tell you this, but Staci's at a volleyball tournament in Wisconsin this weekend. The kids were never here."

Deirdre's stomach plunged. "I...I'm sorry I woke you."

"Don't worry too much. Emma's probably fine. Not much trouble they can get into in a small town like this. Unless she gets up to *your* old tricks, eh, Deirdre, and ends up at Sullivan's Point." Staci's dad chuckled. He must have heard Deirdre choke.

"Emma's not going to do anything crazy," Deirdre said, more to herself than Staci's father. "She knows what she wants."

Deirdre had thought so. Now, she wasn't sure. Drama school was months away. But Drew Lawson...

Deirdre hung up the phone. Her hands shook as she scrambled through the phone book, found the Lawsons' phone number. Maybe Emma was there, having one of those "teen crisis" talks Deirdre had had over the years with her daughter's friends, where they poured out all the poison, how their own parents weren't fair, didn't understand...

Was Emma close enough to Drew or Drew's family to be over there this late? Deirdre dialed, still torn, needing to know where Emma was. Whitewater was a small town, but a lone teenage girl could be a target for some lunatic even here.

A firm voice answered. "We're having calls traced, so just stay on the phone and the police will—"

"I'm not a prank caller. I'm Emma McDaniel's mother."

"Oh, I...I'm sorry!" the woman apologized. "We've been getting some prank calls lately—girls at slumber parties playing jokes. An occupational hazard when one of your sons is the biggest catch in junior high, I'm afraid. Heaven forbid the girls just say they have a crush on Reece. He's our youngest, and quite a charmer. But you didn't call at...oh, Lord, two in the morning to hear my tale of woe. Is something wrong?"

"I was wondering if Emma is at your house."

"At this hour? No. I'm sure not. The house has been dead quiet all night. Reece is staying with friends after the football game and Andrew went to bed early. He said he wanted to take Emma out, but there was some reason she couldn't go."

"Family night."

"You know he's crazy about your daughter."

"He told you that?"

"Heavens no! You can hardly see the two of them together and not guess they're head-over-heels for each other. I've been wanting to meet you, but Drew said things were a little—" Mrs. Lawson hesitated a beat "—intense over at your house at the moment."

These complete strangers knew about the strain between Deirdre and Emma? Deirdre felt angry, embarrassed. She wanted to hang up and move someplace where she'd never have to see Drew Lawson's mother again.

Too bad, she told herself. *You're the mom. Suck it up.*

"Emma...well, apparently she sneaked out. I'm worried."

"Of course you are! This is definitely not good."

Deirdre heard a male voice, then Drew's mother's muffled objections. "Safe sex? I can't say that to a girl's mother!"

"Mrs. McDaniel?"

"I'm not married."

"Oh, I...I remember. Some of Drew's friends said, well...it doesn't matter. Maybe Emma and Drew are just talking."

"Carson, I *know* they can talk on the phone. Carson says...don't worry. He talked to Andrew about—"

"Safe sex?" The top of Deirdre's head felt ready to blow off. "There *is* no such thing!"

"We feel the same way. Hope it doesn't come to that, but...well, closing your eyes to the possibility doesn't solve anything. With all those hormones zinging through their systems... Have you talked to Emma?"

"Emma is sixteen! She never even talked to a boy on the phone until your son started using Shakespeare as an excuse for—"

"For what?" Mrs. Lawson asked sharply. "Ms. McDaniel, I understand you're alarmed. But my son is hardly a maniac ready to hurt your daughter. Drew will take care of her."

"That's what I'm afraid of!" Oh, God, Deirdre thought, she sounded like a lunatic. "There isn't a teenage boy in the world who isn't trying to get—"

The woman's voice took on a distinct chill. "Ms. McDaniel, Brandi Bates said something about...well, I'm not one to credit town gossip. But don't you dare be judging my son by whatever happened to you in the past."

"You just told me to talk to my sixteen-year-old daughter about birth control. What was I supposed to think?"

"Drew is always telling me I go overboard talking to his friends about things like that," Drew's mother said quietly. "But one mistake can be so costly. Surely you of all people should understand that."

"That's why I need to find my daughter. Please, just wake Drew up and ask him if he's heard from her. Knows where she might be. I'm worried sick."

"Of course." Deirdre held her breath, waiting as the woman made her way to her son's room. Deirdre heard a door creak, figured Mrs. Lawson had opened Drew's door.

"Drew," his mother called softly. "Drew, Emma's

mother is on the phone and— Drew? Ms. McDaniel, he's gone!"

Deirdre's stomach hit the floor. She tried to decide whether to be even more terrified or a little relieved. Emma wasn't alone out there somewhere in the dark, she was just with a boy who could ruin her life.

"Carson! Drew's gone!" the mother called out, sounding alarmed.

Deirdre heard a man's voice in the background, gruff with sleep, yet resigned. "My husband says kids do that sort of thing. He did it when he was Drew's age. They'll both show up in the morning. It'll give the girls something to gossip about besides the fact that Emma got the part of Juliet."

"By then it might be too late!" Deirdre slammed down the phone, feeling like she was going to retch. Oh, God.

Deirdre pressed her fingertips to her mouth, trying to force back the bile rising in her throat. She knew Emma had heard whispers about her mother's wild past. Was Brandi Bates gossiping about Emma the way they'd talked about Deirdre so many years ago? There was no creature in the world who could be crueler than a teenage girl. Deirdre wanted to hug Emma, wanted to shake her, wanted to shield her from jealous little bitches like Brandi.

But Emma wasn't confiding in Deirdre anymore. She'd run off to Drew, her emotions raging, feeling hurt and angry and outcast. What might Deirdre's little girl do to feel like she belonged?

Images flashed through Deirdre's memory, steamed up car windows, the crushing weight of a boy on top of her, the slicing pain as he—

No!

Cade...she'd call Cade...he'd find Emma. But Cade

was a whole sky away in Montana, and Emma had taken the van, leaving Deirdre stranded.

She had to get help. Call someone. She was scared…so scared. And yet, Staci's father's jibe and Drew's mother's words chilled Deirdre…. If word got out that Emma had gone missing…

Deirdre had to protect her daughter. She couldn't wait here, helpless, until Emma showed up. If Emma and Drew were at Sullivan's Point that might be too late.

Then who? Who could she call?

Stone.

The private investigator's face rose in Deirdre's mind, those shrewd gray eyes that missed nothing, his inner strength, his humor. His hands, so warm when he touched her. God, she needed someone to lean on just a little.

Deirdre dug through her purse for the page she'd ripped from the phone book weeks ago and dialed the P.I.'s number. Jake answered, sounding awake.

"Stone here."

"J-Jake?"

"Deirdre?" She heard a rustle, imagined Stone sitting up in bed. "What's the matter?" She almost cried at the sound of his voice, so strong, so sure.

"It's Emma. She's gone. Took the car and…and sneaked out. We've been having terrible fights. Her bed's empty and so is Romeo's. I'm so scared."

"Sit tight. I'm on my way." The phone clicked, went dead.

Numbly Deirdre pulled on jeans and a T-shirt and shoved her feet into tennis shoes. She couldn't stay in the house. She walked outside into the dark of the night to wait for Jake alone.

Please God, let Emma be all right, please God please God, please…. She gazed out into the blackness, wondering if

Emma was crying. She started running down the driveway, out onto the road, remembering when she'd cried and nobody heard.

JAKE DROVE THE CAR like he'd stolen it, racing along the roads he'd imagined crossing for so long, retracing the path to Deirdre's house.

She needed him.

He tried not to be glad, even a little. The woman was scared to death, her daughter God knew where in this vast, black night.

A picture of Emma rose up in his mind, the girl so fresh and innocent, so all-fired sure she could handle anything life threw at her.

But Emma didn't know the creeps who owned the streets this time of night. Jake Stone did.

He'd seen how nights could gobble up a kid. Some clueless teenager who'd cut loose from their parents, thinking it was fun. Kids whose parties had ended up with them dead on a highway—or worse.

Crazies came out at night in any town, and drunks. They owned the shadows where light couldn't reach. Maybe this wasn't St. Louis or Chicago. Whitewater was a sleepy little town. Unfortunately, that wasn't always enough to keep a kid safe.

"Damn it, Deirdre, why didn't you pick up the damned phone when I called?" Stone grumbled. "Maybe I could have defused things before you and Emma drove straight off a cliff."

Right, Stone. He grimaced. Mr. Family with all the right answers.

Maybe he'd have handled things all wrong, but at least Deirdre wouldn't have been shouldering this mess alone.

But she wanted him now. Needed him. She was going to let him help her. God, she'd sounded so damned afraid.

Jake veered onto Jubilee Point, slammed on the breaks as a woman popped into view. Hell, he'd almost hit... Deirdre! She ran to the passenger side, climbed in. She looked like holy hell. Locks of her rich dark hair stuck out in windblown disarray, tousled from running, her eyes huge in her delicate face, dark circles smudging high cheekbones. Her features too pale, too sharp seemed as if bone and raw nerves lay too close to the surface.

"You idiot!" Jake snapped. "Running down the middle of the street! I could have hit you!"

"Don't...don't yell. I couldn't just...just stand there...I kept thinking..."

Whoa, baby! She flung herself against him. Held on hard. He gathered her in his arms, kissing her temple, her face. "Easy, there. We're gonna find her. Emma's gonna be fine. Grounded for life, but fine."

"You don't know that! What can happen! They talked about safe sex! My God, Jake, like...like they expected..."

"Who talked about safe sex?"

"Romeo's parents, when I called them. But the boy doesn't—doesn't ever pay. Not like the girl..."

Stone stroked her hair. "I know you're scared, but Emma's got a good head on her shoulders."

"She's brain-dead! Thinks she's in love! She took the van and sneaked off, and Emma would never have done that before. Does that sound like she's got any head at all on her shoulders?"

Damn, Jake wasn't going to laugh. Deirdre meant it. She was terrified. Romeo might as well have been Ted Bundy, crazy scared as Deirdre was. What the hell was up with that? Sure, Deirdre didn't want Emma knocked up. That was easy to understand. But shouldn't that safe-sex thing calm her down at least a little?

"Come on, Deirdre, think. You've lived here your whole life. Where do kids go around here? Hotels? Make-out spots? Anywhere they might go to be alone?"

"There's a Super 8 out on the highway and—and…Sullivan's Point." Her voice caught. Jake's brows crashed together. He wished like hell he could see her face.

"Sullivan's Point?"

"Up in the bluffs, near the river. It's this deserted…oh, God. Didn't some serial killers murder kids at a place like that last year?"

From sex to serial killers in ten seconds. Yeah, the lady was losing it.

"Tell me how to get there."

Deirdre gave directions, deadly silent as Jake broke every speed limit posted. It seemed like an eternity before they took the faded tire tracks uphill, having to all but crawl along because of the ruts.

"Somebody's been here recently," Stone said. "The grass is crushed from tires."

"Yes. I…I see."

Stone squinted, trying to penetrate beyond the headlight beams, hoping like hell the noise of their approach would give the kids time to put themselves back together before Deirdre got out of the car. Stone didn't even want to think about the price Deirdre would exact from Drew Lawson for any piece of Emma's clothing the kid might have taken off.

Hell, he thought, suddenly grim. He'd been a horny teenager himself once. Had his share of excitement in back seats. But he wasn't feeling any too understanding at the moment where Drew Lawson was concerned. That is, if the kid was taking advantage—

The beams of light bounced, landed on Deirdre's van.

Windows steamed up so thickly it would be a miracle if Emma or Drew came up for air long enough to get the heads-up that they had company.

Stone bopped the horn with the heel of his hand. Deirdre nearly went through the roof. She swung the door open and was scrambling out before he'd even hit the brakes. Blast the woman, what was she trying to do? Get herself killed?

The light beamed across her face. Stone reassessed his position. No, the woman was plain old bent on murder.

She stormed to the car, yanked the door. Emma came tumbling out, Drew on top of her. Emma shrieked and Stone noticed Drew rolling to take the brunt of the fall himself. It was a helluva long way down. Stone hoped the ground was soft when they hit.

At least nobody had broken a leg, because Drew scrambled to his feet. He helped Emma up and drew her protectively into his arms, glaring and defiant.

Oookay, Stone reasoned. They'd been kissing plenty— lips all red and puffy. Clothes mussed up, but none missing. Shirts and jeans all accounted for. Of course, no way to tell if her bra was still where it belonged. But it looked like they'd gotten up here before the PG-rating guys would have faded the picture to black.

"Mom." Emma's voice cracked.

"Get in the truck," Deirdre said so sternly Stone almost climbed in himself.

"Mrs. McDaniel, nothing…nothing happened," Drew insisted. "Emma was upset. We were just talking."

"That's why her blouse is buttoned wrong?" Deirdre asked, glaring so hard at the kid he should've been a pile of ash.

"Mom, I— That wasn't Drew's fault. It was mine."

"I'm the one who taught you to start at the bottom, one button to each hole until you got to the top. Remember? I think you were about three."

"I'm not a baby! If you hadn't been so hateful—"

"You think I was hateful before, missy? You're grounded until you're thirty. And maybe you should hand the part of Juliet off to the understudy. Somebody who can tell the difference between fiction and real life!"

"No! You…you wouldn't dare! Hand Juliet over to Brandi?"

"Since you got cast you started sneaking out of the house, making out with boys in public places. You won't even talk to me! Damn it, Emma, I'm trying…"

"Oh, yeah. You're trying. To lie. To keep things from me. Like him!" Emma pointed to Jake. Whatever crush the kid had had on him was definitely over. She looked at him as if he'd burned down Broadway.

"Emma, Mr. Stone—"

"Oh, yeah. *Mr. Stone.* Mr. Stick-his-nose-in-everybody-else's-business Stone. I know all about him now."

Deirdre sucked in a breath as if she'd taken a punch.

"He's the guy who blew Uncle Cade's wedding out of the water when I was ten. He's a private investigator you hired to ruin my life! You're a liar and I can never trust you again! So don't you dare look all sad and say, 'Emma sneaked out and I can't trust her. Emma didn't do what I told her, so she's a brat.' And if you're thinking about locking me in my room you'd better board up the windows, because I swear, I'll climb out!"

Deirdre stared at her daughter, the color draining from her face. Jake could see Deirdre shaking. "My God, Emma—"

"Grandpa knows, too. We all know."

Jake stepped between them, held up his hand. What he

wouldn't give for a boxing ring with two separate corners. "Hold on, there. Both of you. Take a few deep breaths before you say something you're going to regret."

Hell, he wondered, was there anything left to say?

"I have something to say," Drew said, sounding remarkably levelheaded for a guy who'd just had Mommie Dearest descend on him, wanting his balls on a platter.

"I know this looks bad—"

"You think?" Deirdre demanded, incredulous.

"I want you to know I love Emma."

"Oh, for God's sake!" Deirdre snapped in disgust.

"We were…well, making out. Kissing and…stuff."

Stuff like rearranging those buttons on Emma's blouse, Stone thought.

"But I'd never…never hurt her."

"So you brought my daughter up here to Sullivan's Point so you could talk? Give me a break."

"*You* sure haven't been talking to her!" Drew accused.

Stone grabbed Deirdre by the arm, held on tight. He figured if she got her hands on the kid it would be manslaughter—unless she got a jury full of parents of teenage girls. Then no question, they'd figure ol' Drew had it coming.

"My relationship with my daughter is none of your business. I've loved her for sixteen years, mister. A few weeks of infatuation doesn't hold a candle to—"

"If you love Emma you should have known better than to lie to her. She's freaked about it, and I don't blame her. After you dumped her for nine months—"

Deirdre's other hand flashed out, would have connected hard with Drew's face if Stone's reflexes hadn't been so good. He yanked her out of reach just in time.

Emma screamed, went ice-white. "I don't even know

you anymore! I want—want Uncle Cade. I never should have told him I...I wanted to try..."

"Try what?" Deirdre sounded half-dead.

"You lie and you sneak and you...you... Aunt Finn wouldn't have left me! Not ever! She would have told me the truth about this jerk!"

Emma pointed at Stone. Aw, hell. Stone figured the kid was right. He could see from Deirdre's face regrets racing through her head. Finn McDaniel had probably hammered on Deirdre plenty to tell the kid what was up. That didn't mean Finn loved Emma more. It just meant Deirdre had more to lose.

"Why are you being so hateful?"

"I'm trying to keep you from ruining your life. Emma, you're so close to drama school, everything you always said you wanted."

"And you know all about dumping your dreams, right Mom? Because you had to stop singing because of me."

"Emma—"

"Well, it's true, isn't it? Since you came back to Whitewater, I haven't heard you sing a note. Not even in the shower. You used to sing all the time."

"The price was too high. It cost me nearly a year of your life."

"Yeah, well, you might have asked me what I missed most when you were gone. Talking I could do with anybody. But when you sang songs to put me to sleep... that was just you and me."

Deirdre's voice caught, thick. "I thought you hated it. If I'd been you, I would have—"

"But you're *not* me!"

"I had to choose between the music I loved and the person I love most in the world. You deserve better than that, Emma."

Stone looked down into Deirdre's face, asked her softly, "And what did you deserve?"

"Exactly what I got," Deirdre said dully.

"What about Grandpa?" Emma challenged. "Does he deserve to have his whole life ripped up? He's sick, Mom. And old. All these years you claimed it didn't matter who my father is. And I believed you. Now you're breaking the Captain's heart, looking for some stranger! Fine. As soon as I'm old enough, I'm going to find *my* dad. Then you can see how it feels."

Stone could feel that silver bullet hit Deirdre square in the heart. Deirdre stammered. "Emma, don't be..."

"Don't be what? Stupid, like you're being? Selfish? Maybe I don't have enough money to pay some snoop to dig stuff up now, but you can't stonewall me forever, Mom. I wonder if my father has hair like mine? Does he? Is he some guy running around town that I see all the time? Does he even know I exist?"

Deirdre staggered. Stone reached out to steady her. He expected more temper, raging, desperate attempts to reason. But Deirdre stood there, as if her daughter had ripped out her very soul.

"Emma, it's complicated—"

"And your digging around in the past for your father isn't? I never knew you were such a hypocrite. Why are you looking so weird if this 'finding your father' gig is no big deal?"

Stone glanced down at Deirdre, her face gray in the beams of his headlights, her eyes like wounds. Hell, she looked as if her knees would give out any moment. Or her spirit...hell, he'd never believe anything could have the power to break it. He wanted to hold her, knew he didn't dare in front of Emma. At least not yet. He had to buy

Deirdre time to pull herself out of whatever hellish chasm she was falling into.

For that, she needed a little time apart from her daughter.

"Kids, get in the van," Stone ordered. "I'll follow you back to March Winds, then I'll take Drew home."

He expected Deirdre to protest. She was too shattered even to argue. She slid into his passenger seat, silent.

Stone's gut clenched. He'd seen Deirdre fighting mad, lashing out, hurt and vulnerable before. But speechless? The woman had a mouth on her that could break the sound barrier. What the devil was going on?

One thing he knew for certain. After he dropped Drew Lawson off, Stone was sure as hell going to find out.

CHAPTER 11

EMMA STORMED INTO THE HOUSE, Deirdre in hot pursuit, neither McDaniel woman bothering to see if Jake and Drew had hit the road. The kitchen light was still blazing, forgotten when Deirdre had run outside in a bundle of nerves to meet Stone on the road. Deirdre clenched her hands in the fabric of her long T-shirt, hating that the man had seen her so vulnerable, not sure what to do with the rebellious young woman who'd replaced her beloved daughter. Deirdre wasn't sure raking over everything right now was going to do any good. But she had to try something or go crazy.

"Emmaline Kate, you sit down at this table and we're going to talk."

Emma didn't go into her regular "I'm in deep shit" dramatics. She just pulled out a chair and sat, her blouse gaping between the mismatched buttons, her eyes narrowed, glowering.

She'd wondered if she had her father's hair? Now she looked so much like Adam that Deirdre felt like throwing up. Why hadn't she noticed the similarities before? Had she blocked them out of her mind on purpose?

Deirdre sank down across from her daughter, feeling farther away from Emma than she had when she'd been singing eight hundred miles away. Deirdre swallowed hard, searching desperately for the right words, but Emma wasn't waiting.

"I know what you're going to say, Mom."

Did she? Deirdre thought, peering into her daughter's eyes. The kid must be some kind of mind reader, since Deirdre didn't have a clue herself. But the claim did give Deirdre an out of sorts. "Okay, what am I going to say?"

"All that stuff about saving myself for the right guy, not letting myself get sucked into doing something reckless that can wreck up my life. That sex is a big deal and I'm not old enough to handle the responsibility."

"That sounds about right."

"You've told me all that stuff before, but you never even once asked how *I* felt about sex."

That's because I didn't want you feeling anything about sex, period. "You always made it seem like you agreed with me."

Emma raked her hands through her disheveled hair in exasperation. "Maybe that's because I wanted you to let me get up from the blasted table sometime before I was old enough to vote."

"Emma—" Deirdre started to protest.

"Come on, be honest. You would've kept hammering me and hammering me until I said, 'yes, Mommy,' like a good little girl."

Deirdre winced. Emma was right. Deirdre clasped her hands together, squeezing back the panic. *Don't screw this up!* A voice screamed inside her head. This might be the most important conversation she'd ever had with her daughter, except for the one she'd had in this same kitchen when she'd returned to Whitewater to reclaim her child six years before.

"Okay," Deirdre said. "I'll bite. What do *you* think about sex?"

Emma met her gaze unflinchingly. "I think if I decide I want to have sex you can't stop me."

Deirdre's hands trembled, iron bands crushing her lungs. Then suddenly air rushed back into her system. *If.* Emma had said *if* she decided to have sex. That meant there was still time....

"That means you haven't?" Deirdre ventured.

"Not yet. But I'm thinking about it."

"Oh, God, Emma. You barely even know Drew. I want so much more for you than—than what you can find at a place like Sullivan's Point. Trust me, no girl ever got the best of the deal in the back seat of a Chevy."

"It's my decision, Mom. My life."

"I know. That's why I'm so damned scared for you. Emma, you sneak out in the middle of the night, and—"

"You act like Drew is a serial killer or something. Make him feel as uncomfortable as possible whenever he's over here. But you're such a control freak you won't let me go to his house. You won't even meet his parents and give him the chance to—"

What? Tell me how he knows all about safe sex?

"Emma, you barely know this kid!"

"We've been in the same class since sixth grade, and in every high school play we've ever done. I've been crazy about him since I was a freshman, but I didn't think I had a chance in hell with a boy like him."

"Like him? What do you mean 'like him'?"

"He's going to be valedictorian, Mom, and he's first seed in the varsity tennis team. Everybody knows he's going to be prom king."

"That's what makes you want to have sex with him? Because a school full of idiot kids who tortured you think he's terrific? When did you start basing your life decisions on what girls like Brandi Bates think?"

Anger reddened Emma's cheeks. "This isn't about Brandi or any of those nasty witches. It's about Drew. He's not like them at all. And he never dated Brandi. They went around with the same crowd of friends, and people just assumed they were together."

"It never occurred to him to tell Brandi they weren't? Sounds like a line of bull to me. I just want you to be careful."

"So careful I end up like you? Thirty-three years old and alone?"

Deirdre tried not to let Emma see how deep that cut. "I had you to take care of. I didn't have time for...for—"

"Sex?" Emma supplied.

"A relationship. That takes time. Time to get to know each other, see if you have the same core values, the same dreams. See if you're sure enough to risk not only your future but your child's. There was never a man I trusted enough to risk letting him be near you, Emma."

"Right, Mom. Blame it on me. Truth is, you're scared. Of sex. Of life. So you're hiding out in the middle of nowhere, pretending you're making all these sacrifices for me."

"That's not true, Emma! It's no sacrifice!"

"That's what makes me saddest of all. You don't even have the brains to realize what you're giving up! It felt so good when Drew held me. I felt so...alive." Emma hugged herself. "So safe."

"Safe? For God's sake, Emma—there is no safe in a situation like that!"

"You're wrong. I love Drew. And he loves me. I want my first time to be with him."

Temper flared in Deirdre, cutting through fear. "Maybe you think I should just fling open your bedroom door, set a box of condoms on the bedside table next to your *Phantom of the Opera* poster and tell you both to have at it?"

Emma made a face. "I hardly expect you to go that far."

"What kind of mother would I be if I—"

"One who knew when it was time to let go." Emma stood, crossed to the door leading to the hallway. She paused, turned back toward Deirdre. Black curls tumbled about her face, big, dark eyes filled with accusation. "As for the condom suggestion, why don't you pick up your own box? That Stone guy is hot for you. Too bad he's a nosy jerk who runs around wrecking decent people's lives."

"Emma—"

"But then, after all the lies you told me, maybe you guys are a perfect match."

"I'm sorry, Emma," Deirdre said, remembering all the times Finn warned her that the secret was going to blow up in her face. Wondering why she hadn't listened. "I was going to tell you the truth."

Emma rolled her eyes. "Of course you were. About the same time you were going to have sex, probably. If I knew setting a box of condoms on your bedside table was all it would take, I would've bought you some years ago."

"This isn't about my sex life, Emma!"

"Too bad. At least that would have been your business."

Emma squared her shoulders. "As for the bit about handing my part over to Brandi—just try it. I'll be out of here and on my way to New York so fast your head will spin."

"Maybe that would be a good thing." Warring emotions

washed over Deirdre—heartache at Emma's leaving, fear about what would happen if she stayed.

"It's up to you, Mom," Emma said softly. "But if I go like that, maybe I won't come back."

Deirdre watched, helpless as her daughter went up the stairs, not running, slamming doors, performing the familiar theatrics that would have been strangely comforting at a time like this.

No, Emma's tread was measured, quiet, so decided it made Deirdre's blood run cold.

Oh, God. Unable to bear staying in the kitchen, Deirdre wandered through the first floor of March Winds, Emma's accusations echoing in her head. *Had* she been hiding out here, in the middle of nowhere? Using Emma as an excuse for...what? She didn't want a man in her life. It was that simple.

Or at least it had been until Jake Stone had almost run her over in the middle of the road tonight. A knight in tarnished armor, coming to her rescue. The man was as cynical as they came, hard-edged, arrogant...but beneath the exterior he showed to the world, he was so much more. He'd painted his grandmother's house pink, for God's sake. And he'd jumped out of bed at two in the morning to help Deirdre track down her daughter. He'd been so strong, so kind, that Deirdre hadn't minded leaning on him just a little. A little?

Liar! a voice accused deep inside her. *You were glad to lean on him. So damned grateful that you wish he was still here. Wish he could fold you into his arms, tell you everything is going to be all right. Wish you could spill out everything....*

Deirdre's knees felt weak. She sank down into a chair in the dark living room and curled her body tight, hugging her bent legs, her stomach churning, her hands shaking. Seventeen years of scar tissue torn away until she felt small and battered and more afraid than she'd ever been in her life.

THE LIGHT WAS STILL ON. Jake slid his truck into Park, killed the engine and knotted his fingers around the steering wheel, wondering if this was the time he was going to drive right off the cliff.

He'd dropped off plenty of clients at the brink, knowing the secrets he'd uncovered would push them over the edge. He'd only hoped that when they pieced their world back together again, their lives would be better.

No sense tearing the messenger up with guilt, Stone had rationalized. *He* hadn't instigated the search they'd sent him on. And yet, in all the years since he'd hung out his shingle as a private investigator, he'd never felt the suicidal impulse to grab on to a client's hand and jump with them into the hellish world of consequences, into the belly of the beast he'd set loose at their command.

He'd left clients alone to deal with their changed worlds on their own, while he went off to paint Trula's house pink or take Ellie May hiking so she could smell critters in the woods. He'd headed for the dojo, where he could practice tae kwon do, immerse himself in discipline, predictability, grateful for his uncomplicated life as a single guy who could do exactly what he wanted. Keep all that angst and human misery that had become his stock-in-trade bottled up, where it belonged.

He'd felt bad a couple of times for the people caught in the cross fire of his cases—like Cade and Finn McDaniel. But he'd never felt the slightest temptation to cross the line from business to personal until Deirdre had charged through his agency door and rocked his world.

Now, here he sat like an idiot, parked in front of her

house, ready to march headlong into all that private pain he'd witnessed at Sullivan's Point and demand to know what lay beneath all that McDaniel bravado.

What made Deirdre the bundle of contradictions that gave him night sweats and kept him edgy with wanting her in his bed, confused as hell by wanting far more than that? He wanted to get inside her skin where the pain lived.

And do what, Stone? a cynical voice demanded in his head. Screw up her life even more than it already was? Deirdre's kid hated him now—he was living proof her mom had lied to her. Stone doubted he could buy enough tickets on Broadway to appease Emma's wrath.

Logic screamed that he should stay as far away from this house and the women who lived in it as possible. Knowing Deirdre and Emma, they were probably in the middle of the kind of emotional scene Stone hated. Odds were his arrival would only make it worse. And yet…

Stone glanced over at Cade McDaniel's deserted cabin. Who else did Deirdre have to turn to?

Stone fought the strange feeling in his gut. Damn if it hadn't felt so right when Deirdre had needed him. Her call cracking the hard shell around him, making him feel stronger, a better man, like the cocky kid he'd been when he'd graduated—the police academy's best and brightest, the whole world laid out before him, shiny and new as the badge he'd been so proud of.

He wasn't that kid anymore. He knew things that that kid hadn't: that there were things he couldn't fix even if he wanted to; that doing the right thing wasn't as simple as it seemed; and how fast a man could lose everything.

There's still time to turn around, the voice of self-preservation tempted Stone. *Just get the hell out of here….*

But if he did that, he might never get to the bottom of

Deirdre McDaniel. He could sense an opening inside her, a rare moment when defenses tumbled down, when a client would tell him the truth. Gut instinct for recognizing that moment made Stone good at what he did, who he was—a ruthless bastard who didn't hesitate at closing in for the kill.

Deirdre was right about one thing. He was ruthless enough to use that instinct in dealing with her and bastard enough to knock on that door.

Not just to satisfy curiosity this time, or even to close a case, Stone tried to rationalize. To help her. To comfort her. To get closer…

What are you, crazy? Go poking around in her secrets and you might betray some of your own.

There's not a relationship in your life you could be honest in. There will always be truths you can't tell. And a woman like Deirdre would sense that you were holding something back. She could never, ever trust you.

But this wasn't about him. It was about the woman who had haunted his dreams for so damned long. He couldn't shake the sense that something was terribly wrong. Not the surface crap he already knew Deirdre and her daughter were going through. Something so deep inside Deirdre McDaniel that it was fused into every cell. And whatever it was, it was ugly enough to bring the strongest, most passionate woman he'd ever known to her knees.

The pizza Stone had eaten for dinner the night before lodged in a burning lump of acid in his throat, his imagination raging over time. His job had given him plenty of material regarding hellish secrets. Who was Emma's father that he could still shake Deirdre to the core?

She'd been a kid herself when she'd given birth to Emma. Was the man who fathered Emma dangerous?

Violent like Trula's mob boss? Was he in prison for God knew what and Deirdre was afraid Emma would find out? If he'd ever touched Deirdre in anger, by God, Jake would teach the son of a bitch the meaning of pain.

Grim fury settled in Stone's very marrow, mingled with a protectiveness so fearsome no one but Trula had ever inspired it. He couldn't shake his feelings of impending disaster as the expression contorting Deirdre's face up there at make-out point hit Instant Replay in his mind.

His fiery-tempered, fierce lioness of a woman stark, shattered. Scared out of her mind. So damned alone it had cut Stone to the core. Hell if he was going to let her stay that way.

Resolved, Stone opened his truck door, then reached for the cardboard box on the seat beside him and retrieved two cups of hot coffee from the cup holders on the dashboard. Balancing cardboard containers, he climbed out of the truck and mounted the steps up to the veranda, the porch swing swaying gently in the breeze.

Only Deirdre's van was in sight, so it seemed as if, blessedly, there were no guests at the bed and breakfast at present. Stone couldn't imagine how hard it would have been for Deirdre to have to smile at strangers, fix breakfasts, help plan itineraries for day trips as if she gave a damn whether or not the tourists would see eagles or find wildflowers in bloom.

With March Winds' guest rooms empty Deirdre and her daughter could be alone for a while, to sort things through. Setting the coffee cups on top of the box in one hand, Stone knocked softly on the door with the other. His heart slammed against his ribs as Deirdre opened it.

She looked raw, nothing but nerves and heartbreak, still dressed in the jeans and T-shirt she'd been wearing when she'd leapt into his headlights on the road hours before. Except the lights inside the house made one thing clear he hadn't known before. That she'd been in such a rush to find Emma she hadn't bothered to put on a bra.

Don't be a jerk, Stone. You didn't come here to stare at the woman's breasts. Even if they were lush and soft, the pink of her aureoles a shadow against the thin white cotton.

"What...what are you doing here?" she asked so numbly Stone jerked his gaze back up to her face, feeling like a first-class lech. She looked like holy hell, and he was grateful for the coffee he was juggling. Hoping the jolt of caffeine would put some life back into her.

"I'm probably being a complete dumb-ass," Stone mumbled. "Not that I seem to be able to help it."

Deirdre's forehead crinkled in weary bewilderment. She raised a hand to knead her temple. Stone wished he could take her in his arms, but he'd scald her with the blasted coffee.

"Krispy Kremes," he said, nodding toward the box. "I didn't know what kind you liked, so I just got one of everything."

She looked like the mere thought of doughnuts made her sick to her stomach. "Stone, I know you mean well, but—"

"Don't try to wheedle any more junk food out of me," he said, stepping around her into the house. "I don't share my stash of Twinkies with anyone."

God, was that a shadow of a smile?

He wanted to say something smart-ass, but all that came out was, "How are you?"

"Scared out of my mind. Trying to figure out how my life got so screwed up. And where the pod people put my real daughter."

"I can see the headlines in the *Enquirer:* Small-Town Juliet Has Brains Sucked Out By Alien Posing As Romeo. Mother Wages Valiant Effort To Stuff Brains Back In."

Stone headed for the kitchen, Deirdre a few steps behind. "If you can figure out some fail-safe technique for pouring brains back into teenagers' heads you'd be an instant billionaire. Get yourself one of those infomercials on TV at three in the morning when moms everywhere are waiting up for kids who broke curfew."

He slid the Krispy Kreme box onto the sparkling-clean counter, grabbed a cup and turned, pressing the coffee into her hand. The gratitude in her big, sad eyes made him damned glad he was here.

"Stone, I...thank you. For helping me find her. For bringing these." She gestured to the box with her free hand.

He shrugged, popping the lid open. "What can I say? Hormones are hell. But the real Emma is in there somewhere. Kind of like the jelly filling in one of these damned things." He poked at a likely looking doughnut.

"I forgot you're such an expert on teenage girls."

"Yeah, well. You want any info about kids, junk food or the best divorce lawyers, I'm your man." The half smile on his lips died, Stone the notorious smart mouth suddenly dead serious. The mood fit him like a cheap suit, but what the hell could he do? Deirdre needed to hear the plain truth.

"I know how much you love that kid," Stone told her. "She knows it, too, even if her opinion of you at present puts you somewhere between Mussolini and the witch in the musical *Into the Woods*. What was it Bernadette Peters said in the version Trula taped?"

Deirdre sipped at her coffee, a mere act of politeness, then set it down. "Stone, I'm really not up to reciting Broadway trivia right now."

"Rapunzel wailed that the witch had locked her in a tower, blinded her prince, thrown her out in the desert to bear twins alone. And the witch said...?" He raised his eyebrow, letting her know he wasn't going to let her slide on this one.

"'I was only trying to be a good mother,'" Deirdre quoted. "Emma and I used to laugh ourselves hoarse over that line. Somehow I don't find it nearly as funny as I used to."

"That's why people love good theater. It touches the truth in all of us." Hell. Had he said something serious? Aloud? Let someone glimpse the part of him that still loved the stage, even if it wasn't the usual tough-guy fare? Way to ruin his image!

"Don't go philosophical on me now, Stone," Deirdre said, looking pale and worn. "I don't have the energy."

"Yeah, well, how about I play good cop, then? And you tell me what this whole blow-up between you and Emma is really about?"

Deirdre hugged herself. "If I did, I'm afraid I'd have to kill you. Or you'd have to go into the witness protection program. Trula would never forgive me."

Thank God. A little humor. "I knew my Deirdre was in there somewhere."

My Deirdre? What the hell was he thinking? And yet, somewhere in his gut he'd felt that way about her forever. From the first time he'd seen her, he'd wanted... Things to be different. Impossible snarls smoothed away. Wanted her fire and courage and passion in his bed. But in the past weeks, he'd found he wanted something else even more— the places inside Deirdre where her wounds lived, wanted her heart wide-open with loving him.

Loving him.

Hell, he was in big trouble here.

He laid his hand against her cheek, savoring the soft of her, the warm. Wishing he could kiss her eyelids and smooth away all her fears. Wishing she would be brave enough to let him in.

"I know I act like a real hard-ass," Stone confessed. "A son of a bitch with a heart like steel. But it's pretty much bullshit, at least where the people I care about are concerned. That's why I keep the list to a bare minimum. Trula, my old partner on the force and his wife and kids. My dog."

Deirdre rolled her eyes heavenward and shook her head. "Stone, I'm honored to be on the same list as your dog. Really. But—"

"Actually you and Emma have edged poor Ellie May down a couple of notches. She would have been heartbroken if I hadn't bribed her with a really big bone."

He couldn't help himself. He drew Deirdre into his arms for just a moment. She was stiff, her whole body tense. He tried to rub the isolation out of her, smoothing his hand up and down her back.

She stilled for a moment. He could feel the second that need won out over wariness. She melted against him, her face buried against his chest. Her arms folded up between their bodies, not holding him, but burrowing into him, as if she were trying to bury herself deep.

The trust she offered shook Stone. Elated him, terrified him. God, she felt so fragile in his arms.

"Hey, did I tell you one of the great rules about being a private eye?" Stone murmured into the fragrant silk of her hair. "In this case, I mean. With you?"

He felt her shake her head no.

"I can't tell a soul anything you say to me in confidence. It's privileged information."

He was trying to draw her in. Feeling like a bastard for using what he knew of Deirdre McDaniel against her. A trust he knew in his gut was incredibly rare.

Why didn't he just say it? Spill his guts now. *I can't figure you out and, crazy as this sounds, I really need to know, see, because I…love you.*

Oh, yeah. That would send the woman screaming into the night.

He hooked his finger beneath her chin, gently urged her to meet his gaze. Her eyes were so blue he could swim in them. Filled with secrets.

Don't hide from me, Deirdre. I'm strong enough to handle whatever is torturing you. Let me help you. Stone feathered the pad of his thumb over her cheek, savoring the softness of her skin, the stark vulnerability in her eyes he knew few men had seen.

"It's obvious that stuff Emma said about her father shook you up," Stone said. "You've got to admit that seems kind of strange, since you're so dead set on tracking Jimmy Rivermont down."

Deirdre went rigid in his arms and pulled away. He hated letting her go.

She paced a few steps away from him, putting distance between them. Her mouth twisted, a strange mixture of bitterness and resignation. "So I'm a hypocrite. Just ask Emma."

"Bull. You need to be able to lie to yourself to be a hypocrite. And you're the most up-front person I've ever known—except for Trula, that is. Whatever you're thinking usually spills right out of that pretty mouth of yours. That's why this whole case isn't making sense to me. You're holding back, and that's damned well not in your nature."

"Looks like you're not nearly as gifted a detective as I thought you were. If you only knew." She stopped, rubbed her eyes, her voice dropping low. "I've never—never talked about…"

"The man who made you pregnant?"

"Boy. He was a boy. And I was so stupid…" Self-loathing burned in her face. Hell, was she still beating herself up inside after seventeen years? Why hadn't she let it go? Because whoever this boy was, he'd left Deirdre full of guilt and self-recrimination, left her somehow broken.

Stone seethed at the very thought of what some jerk had done to her. He had to struggle to keep from slamming his fist into the wall. He tried to keep his voice level, keep from spooking her, but even he could hear his outrage leaking through.

"Emma's father hurt you, whoever he was," Stone insisted. "Damn it, Dee, I can see the scars he left every time I touch you, kiss you. Fear is so strange in a woman brave as you that I can't help wanting to know why."

"No. What's strange is that…that I want to tell you."

Stone took a step toward her, wanting to hold her while she ripped open her heart. Deirdre held splayed hands up in front of her, warning him off. "Don't…don't touch me. I don't want you touching me.…" she said, wedging herself into a chair. He sank down across from her.

"Okay," Stone soothed. "We do this your way. Whatever you want."

"I want it to go away," Deirdre said. "I want it never to have happened."

"But then you wouldn't have Emma," Stone said gently.

"Emma," Deirdre echoed, the pain softening a little. "I was just sixteen. Emma's age. I was a baby myself. I just didn't know it." Deirdre clasped her hands together, stared at them as if she were trying to gather enough courage to open them, and let her secrets go.

Stone watched her, listened, begging silently for her to trust. Him? He was the last person any woman should have faith in. He didn't even trust himself.

"I kept thinking it was a mistake," Deirdre began softly. "I took three pregnancy tests, desperately praying the other two had been wrong."

Stone fell into Deirdre McDaniel's eyes, and she carried him back until he could feel the fear in her. How young she was. How damned alone....

THE CAPTAIN WAS MOVING AROUND downstairs. Deirdre listened, terrified she'd hear his footsteps on the stairs, his knock on the door demanding he be able to use the only bathroom in the house. The bathroom where she'd been throwing up every morning.

She couldn't be pregnant, she assured herself. This whole big scare was just some crazy reaction to stress. With Mom dead just three weeks past, the Captain drowning himself in Jack Daniels and Cade keeping the skies of America safe, it was no wonder she was such a mess.

As for her period—it had always been screwed up, just like she was, never behaving itself and holding to a schedule like the other girls' did.

Deirdre shivered, her hand touching the swell of her stomach tentatively, as if it belonged to someone else. She hadn't been eating, so she sure shouldn't been gaining weight. It was just her imagination that her clothes were getting tight.

Oh, God. Please don't make me pregnant, she'd pleaded. *I know this was all my fault, but I'm so scared. What do I know about babies?*

She was the least maternal girl she knew. When they'd had to lug around eggs in junior high, take care of them like babies, she'd dropped hers and smashed it all over the music room floor. She'd been playing the piano, working on a new song. The vibrations had jiggled the egg off the glossy ebony edge and *splat,* she'd failed home ec.

She stared at her watch, the seconds ticking by so slowly she wanted to tear out her hair. If Cade was here, she could have told him. He would have waited with her, waiting for the plastic stick to show its colors. He would have hugged her and told her everything was going to be all right. He would have been her rock, just like he had when she was small and confused and trying to figure out why her parents didn't love her as much as they loved him.

Just by loving her, Cade would have made everything okay. Deirdre blinked back tears. Who was she kidding? The Cade who had been her dragon slayer, her hero, her best friend was as dead as their mother.

No matter how desperate Deirdre was, she'd lost that invisible connection a family full of secrets had forged between them. The accident had changed everything and there was no going back. Grief ripped through her. Cade was rid of her and the Captain and the craziness at the house on Linden Lane, just like he'd always wanted to be. He'd have to be out of his mind to come back.

But she needed him. Needed somebody.

Suck it up, she shamed herself. *You've spent your whole life saying you don't need anybody.*

I lied.

Her eyes filled with tears, her hands aching for somebody to hold on to.

She needed…needed her mom. Needed Cade. Needed Spot. She would have traded everything she owned for the chance to bury her face in the stray's mangy coat, feel the dog lick the tears off her cheeks like Spot had so many times before. He'd loved her madly, unconditionally, from the first day she'd taken him in. Her solid black dog. Her one soft spot. But he was gone, too, buried under the oak tree out back.

Deirdre closed her eyes tight, trying to remember how soft Spot was, how sweet. She'd loved the dog desperately. Did that mean she could love a baby?

She glanced at her watch again, her stomach knotting. It was time. Whatever the results were, they were there on the little white stick for all the world to see. No, just for her to see if it read negative. That way nobody else would have to know how close she'd come to disaster, how scared she'd been.

She wouldn't have to tell her father, write to Cade, hear the kids gossiping about her at school. She knotted her hands so tight her fingernails cut into her palms. She sucked in a deep breath, feeling as if she was juggling a live hand grenade, not knowing if fate had pulled the pin.

Mustering the last scrap of her courage, she turned to the windowsill where she'd placed the test minutes before. She swallowed hard, uttered one last desperate prayer, then forced her gaze inexorably down.

The bright pink plus sign hit her like a baseball bat. Positive.

No! Let this be a bad dream! I'll be better from now on. I won't fight with Dad or sneak out or break rules. I won't be hateful to Cade so he'll stay away. I won't care what the cheerleaders think of me or believe I might be pretty enough, talented enough, interesting enough for a boy like Adam to love. I won't ever try to pretend I'm like the other girls. I promise, God. Never again.

She stared at her ice-white face in the bathroom mirror, cold sweat dampening her skin. Terrified.

For a heartbeat, she imagined just walking into the river, floating away where nothing else could hurt her.

Coward! She could hear her father's disgusted voice in her head as he watched the neighbor cat perched on the yowling Spot's back.

Two hot spots of shame burned Deirdre's cheeks. Why

should she care if he thought that about her? She wouldn't be around to listen to his raging.

But Cade...Cade would be so sad. Feel as if he should have fixed her. As if anyone on earth was strong enough for that!

Think, she could hear Cade urging her when she'd gotten in deep trouble as a kid. *Come on, Dee, think your way out of this! You're the smartest kid I've ever known!*

Right. There were things she could do, ways for girls like her to get out of trouble. She could sell that emerald ring that had been her great-grandmother's. Tell the Captain she'd taken it out just to wear for a little while and lost it. He'd be furious, but it wasn't like she'd be stealing. The ring was supposed to be hers someday.

She could take the money, go to one of those clinics where the baby inside her could just disappear, and no one would ever have to know.

Deirdre pressed her hand against her stomach, wondering if it would hurt, imagining the relief she'd feel making this nightmare go away.

I'm sorry, baby, she cried to the tiny life inside her. *I'm going to cut platinum records, be on every radio station in the world. I'm going to be famous. Don't you understand? I can't be just a mom.*

But awareness shivered through her.

A baby. *Her* baby. Alive in there...

Someone who would love her back. Love her better than Cade or the Captain. Better than anyone in the world.

Deirdre walked downstairs in a daze, saw the haphazard decorations she'd stuck around the house, so different from her mother's delight in making the place look like House Beautiful. She'd do better next year when the baby came.

She bumped her chin up a notch as she faced her father.

"I'm pregnant," she said. "Merry fucking Christmas."

The Captain staggered back a step, color draining from his face, shock giving way to fury. "What the hell are you going to do with a baby, missy? You can't even take care of yourself!"

She tried so hard to look like she didn't give a damn as she slid past her father and began to assemble the traditional Christmas-morning cup of cocoa.

"Who the hell did this to you?" He demanded. "Tell me his name!"

"I can't." She fought to keep from spilling the hot chocolate, her hands shaking as she squirted whipped cream into the Santa Claus mug.

Anguish blazed in her father's eyes. "What do you mean, you can't?"

She forced her lips into the smart-alec smile he hated. "What do you *think* that means?"

The Captain reeled as if she'd kicked him in the gut. "You don't even know who the father is?"

She didn't answer.

She didn't have to.

He'd already made up his mind.

So had the rest of this stinking little town, at least when it came to wild child Deirdre McDaniel.

CHAPTER 12

STONE REACHED OUT, took Deirdre's hand, shaking her out of the past, bringing her back into the living room at March Winds again. Into the path of Jacob Stone's laser-sharp eyes. That mouth, so drop-dead sexy, ridiculously sensitive at the moment, as if he were the one hurting.

What in heaven's name was she doing, baring her life to him? A warning shrilled in Deirdre's head. She'd been so close to spilling the rest.... Shame seared her cheeks, her stomach roiling. She pressed her fingers to her lips.

Don't fall apart, she told herself. You can't fall apart. You have to hold yourself together or how on God's earth are you going to help Emma?

"There's more to this whole thing than you're telling me, isn't there?" Stone prodded, his gaze so disarming part of her wanted to tell him he was right.

She levered herself out of the chair, paced to the window to escape the irresistible pull of Jake Stone. Moonlight filtered through the trees, tangled black webs as twisted as the secrets she'd kept for so long.

Don't touch me, she'd told Stone. *I don't want you to touch me.*

She'd lied. She wanted his hands on her, wanted his mouth eager and hot on her skin. Wondered if he'd possess some kind of magic that could make her forget...

She could feel his gaze like a touch, blunt, callused fingertips peeling any covering away, leaving her heart naked, the way some crazy, fatalistic part of her wanted him to make her body.

"You know who Emma's father is, Deirdre," Stone pressed her. "Otherwise the things she said wouldn't have shaken you up so badly."

Deirdre tried to draw her tattered defenses around her, closing her eyes, shaking her chin-length hair back from her face. "Don't be so greedy," she said. "I told you all the best parts."

"What about the worst?"

"My story isn't bad enough for you?" Deirdre wheeled on him, eyes blazing. "You need all the gritty details? The Captain went crazy. Cade came back home to keep us from killing each other. He'd been in Whitewater when Mom died. Some kind of leave you can get when your family's dying. But he'd headed back to the Air Force before I came up pregnant. One of my greatest achievements is that I single-handedly ruined my big brother's life."

"His life looks pretty damned good to me." Stone looked a little surprised as he said so.

"Sure it does. His life's terrific now that he has Finn and his babies. If you'd known him before that you'd realize how bad things got. God, Jake, you should have seen him the night I broke into his house and surprised him. I'd been gone five years. Left him to handle the Captain alone. I just cut out of town, stranded Cade in a place he hated."

"Your brother seems to me the kind of man who makes his own decisions."

"He sure decided he didn't want his sister's kid to raise. He told me that in no uncertain terms. Cade promised he'd help me, give Emma and me a home until I worked things out. But he didn't know anything about kids. Truth to tell, Emma scared the life out of him." Deirdre grimaced. "But then it's easy to see why. She *is* my daughter."

"He adores Emma."

"What choice did he have? I dumped Emma on his doorstep and ran off." Deirdre laughed, a harsh, tortured sound. "You want to know the funniest part of this whole blasted fiasco, Stone? Deirdre McDaniel, the wild child of Whitewater, the bad girl of the senior class… You know that roll in the hay that got me knocked up? The sex stunk so badly I haven't been able to get it right since."

Empathy welled up in Stone's eyes, and something more: something that scared her, enthralled her. "Damn it, Dee, I'm so sorry."

"Me, too. But that doesn't change anything. Emma's right. I'm dried up inside. Barely even a woman. It's not that I didn't try to work through it—at least when I was on the road. But what can I say? I crashed and burned every time. I haven't even wanted to bother with sex since then, until…you bullied your way into my life."

Stone froze. *She wanted to have sex with him?* And he'd thought he was in deep shit before. He had to be careful. She was half a second from being major league spooked and fleeing up the stairs. That was no surprise. What shocked the hell out of him was realizing that some part of her wished he'd come up the stairs after her and take the whole thing out of her hands, show her what she'd been missing.

Instinct curled, tight in his throat. No...any macho crap like that would panic her. Keep it light, Stone. Hell, it felt like talking a jumper off a ledge.

"You're the one who showed up on my doorstep, as I remember."

Deirdre grimaced. "You would bring that up now. You're such a jerk."

"Yeah. I am. But I'm a jerk who..." *Who's crazy in love with you.* Yeah, right. Say that, you jackass. "Who wants to..." *Screw your brains out. Show you just how damn good it can be between us.* Arrogant ass. Was there any man who had the guts to tell the truth, to say, *Let's just give it a try, maybe we can work this sex thing out. Even if we don't get it right the first time....*

"What is it you want to do, Stone? Rock my world? Show me the greatest sex in the free world? Show me how it will be different with you because you're such a kick-ass lover you'll blow my mind?" She glared at him, daring him to deny it, making him ache to kiss her, show her he *was* different. Bet she'd never heard a man spout that line before.

"Ouch," Stone said.

"Do you know how desperately I wish that stuff were true? That you really could make me feel...what was it Emma said about Drew? Make me feel safe...alive." Tears welled up in her eyes. What the hell had Emma's father done to her? Stone needed the guy's name so he could kill the bastard.

But as satisfying as cold-blooded murder would feel, it wouldn't help Deirdre right now. Stone swallowed hard, torn by indecision. They were so much alike, he and Deirdre: never let them see you sweat; never blink in a stare-down; never be the first one to swerve out of the path of the other car when you're playing chicken; never let anyone see past the wall where you kept all your insecurities hidden away.

Hang on to all that pride, you bloody idiot, Stone warned himself. *And you'll never, ever reach her.*

Why not just do it? Stone asked himself. Risk the humiliation of failing her. Give it to her straight. He flexed his fingers, wishing he could shake the trapped sensation that was making him want to beat feet to the door. Didn't Deirdre McDaniel deserve better? Look how brave she'd been. How honest. She'd stripped her soul naked for him, every flaw, every mistake, every regret. Even admitted she didn't feel like a woman....

Passionate, brave, beautiful Deirdre, the most desirable woman Jake had ever known. How the hell had she lost all faith in herself? What in the name of God had happened to her?

Stone drew himself up, being ruthlessly honest, even to himself. "I don't know if things would be different with us," he admitted slowly. "But, hell, Deirdre...don't you owe it to yourself to try?"

She stood so silent, so pale. Watching him with those big blue eyes. He tried to remember how to breathe, so much hung in the balance.

"I know what you're thinking," he said. "You're thinking that I'm just another guy who wants to get in your pants. If that was true, I'd find a woman with a lot less baggage. I'm not the 'tell me about your dark night of the soul' type. And when it comes to sex, my first instinct is to say I'm damn good at it."

"Don't be so modest, Sugar Bear."

Good sign. At least she was fighting back—a little.

"I can't promise you we can get past...well, whatever you're holding back. But I can tell you this. I care about you. And I want you more than I've ever wanted any woman. I want you enough to stop whenever you tell me to. I want you enough to give this a try, you and me together, knowing I might fall flat on my face. Not a fun prospect for any guy's ego, let me tell you."

Jake almost turned hero, almost walked out the door and turned his back on the need clamoring in his veins. Almost.

But she moistened her lips, peered up at him from under those incredible thick lashes, her breasts swelling, so soft, so tempting against the white of her shirt. She grabbed his hand, and he wondered where she was leading him.

"Emma's upstairs," she said softly as they slipped out the back door.

One thing was sure. Deirdre wasn't seeing him safely into his truck. The garden was dimly lit, smelled sweet, whatever flowers were growing there filling the air with something exotic. The soft sound of waves lapping the shore whispered from the river beyond. He stumbled over a root. Deirdre tightened her hold on his hand.

That gazebo thing—that must be where she was headed.

"For years I've been hearing lovers tell me how magical the gazebo is," Deirdre said, obviously talking to calm her nervousness. "Maybe because my brother was falling crazy in love the whole time he was building it. I believed the magic was true, but fairy-tale endings were for women like Finn, so good even fate couldn't deny them happiness. I knew I could never be a Cinderella—I would have dumped a bucket of ashes over somebody's head long before I got the glass slipper."

Jake squeezed her hand. "I always did think Cinderella should have fought back. Like you're doing, Dee. Right now."

"Finn said the gazebo was her and Cade's lucky place." Deirdre seemed so shy, so uncertain as she drew him up the wooden stairs. "She's dead sure that's where they conceived the twins. Maybe some of that luck will rub off."

Whoa, Stone thought, picturing two squalling, red-faced babies. Way to take the edge off a guy's hard-on.

He'd never wanted kids of his own. At least, that's what he'd told himself, satisfying any bouts of insanity by playing uncle to his old partner Tank Rizzo's brood. And yet, part of him couldn't help wondering what it would be like, hovering at the nursery door, unseen, watching the woman he loved nursing the child they'd made together.

The image had always been hazy when he'd been fool enough to think about it. A woman's body silhouetted against the cushions of a rocking chair, moonlight streaming in from the window as she cuddled the baby against her white breast.

His own mother must have done the same with him. If he could just remember…

But those memories were gone along with his parents' faces, lost to time and a bewildered two-year-old boy's need to move on. When he'd hooked up with Trula, well, she hadn't exactly been the peaceful, rocking-chair type. She'd been all sequins and games and laughter. He hadn't thought he missed anything else.

Until he pictured Deirdre, her beautiful face suffused with a sweet, rare peace, secure in his love, in the home he'd made for her.

Fool, he warned himself. You can't have her. You can never have a wife and a baby and the kind of future Cade McDaniel found for himself. That kind of love took complete honesty. And the last time he'd trusted a woman with the truth, she'd nearly destroyed the lives of people he loved.

Spousal privilege had been the only thing that saved him. That and the steely danger Jessica had seen in his eyes.

What was he? Crazy? He was about to make love to Deirdre McDaniel out here in the garden while the sun started to rise. He was finally going to get his hands under her blouse, into her hair, feel the excruciating pleasure of sinking himself deep inside her. And he was thinking about his blasted ex-wife?

He blocked the past from his mind, glad his mess of a marriage was gone, glad he was free to hold Deirdre in his arms. At least for a little while.

The garden structure's gingerbread-decked walls shone white against the mauve tinted sky, like lace, unearthly, as if part of another world. A world in which Jake Stone could love the passionate woman in Deirdre McDaniel back to life. Or screw things up so badly she'd never let a man touch her again.

The thought of any man besides him touching Deirdre made him crazy. He wanted all of her for himself. More than he could ever hope to have.

The enormity of what they were about to try made Stone's stomach cold. Fortunately, Deirdre chose that moment to curl her fingers into the hem of her T-shirt and sweep the soft cotton garment up over her head. The moment all that creamy, pale skin filled his vision, his stomach was the last part of his anatomy he was thinking with.

"God, you're beautiful," he rasped.

She was. Sweet, lush curves made all the more sexy by her sudden shyness. He must be staring at her. She gathered the T-shirt up tight against her, hiding the shadowy cleft of cleavage so velvety rich it made Stone's mouth water.

"It's okay if you change your mind," Stone said. *I'll go completely crazy if you do, but it's okay.*

Her eyes glowed, huge in the first kiss of dawn. "Jake...help me?"

Gently, he took hold of a fold of her shirt and tugged it out of her hands. His fingers clenched in the fabric, still warm from Deirdre's body, still smelling like her, oranges and spice.

The sight of her breasts made his mouth go dry. They were perfect, like cream, and in the filtered light the tips looked the color of milk chocolate. He wanted to take them in his mouth, wanted to drown in her, quench the fire in him even six long years hadn't put out. But he couldn't move too fast. Couldn't startle her. Scare her off.

That seemed absurd, knowing Deirdre's courage. But then, if she'd had bad sex and ended up pregnant at sixteen, that would be enough to scare plenty of women he'd known. And yet Deirdre wasn't like anyone he'd ever dated. She was braver. Indomitable. At least, he'd thought so before...before tonight when she'd let him see beyond the face she showed to the world, into the shadowy places inside her where the monsters lived.

Fighting for control, Stone dropped the shirt, reached out, curving his fingers against the bare skin of her arms. It had been too damn long since he'd felt a woman's softness. He gritted his teeth. He couldn't let her know she was making him crazy, making him want to push her down onto one of those wooden benches and take her, hard, fast, all passion and wildness and heat, the way he'd fantasized taking her for so long....

So he could get Deirdre McDaniel out of his system, stop dreaming about her and get on with his life.

But this moment was so damned different from the one he'd imagined. He hadn't expected how fragile she'd be, how much his chest would ache because she trusted him. How damned scared he'd be that he might blow it.

That's a first, he could almost hear Trula say. But then, Deirdre had never been like any other woman he'd known.

She shivered under his touch. And he wanted his clothes gone. Wanted to feel her, skin to skin. For once, not just because of his own sex drive—but because in some crazy way, it would make him as vulnerable as she was. And he wanted to lay himself bare to Deirdre. Insane as it was. Knowing he never really could.

What would it feel like to lay the whole truth in her lap? Take a chance—

Don't think, Stone, he warned himself. *Do not think. This is going to be risky enough without you getting distracted.*

Still, he pulled his own shirt over his head, the breeze from the river teasing coolness over skin fire hot with wanting the woman so still, so quiet before him.

He drew her into his arms, her breasts flattening against him, exquisite, as he found her lips with his. He wooed them, cajoled them, tempted them with every skill he possessed. He ran his tongue lightly along the crease, a soft groan rumbling in his chest.

Damn. He'd never been this hard. He felt himself growing, thickening. He wasn't a small man. Anywhere. And he didn't want to scare her. Though he longed to grind himself against all that womanly softness, he eased his hips away from her, concentrating on Deirdre's luscious mouth.

That was something he could take his sweet time with, memorize every curve and nuance and taste in her delectable mouth.... But damned if Deirdre would cooperate.

For a woman on the edge, she wasn't holding back, making him do all the seducing while she held her breath, waiting for him to take charge. No. She made her own foray into the sensual web weaving around them, running her fingertips lightly over his bare chest, skimming over the light dusting of hair, sensitizing him beyond bearing until he thought he'd go crazy if she didn't open her mouth and let him kiss her inside.

The edge of her little finger brushed over his nipple, jolting sensation through him so he growled with pleasure.

He should have done it sooner. Deirdre opened her mouth. Stone nearly lost it as her tongue oh-sotentatively touched his. He let her take the lead, exploring him with her mouth, her tongue, her hands as long as he could hold himself still. Letting her immerse herself in sensation.

"I want to feel you," he whispered against her cheek as he drew her down onto the makeshift nest of their cast-off shirts. "All of you." He slid his hands up to cup her breasts. Her nipples pearled, hard against his palms.

A frisson of excitement seared through him, knowing her body was responding, wanting him as badly as he wanted her. He trailed his lips down the curve of her throat, lingering on the pulse point, drinking in the scent of her, the impossibly erotic contrast between silky skin, satiny hair, the damp searching of his mouth tasting her at last.

She gave a faint cry of pleasure, and he dared to trace his way down to the soft slope where her breast began, kissing and gently nipping until his mouth reached the dusky crest.

Opening his lips he took her nipple in, to the dark and wet and heat of him, suckling until she arched up against him, her fingers threading through his hair, holding him there, too shy to tell him what she wanted. Too fiercely full of need to let him go.

He made a hungry sound, low in his throat, building the connection between them, daring her to be reckless enough to trust him. Trust them. Together. Here. Now.

Deirdre felt the insistent suction of Stone's mouth upon her breast, his tongue teasing the sensitized crest, wringing moans of pleasure from her. He was pulling her under with his hands and mouth, into swift waters of a desire so intense she'd never known it existed, into storms so wild, so consuming she couldn't hold herself back. She knew she should let go, let it carry her away, to a place where there was only this—sensation, elation, desire. But to do that meant surrender so complete just thinking about it terrified her.

Remember...remember what it felt like to crash back down to earth. The pain of it. The humiliation. Remember trying to sweep pieces of your soul back together, knowing they were broken. Do you really think you're strong enough to put yourself back together again?

Desperate, she clung to the part of herself she couldn't afford to lose. The part that had been naive enough, bold enough to surrender the last sliver of herself.

*I dare you...*a mocking voice whispered in her head.

Dare what?

To let him use your body and then see if he walks away, laughing. To be reckless enough to believe that maybe, just maybe there is something inside you worth loving.

Don't think! she told herself, trying to pull away from memories still too vivid, failures still fresh when they should have faded years ago.

*Oh, God, I want to run...*panic fluttered in her throat.

Coward.

No, she wasn't going to chicken out. Wasn't going to turn back. She wanted Jake. Wanted sex. Wanted to take back the part of her life she'd feared was lost to her forever.

Hastily she reached for the snap of her jeans, popped it open, slid the zipper down. Stone reached out, stopped her, his drawl lazy so sexy she shivered.

"What's your hurry?"

"I…" She almost lied. Then she looked into Jake Stone's eyes. "I'm scared I'll chicken out. Figure it'll be harder to bolt once my jeans are off."

Stone sobered, gentled, the corners of his beautiful mouth curving down. "This isn't a test, Deirdre. It's just the two of us, taking pleasure in each other, going wherever that leads us."

"Easy for you to say." She pulled away, shoving the jeans down her legs. She should have seduced Stone closer to the river. She could have thrown her clothes off the dock so there could be no turning back. "The way you look you probably have women throwing themselves at you all the time. Mr. Alpha Male. Irresistible. I can imagine how you must turn other women on if you can even get me thinking nonstop about sex."

She kicked her jeans off, feeling exposed in ways that had nothing to do with the fact that she was now wearing nothing but simple white cotton panties. "It's a little intimidating, if you want to know the truth."

"Okay. If we're being honest, how about if I tell you this? My job played havoc with my sex life. Nothing like seeing marriages shattered by cheating husbands and wives, nasty divorces tearing families apart and gathering evidence for paternity suits to convince a guy to keep his pants zipped."

"A confirmed cynic, huh?"

"I just want you to know it's been a long time for me, too. At some point—" he looked away from her, quiet, suddenly. Dead serious. She could see secrets in his eyes "—I…decided that sex for sex's sake wasn't enough. That it should mean something."

He'd surprised her. Again. But wasn't that what Stone was best at?

Smart-alec comments flashed into her mind. *Sugar Bear Stone, last of the great romantics.* But the words wouldn't come out. This was too important.

"Does it? Uh, mean something? This time?" she asked, feeling like an idiot, fishing for reassurance. Her muscles tensed, and she knew she was headed for disaster unless she could relax. When had her own body become her enemy? But Stone regarded her, so sincere her throat felt tight.

"Oh, yeah, it means something all right." He lifted his hand to her face, skimmed his fingers across her cheek. "After all, you did bite me and stomp on my foot and get me out of bed at two in the morning and I came back for more. Some people would doubt my sanity, all things considered." Damn the man, he actually winked at her, let tender amusement fill eyes smoky with desire.

She was doomed, Deirdre thought as his lips parted, flashing white teeth. That smile of his should be registered as a lethal weapon. Stone didn't need a gun, at least when it came to female suspects. He could just mow them down with that bone-melting grin, and they'd be begging for him to haul them in.

Into his arms.

Into his bed.

Of course, then she'd have to kill him. Or them. Or…oh, Lord, what was she thinking? She'd never been the possessive type.

"I…I really hate being the only one naked," she said.

The corner of Stone's mouth crooked. "Quit complaining and do something about it."

Gratitude welled up inside her. He knew her so well. Knew when feeling grew too much, when it stung and burned and threatened to suck her under. He knew how to make her laugh, even when she was shaking inside.

"Typical male," she shot back. "Completely helpless. I have to take off my own jeans, but you—"

"Do you know how many times I've imagined this? In my fantasies your hands are on my zipper, your hands are stripping my jeans away."

Heat flooded through Deirdre, infusing her with daring, the need to please him. She placed her palm over his heart, drinking in the pounding rhythm, the racing of it, his need stripped bare. She slid her palm down Stone's flat belly. Her finger dipped into the tiny hollow of his navel, then traced the prickly ribbon of dark hair until it disappeared beneath his waistband. His jeans strained over his arousal, and Deirdre explored the hard ridge through the denim. Her eyes widened, her breath caught. Was all of that him?

Stone growled. "If you don't touch me I'm going to go crazy. Skin on skin, Deirdre. Your hand on my—"

His urging shattered on a groan as she opened his fly, folded back the denim from flesh warm and roughened with hair. She was melting inside, throbbing between her legs, as her fingers came in contact with the velvety tip of his sex.

Stone went still. She hooked her thumbs under the elastic of his black boxers, pushing jeans and shorts down Stone's muscular legs.

She lay back against the shirts, pulled Stone with her, quiet desperation fueling her every move. She tried to blot out the ghosts, fill herself instead with what was real. Jake…the feel of his blunt-tipped fingers roving across her skin. His body, long and strong as he lay beside her.

He'd brushed his hair carelessly back into an elastic band before he'd returned to March Winds. She wanted it loose around his broad shoulders, wanted to delve her hands into it, bury her face in the fresh smelling waves.

She fumbled with the elastic until she worked it free. His gaze held hers, fiery hot as his hair tumbled down, making him look like a modern-day Samson to her Delilah. Invincible with all those rippling, tanned muscles. Primal, his face hard planes and angles. Fully aroused, his heart thundering as she flattened her palm against his chest.

She wanted him to pull her full length against him, until there was nothing between them, until they were both too far gone to stop.

She urged him down on top of her. Stone braced most of his weight on his elbows, only his hips settling in the hollow between her thighs. She instinctively clenched her legs together, but Jake all too persuasively moved as if he were already inside her.

Just do it. Deirdre told herself. *All you have to do is open your legs and…*

And he'd do what she wanted him to. Open her, take her, push into her and the worst would be over. She wouldn't have to be afraid anymore.

It was amazing, the sensations Jake was building, making her feel soft down there, wet. That had never happened to her before.

But Stone eased his big body to one side, slid his fingers down to where she felt so strange, so aroused, so…

Oh, yes! Touch me…no, don't… You'll know how far gone I am…how much I want you…need you… If you find that out I won't ever be able to take it back...hide behind the wall I built to keep me safe.

"Just...just do it," she said, trying not to cry.

But Stone, made soft, hushing sounds against her cheek. "We've got all the time in the world."

It was like he knew how scared she was. His big hand eased over soft, dark down, his middle finger seeking out the sleek center where all her need pulsed. Her cheeks burned as Stone circled that tiny nub, seducing her, hypnotizing her, sucking her deeper into raw sensation.

"Trust me, Deirdre. Spread your legs for me, love. Just a little. *There.*"

She managed to unclench her muscles, edge her legs apart, giving him room. Room enough to touch her, room enough to make her fall apart.

"Just feel," Stone urged her. "Let me show you..."

Stone groaned, and slid his finger inside her.

Deirdre stiffened, waiting for pain, expecting it to hurt...too scared to breathe. But Stone only angled his big hand so he could still tease the part of her pearled and burning under the callused tip of his thumb.

She caught her breath, rocked instinctively against his hand, driving his finger deeper, feeling as if she were going to fly apart. Wanting to...

"Come on, Deirdre, let it happen. I'm going to bury myself inside you, and you're going to come the way you're supposed to. All that passion, all that fire...you're going to come for me."

He grabbed her, rolled them both over so his back was against the gazebo's floor, and she was straddling him.

Oh, he felt so good, so hot and hard and male. Her body softening and melting into curves and hollows, yielding in ways she'd never imagined. His hardness cradled in the hollow between her thighs scared her, thrilled her, made her wonder…would it hurt the way it always had before? Would she tighten up and—

She could feel him, trapped between her slickness and his body. All she had to do was move just a little, pull back, so he could push himself inside her.

Once she managed that, Stone would take care of the rest. She could just…just zone out if things got too intense, too terrifying. Like the other times.

"Look at me!" His eyes were fierce as her gaze found them. "It's up to you, Dee. Take me. Or don't. It's your choice."

"Don't…don't make me— I can't… Will you please just…just do it." Oh, no! She was going all cold inside, closing up like a fist. She closed her eyes, felt tears leaking out. "I'm ruining everything."

Stone went still. His arms surrounded her, drew her gently down onto his chest.

"I…I'm sorry," Deirdre said brokenly. "Just finish. It's hardly fair for you to get…well, this far and—"

"Is that what some selfish bastard told you? When we come, I want it to be together," Stone said, wiping away her tears. "You and me, both falling apart, both stripped down until there's no one else between us. Just you and me, Deirdre, and the way I love you."

Love? Not possible. Deirdre told herself. Stone hadn't meant it the way it sounded. Make love…that's what he'd been trying to say. A pretty euphemism for "screwing your brains out." It was a good thing she and Jake understood each other so well or she might have been misled into thinking he meant something far more important, far more terrifying.

But she and Jake Stone understood each other. They both needed plenty of room in between them to be separate. Safe. Neither one of them would ever be able to tolerate that joined-at-the-hip, crazy-without-each-other feeling of being in love. That was for the lucky few like Finn and Cade. The most Deirdre had wished for, hoped for, was that she and Stone could bridge the distance between them for just this one brief, precious space of time before they both moved on.

Deirdre rolled away from him until she sat with her back to him, trying to hide how bereft he'd left her. If she couldn't make love to Stone, who could she make love to? Nobody...ever....

And yet, what was it Stone had said? Something that had jarred her? Something unexpected?

When we come, I want it to be together. You and me, both falling apart, both stripped down until there's no one else between us....

"Wh-what did you mean? No one else?" Deirdre asked.

"The man who made you afraid. He was there, Dee, between us. I could feel you thinking about him, trying to close him out." Stone flattened his hand against her back. She knew the moment he felt her scars.

He skimmed his hands over the raised white lines. "Good God, your back. Did he...did he do this to you?"

Stone turned her toward him so gently, and yet she almost cried out, so cold after being enveloped in so much heat. "What's his name?" Stone demanded, his voice dead cold. "Tell me his name so I can kill him."

A shiver of something primitive raced down Deirdre's spine, and she wondered what it would be like to have a man like Stone know everything about her, defend her, love her. What would it have been like when she was sixteen and scared to hear him say those same words?

But the scars from that night were far uglier than the faint white lines from the surgery the night her family had fallen apart.

"I think Finn would object if you killed the father of those babies of hers. Besides, it wasn't Cade's fault. I just fell off a plane onto a toolbox. The scars are from the accident you read about in Mom's letter."

"Emma's father...didn't do this."

"No." Deirdre looked away.

Stone hooked his finger under her chin, forced her to look at him. "Maybe it would have been easier if he had."

"Wh-what?"

"Scars you can see are easier to deal with than the ones on the inside, the ones nobody else knows are there." Stone slipped her T-shirt over her head, covering her so tenderly her throat ached.

"Stone, let's just...just admit defeat and get dressed. Head back up to the house and I'll make us some coffee. Leave what little dignity I have left intact. It's not your fault I couldn't— You were a terrific lover, really. I just—"

"He raped you."

Deirdre's stomach plunged. "What?"

"That bastard raped you, didn't he?"

CHAPTER 13

"Raped?" Deirdre echoed. She clambered to her feet, crossed to the far side of the gazebo, trying to put as much space between her and Stone as she could. "I went up to Sullivan's Point of my own free will," she said, her voice sounding brittle even to her own ears. "I knew what kids did up there. Sort of, anyway."

"Is that what he told you?" Stone asked, shoving his legs into his jeans. "The lowlife sonofabitch."

She crossed her arms tight across her chest, the T-shirt skimming her thighs. "Well, it was true. It's just…thinking about things and *doing* them are a lot different. Even with a guy who claimed he loved me. He was going to drop all of his popular friends, all the perfect little homecoming princesses and marry me. We'd travel all over the country while I sang. Maybe even then I knew it was a line of garbage. I mean, I wasn't ever exactly the type of girl who made men start thinking of white picket fences."

She glanced over her shoulder at Stone. God, the man was beautiful, bare-chested, jeans slung low on his hips. He'd zipped them up but hadn't bothered with the button at the top of the waistband. His feet, silhouetted against the dark-gray painted floorboards were long, narrow, exquisitely shaped like the rest of him. She saw a strange expression dart across his face, as if he felt he should jump in with some worthless comment to reassure her. In the end he obviously thought better of it and didn't say a word.

"When the make-out session went further than I was ready for, I got scared." Deirdre continued, remembering the metallic taste of panic, the terrible realization of how helpless she was, how far from home. And that no one on earth knew where she was.

Stone's thick, dark brows dipped low as he scanned her face, and for an instant Deirdre felt transparent, as if he could see the whole ugly scene through her eyes, the steamed-up windows, her torn blouse, her face, white with shock.

"You were a virgin." It wasn't a question.

Deirdre forced a raw laugh. "Yeah. Who would've believed it? Nobody at Whitewater High, that's for sure. Everybody thought I lived by the musician's credo—sex, drugs, rock and roll. And I let them. Didn't all musical genius come from being an outsider? I mean, think of all the greats—Van Morrison, Jimi Hendrix. Hey, even Judy Garland was drugged up and crazy. And Janis Joplin wasn't exactly pushing pompoms and making cupcakes in home ec when she was in high school."

Stone regarded her intently. "I suppose not. Of course, they're all dead."

"Live hard, die young...the price of genius and all that. Except it's a little harder to go down in a ball of selfish flames when you have a child who needs her mother. Know what the real joke was?" Her voice cracked. "I thought he loved me. Mr. Football Star. Gorgeous, rich, the king of the school. He and his friends must have been laughing their asses off."

"So that's why you went postal when Drew Lawson started hanging around Emma," Stone said, raking his hair back from his face with one large hand.

Deirdre shuddered, bone deep. "Drew is so much like *him* I can't look at the kid without feeling sick. It all floods back, you know? The night Emma was conceived. Just the thought that anybody might hurt my baby like that—God, Stone, I get so crazy I'd do anything to protect her."

"I wonder if Drew knows how lucky he was when we interrupted the two of them up there on Sullivan's Point. All things considered, you showed remarkable self-restraint. If Emma had any idea what happened to you she'd understand why—"

"Oh, yeah, Stone. That would be terrific." Deirdre grabbed her own jeans, dragged them on, her panties lost and forgotten somewhere on the gazebo floor. "I can just imagine that hellish chat. 'Hey, Emma, here's a little factoid for that family tree project you're doing in English class…'" She slammed her hand against the railing. "Forget it, Stone. No way."

"I don't pretend it would be easy, but—"

"There are no 'buts' about this one. If Emma ever found out the kind of man her father was it would destroy her. I'll never tell her. And that's the end of it."

Stone looked at her so intently Deirdre felt more naked than she had minutes before. She hugged the soft cotton of her shirt tight against her unbound breasts.

"Who *did* you tell?" Stone asked. "Your father? Cade?"

"You're kidding, right?" Deirdre snorted in disbelief. "And here I thought private eyes were students of human behavior. Announce in the hallowed halls of Linden Lane that I'd sneaked off to Sullivan's Point with some boy and he forced me to have sex with him?"

"It's called rape," Stone insisted.

Deirdre still couldn't get the word out of her mouth. "One word back home would've lit off an explosion to rival Hiroshima. If Cade had ever gotten the real story, Adam sure wouldn't have gotten any *other* girls pregnant, *ever*. And the Captain would have murdered the kid with his own hands."

Deirdre made a face, still recoiling from the scene she'd avoided at such grim cost to herself. "Things were bad enough for me already, Jake. My brother and father going to jail for the rest of their lives would've topped the whole sordid mess off perfectly."

A McDaniel should be resourceful, able to take care of herself. Admitting how miserably she'd failed would have made her seem weak, so pathetic—the tough girl who couldn't even fight off a boy in the back seat of a car. Why heap on the final humiliation by telling the Captain how helpless she'd been, how scared. What had it mattered anyway? By then it was already too late.

She started, surprised when Stone touched her, gently laying his hand on her arm. She wasn't used to being touched. Only Emma and Finn and occasionally Cade daring to slip past her natural aura of reserve.

Her gaze leapt up to Stone, her first instinct to draw back, but something in those mesmerizing tiger eyes held her still, made her ache, willed her to surrender her fierce independence for just a moment in time as Jake gathered her into his arms.

Heat from his naked chest seeped through the thin cotton of her shirt, banishing at least some of the chill. Her hands slid around him to link together at the small of his back, the sensitized skin of her inner arm seeming to melt into his tautly muscled waist. He dipped his chin down, leaned his forehead against hers.

"What happened to you in that car seventeen years ago wasn't your fault," he said, his eyes so close, so intense they seemed to fill her world. "You told that little bastard no. You were raped, Deirdre. Do you hear me? Raped."

The word cut a jagged path, tearing at everything she'd believed, a lifetime's worth of guilt, shame and self-loathing.

"No wonder you can't relax when I touch you," Stone said. "He hurt you."

Did Stone's voice break? The words sounded so thick, so strange in his throat. He stroked her hair, threaded his fingers through the feathery, chin-length strands. It should have felt so delicious, Stone's big hands touching her that way. She should have let herself be pulled under by contact so sensual, so enticing, feelings women all over the world took for granted.

Soft, silken skeins of sensation binding woman to man, the way nature meant it to be. Pleasure. Pure, unadulterated bliss, slowly immersing two people so deeply in each other they became one in some mystical alchemy called love.

But Deirdre had lost that brand of magic. No, it had been taken from her. Stolen. And she could never get it back. The innocence. The dizzying excitement. The leap of faith that would let her surrender herself completely into her lover's hands.

Grief settled in a lump in her throat. "I'm sorry, Jake," she said. "For both of us. Tonight could have been so different if only—" She hesitated. "There's something broken in me, you know? I can't..."

"That son of a bitch hurt you, Deirdre, but he didn't break you. You're too strong inside to let him do that."

"I don't have much patience with revisionist history. I was there, on that gazebo floor with you when...well, everything fell apart."

"Maybe it didn't end the way we both wanted it to. But you were so close to letting go, Deirdre. You can't deny it. I could feel you turning all hot and wild in my arms. Then, just a heartbeat before the point of no return, you pulled yourself back from the edge."

"I'm hopeless, Stone," Deirdre confessed, sagging against the hard wall of his chest. "If I can't...with you... when I want you so bad...then I'm hopeless."

Stone drew away from her, his hands curving about her upper arms. "I won't believe that," he said fiercely, looking into her eyes. "It was *my* fault we got snarled up. I didn't know what you were dealing with. I mean, I knew it was something bad, but rape? Hell, you were just a kid. God, it kills me, thinking how damn alone you were. Pregnant, and not telling anyone what happened."

Deirdre grimaced. "About four months into the whole process words weren't exactly necessary, if you know what I mean."

Stone sucked in a steadying breath. "It's no wonder you reacted the way you did when I had you in my arms. We went from zero to overdrive way too fast, all things considered. It's just...I've wanted you for so damned long. You're the hottest woman I've ever seen, Deirdre McDaniel. Just thinking about you burns me up."

The heat in his eyes made her tingle all over, wish she could shed her past, step toward him, naked and new. But that was just one more dream that could never come true.

"That woman you say is so hot—it's not the real me, Jake. You want some fantasy you've dreamt up about who you *think* I am. The hard truth is that you don't even know me."

243

"Don't I?" He looked genuinely bewildered, uncertain, so different from the cocky Jake Stone she'd come to expect. "I know it sounds nutty, but sometimes I feel like I've known you forever. Trula had this friend, a crazy old bird who thought she was a psychic. Talked about past lives and past loves, so strong they wandered through time until they found each other again. That somehow, when they looked into each other's eyes, their hearts remembered..."

His voice trailed off, his cheeks darkening. "Sounds sort of hokey, huh?"

"Sort of." Sort of hokey. Sort of wonderful. Sort of romantic. And as unlike Jake Stone as anything that had ever come out of the man's mouth before.

Stone shrugged. "I guess when it comes right down to it maybe you're right. Maybe if we take a little time to get to know each other better, if you learn to trust me, we can get past this mental block you have about making love."

And then what? a cynical voice inside her asked. *The only way you know how to live is alone.*

"I don't know if that's such a good idea," she hedged.

"We'll never know unless we try it." Stone laced his fingers with hers. "How about this? I take you out on dates. We see some really bad movies. Eat dinner at some really good restaurants. I take you dancing at Amandine's."

"Aman—what?"

"Classiest nightclub in Chicago. I put on my tuxedo and take Trula dancing there a few times a year so she can strut her stuff and wow everyone in the joint."

Deirdre's eyes burned at the image of Jake dressed to the nines, escorting his grandmother on a trip to Chicago, wining her and dining her and making Trula feel young.

"She must love it," Deirdre said softly.

"It appeals to the devil in her. She makes sure everyone there thinks I'm her boy toy. When I sweep in there with you on my arm we'll set the place on its ear."

Deirdre's heart squeezed, picturing Jake and his grandmother, sharing their private joke, loving each other so much, no walls or angry words or ugly secrets between them. But then, Deirdre had seen with her own eyes how Trula and Jake handled confrontation. They raged at each other, laughed with each other, talked even when they wanted to shut each other out.

If only the McDaniels could be like that.... If Deirdre could have gone to the Captain and Cade, inexorably reasonable. Explaining why she felt the need to find her birth father.

You were the one who charged in like a wounded bear, she told herself. Who knows what might have happened if you'd given them a chance.

But she'd blasted her family right out of the water with her outrage, her temper—

Just like your father, Emmaline McDaniel would have said. Deirdre couldn't help wondering now which one.

"Come on, Deirdre," Jake urged, drawing her back into the present, the dawn-kissed gazebo filled with his big, hard body, his soft, sexy mouth, his dangerous, persuasive eyes. "Trula browbeat me into all those lessons by promising that women can't resist a man who can dance. She'd get really ticked if you proved her wrong."

"She's not wrong, exactly. It's just that her theory needs qualifying. As in *most* women can't resist dancing men. I would be the exception. I was always singing onstage with the band while other girls got swept around the gym floor by some Prince Charming type with acne and an ugly carnation boutonniere."

"You're kidding me, right?" Stone actually looked

stunned. "The way you love music you'd be a natural dancer. You'd feel it all the way down in your soul." He regarded her so earnestly she could almost see him at Emma's age, charming the socks off any girl who caught his eye. "I know we'd be good together," he insisted.

"Oh, you do, do you?" Deirdre gave him her most skeptical look. "What's with you, Stone? Are you a glutton for punishment?"

But he just continued in that low, seductive voice, painting pictures in her head, making her want things that were out of her reach. "After we close the nightclub down, we can walk by Lake Michigan in the moonlight. I'll hold your hand because it feels so damned good just to touch you. Then maybe I'll steal a few kisses."

Deirdre's mouth went dry. "Stone, I know you're trying to be a nice guy, here, but you'd be putting yourself to a whole lot of trouble for what? A few less-than-stellar rolls in the hay before this case is over and we say goodbye?"

A stubborn glint shone in Jake's eyes. "You don't know they'd be less than stellar. Maybe they'd be the best sex of your life."

"Oh, yeah, that would be a real stretch." Deirdre gave a snort of laughter. "Reach for the stars, Stone."

"How about the best sex of *my* life, then?" Jake flashed her his irresistible grin. "That would give us something to shoot for. We'll start slow, though. My old partner, Tank Rizzo, is having a picnic a week from Saturday."

"You still see your old partner?" Deirdre blurted out, surprised.

"Yeah. Why?"

"Isn't it kind of awkward…after you shot that guy." Great, she thought as Jake's expression darkened. Deirdre McDaniel, the queen of tact. "Knowing you now, Stone, I'm sure he deserved it, or…or it was a big mistake." She cringed inwardly. *That* made it sound so much better! "After all, cops are only human."

"Are they?" Stone's mouth set, a little grim.

Deirdre wanted to kick herself. When would she learn to keep her big mouth shut? "It's not like it's any of my business, I guess you just surprised me. When most people screw up big-time, they stay as far away from all the people who saw them crash and burn as possible. I know I sure did. That way it's a lot easier to pretend it never happened."

Was it her confession that she tried to use to blot out her own mistake that made the tension in Stone ease? His eyes filled with a depth of character that surprised her, a quiet strength, unflinching honesty, a weary acceptance of flaws he understood all too well.

"There was a time I thought about closing the door on our friendship. It might have been easier on me and on Tank not to have to see things that we'd just as soon forget. It still gets rough sometimes. But he's the closest thing to family I've got besides Trula. Guess I figured that was worth fighting for."

"I never really had a lot of girlfriends as a kid. I hung around with Cade and his buddies, and then with different bands I'd try to put together—I was always the only girl. Until I met Finn I didn't know how it felt to be able to share almost everything with someone. You're right. True friendship is worth fighting for."

"Some things are."

A shiver of awareness prickled Deirdre's nape, Stone's gaze suddenly solemn, holding hers. She pulled her gaze away, the contact too intense, confusing her, unnerving her.

Stone touched her cheek. "Does that mean you'll come with me to the picnic? Bring Emma?"

Deirdre tried to put emotional space between them with a nervous laugh. "In case you missed the latest newsflash, Emma isn't exactly crazy about you anymore. When that girl gets herself into a royal snit, even I don't want to be in the same county."

"She's got a whole week to cool off. It'll be okay, Dee. I promise. Nobody can be around the Rizzos and stay mad."

"You don't know my daughter. Sometimes she can even trump the Captain in stubbornness." *But somehow in the past I could always reach her.… Why is this time different?*

"Trust me. Emma will be crazy about Tank and Lucy and the boys. Besides, Trula's invited. She'll be a little miffed she won't be my official date this time. But she'll forgive me when she hears Emma's going to be there. The two of them can talk theater until their ears fall off. I'll even tell Trula to bring her dancing shoes."

Maybe that would be a good thing, if Trula and the prospect of dancing lessons could distract Emma from her obsession with Drew at least for a little while. Restore Emma's sanity so that maybe, just maybe, Deirdre could find a way to break through this wall of hurt and resentment cutting her off from her daughter.

And yet, Deirdre couldn't deny the gnawing anxiety in the pit of her stomach. She caught her lower lip between her teeth. She was being ridiculous, feeling so shy and awkward at the thought of meeting Jake's friends.

"I don't know if this is such a good idea," Deirdre admitted. "I don't…well, I'm not real big on—"

Meeting new people, going into new social situations. I've got more than enough people to love and care about and worry over. I'm big on personal space.…

"Stone, I really kind of like to keep to myself. I'm used to it. I have to deal with my family and the guests at

March Winds, but that about uses up what few social skills I have. My mouth tends to get me in trouble when I'm edgy or bored."

Stone crossed his arms across his bare chest. "You're so sure my friends are boring, huh?"

"No offense intended, Stone. It's just—"

"Lucy looks like a Botticelli Madonna and writes romance novels so steamy smoke comes out your ears when you read 'em. And Tank spent three years in the army as a spy."

Deirdre rolled her eyes. "Sure he did."

"He opted out because he was scared some subversives from a third-world country might kidnap the boys while Lucy was on deadline. Of course, Tank says the kidnapping would probably end up like that short story he read in high school—'The Ransom of Red Chief.' The terrorists would be begging Tank and Lucy to take the kids back."

Deirdre actually managed to chuckle. "Stone, you are so full of it."

He arched one brow, looking unbelievably sexy and—damn, this was downright dangerous—sweet. "You don't believe me?" Stone challenged. "Why don't you come to the picnic and ask them? Besides, Trula's giving me no peace, wanting to start Emma's dance lessons. She hasn't been this excited since the day she decided to paint that damn house of hers pink."

"Well…"

"You know, this romance novelist, spy stuff is going to drive you crazy if you don't verify it for yourself. Besides, what better place to get a new perspective on this whole illicit sex deal than at the Rizzos, with Emma and Trula and the five pint-size monsters running around. We'll have to watch Lucy and Tank, see if we can get any pointers. They're experts at stealing kisses—and, from what Tank says, a whole lot more than that right under the kids' noses. Come on, it's just one little picnic. What have you got to lose?"

For a fleeting instant the word *plenty* rose in Deirdre's mind. But she shoved it aside, and stopped to consider. What did she have to lose, besides seventeen years of inhibitions? Too much time to hear the deafening silence where Emma's eager chatter used to be? And the crowding of self-doubt every time she happened to glimpse Cade's cabin on the opposite end of the garden?

The best thing about this relationship with Stone was that it had finite limits. Once Jake found Jimmy Rivermont, Deirdre's partnership with the private eye would die a natural death. No expectations of more.

Maybe that's what made her willing to take a few risks. She could have a fling with the sexiest man she'd ever known, then go back to her real life, the life she felt safe in, the life she understood.

Deirdre shook off a niggling sense of loss. No sense being melodramatic. Neither she nor Stone were dewy-eyed romantics. They both preferred to look the truth coldly in the eye. And yet, as she thought of Jake Stone, there was nothing cold about it. He was heat and fire, the way he'd devoured her with his gaze, his big, hard hands hungry, as if he could never get enough of her.

Stone frowned. "You're thinking mighty hard considering the question just needs a simple yes or no."

"Fine. Okay. I'll go." She was probably going to regret it, but he'd managed to pique her curiosity. Besides, he was right. It *had* been quiet with the other McDaniels in the wilds of Montana and Emma so preoccupied with Drew Lawson and the play. Sadness tugged at Deirdre's bravado.

Truth to tell, it had been too quiet even before Cade had loaded everyone up in his SUV and hit the road, since the fateful day Deirdre had stormed into the cabin, Emmaline McDaniel's letter clutched in her hand.

Deirdre shoved back the hurt and loss, grabbed on to sharper emotions far more comfortable and familiar. "But you can just quit being ridiculous and deep-six the whole stolen-kisses idea, Stone. You can't ignore the fact that we've already done everything except—" Full-out, burying-to-the-hilt penetration.

Take me…

Her cheeks burned at the memory of his passion-rough voice, urging her on.

She tried not to wonder what would have happened if she'd steeled her courage, forced herself to lower herself onto him, inch by inch; accustomed herself to the feel of all that maleness; let Stone bracket her hips with his hands as he thrust up, into her.

Just the fact that he'd drawn her that far into a sensual haze proved he was right about one thing. He was a damned good lover. If she'd forced her way through her fears would she have been able to just feel? Would she have been able to let go?

She tried to blot out the image of Stone glistening with sweat, his muscles straining, his heart thundering, his eyes burning beneath her. She fought to focus instead on what she needed to say right now.

"You know, Jake, our whole rolling-around-naked-on-the-ground thing may not have ended in fireworks tonight, but we zoomed way past the stealing-kisses stage of the relationship and headed straight to naked body parts and your tongue in my mouth."

"Yeah, well, I won't be making that mistake next time." His gaze dipped to her lips, held there a long moment. "In spite of how good it felt to put my tongue in your mouth."

Deirdre fought back a shiver of need. Oh, perfect, she thought with grim humor. Her libido was working just fine, at least where Jake Stone was concerned. It was just her follow-through that stunk. Still, she couldn't keep from asking, "Is there going to be a next time?"

"Oh, yeah." Stone feathered the pad of his thumb over her bottom lip. "You're a woman worth waiting for, Deirdre McDaniel. And you're gonna find that I can be a very patient man."

CHAPTER 14

JAKE STARED AT THE WHITEBOARD he'd used to trace Deirdre's case, notes from the leads Norma Davenport had given them, employment records reconstructed from the fuzzy brain of the old man who'd once owned the town music store where Emmaline McDaniel's lover had worked.

Stone was close—damned close to finding Deirdre McDaniel's birth father—and if he proved to be the man Jake was starting to suspect he might be, he could imagine Deirdre's reaction.

Stone shoved back his desk chair, Ellie May moaning in indignation as one of the wooden legs bumped her shoulder. The bloodhound had a complete aversion to any fast moves. She thumped her tail twice to let Stone know she forgave him, gazing up at him with adoring eyes.

"Yeah, yeah, I know. I'm supposed to be glad, like you are, when I'm hot on the scent. The end of a case is a good thing. We get paid. Right? Trula's pink house is safe for another few months..."

Ellie May nosed at his hand, pleading for him to pet her. Pulling a wry face, Stone hunkered down, scratching the dog's sweet spot behind her droopy right ear. "Okay, I'm exaggerating. I admit it. The agency's doing great. The pink house will be paid off next June. You and me are on Easy Street, babe. We can have all the wild parties we want. Invite all your doggie friends and the cat next door. Trouble is, there's only one person I want to have over here, and she's made it pretty clear that the minute I hook her up with this Jimmy Rivermont guy, she and I are history."

Ellie May whined. Stone was sure it was in empathy and not just because he'd gotten distracted and quit scratching her ear.

"What would you say if I told you I love her, Ellie May?"

The dog crumpled onto the floor and rolled onto her back, legs up in the air, tongue lolling out ridiculously from the corner of her mouth. He'd always called it her "dead dog" trick.

"That's real encouraging, Ellie. Either you've died from shock or you think I'm dead in the water. And to think I rescued you from certain death. You're supposed to be man's best friend."

Ellie wiggled her wrinkly body into an impossible curve so she could lick his hand. "I know. That's what I thought, too. You and me, kid. A couple of washouts from the force, living on the edge. Cold pizza for breakfast, watching old gangster movies all night. Nobody to nag when we went to play a pickup game of basketball at the gym. I didn't know I was lonely, Ellie. Then she walked through that door."

Ellie rolled to one side and heaved a wrinkle-shaking sigh. "No, she did not deliberately miss and whack me over the head with that statue instead of hitting the con. She just…trusted me. You know? Out there in that gazebo. The things she told me…"

Stone buried his face in one hand.

"I forgot what that felt like, to have a woman look at me with eyes like that. It made me wish…hell, made me wonder if it would be such a terrible thing if I didn't push this case through, you know? Pull back just a little. Buy myself just a little more time. She'd never have to know."

But you'd know.

"Cut it out, Stone. You are a jerk. A jerk half in love with the woman, whatever that means."

It means nothing, he warned himself. He couldn't change that. Even if he was reckless enough to try to make all the stuff he felt about her mean something, she'd never let him. She talked about wanting to put Emma in a tower like Rapunzel? Hell, Deirdre was the one locked up in a tower. Except she'd bricked up the door to it herself.

She blocked out all chance of love, of a husband, a home. Now she'd even bricked out her brother and her father—and yes, damn it, Martin McDaniel would always be that to her, if she'd quit being so stubborn and let him.…

Let him love her.

Let *anyone* love her. Why was it so hard for her to see? The courage Stone glimpsed every time her eyes flashed in anger, the passion he felt when she defended her daughter, when she talked about her music, when she kissed Stone and he touched her.

Had the son of a bitch who raped Deirdre taken all hope away from her? She'd wanted Stone, wanted passion, wanted to drink it all in. Stone would've given his right hand to be able to be the man who gave her sexuality back to her.

But the most he could do was move on this case as quickly as possible, navigate Deirdre through all this confusion with as little pain and lasting damage as he could, deliver her back to her family—her *real* family: her fiercely protective brother and dreamy-eyed Finn, the nieces and nephews that would fill at least some of the place in Deirdre's heart where more of her own babies should have been, and the father who had loved her all the years of her life, who, please God, would be able to forgive her for showing him that that wasn't enough.

Stone straightened. Picked up the phone to call March Winds the way he had every night since the gazebo, taking her out for dinner, to the movies, hiking in the park with Ellie May. He didn't feel much like eating, but he'd go through the motions if Deirdre was across the table.

Time was running out.

He'd just have to make the most of whatever he had left.

"Don't tell me you're going out with him again?" Emma scowled over her chemistry book as Deirdre hung up the phone. "God, Stone, get a life!"

"Actually, I'm the one trying to get a life here, Emma." Deirdre tried to hold on to her patience. "There's no reason I should stay home. You're going to play practice, everything's ready to go for the guests' breakfast tomorrow morning, the table's set, muffin batter's in the fridge. I could sit and watch dust bunnies grow in the corner, but for some reason that doesn't appeal to me tonight."

"Or any night for the past week," Emma complained. "It's bad enough you're spending time with that nosy jerk, but forcing me to waste a whole Saturday at some lame picnic with people I don't know is cruel and unusual punishment."

Deirdre smoothed her fingers through her unruly hair, trying to tame it down. She flushed, remembering the other night when Jake had told her he liked it a little wild. It suited her. Her cheeks tingled at the memory of the kiss he'd nuzzled against her throat.

*Leave it like that…*he'd murmured. *It's so damned sexy…*

Emma…Deirdre reminded herself. She was supposed to be talking to Emma. Reasoning with her about…what? Oh, that was it. Saturday. She wondered what Stone had in store on that day. The man had perfected turning on Deirdre into an art form, teasing her, taunting her, pushing hot buttons she hadn't even known existed.

Focus, Deirdre told herself. *You're supposed to be convincing Emma not to be a total brat at the Rizzos'.*

"Taking a few lessons from a professional dancer would have thrilled you a month ago."

"There's a dance school on Maple Street. I could go there."

"And mince around with all the other little cheerleaders in tutus? Trula knows what it takes to audition and make it in theater, just like you've always wanted."

"What I *want* is for you to quit trying to ruin my Saturday!" Emma slammed her chemistry book closed. "I don't care if Stone's grandma is Mikhail Baryshnikov in drag, I don't want to go to some stranger's house with a bunch of stupid little kids and eat potato salad that makes me feel like I'm gonna barf even before I have to look at that—that nosy jerk Jake Stone's ugly face."

Deirdre wished she'd put in a pair of earplugs. Smile and nod. Smile and nod. Come Saturday, duct tape the kid's mouth and drag her to the Rizzos' by her hair. "I thought you said Jake was movie-star gorgeous the first time you saw him." She grabbed a lipstick from her purse and squinted at her wobbly reflection in the chrome of the toaster as she smoothed color on her lips.

Emma scoffed in disgust. "Yeah, well, aren't you the one who always tells me first impressions are deceiving? Besides, Drew and I have to practice—"

"I checked the practice schedule the school sent home, and you have the day off. A few hours won't kill you."

"No, but it might kill you," Emma muttered. She dragged a pile of dusty books from her book bag and thumped them onto the kitchen table.

"More homework?" Deirdre asked, glad to change the subject.

"Nope." Emma said, spreading the top book open. "They're yearbooks."

"Yearbooks?" Deirdre echoed, a little uneasy. "What do you want to look at old yearbooks for?"

Gravel crunched outside as Stone pulled up.

"Stuff for some stupid old class reunion that's coming up. The drama department is supposed to dig out old pictures. You know, a picture of me as lead in the senior play, a picture of whatever old chick got Whitewater High's top billing back in the Dark Ages."

"Hey, I resent that," Deirdre's brow furrowed.

"Yeah, well, it's your Dark Ages I'm supposed to find this stuff in. Your graduating class. Remember? Aunt Finn said you threw the invitation away."

"Did I?" Things had been so crazy she could barely remember her own name lately. But Finn had shown her some kind of invitation that had come in the mail a few weeks ago. It *was* her class that was reuniting. She'd thrown the invitation in the garbage.

One session in hell was enough, she'd told Finn. There was only one way she'd ever show her face at a class reunion: that was if Stephen King could hand over all those psychic powers he gave Carrie. There were some people in the graduating class Deirdre had always figured would look good in pig's blood.

"So this was your graduating class, huh?" Emma asked, looking up, suddenly a little quiet, a little unnerving.

"I guess so." Deirdre looked at the images on the yellowed pages, felt a jolt of recognition. Her senior year spread out across the page—the dorky float the music teachers had made them work on, the homecoming court lined up, smiling their toothpaste smiles.

Her stomach lurched.

"What's the matter, Mom?" Emma asked, her eyes far too keen, her mind too sharp.

Don't let her see, Deirdre thought desperately. *Don't let her guess...*

"I got a speck of dust in my eye," Deirdre lied. "Don't they ever go in the library stacks and shake all the crud off these old books?"

"I wouldn't have had to drag them home from the library if you'd just kept your own yearbooks like everybody else in the world."

I didn't want anything that reminded me of him. Didn't want to remember—

She fought the urge to snatch the book away, slam it shut, shove it into the fireplace and burn it to ash.

Instead she turned and walked away, trying to blot out the image from her mind. But even later that night as she sat across the table from a worried Jake Stone, she couldn't tell him what had shaken her so badly. Couldn't tell anyone how a split second could have torn her world apart. The heart-stopping instant she'd realized that Emma's fingers lay carelessly across the picture of her own father.

NEVER TAKE YOUR EYE OFF THE BALL. Hadn't some high school coach of Jake's a jillion years ago dropped that little gem of wisdom into Stone's hormone-crazed brain?

Jake doubled over, struggling to breathe. What the coach should have said was keep your eyes on your *own* balls, at least when Frankie, J.J., Ricky and Tommy Rizzo were practicing the karate kicks Stone had taught them last time he'd been at the house.

Even five-year-old Joey, lured away from roughhousing by his fascination with the fire that Tank was starting in the grill, stared at Uncle Jake in awe.

"Frankie kicked him right in the nuts, Daddy," Joey shrilled in a voice that could be heard in the next state. "Man, I bet that hurts!"

Tank roared with laughter. "This lady friend Uncle Jake invited must really be something, boys. His concentration's shot to hell," Tank muttered, sotto voce, "along with any extracurricular activities you might have had planned after dessert, eh, Jakey boy?"

"Rizzo...you're a real...comedian." Stone scowled at his best friend, surprised at the wave of protectiveness that swept through him. "Lay off when Deirdre's here, man. No sex jokes."

"With my children's tender ears about?" Tank tried to look innocent as he tended the charcoal. "I'll make sure my manners would measure up at Sunday Mass."

"That's a hell of a comfort, considering some of the stunts I've seen you pull during the boys' baptisms and first communions."

"Only when Father Casey isn't looking and Lucy's busy trying to keep the kids from killing each other. Somehow they don't quite get the spirit of that go-in-peace, serve-the-Lord stuff."

"Yeah, they're chips off the old block." Jake limped over

to the picnic table he and Tank had built for Lucy's Mother's Day present the year J.J. had been born. "I mean it, Theodore Patsy."

Tank scowled and thwacked Jake on the arm, his usual reaction to hearing his loathed formal name. "Call me Theodore Patsy in front of this chick and the boys and I will pants you. I mean it, Jake. No mercy."

Jake hated the strange tension in his nerves. The edginess that had only grown worse in the time that had passed since Stone had *not* made love to Deirdre McDaniel at the gazebo. Maybe Frankie had done him a favor after all with that well-aimed kick. He'd had a perpetual hard-on for almost a week. Surely pain would take the edge off it.

Then again, maybe not, Stone thought as he saw Deirdre's van pulling up to the Rizzos' cozy ranch-style house. The place, on its spacious corner lot, had been advertised as a fixer-upper when the Rizzos bought it. Tank and Jake had remodeled the whole damned place, room by room, until now it was everything Lucy Rizzo had dreamed of.

Stone grabbed Tank by his meaty forearm and glared into his mischievous eyes. "Do *not* screw this up for me," Jake warned, his heart skipping a beat as he heard Deirdre's car door slam. "The lady...she's a little skittish about, well, sex. I don't want you spooking her."

"No wonder you've got such a foul temper if you haven't been getting any—ooph!" Tank gasped as Jake elbowed him in the gut.

"I heard that," Lucy said as she swept through one of the sliding glass doors. Her green blouse and khaki shorts set off her slender frame, her long golden hair caught up in a ponytail that made her look far too young to be the mother of such a rowdy pack of boys. The heaping platter of burgers and hot dogs for the grill demonstrated she had a healthy understanding that the Rizzo men plus one would soon be descending on her table like a swarm of army ants.

"Jacob Stone, you're a wreck," she said, giving him the once-over. "This woman must be really special."

Stone was amazed to feel his cheeks burn. "She is."

"All right, then." Lucy rounded on her husband. "Theodore Patsy Rizzo, step out of line once tonight and I swear, I'll put so much starch in your underwear you'll be walking like a penguin when you go back to work on Monday. Jake is your best friend, and he's actually bringing a lady over for the first time since...well, in years."

A shadow crossed Lucy's face, even Tank's ornery grin looked stiff. Jake hated the haunted quality in his friends' eyes.

"Go ahead and say it. I haven't brought a lady over here since I got divorced," Jake supplied. "Actually longer than that. Trula always said that Jessica was no lady. I should have listened."

He almost got a smile out of Lucy. "Men," Lucy groaned. "Why is it you're always chasing after these delicate little flowers with big boobs and the brains of a china doll?"

"Hey," Tank objected. "I chased after you from the time I was an altar boy, and you're so much smarter than me sometimes it's scary."

"Lucy Rizzo, the last of the genuinely good women." Jake mourned. "It's a pity that polygamy is illegal in this state since you conned Lucy into marrying you first, Tank. Of course, I'm the one she comes to when she has questions to research in all those love scenes."

It felt good to see them both laugh, Jake thought. Deirdre's blunt questions the other day had reminded him of far darker days. When they'd all three been tense and edgy, the friendship they'd taken for granted changed forever.

He'd been so damned grateful when they'd eased their way back into some of the old patterns, sparring back and forth again, no one missing their cue. But tonight was different.

"Hey, Tank," Stone said, his voice unsteady. "Seriously, man. Take it easy on her. I kinda love her."

"Holy shit!" Tank exclaimed. "You hear that, Lucy? Jakey here kinda—"

Lucy scooped a hamburger bun from a nearby basket and jammed it into her husband's open mouth. "Behave, or no sex for a week," she said under her breath.

Tank mumbled around a mouthful of bun. Stone knew from a dozen other play fights Rizzo's line was "At home?"

But Stone was too shaken to give a damn about the rest of the exchange. His heart was thundering in his ears like a nine-pound hammer as Deirdre walked toward them, a Tupperware bowl of fruit salad clutched in one hand, a bottle of wine in the other.

Trim denim capris accented her shapely legs, a soft, flowing poet's shirt in poppy orange making the rich tints in her dark hair glow. Emma, obviously pouting, clutched the play script in her arms, a built-in excuse to barricade herself in a corner, so she could make damned sure she didn't have a good time.

Deirdre looked tired and wary and so beautiful Stone had a hard time coming up with something to say.

"Hey," Joey piped up. "You look like a pun-kin. They're orange, too. Frankie kicked Uncle Jake right in the—"

"Hey, there, partner!" Lucy swooped up her big-mouthed son and smacked a kiss on the kid, drowning out his little announcement. "How about if you and J.J. check to see if any tomatoes are ripe in the garden? We'll need some for the burgers and nobody's better at picking them out than you are."

Joey wriggled in delight. "I get to pick 'em. I'm the best!" He raced around to the vines by the side of the house, his brothers in hot pursuit.

Lucy swept over and gave a surprised Deirdre one of her ubiquitous hugs. "I really hope we're going to be friends, Deirdre, because I just sacrificed the rest of this year's tomato crop to keep my son from embarrassing you so badly you'll never set foot in our yard again. He'll pick every tomato on the vine and expect us to eat them— especially the green ones."

Deirdre set the fruit salad on the picnic table. "The green ones are my favorites." She held out the wine a little awkwardly. As Lucy accepted it, Deirdre nodded to the Ice Princess. "This is my daughter, Emma."

Jake had a moment to wonder if Emma would be the first one in recent history not to melt under the warmth of one of Lucy Rizzo's smiles. But he never got the chance to find out.

Heels clicked across the concrete patio, Jake recognizing his grandmother's rhythmic stride before he caught a glimpse of her fire-engine-red hair.

"Oh, my, you must be Emma!" Trula gasped, her blood-red fingernail polish flashing as she clasped her wrinkled hands. "Look at the legs on this girl, Lucy!"

Trula looked the kid over as if she were a prized cow or something. Emma took a step closer to her mom, but Trula didn't miss a beat, God bless her.

"And what presence!" Trula said, enraptured. "You know, Emma dear, presence is something even the finest masters in the world can't teach. You must be born with it...here." Trula touched the center of the startled teenager's chest.

Jake almost laughed aloud as Deirdre's jaw dropped open. Must be weird, he figured, watching your daughter fall under Trula's spell.

"When did you know you were destined to be an actress?" Trula inquired.

"I...I guess I never—I mean, I always..."

Jake almost felt sorry for the kid—caught like a deer in the headlights—staring at Trula's spectacularly red hair. Emma clung to her script almost as tightly as she was hanging on to her rotten mood. "I've got lines to learn."

"Oh. Lines." Trula waved her hand as if saying, Oh, you're taking out the garbage.

"I promised her she could sit in a corner somewhere," Deirdre said, looking uncomfortable. "Someplace far away, where she wouldn't bother anybody."

Jake threw the kid an appraising look, filling in the blanks with what Deirdre hadn't said: *Emma can sit far away where she won't wreck the party with her Oscar-worthy performance of a little black cloud.*

But Trula wasn't backing down. "Jacob and your mother said you are playing Juliet in the school play." Trula walked around Emma. The old woman laid one finger along a brightly rouged cheek in appraisal. "You know, I lost my virginity to—"

"Trula!" Stone exclaimed while Tank roared out a booming laugh.

The ornery old woman gave the two men a look filled with wide-eyed innocence. "Ah, well, fine, then. Plenty of time to get around to losing your virginity *after* you learn how to dance. Theodore has been kind enough to clear space in the boys' roller hockey rink in the basement."

"It's, uh, *Tank*, Miss Trula," Rizzo said, tugging at his shirt collar.

"Why, thank you for reminding me of that, Theodore. I do forget things now and then."

Lucy affectionately grabbed her husband's hand. "So

what are you two drama queens going to do tonight?" she asked Emma and Trula.

Trula stopped to consider. "I thought before dinner I'd start Emma out with some combinations Twyla Tharp designed specifically for me."

"That's very kind of you," Deirdre began, "but I don't think Emma—"

"Twyla..." Emma cut her off. "You mean *the* Twyla Tharp?"

Trula did Jake's eyebrow trick. "I hardly think there could be more than one."

"She's the most gifted choreographer alive, in Trula's humble opinion," Stone said. "She can go on about it for hours."

"Twyla is an original," Trula informed her audience. "Just as I am. That's why we adored each other on sight. True originals are depressingly rare in the world of the stage. However, if I were to hazard a guess looking at you, Emma dear, you stand a fair chance of becoming an original, too."

Nothing original about this kid at all, Jake thought. She's as damned mule stubborn as the rest of her family. It was part of the reason he liked the kid so much.

"Of course, I was hoping to pass my knowledge on to someone deserving," Trula said, playing it to the hilt. "I *am* getting older, dear. I won't be around forever. What a shame, should Twyla's brilliance be lost. But maybe you should spend this evening just running those tedious lines until they're dull as sawdust in your mouth."

"No!" Emma piped up, obviously surprising even herself with her eagerness. "I...I'd love to learn some dance steps. Really."

"Well then," Trula said with a flourish, sweeping Emma toward the sliding glass doors. "To the stage."

"Thank God," Deirdre breathed, looking visibly relieved as her daughter disappeared inside.

Lucy grinned. "I feel like we all should applaud."

"I think Trula deserves an Oscar," Jake said, marveling at the old woman's panache.

"No way," Tank grumped. "No Oscars. I can just hear her announcing over international TV, '…and a special thanks to Theodore Patsy Rizzo.' The guys at the station house would turn my life into a living hell."

They all laughed. Deirdre seemed to have quit grinding her tooth enamel to dust. Jake blessed the old woman for her skill at handling pouting teenage drama queens, and hoped he'd have half Trula's luck putting Deirdre at ease.

"Remind me to thank your grandmother for that." Deirdre slipped her hand into Stone's. "Emma's moved from playing Juliet onstage to performing the death scene from *Camille* in real life. I was scared to death she'd turn today into a disaster."

Jake felt Lucy watching them. He tried not to show how much Deirdre's simple act of trust moved him as he curled his fingers protectively around her smaller ones.

"No worries," he said. "Trula's got a real gift. Besides, I bribed her to keep Emma busy the rest of the night."

"Maybe," Tank warned, "but that Trula strikes a hard bargain."

Jake grinned at his best friend. "The way I figure it, I'm gonna be eating lunch at the pink house every afternoon until I'm eighty."

"Yoo-hoo! Rizzos!" A woman's voice called from the street. Stone felt Deirdre stiffen, release his hand. Feeling an odd sense of loss, he looked up to see a Barbie doll in a lavender-colored running suit jogging by, her white-blond hair caught back by a matching sweat band. "Lucy, if you eat one of those burgers you'll have to run for a week to work off the calories!"

"Yeah, well, I think I'll risk it, Liz," Lucy called back, glancing back at Deirdre and crossing her eyes. "The woman's obsessed," Lucy whispered to Deirdre under her breath. But before she could finish, Liz shrieked in excitement.

"Don't tell me that's Deirdre McDaniel right here in my very own neighborhood!"

Stone glanced at Deirdre. Her tooth enamel was toast.

"Hi, Liz," Deirdre said with forced ease. "It's been a long time."

Not nearly long enough, Stone guessed, considering Deirdre's expression. He hated Barbie on sight. And not just because her untimely arrival had made Deirdre let go of his hand. Stone figured the feeling wasn't mutual considering the way Liz's beady mascara-clad eyes raked over him.

"I've been trying to get these last few pesky pounds off before the class reunion." Liz planted her hands on her teensy little waist. "A bunch of us are going to wear our senior prom dresses. You know, show we've still got those cheerleader shapes all the guys drooled over."

Stone wished the woman would run into the path of an obliging semi.

"Why, who on earth *is* this gorgeous man?" Liz asked, giving Stone a come-hither smile.

"I'm Deirdre's date." Stone closed the space between them and slipped his arm casually around Deirdre's waist. He hoped like hell she wouldn't take exception to what he'd done and elbow him hard in the ribs.

But she actually seemed to edge a little closer to him.

"You are coming to the reunion, aren't you, Deirdre?" Liz cooed as if the question was a no-brainer and the reunion was the social event of the century.

"I don't think so."

"Yeah," Stone said. "We're pretty busy." Deirdre flashed him a quelling glance. He took a step back, taking his toes out of stomping distance. But hell, he wished they could get busy with all that kissing, touching and tasting he was still hoping would lead her to the big bang theory of orgasms.

"But you *have* to come. Both of you!" Liz actually seemed distressed.

Stone tried to look as if he hadn't just been thinking about sex. From Tank's sly look on the other side of the grill, he figured his friend had pegged him dead to rights. And Lucy—she was looking downright suspicious.

"Peter Jessup and the guys are getting the band back together to play," Liz said. "They're really good. We're trying to feature people in little vignettes, like we did in the yearbook...you know, 'First To Marry a Doctor,' 'First Boy To Lose His Hair,' 'The Girl Most Likely To Become Famous.'"

"I was 'the first girl likely to be knocked up' in my high school," Lucy said. She looked from Jake to Deirdre to Liz, obviously bewildered at the sudden strange expressions on their faces.

Jake tried to think of some quick comeback to get the spotlight off Deirdre, but all he could think of was this witch of a cheerleader giggling with her friends as Deirdre walked past in the hall, her books balanced on her growing belly.

Thank God Tank was quick on the uptake, jumping in with his Italian good humor. "Considering I got you pregnant the day after we got married, I guess I came through."

Jake gave him a wan but grateful smile. The corners of Deirdre's mouth tipped up.

Liz regained her composure and flashed Stone a smile. "Deirdre was really something in high school. When she sang—well, it was spectacular. When my yearbook committee was picking for the different categories, 'Most Likely To Be Famous' wasn't even a question. We all expected to hear her on our radios someday."

"Yeah, well, it seems like another lifetime ago," Deirdre said.

"Thank God," Lucy said. "I wouldn't go back to high school for a million dollars."

"I would, Lucy," Tank said. "You were *hot*. I spent so much time in confession for impure thoughts, I about wore out my knees. But, hey, my intentions were honorable. I married you the day after graduation and I'm *still* having impure thoughts about you."

"Father Casey must be so proud," Lucy said, evidently picking up on Deirdre's discomfort. "Really, Liz. You'd better get your run in before—"

Liz astonished Stone, her plastic face softening a little, as if she really were a little bit sorry. Maybe Barbie had remembered tormenting Deirdre and she'd moved up on the evolutionary scale at least enough to feel a little bit ashamed.

"Deirdre, I know things weren't great when you were...well, your senior year. But people really have been asking about you. Come to the reunion and sing. Everybody will be dying to hear you. They're already going to be disappointed. The most valuable athlete isn't going to be able to make it. He's in the middle of moving his medical practice or some such."

Stone sensed a flicker in Deirdre, something sharp, cutting. Relief? Regret? He thought about what she'd told him, that last hellish year of high school, growing more pregnant every day. He could imagine the whispers, the cruelty, how much it had hurt this proud woman he'd grown to...what had he told Tank? Kinda love?

She deserved to walk back among her classmates, looking like a queen with her head held high. He'd sweep her into the room on his arm and charm the whole goddamned room, make damn sure every woman there wished to be in Deirdre's place, and every man envied Stone the woman they'd whispered was a slut.

Oh, yeah. Deirdre's last year in high school might have been miserable. But if it took Stone's last cent he'd make sure at this reunion, his Deirdre was damned well going to shine.

He turned her toward him, smiled down into her eyes. "What do you say?"

"In case you haven't noticed, I'm not famous," Deirdre murmured for his ears only. "I don't even have a husband to show off."

"How about a really hot date? Come on. Let's give them something to talk about."

Deirdre's throat worked. Her lips trembled. Stone bumped his thumb up under her chin, nudging her until her head was held high.

Blue eyes held his long moments. Then she smiled. "Just remember, I can't dance."

"Wanna bet?" Stone twirled her out, then swooped her into his arms.

Lucy and Tank burst into applause. Deirdre laughed, looking back at Liz.

"We'll be there," she said.

From the moment Reunion-Hell Barbie jogged off, Deirdre relaxed. Stone delighted in watching her animated face, listening to her snappy comebacks as she traded jokes with Tank and asked Lucy about the books she'd written. Maybe there was still a little tension underneath Deirdre's sparkle, but Jake bet he was the only one who knew it.

The burgers were burnt, the hot dogs cold in the middle and the tomatoes Lucy and Deirdre sliced were frog green. Stone could never remember a meal he'd enjoyed more.

He smiled across the table at Deirdre, amazed at how strong she was, how funny and bright with her take-no-prisoners sense of humor. He felt so damned proud to know she was here with him. This night was worlds different from those times years ago when Jessica had been at this same house, looking down at the benches as if she was afraid the splinters might snag her silk pants or one of the boys might smear dirt on her skin.

She'd thought the Rizzos far beneath her social standing. After all, she was the chief of police's only daughter. The wife of the star pupil of the police academy. Her husband was the force's best and the brightest. It wasn't that she wanted to be snobbish, she'd assured Jake, peering up at him with big green eyes. It was just the way things were done at her daddy's house.

Blinded by Jessica's neediness that made him feel strong, wanting to build the family he'd never had, Jake had made excuses for her. She was very young. Overprotected. It wasn't her fault her parents had filled her head with that garbage. There was no question she worshiped Jake. Told him time and again he was everything she could ever ask for. She just knew he'd take care of her.

And he wanted to. God, how he'd wanted to take care of someone then. His wife, his kids, even a damned dog. Sure, Jessica was a little self-absorbed, he'd told Trula when the old woman had been less than thrilled about his engagement. But Jessica would grow out of it. Once they were in their own house, raising their own babies, she'd be able to see the world from his perspective—realize Trula was a treasure and the Rizzos were solid gold.

He grimaced, remembering the arrogant dope he'd been, so damned sure life would go along exactly the way he planned. But nothing about his marriage was the way he'd pictured it.

Jessica's attitude toward the Rizzos had only gotten worse as she watched Lucy go through her frequent pregnancies, faintly repulsed by a process that left Jake awestruck. Maybe his marriage had been doomed long before he lost his badge, when Jessica made it plain she didn't want to have his babies.

She wasn't going to turn into a baby factory like Lucy Rizzo, she'd informed him after J. J. Rizzo's birth. Jake was never home, anyway; he was always on the job. She'd be the one stuck with dirty diapers and baby barf staining all her clothes. She wasn't going to be a drudge and waste her life like that.

Was it hurt? Anger? Or just brutal honesty that had made Jake snap, tell Jessica that she wasn't worthy to wash Lucy Rizzo's dishes. Truth was, he'd mourned the loss of his badge far more than the loss of his wife. And if the gunshot that detonated his career had cost him the friendship of Tank and Lucy—that would have been the greatest heartbreak of all.

But Deirdre was Jessica's complete opposite—*real* in a way those china-doll types never could be. She's a woman's woman, he could hear Lucy say. Her highest compliment of all.

The kind of woman a gem like Lucy could respect.

But it was obvious the feeling was mutual. Stone could see how much Deirdre respected his friends. And for the first time since he'd lost his badge he closed his eyes, imagined cooking out on his own grill, at his own house, with his own wife warning him he was going to burn the hamburgers.

He could even see a couple of little girls mixing it up with Rizzos' brood. Deirdre's daughters? Hell, yes, they'd hold their own.

Lucy scooped up a stack of plates, starting for the house, as Deirdre bundled half-empty glasses and bottles of ketchup and mustard onto a tray that read, I'm The Mom, That's Why.

Jake watched the two women disappear into the house. His jaw knotted. Maybe if he told Deirdre about his past she would understand what he'd done. Maybe she'd even be glad...glad that what? He'd taken his future on the police force and thrown it away? He'd flushed away all the respect he'd earned. The pride he'd seen in his step-grandfather's eyes? He'd never wanted to mention another word to anyone about what had happened in that dark, despair-filled crime scene. And he'd never felt a pinprick of goddamned self-pity over the whole fiasco.

Until he watched Deirdre McDaniel tonight.

Suddenly he was aware of heavy silence. Stone turned and glared at his best friend.

"What's the matter with you?" Jake grumbled. "This is headline-news material—Tank Rizzo keeping his mouth shut."

"I was just thinking. It must be love, buddy, if you're putting yourself through going to her high school reunion."

"Might as well." Stone shrugged. "I sure as hell won't be going to any of my own. I don't think they'd exactly roll out the red carpet for me at this year's Policeman's Ball." Jake regretted the words as soon as they slipped out, but there was no way to take them back.

They hit Tank with sledgehammer force, driving all

merriment from his eyes, replacing it with dark brooding so quickly it betrayed the big Italian's secret. That sometimes at night he still thought about what had gone down in that miserable dark apartment eight years ago. Rizzo's jaw clenched. "Jake, if I could change what happened..."

But there was no going back for either one of them. Not now. Not ever.

He clapped his hand on his friend's back, his voice strong, sure. "Don't even think about it, Theodore. I wouldn't change a thing."

CHAPTER 15

DISHES WERE WASHED, food put away, Lucy Rizzo's cheery kitchen sparkling clean and so warm Deirdre wished she could sit there forever. The picnic had been an unqualified success, Trula performing a minor miracle by maneuvering Emma into talking to Jake about the time Trula had gotten him a brief gig as a child actor.

"I stunk," Stone had admitted, winking at Emma. "But when you get in front of the camera, kid, you won't. Trula's right. Whatever 'it' is, you've definitely got it."

Emma had actually smiled, the old dreams shining bright in her eyes, and Deirdre had dared to hope somehow Drew Lawson might fade to the background.

And Emma would go to New York. Leave March Winds and her mother and the small town of Whitewater behind.

Deirdre tried not to think about how quiet the house would be—how empty her life would be without her little girl. She crossed to the refrigerator that obviously served as the Rizzo family art gallery.

The boys' paintings were stuck on the shiny white surface with magnets of all shapes and sizes, while Lucitecovered photographs gleamed, rich with color, under a row of rainbow colored magnetic alphabet letters that said Rogues' Gallery.

Deirdre perused the photos of the Rizzo family, trying not to feel too envious of the easy camaraderie of the brothers, the obvious love and security to be found in Lucy's houseful of men.

Lucy had shots of all the boys at different ages, in diapers and taking a community bath, lined up like little stair steps, from oldest to youngest. A much-younger Lucy in a simple, white knee-length dress beamed over what must be her wedding bouquet, while Tank, in his dress army uniform grinned like he'd won the lottery.

Deirdre wondered if he knew that he really had. A new bride. Life as a spy. It didn't get much better than that.

Maybe there is such a thing as a happy family, Deirdre thought wistfully. Cade had created one. It was obvious Tank and Lucy had. But then, Finn and Lucy were warm, Earth Mother types. Nothing at all like her.

Deirdre tried not to mind too much, distracting herself by viewing the rest of the Rizzo's treasured pictures. Jake was in three of the shots—half-naked and full of sawdust as he and Tank knocked out a wall to make the kitchen more spacious, swinging from a tree as he and Tank hung a Tarzan swing. Another, the shot a bit fuzzy, showed Tank and—God, was that Stone?—with their heads shaved completely bald!

Deirdre's breath snagged. No, that was impossible! It must've been some kind of costume party, Halloween or… The thought of all Stone's gorgeous thick hair lying on the floor of some barbershop was almost more than Deirdre could take.

"What was that gasp for?" Lucy came to look over her

shoulder. "The kitchen shot of Jake's fantastic bod? The man does keep himself in great shape with that martial arts stuff he does. Tank wants him to teach the boys, but I'm scared they'll kill each other. And I already know the E.R. nurses by name. We'll see when the kids get older."

Deirdre's curiosity was killing her. She pointed to the picture in question. "Were they—they going to a costume party or something?" she asked, knowing her dismay must be showing. "Dressing up for some joke?"

Lucy was quiet for a moment. Deirdre squinted. It looked like a balloon was drifting just above their heads in the snapshot, a white one with big, dark circles like eyes.

Lucy took the picture down, ran her finger along the edge tenderly. "I pulled this out of the photo album when I heard you were coming. I don't keep it out as a rule. The little boys, they don't remember much. But it makes Frankie and Tommy upset."

"I'd get upset, too, if Jake cut his hair."

Lucy smiled softly down at the photograph. "Neither one of those guys ever looked more handsome. At least not in my eyes."

"You're serious?"

"Frankie took the picture, so it's a little blurry, but see this blob up at the top of the picture?" Lucy pointed. "That's me."

Deirdre squinted, made out Lucy's brown eyes, a smear of nose, but not a wisp of her rich spun gold hair. Deirdre looked up, meeting the other woman's gaze. "You?"

"I'd just finished chemo. My hair was coming out in clumps. So I went to the hair stylist and just had her shave it all off. She put it in an envelope and I took it home with me. Why, God alone knows. Tank and Jake found me crying over it, like a baby."

"I'm so sorry."

"I'm not. Those two knuckleheads ran out, saying they were going to pick up some ice cream. They came home looking like this, grinning like complete idiots. That Halloween, the three of us painted our heads different colors and went out disguised as pool balls. The boys thought it was awesome."

Deirdre swallowed hard, emotion squeezing her chest as she peered down at Jake Stone's face captured on the bit of film. It was so easy to imagine him, trying to make Lucy feel better. Loving his friends so easily, the way he loved Trula and the pink house and that ridiculous-looking dog of his with its skin six sizes too large.

"Jake's one in a million," Lucy said. "Any woman who gets her hands on him is damned lucky."

Especially if she knows what to do with him once she does, doesn't freak out and go cold. "They must be standing in line," Deirdre said, a little wistful.

"Pretty much," Lucy told her. "Not that he's been interested. Tank even quit trying to set him up with my friends. He'd just tell them he was already seeing someone else."

"When I came to his office to hire him, he tried to convince me he had two bimbos on the string—Trula and Ellie May. Of course, it was easy to believe he had a whole harem of women crazy about him. God. That man has a gorgeous smile."

Lucy sobered. "None of us had much to smile about back when we took this picture. I lost my breast, Tank lost his pride, my boys lost their belief that Mom would live forever and Jake…sometimes I think Jake lost most of all. Has he talked to you about, well, about how he lost his badge?"

Deirdre looked into Lucy Rizzo's earnest brown eyes.

"I know the bare bones. He and Tank were partners. Stone shot a suspect. The guy was unarmed. So he became a private investigator when he was kicked off the force."

"And you believe that's all there is to it?"

Deirdre felt the weight of Lucy Rizzo's gaze on her, the woman seeming to measure her somehow, searching for something Deirdre couldn't name.

"No. There's something more. Sometimes I see it in his eyes. He wanted me to believe he didn't give a damn about the man he shot, about losing his badge. And yet, that lack of honor…it seems so…so strange on Stone. It doesn't fit."

"No. It doesn't."

Deirdre regarded this woman who was Stone's friend, a woman Deirdre had come to like and respect in a short time, in spite of her own usual reserve. "I wish he'd tell me…what happened. I'd believe him."

"He never will." Lucy set the picture down and perched on the edge of a stool at the kitchen island.

"Will you?" Deirdre asked. What was she? Crazy? She didn't want to know any more about how wonderful Jake Stone was. It would just make it harder when he found her father, and she had to walk away.

Lucy patted the stool beside her. Deirdre scooted up on it to listen.

"One thing you can always count on with Jake. He'll let people think the worst of him and take the fall himself before he'll risk letting down someone he loves. For Tank and me, it's been one of the luckiest things in our lives that Jake Stone loves us."

What would it be like to be able to say that so certainly? Deirdre wondered with a twinge of envy. Jake Stone loves us. Loves me. Loves Emma.

"Eight years ago Tank had just brought me home from

my mastectomy. They had to do a radical, lymph nodes, the whole ugly deal. Trula stayed with the boys and me while Tank and Jake were at work. There was no way Tank could take any time off. We needed the money too badly. But with me so sick his head was—well, you can imagine. Tank's mind wasn't on his job."

Deirdre tried to imagine the burly Italian who'd loved Lucy since he was an altar boy facing the possibility of losing her.

"The doctor had done his best, but he wasn't sure he'd gotten all the cancer. I was so young, you know? It took everyone by surprise. Tank was out of his mind with worry, scared he was going to have to watch me die. Feared he'd have to raise our boys on his own. God, Deirdre, if you could have seen him—this big strong man, crying at night when he thought I was sleeping."

Deirdre's eyes burned. "You're lucky. To have a good man like Tank love you that much."

Lucy smiled. "I remember him leaving the house the night it happened, Frankie clinging to his leg, begging Tank not to go. You know how kids get crazy things in their heads sometimes? Frankie believed with all his heart that Tank had to be home to keep God from stealing Mommy away. Jake had brought Trula over to help. He could see Tank was on the edge. Yelling… Tank almost never yelled at the boys. Jake sent Tank outside to cool off, then he picked Frankie up."

Lucy wiped away tears, unashamed.

"Jake looked right into my little boy's eyes and told him I wasn't going anywhere. He told Frankie that a fire had taken Jake's mom away before he even got to know her. So it would be cheating for God to take me to heaven, too. Like on game night when J.J. tried to pick too many cherries in Hi Ho Cherry-o."

"If only the world were that simple."

"Frankie's world was. The logic made my brain ache, but Frankie figured there was no way God was going to cheat like his rotten little brother. Not with Uncle Jake around to keep things fair. Jake was so patient with my boy, like he really understood. But it made me so sad. I kept thinking Jake was so much younger than Frankie when his own mother died."

Deirdre imagined how strong Jake would have felt to little Frankie Rizzo, how wise. The uncle who loved him, who'd always be there for him. Who loved Frankie's mom and dad.

"After Tank and Jake headed off to their beat, they answered a domestic violence call. The boys had been there a half-dozen times before. This time was worse than the others. They found the woman stabbed in the breast. Her husband was laughing, telling Tank to go ahead and arrest him. The minute he got back out of jail he'd find his wife, cut her again. Make sure she died real slow, a piece at a time."

Deirdre's stomach lurched, imagining the blood and the threat and the helplessness Tank and Jake must have felt, knowing that the monster would keep his promise.

"'There's nothing you can do to stop me,' the husband had said, and laughed and laughed and laughed, his wife out of her mind with pain, waiting for the ambulance." Lucy's fingers clenched on the top chair rail. "What I'm going to tell you is grounds for arrest. That's why Jacob never will…"

She paused for a moment, seeming to steady herself to take the risk Deirdre could see was weighing on her.

"Tank shot the husband," Lucy said, meeting Deirdre's eyes. "He pulled the trigger and killed him."

Deirdre stared.

"Tank was crazy with fear and grief and hadn't slept in weeks," Lucy defended. "Not since I'd gotten the diagnosis. Hearing that animal delighting in his wife's pain was more than Tank could stand."

"But Jake...Jake is the one who killed the guy," Deirdre stammered. "He lost his badge—"

"Jake knew the kind of trouble Tank would be in. God, sometimes I still can't believe this. Jake grabbed this little end table the woman had sitting by her couch and whacked Tank over the head with it. Knocked him out cold. Tank had a nasty gash, and was still so out of it when the ambulance got there the EMTs insisted he go with them to the hospital to get stitched up. Jake took Tank's gun and told Tank to go home once the docs checked him out. Jake would come by our house after he filed the report."

"He lied," Deirdre said, knowing it was true.

"He claimed the perp surprised them, came after them with the table, knocking their guns out of their hands. When the perp bashed Tank over the head, Jake grabbed the first weapon he could reach and fired the fatal shot."

Deirdre tried to make sense of it. "But Tank loves Jake. Why would he let that story stand?"

"Tank went crazy, he was so furious. Ready to charge out of the house, go to headquarters and set things straight. Jake blocked the door, saying it was too late for that. Telling the truth now wouldn't save Jake. He'd already perjured himself. He was off the force either way. If Tank said he'd fired the fatal shot now, they'd both go down."

Tears welled up in Lucy's eyes. "Tank swung at him, out of his mind, so broken by all of it. They fought—God, I've never been so scared. Jake tried so hard not to hurt him, but Tank was crazy, you know? Trying to beat the pain out of him. Finally Jake pinned him to the floor. 'Think, you bullheaded Italian,' Jake said. 'You admit to firing that shot, they won't just take your badge, you'll lose your medical insurance. How the hell is an unemployed cop with no coverage gonna pay for chemo and checkups and God forbid, more surgery if it comes to that?'"

"Oh, Lucy." Deirdre could see the two friends, shirts torn, noses bleeding, forced into doing the unthinkable.

"I hobbled out of my room, crying. Knelt down by Tank. I told him we had no choice. He had the boys to support, and if I died... Deirdre, there was no way to know if I'd live out the year."

Deirdre crossed to the window, looked out to the man roughhousing with the Rizzo boys, her heart breaking as she remembered the convicts jeering at him, imagined the shame of seeing his name smeared across the news.

He'd said he was grateful the cop who'd loved Trula hadn't lived long enough to see Stone's shame. Deirdre was sure up in heaven the man was beaming with pride. She flattened her hand against the cool glass, wishing she could touch Jake, feel the warmth in him, tell him how much she admired him, respected him.

"Thank God," Deirdre said. "Thank God you're all right. You are, aren't you?" It astonished Deirdre to realize how personal her stake was in the question. She'd only known Lucy for a few hours, but imagining the world without her was unthinkable.

"It's been eight years and counting. When we hit ten, Tank and I are going to do something wild and crazy to celebrate. He's been saving to take the boys and me on a Disney cruise."

"You all deserve it."

"I wish there was something we could give Jake, to

make up for everything he sacrificed that day." Lucy fought to steady her voice. "He gave up everything he'd worked so hard for because he loved us. Even his wife, Jessica, left him when he'd told her what he'd done. How he'd saved us."

"Then she didn't deserve him," Deirdre said, hating a woman she'd never seen. The woman Stone had given his name. How could she have flung it back at him?

But Lucy Rizzo had just met Deirdre. How could the woman be sure Deirdre was any different? "Considering everything that happened, how dangerous this information is, I guess I'm trying to understand… Why take the risk of telling me?"

Lucy took Deirdre's hand in her warm one. "Jake Stone is our best friend. The most honorable man I've ever known. And the kindest. He'd never tell you any of this himself because he's still trying to protect Tank and the boys and me, no matter what the cost to himself. I keep hoping, praying that maybe he can find a woman strong enough to love him the way he loves. Through fire and storm, with all his heart." Lucy's eyes locked with hers. "I'm hoping that woman is you."

Deirdre peered up at Lucy, her heart aching. "You don't understand. I can't…" How could she ever explain? "I live alone. I've always been alone."

"So has Jake," Lucy said, peering out into the sunshine where her children were howling with glee in a wild game of football with their uncle and father. "He deserves better than what life's dealt him. A family of his own." She walked out to join the mayhem.

Deirdre watched as the Rizzos' youngest got hold of the football, his eyes saucer wide as his big brothers charged to make the tackle.

At the last instant, Jake scooped the little boy up onto

his shoulders, carrying the triumphant five-year-old in for a touchdown.

The other boys fell on Stone in a howling mob, trying to take him down. Deirdre's heart ached as the big, hulking man surrendered, carefully setting Joey on his feet before collapsing under the weight of the rest of the Rizzo brood.

"Oh, Jake," Deirdre whispered, dreading once this case was over, thinking just how badly she was going to miss him.

She saw Jake call something to Lucy, Lucy wave back toward the house in reply. Jake disentangled himself from the five rowdy boys and ran toward the kitchen's sliding glass doors, his body working with the effortless grace of an athlete.

He was beautiful, Deirdre thought, her throat tight. Inside and out. Far more heroic than any badge could ever make him, far more selfless than anyone except Tank and Lucy knew.

Not anymore, Deirdre corrected herself. I know.

Jake slid open the door, his hair tousled, his eyes shining, a little anxious, a little uncertain, hoping she was having a good time. "Hey, the party is out here," he said. "Or are you ready to go home?"

Home? To a big house she never wanted, filled with people she didn't know. Where Emma's room would soon be occupied only by her cast-off stuffed animals and posters of Broadway shows she hoped to star in someday.

Where Deirdre's bed stretched, big and empty except for nightmares that turned her cold. Where not even Jake Stone's beautiful strong hands could warm her.

"Dee?" Jake's brow furrowed, his hand brushing lightly across her face. "Did Joey stick a fake tattoo on my forehead or something?"

"No," Deirdre said, her eyes stinging.

Stone's mouth crooked in a smile. "Then what are you looking at?"

"You."

The way your eyes sparkle, the way you grin like you really mean it, the way you handle Lucy's little boys so perfectly it makes me wish that you had your own....

She tingled, imagining what it would be like to make those imaginary babies with Jake, the picture in her head so vivid she could see the wonder, the awe on his face when she told him...

When she told him? Deirdre drew back in horror. She wouldn't be telling Stone any such thing. Some nameless woman who wouldn't chicken out on Stone at the last minute would be the one to put that joy on Stone's face, tell him he was going to be a father....

Oh, God, Deirdre thought. She was losing it. And Stone was so damned good at reading people that he'd be able to tell.

Maybe he could tell that something was wrong, she assured herself, but not what she was thinking. Even Stone wasn't mind reader enough for that. Her eyes dipped down, relief washing through her as she glimpsed a triangle of tanned thigh showing through worn denim. The perfect excuse for her staring. "You tore your jeans."

"Oh. So that's it." Jake brushed off the worst of the grass clinging to his leg, a smear of dirt dark where he'd gone down on one knee. "If you're worried about that reunion of yours, don't. I clean up pretty good. And we'll start on those dancing lessons of yours tomorrow, all right?"

Deirdre nodded. She couldn't squeeze words past the lump in her throat.

"Dee," he said, taking hold of her hand. "What's the problem? You're still looking at me all weird."

Don't you see? You're my problem, Deirdre wanted to say. *After today I can never look at you the same way again.*

She couldn't tell him that, so she reached up on tiptoe instead and kissed him softly on the cheek, wishing for a life she could never have.

CHAPTER 16

JAKE PROWLED HIS LIVING ROOM, more nervous than he'd been in the stuffy room at the courthouse, waiting for the verdict in his trial eight years ago. He scowled down at Ellie May who was staring up at him soulfully.

"So she's coming over here for the first time since we started dating. Big deal. It doesn't mean I'm going to get laid."

So why did you change the sheets? Ellie's big brown eyes demanded. *And you won't let me take my afternoon nap up on the bed.* Sometimes Stone hated it when his dog started to think too loud.

"My motto is Be Prepared," Stone told her. "I was a goddamned Boy Scout when Trula dragged me to Illinois. She and Manoletti thought it would be good for my character."

Ellie tilted her head to one side, the wrinkles on her face sliding toward the floor. She looked so ridiculous, Jake had to chuckle.

"Yeah, I know that at first glance it looks like not much good came of it. But some of the damned stuff must have rubbed off on me or I'd never have survived the past fourteen days."

The days since the Rizzos' picnic; since something in Deirdre had changed. Jake's heart skipped a beat as he pictured the new softness in her eyes when she looked at him, the new tenderness when she touched him, the sweetness in her kisses. What had changed? She hadn't said. He'd been too cautious to ask. Maybe she wasn't even aware of how different she was acting.

Deirdre, his strong, defiant, in-your-face Deirdre... letting her guard down little by little, until tonight...

"It doesn't mean a damned thing," Jake told Ellie. "At least not necessarily..." *The hell it doesn't,* the horny bastard inside Jake snapped.

Deirdre had surprised him, no question, when she'd called to tell him that Emma was spending the night with her best friend. He'd tried so hard to sound casual, while his imagination went into overdrive. "Great, yeah, that's great. Terrific," he'd said. "She could use a good time...."

And so the hell could we...let me show you one....

Deirdre had hesitated, then her voice had grown suddenly shy. "I thought maybe we could have our dancing lesson over at your house. Finn and Cade got back, and they said they could handle things at March Winds tonight."

He'd wanted to ask Deirdre why they'd volunteered. Had she asked them? But he didn't want to spook her. "Great. My house. What time?"

"The usual?"

It made him feel so damned good. He and Deirdre had a usual time. And after weeks of dating, she was coming to his house. Where they could be alone.

Jake looked around the bungalow he'd fallen in love with the first moment he'd seen it. The clean lines, the comfort, the simple beauty spoke to him when life as a cop had seemed so damned complex. But tonight, as he prowled the house he'd perfected for ten long years, he didn't see the wood trim richly glowing, or the classic lines of his Stickley-style furniture, he didn't see the plush rugs or glassed-in bookcases or the tiles on the fireplace some artisan had made by hand.

He saw tiny flaws he'd never noticed before, imagined imperfections as he tried to see the place through Deirdre's eyes. Oh, she'd seen his front office that first day, but during the past weeks of their relationship, they'd always met at March Winds. With Finn gone to Montana, Deirdre was shouldering all of the responsibilities at the thriving bed and breakfast, and after Emma's foray up to Sullivan's Point, Deirdre was determined to be home whenever her daughter's boyfriend came around.

There was simple logic to Deirdre's insistence that he pick her up for their dates at the old Civil War–era mansion, Jake had to admit. But in spite of all that, it hadn't taken him long to see beneath that whole smoke screen to get a glimpse at the fear that lay beneath.

Deirdre was scared. Pure and simple. Avoiding the chance that they might be alone with a bed nearby. She didn't want to risk trying to make love with him again, risk failing.

He'd done what he could to build her confidence. Touching her any chance he got, teasing her, playing at love the way he'd seen Tank and Lucy do for so long. He'd talked and listened and let her know she was beautiful, made her laugh and pulled her chain just to get her fired up so he could kiss her.

And their dancing…from the moment he'd taken her in his arms she'd been pure sin. Just moving with her across a floor was sexier than anything he'd ever done before.

The music was in her blood and bone, under her breasts where her heart beat, in her slender legs where they touched his. He tangoed with her, played salsa music, teaching her steps so sensual it left his good intentions hanging by a thread. He'd promised himself he wouldn't push her, he'd let her tell him when she was ready to take their relationship to the next level. He would just build the fire, win her trust, let her find the passionate woman he knew was in there hiding.

He'd been taking so many cold showers Ellie May was starting to question his sanity, and the hit he'd taken in the crotch at the Rizzos' was seeming like no big deal since he was in a constant state of arousal.

Until just the sound of her voice on the phone, just the scent of her on the sweater she'd forgotten in his car, just the thought of her before he fell asleep alone in his great big bed left him hard and aching and wanting far more than she was ready to give him.

He'd wondered if frustration was ever fatal. If she lay awake at night remembering where he'd touched her.

But all his waiting and wondering might be over tonight. A sudden sadness dogged Jake. Sex wasn't love, and love took absolute honesty about things that mattered. Telling Jessica about the choice he'd made eight years ago had left him wary, a part of him forever cut off in secret and shadow.

If he'd be the only one in danger, he'd tell Deirdre the truth in a minute. But there was so much more to it than him. The danger to Tank's career, the Rizzo family's security. The insurance that they'd need if, God forbid, Lucy's cancer came out of remission. Not to mention Tank's pride. Jake knew how much it cost Tank every day to live with the sacrifice Jake had made. Knew if the survival of Tank's family hadn't depended on silence,

Tank would never have been able to bear the burden Jake's actions had left on his friend's sense of honor.

Sure, it was a done deal now. They'd all made their peace with it as best they could. Not as if they had any real choice. But to expose Tank that way, even to a woman Jake loved… It would be the final betrayal. One step Jake could never make.

The doorbell rang, startling Jake from his reverie. He jumped as Ellie May roused herself enough to bay at the door.

"I know, I know. She's here." Jake's heart hammered under his ribs. "It's no big deal."

Yeah, Ellie May seemed to say. *And a Chihuahua is a hell of a watch dog.*

Jake crossed to the door, wiping his palms on his black slacks. Damned if his palms weren't sweating. Sucking in a steadying breath, he opened the door.

The porch light drenched Deirdre in a golden glow from her crown of dark hair to her toes. She wore a flame-red silk tunic and matching pants that flowed in liquid sensuality down her legs. Silver hoops dangled from her earlobes, and her lips glistened red.

Have mercy, Stone thought, trying to remember how to breathe.

"You said I needed to wear something that I could move in so you could teach me that lift and stuff…you remember? The one where you almost ripped out the seat of my jeans?"

"I remember." He remembered every brush of her body against his, hard against soft, man against woman, where touch conveyed more than words ever could.

"You meant a dress, but I don't own one. I just…always feel silly in them."

Maybe, Stone thought, *but you'd look like the hottest dream I ever had.*

"What you're wearing is great. So, uh, come on in." He stood aside, gestured toward his living room.

She entered, her gaze traveling slowly over everything he'd worked so hard to make home. "This place is really amazing. So...I don't know. It's easy to breathe in here. Sometimes all that Victorian clutter makes me feel claustrophobic."

Stone smiled. "It doesn't really seem your style."

"It's right for the house, for the business. I just have to deal." She hunkered down, stroking Ellie's velvety ears. "Hey, wrinkle puss."

Ellie gave a moan as if saying, *He's been driving me crazy. For God's sake, put him out of his misery, will you?*

Stone crossed to the turntable he still kept in tip-top shape, grabbed one of the vinyl records he'd set out for the night's lesson. "I thought we'd start with—"

"Jake," she cut in.

He looked at her, saw tension in her, like a string about to snap. "Yeah?"

Color flooded into her cheeks, until she almost matched her shirt. "I didn't come over here to dance."

Stone's fingers clenched on the record so hard it should have cracked, his mouth suddenly dry.

Deirdre straightened, hugged her arms tight around her middle. "Staring at me like that isn't going to make this any easier."

Jake put down the record and fumbled with the CD player instead. The music was an easy call. He'd been listening to it nonstop since the first time he'd kissed her. "So you're, uh, wanting to..."

Her eyes turned pleading. "Don't make me say it."

"No." Jake hit the play button. Jazz poured into the room like dark chocolate, powerful, sensual, a melding of pain and strength, power and survival, hope...

He closed the space between them, drew her into his arms. "You don't have to say anything. Just feel."

"Stone, I'm scared out of my wits, here. Maybe you've got some Scotch to take the edge off?"

"No way, baby. I want every cell in your body awake when I take you. I want you to remember every touch, every time I taste you. How about instead of a drink we just dance a little, see if that relaxes you?"

"Easy for you to say."

"I've been a nervous wreck. Just ask Ellie May. I even changed the sheets just in case... Otherwise, I figured I'd take another cold shower. You've been saving my water heater a lot of mileage."

She laughed. It was a little strained, Stone gauged, but a laugh was good. She hadn't figured it out yet, but sex was supposed to be fun.

"Have I mentioned you take my breath away tonight?"

Her dark hair tousled about her catlike face, all elegant bones and big, wary eyes and attitude. Her lips gleamed red under a thin coat of gloss, blusher highlighting her cheekbones. The red silk skimmed her body like his hands would soon, memorizing Deirdre by touch.

"Stone, you are so full of it." The sparkle came back into her eyes. "You just want to get me in bed."

"Oh, yeah. There's nothing in the world I want more." *Except to keep you there forever. To tell you I love you. Beg you to be my wife. Marry me...*

Way to kill the mood, Stone. It would scare the lady to death.

Dance. He could almost hear Trula's voice in his head.

Deirdre cocked her head, listening. "Who is this?" she said, pointing toward the speakers.

"Diana Krall. Ever since I've known you sing, I can't seem to listen to anything else. She reminds me of you."

"I never sang any jazz."

"I'd think you'd be a natural. It sounds like you."

"My mom loved it, so there was no way I was going to touch the stuff. But it's beautiful. It sounds like...sex. At least the way I think sex should be with someone you... care about."

Go ahead. Say it. I love you and you love me. Do you love me?

The woman trusted him enough to go to bed with him after everything she'd been through, he told himself. Isn't that enough?

Jake slid his hand around to the small of her back, cupped the fingers of his other hand around hers. He drew her toward him until their hips brushed and he could feel her heat.

The track changed and he felt for the rhythm, a pulse in the music matching the beat of his heart. He bent her backward over his arm, her slender neck arched back. He could see a flutter in the hollow of her throat. Her hips pressed tight against his growing arousal as he swept her in a half circle to one side, then brought her face back up to inches away from his, leaving her breathless.

Magic...they moved across the hardwood floor, Stone instinctively leading her around furniture, angling bodies so the tips of her nipples abraded the front of his royal blue dress shirt. He felt her stiffen, stumble. He drew her so close he could breathe words in her ear.

"Trula was right. She always told me someday I'd find a woman who would make all those dance lessons worth it. If those jocks who used to laugh at me saw me now, they'd be so damned jealous."

"Tell 'em to get in line, Stone. I could step on their toes, too."

"You wouldn't make one misstep if you'd just trust

yourself. You feel the music just like I do. Your body knows what to do when it's this close to mine. Look at me, Dee. Right here. Into my eyes."

She swallowed hard, and raised her gaze from his chest up past his chin, his lips, to where he knew his eyes were hot for her.

A sizzle of awareness shot through his palms, his arousal rock hard where it met her softness. She caught her lip between her teeth, the sight so delectable Stone could barely keep himself from kissing her. She wasn't ready. Not yet. But she would be.

He whirled her into the sensual combinations he'd taught her, his muscular thigh slipping between hers, her inner thigh ghosting across his, the contact electric. He bent her back over his arm again, this time flattening his other hand on her ribs, sliding his spread fingers up, between her breasts, along her throat, then back into her hair.

She was melting now. He could feel her resistance softening, opening, urging him on.

When he swept her up again, he dragged her full length against him, his mouth fastening on hers.

She moaned, opened her lips, all vulnerability and wanting. Stone scooped her up in his arms, carried her to his bedroom. Laid her down on his big bed. Red silk against teal-green bedspread.

His hands went to the buttons on her tunic, the slippery fabric sliding down her sides as he bared her breasts.

Her bra, black lace, let glimpses of soft, peachy skin peep through, the disks of her aureoles darker, even more enticing through the openwork pattern. Stone knew damned well Deirdre was a white cotton kind of girl, as simple and straightforward as she was. This black lace—she'd worn it for him. He was awed by her courage, humbled by her trust, half out of his mind with wanting her.

He groaned, his long fingers hooking the fastening between Deirdre's breasts. It popped open, and Jake buried his face in the cleft where it had been. He kissed her, a hot, slow, wet kiss on velvety skin, then edged the bra cup aside with his mouth and nose, drinking in the spicy woman scent of her breast.

His hand cupped the other breast, bared it, his thumb teasing the nipple until it pebbled against his thumb. His mouth fastened, hungry and hot on her other nipple, sucking it deep into his mouth, drinking her in.

He slid his hand down her belly to the waistband of her pants. Bless whoever invented elastic. He only had to pause a heartbeat to insinuate his fingers under the band and then…heaven. He was underneath her panties. Skin impossibly soft, silky down. His fingers dipped lower into all that wet heat.

Her body was ready for him…if he could only keep her from thinking of that other time…that other man.

Stone slid the pants off her. She looked like an exotic flower, the red tunic, spread around her like petals, her pale, slender body its stem.

Stone unfastened the top two buttons of his shirt, then whipped it over his head. He didn't have time to undo buttons all the way. He didn't want to give her too much time to think.

He undid his pants, shucked off shoes, socks and boxers, damned glad to be naked. She sat up, letting the sleeves of the tunic slide down her arms, the bra straps following. Light poured over her naked body.

Cover her up, you damned fool, Stone thought. *Drape yourself over her so she doesn't get shy.* But damned if he could make himself do it. She was fire and passion and strength and light and every dream Stone had ever had, and he wanted to burn the image of her into his mind, so he could keep it forever.

Even if you can't keep her.

The thought knifed him in the chest. He tried to shove it away, but the simple truth stayed with him.

Deirdre had made it clear that once the case was over they were finished. She didn't want anything permanent. Hell, it was a miracle she wanted to have sex with him. Why couldn't he just be satisfied with that?

Because he wanted the whole ball of wax. His ring on her finger. His baby growing inside her. His hands on her every night for the rest of his life.

Hey, Dee, funny thing. You know that great guy you met the other day? I took the fall for Tank eight years ago, so I'd be the one thrown off the force....

Tank would see that she knew. It would be in her eyes. The shame of it. The censure. And Stone—she'd make him some kind of a goddamned hero. When the truth was he just hadn't known what else to do.

"Jake?" Her tremulous voice brought him back to his bedroom, her naked body, this chance to get it right. "You can touch me now."

His hands shook just a little as he lowered himself down onto his bed beside her, angled his body over her side. His shaft against the velvety hot hollow of her hip. He couldn't keep from arching it against her, a groan tearing from his lips.

"I want to do this right, Dee. Everything perfect for you."

"Kiss me. I'm starting to get...cold."

Jake found her sweet, hot mouth with his, kissed the fear out of her, kissed her warm. His hand played across her rib cage, her stomach, her breast, taking her all in.

He'd been thinking out his strategy for weeks, how he'd bring her to the point of no return, every trick or talent or fantasy he could use to break down that last wall inside her.

But the instant he felt her small hand search its way down his body, timidly close around his hardness, his big plans were blown to hell. She was so damned brave, was all he could think, when he imagined how she'd been hurt by some other man. He felt murderous fury, felt crushing responsibility and gratitude so deep he almost drowned in it.

He held his breath, let her explore him until he had to grit his teeth and gently draw her hand away.

Deirdre met his eyes, worried. "Wasn't I...doing that right?"

"Have mercy." Stone gave a shaky laugh. "You were doing it *too* right, honey. Tonight's about you, and I'm not a saint. I'm the bad cop, remember?"

A strange expression came into her eyes, tenderness, and...something a little like love. She cupped her hand against his cheek, kissed along the line of his jaw. "I know all about you, Jacob Stone," she murmured, setting his skin on fire. "I like it that you're bad. I think it's sexy."

Stone swore under his breath, rolled her underneath him, pinning her between his hard body and his bed. His mouth was all over her, tasting her, nipping at her, soothing the place his teeth had teased with his tongue. She kissed him back, her nails against his shoulders unbearably erotic. He arched against her, sweet temptation, feeling how ready she was to take him, knowing he'd only have to shift his hips just a little, spread her legs a little wider and he could drive himself home.

Don't do it, you selfish jerk. This is about Deirdre...she has to be so hot she can't think, want you so bad she can't remember....

Stone kissed her throat, her body, suckled her breast with exquisite care. She moaned, and he knew the sensations were getting too intense. She tried to pull him back up to her mouth.

He glided slowly downward, kissing her belly, her hip, his breath teasing her where she'd never felt a man's mouth before.

"S-Stone...Jake, no..."

"Just let me try it. It'll feel so damned good if you let me. I'll stop if you want me to. I swear it, Dee."

She looked down her body at him, so damned vulnerable. Maybe he'd gone too far too fast. But it just felt so right. He wanted all of her. Wet and needing and mindless, flying apart the way she deserved to.

She nodded. The tiniest damned nod Jake had ever seen. It was enough. He spread her legs a little wider, kissed her stomach and then...

DEIRDRE JERKED as his tongue found her, wicked... wild...so primitive a possession she was drunk with it. He took his time, mouth and hands, until every atom of her body was focused there and she felt herself start to shake. Her legs, her hands, so restless, so intense it was almost pain. She threw her arm over her eyes as she writhed under Jake's strong hands, but the image of his dark head between her pale thighs was burned onto the insides of her eyelids.

She felt empty...so empty it was driving her wild. She arched against him.

His finger teased, slipped inside her. It wasn't enough. She was going to flame, turn to ashes, but she wanted him with her.

What had he said? All of me...take all of me...

With a strength she didn't know she possessed, she

grabbed at his shoulders. "Jake, I want you. Now. I want—"

He sheathed himself in a condom. A heartbeat later, he was on top of her, full length, the hard length of him against the ember he'd stoked to an inferno. He felt so hard, smelled so good, his whole body magic against her. But he was so big…what if it hurt…?

Don't let me think. Please, God, don't let me think….

She felt the tip of him, there, almost there. *This is Jake,* she told herself. *My Jake. He'll take care of me.*

She ran her hands down his back to his hard buttocks. Felt muscles bunch, then the opening of her, the slow excruciatingly pleasurable filling of her, inch by inch. She arched her hips, the power of him, the rippling, hard muscles, the maleness of Jake Stone taking her breath away.

It didn't hurt. It felt… "Oh," she gasped as Stone moved inside her. He rested his forehead on hers, his eyes filling her whole world.

"Shh," he hushed her. "We're gonna take this slow, Dee…" He half groaned, half laughed. "Even if it kills me."

"This is about me, Stone," Deirdre breathed, wriggling against him. "You make me want to…to… Oh, oh, Jake… Not slow. Fast. Hard. I want—" He drove deep, every muscle in his body clenched, and yet she could still feel it. He was being careful.

She didn't want careful. Didn't want to feel breakable and small. She wanted all the power Stone had shown her she possessed, all that passion he'd promised was inside her.

"I won't break," she said, pulling his mouth down to hers. "Not with you."

He lost it. She felt his control shatter. He filled her,

inside of her, all around her, long, strong delicious strokes that hammered at the last kernel of fear inside her. She was splitting wide-open, felt the pleasure building, like flood tides hammering against some dam inside her she couldn't see.

"Come on, Dee," Stone pleaded, so ragged, so urgent. "Do it. Come for me…you're…so damned…hot I can't…hold back…much longer."

Deirdre's head tossed against the pillows, a low scream escaping her lips. Her whole body convulsing, her whole being seeming to fly apart. She was coming and coming and it went on and on and on. Stone swore, driving into her, feeling her stripped naked down to her soul.

He cried out her name. She felt him go rigid, a guttural moan racking his body. Then he collapsed on top of her, his breath rasping in her ear, his heart pounding against her chest, his hair damp and silky on her cheek.

She held him, even as he eased most of his weight off her, his face still buried in the hollow of her neck.

"Jake," she whispered, her eyes burning.

He raised his head up, eyes so dark with concern, so beautiful her tears fell free.

*Don't love me…*part of her said. The other, deeper place begged, *Oh, Jake, do.*

"You're crying." Jake slid all the way off her, his handsome face stricken with guilt. "I'm so damned sorry, Dee. I shouldn't have— I should have been careful. I hurt you."

"I'm crying because…you didn't hurt me, you big…big dope." A sob caught on her breath. "Jake, I…I got it right. After thirty-three years, I…"

Pride and triumph transformed his face, his grin flashing so bright it all but blinded her. "You sure as hell did." He gathered her into his arms, rolled her on top of him, laughing. "I didn't do too bad, either. For a bad-ass private investigator, I mean."

He expected her to laugh. Instead she pulled away from him.

"Uh, about that bad cop stuff," Deirdre said, suddenly so serious he went still. "There's something you should know."

"What? Dee, you're freaking me out here. The sex was great, but your follow-up needs a little work."

"Lucy told me."

Stone jackknifed up in the bed, staring down at her, looking like an angry pirate with his dark hair falling to his shoulders. "Lucy told you *what?*"

She moistened lips still swollen and red from his kisses. "How you saved her family. How you took the fall for Tank. You gave up your own dream of being a cop because you loved them."

Stone swore, climbed out of bed. He stalked across the bedroom, all naked, angry male. "She was a damned fool to do that. Last time I told somebody they almost blew the lid off the whole deal."

"I'm not your ex-wife," Deirdre said.

"She told you about Jessica, too?" Stone said, outraged. "What the hell was she thinking?"

"That you were too honorable to tell me yourself. And that you wouldn't...wouldn't feel right keeping secrets from someone you might...well..."

"Love?" Jake snapped. "Why don't you just go ahead and say it since I'm dead sure Lucy spit it out. Why the hell not, after everything else she blabbed. That's no big deal."

Deirdre was looking at him with eyes so deep and blue he could dive into them. "Do you?" she asked. "Love me?"

"Yeah, so what if I do?" Stone turned, hands on hips,

glaring. "You made it crystal clear that you like your life the way it is. When I find your father we're finished. But maybe I'll get lucky and never find him. Maybe you'll have to deal with me forever. Maybe I'll pay the guy to stay the hell away."

He felt betrayed, felt relieved. Didn't know how the hell he felt, truth to be told. Lucy broke his trust. She'd...told Deirdre all the secrets he'd been sure would keep them apart. Removed the only barricade to the relationship Jake wanted with this woman. Lucy had made "forever" possible.

He was going to shake her silly for the risk she'd taken.

Then he was going to buy her a new red dress and take her and Tank out on the town.

But Deirdre was gazing up at him as if he were some sort of white knight. It didn't sit right with him. His armor was tarnished as hell.

"I'm sure Lucy made it sound like I was...was a hero or something."

"Weren't you?"

Jake raked his hands through his hair. "Hell, no. I just... It happened so fast. Maybe if I'd had time to think about it I wouldn't have had the guts to just cut everything I wanted loose. And then it was too late, you know? It was a done deal. We just had to wade through it as best we could."

"Nice story. But as I've mentioned before, Stone, you're so full of bull."

"Damn it, Dee, I'm telling you the God's honest truth. I've questioned what I did a dozen times. Wondered where I'd be now if I were still on the force. If I'd ever have made police chief, or detective like everybody said I would, instead of making a living following cheating husbands and tracking down con men who swindled old women. That first day when you came here, all the stuff you said about my job—plenty of it is true."

"Except the sacrifice you made to get here. And the courage you had to make a new start with a manslaughter charge hanging over your head. So that cons like those jerks who were here that day could taunt you, torment you."

"Oh, yeah. That's right. They used words," Stone said with burning sarcasm. "*That* hurt."

"My words did. And I'm sorry." She climbed out of bed. She looked so damned small. How could something so delicate be so damned strong?

She came toward him, but he felt too raw. He turned away, grinding his fingers against his eyes. "I swore I wouldn't tell you. I meant it. But I...damn, the last few weeks I wanted to. You'll never know how close I came, because...you're everything I've ever wanted, Deirdre McDaniel. Everything I was so sure I couldn't have anymore. Damn it, I love you. Okay? So...I know this isn't great news to you. You wanted to keep things light—clear up this little sex hang-up you had and have some fun, a relationship with a finite ending, just the way you needed it to be. But that's the way I feel. I can't help it if you don't feel the same—"

"Shut up and listen, mister." She pressed her fingertips to his lips. "Don't even *try* to tell me how I feel, because even I don't know. I'm scared and I'm flattered and I'm all shaken up inside. The only thing I *do* know is...I don't want to go home tonight. Emma won't be home until noon."

She took his hand, tugged him toward the bed. Throwing back the covers, she pulled him down with her. "Can't this be enough? For now?"

Jake had been so sure that it would be—sex, dancing, good times to remember. But now...

He had to be truthful. "I want more."

"I know" was all she'd say as she pulled him into her arms once more.

IT WAS EIGHT IN THE MORNING when the telephone buzzed. Jake rolled over, reached across Deirdre's sated, sleep-softened body to grab the receiver for the portable phone. He grimaced, noticing that sometime after they'd slept Ellie May had sneaked up on the bed. Deirdre was sandwiched between Stone and his dog. He grinned. Good. She couldn't escape.

"Jake Stone," he said, low.

"I'm a representative for Mr. Jim Rivers, calling in regards to your inquiry."

"Just a minute." Stone swore inwardly, splashed awake as if by ice water. Deirdre stirred against him. He sat up, turning his back to her. Careful not to disturb her, he slipped out of bed. He grabbed his dark blue silk robe, slipped it on, then padded, barefoot into the living room.

"I'm right, aren't I?" Stone demanded, keeping his voice low. "He's the man I've been looking for."

The caller cleared his throat delicately. "A famous man like Mr. Rivers gets all kinds of crank calls, people trying to get their hands on a piece of his fame or a chunk of his money any way they can."

Stone's lip curled in disgust. "My client doesn't want his money. She wants to know if he's her father. It's that simple."

The asshole laughed. "Really, Mr. Stone. It never is."

"You listen to me," Stone said fiercely. "I sent you a copy of the letter Emmaline McDaniel wrote to your client. I've spoken to the friend she confided in and—"

"I know all that. You documented everything very professionally. Traced the path to Mr. Rivers quite convincingly. Enough so that he's willing to see this, er, young woman—"

"His biological daughter."

"Well, that's to be established. You may have heard of Mr. Rivers's jazz band, Spunky Bottoms?"

"Anyone who's ever listened to jazz knows they're one of the greats."

"Yes. Well, as it happens, they will be playing a theater in St. Louis day after tomorrow. He'd be willing to see Ms. McDaniel after the show."

"I'll tell her."

"A complimentary ticket will be waiting at the box office."

"Better make that two. I'm coming with her."

The caller hesitated, sounded a little patronizing. "As you wish, Mr. Stone. But if you have any plans to bilk my employer out of money, or blackmail him with some kind of exposé, I think I should warn you Mr. Rivers has a staff of lawyers who will make that impossible."

Rage settled over Stone. His fingers clenched on the phone. "I'll tell you what. You tell your employer to watch his manners. I don't like what you're insinuating. When it comes to Ms. McDaniel, I'm a pretty damned fierce watchdog. You got that?"

The man on the other end of the line gave a nervous laugh, almost as if he could feel Jake's hand around his scrawny throat. "The show is at eight o'clock."

"We'll be there." Stone jabbed the off button on the phone, trying to imagine how he was going to tell Deirdre. What she'd feel. What changes this might set in motion.

What if she called it quits? This thing the two of them had. What if she thanked him and told him she never wanted to see him again? Stone's gut went cold.

He needed to slip back in bed with her. Maybe make

love to her one more time before he told her. He'd made her scream two more times last night. Maybe she'd be too sore to do it again.

But damn it, selfish bastard that he was, he wanted her. Wanted to stake his claim on her. Wanted one more chance to convince her they belonged together before it all came apart.

He turned. His heart dropped. Deirdre stood framed in the bedroom doorway, her red tunic wrapped about her, skimming midthigh, her feet bare and white on the floor, her eyes wide and shadowed by a haunting dread.

"You found him," she said faintly.

Stone swore inwardly. No way out. Damn, why did he have to be so good at his job?

"Who is he?"

"Ever heard of a jazz band named Spunky Bottoms?"

"I think Mom had some of their records. Their sax player is legendary. Does some vocals. Big Jim something or other."

"Big Jim Rivers." Stone watched her face. "He's your father."

STONE WANTED HER TO STAY, but Deirdre stumbled toward home in a haze, needing to be alone to deal with so many things: the fact that Stone loved her; maybe, God help her, she loved him; and that one of the greatest jazz musicians of all times was her father.

The man who'd gotten her mother pregnant and then vanished, leaving Emmaline McDaniel alone to try to piece together her already rocky marriage, and go on with her life as if she'd never recklessly fallen in love and into bed with another man.

If there was ever a warning...against love and marriage beyond the mess Martin and Emmaline McDaniel had made of it—this whole bit with Big Jim Rivers was one.

She turned her car down the road to Jubilee Point, grateful Emma wouldn't be home until noon. The last thing she needed was a bout of her daughter's theatrics, though Emma seemed to be handling things better lately. At least handling Stone better. He'd bribed her by buying five tickets to the local dinner theater with Deirdre, Stone, Drew and Trula completing the party.

Stone had done his best to charm Emma, and yet Deirdre wasn't sure how she felt about it. She'd sworn when Emma was small she wouldn't have men leaping into and out of her daughter's life. Emma needed stability. What about a father?

She'd never been able to even think of the word in connection to Emma without getting a sick feeling in the pit of her stomach. And now Emma was all grown-up, would soon be leaving home.

She still wouldn't have anybody to walk her down the aisle someday, a voice inside her accused. She'd have Cade. The Captain. She could take her pick.

But it was Jake Stone's smoky eyes that rose in Deirdre's mind, his hair loose against the corded muscles of his neck, black silk, tanned satin.

"Oh, God. I'm so confused," Deirdre said aloud as she pulled into the driveway, heaving a sigh of relief when she saw all the cars were gone. The guests had already cleared out for a day of antiquing or rambling along the river. She only hoped Finn and Cade had cleared out, as well. She parked the van and climbed out the passenger door, catching a glimpse of herself in the side mirror. Her lips were pink and a little swollen, her cheek whisker-burned. She hadn't even brushed her hair. She looked as if she'd spent all night in the arms of a very bad man. And then crashed to earth with a bang.

Seemed like her birth father had Deirdre's rotten sense of timing.

But she'd get herself put to rights—a hot shower, her hair washed and tamed. Throw on a pair of jeans and a baggy T-shirt and feel like her usual self again. Except that she would still feel almost painfully tender in all the places Jake had touched her—her body, her heart.

She opened the kitchen door, walked in.

"It's about time you got home." Emma sat at the kitchen table, a thunderous expression on her face, the cotton panties Deirdre had lost in the gazebo in a crumpled heap next to the yearbook Emma was going through.

"What...what are you doing home?"

"Jessie got the flu, so her mom dropped me off last night. When I got up this morning your bed hadn't been slept in. Aunt Finn said you were going over to Jake's."

Damn. Deirdre dragged one hand wearily through her hair. She didn't need this right now.

"Listen, Emma, I've had kind of a tough morning. Stone made some progress on my case." She wasn't ready to share the fact that in just a few days she'd be meeting her birth father.

"Oh, so that's why you were over at Jake's all night," Emma sniped. "Just talking business. That's why your clothes look like they lay on the floor all night and your hair is a mess."

Deirdre took a deep breath and counted to ten. "I'm really tired. I'm sorry you were worried, but I had no way of knowing you'd be home early."

"Or what? You'd have left me a note? Sleepover at Stone's house—don't worry, I packed my condoms."

"Emmaline Kate, I'm the parent here. I'm thirty-three years old and I—"

"So that makes it all right? Do you love him?" Emma demanded fiercely.

Deirdre's cheeks flamed. "I don't...it's not...that simple."

"What a hypocrite!" Emma smacked her palms on the table and jumped to her feet. "You go all crazy on me for letting Drew cop a feel up at Sullivan's Point and then you go have sex with a guy you don't even love."

"Emma—"

"I *love* Drew. But I'm not supposed to have sex with him—"

"You're sixteen, damn it! It's not the same thing at all! Think! If you got pregnant—"

"What if you did?" Emma flung back. "You got knocked up having casual sex before! Didn't you learn your lesson?"

"Emma," Deirdre struggled for patience. "You're crossing the line, here."

"You're the one who keeps crossing the line!" Emma stared at her, wide eyes filled with defiance and pain. "Since this sex thing is no big deal to you, maybe you can help me out. I've been trying to figure out who my father is. I've circled all the likely prospects. Anybody who looks anything like me. Could you narrow it down a little?"

Deirdre's hand shot out. She stopped it an instant before she struck her daughter's face. She clenched her fingers, looked down at the table, fighting for balance. Horror flooded through her. Black marker circled faces, big Xs marked others.

"Emma, go to your room," Deirdre said, fear making her cold inside.

"Fine. I'll go." She slammed the yearbook shut. "But remember this. You can't stop me any more than the Captain could stop you. I'll do what I want. At least I'll be having sex with someone I love. And my father—I'll find him, too. It's all about making choices, right, Mom?

Isn't that what you told me? Just don't you ever dare preach to me about Drew again!"

Emma spun around, yearbook clutched to her chest, and ran out of the room. Deirdre heard her footsteps pounding up the stairs. Deirdre sank down into a chair, her whole body shaking. One of the circles had been around Adam Farrington's face.

CHAPTER 17

THE ORNATE THEATER five blocks from the Mississippi whispered of former grandeur, its ceiling painted in vignettes Mark Twain would have approved, a pair of bright-painted paddle wheelers racing up the river.

But despite the elegance of the venue, none of the patrons leaving could speak of anything but the performance that had filled the room twenty minutes before.

Stone wished he could have concentrated only on music, immersed himself in the smoky ache and longing Big Jim Rivers melted into the lyrics he sang, music that captured the feelings roiling inside Jake when he thought of Deirdre McDaniel.

But during the performance, he'd been far too preoccupied with the woman sitting in the red velvet seat beside him. Deirdre had stared at Big Jim Rivers as if there were no one else in the room, and Jake had spent the time wondering what was going through her mind. She looked so fragile, so uncertain, her vulnerabilities stripped bare, while up onstage Big Jim Rivers vibrated with an almost frenetic energy that made Stone think of other musicians whose genius had burned them up until there was nothing left inside.

A perception a couple of die-hard Jim Rivers fans in the row behind Deirdre and Jake echoed, wondering aloud if the big guy was sick. Rivers had been just a little off, missed a cue or something, they'd complained. It just wasn't like him.

Jake grimaced. If Rivers was feeling anything like his daughter tonight, it was probably a miracle the guy had been able to sing at all. From the moment Jake had picked Deirdre up at March Winds, she'd been edgy and quiet. She'd dressed herself so carefully it wrung Jake's heart. Black pencil slacks flattered her slim legs, a flowing tuxedo-style shirt with inch-wide tucks and pearl buttons giving her a bohemian aura, while an electric-blue, white and black scarf portraying stylized musicians splashed color against her face.

For once, she'd even wrestled every hair into place, the tousled chin-length mane Jake loved as subdued as her spirits. Despite makeup more carefully applied than he'd ever seen it, her face looked stiff, pale with bruised circles from sleeplessness smudged beneath her eyes.

Damn, but he wanted to gather her in his arms, kiss her cheeks and muss up her hair. He wanted her all spice and smart-aleck humor, her eyes flashing and her skin flushed with excitement the way it had been just before he made love to her.

Before the phone had rung the morning after and her daughter had been waiting, furious, at the kitchen table once Deirdre reached home. Before the hopes he'd had the night before all came undone.

Don't turn this into some kind of catastrophe, Stone, he warned himself. So things hadn't turned out the way he wished they had on the morning after—hell, in the *week* after—they'd become lovers. That didn't mean their relationship was heading for a train wreck.

So Deirdre was a bundle of nerves. That wasn't surprising after everything that had gone down lately. Merely facing the prospect of meeting a birth father would be enough to mess with most people's minds. Add to Deirdre's list the latest upheaval with Emma and it was no wonder the woman's nerves were strung so tight.

Didn't it just figure that the kid would come home early the one night Deirdre had actually felt safe enough, relaxed enough to spend the night in Jake's bed? The sex had been phenomenal—the best of his life. And Deirdre had broken through the prison of ice left behind by the bastard who had raped her. She'd been fiery, passionate, so brave Stone was humbled by it. If he hadn't already loved her, he'd have lost his heart as she came in his arms.

The climax had rocked both Jake and Deirdre, unleashing a tempest of emotions. Surprise at the trust spun between them. Shaken by revelations painful, perhaps dangerous. The possibility of complete honesty at last making the future Jake hungered for at least a possibility.

Deirdre knew he loved her. But in spite of the wariness that had filled her eyes, he'd seen awe and disbelief, too. She hadn't told him she never wanted to see him again. At least not yet. That had to be a good sign, didn't it?

"Jake?"

Her voice startled him. He turned, seeing how white she'd grown, except for two spots of color on her cheeks.

"Most of the people are gone. I guess it's time."

He'd suggested they wait a little while, until people cleared out. He didn't want her to have to go through this ordeal with groupies and strangers looking on. This was going to be hard enough without some journalist picking up a story for the scandal sheets. Big Jim Rivers Meets Secret Love Child.

Jake's jaw clenched as he imagined what a headline like that would do to the whole McDaniel family, from Deirdre to Emma to Cade and the Captain. The humiliation would be so damaging Jake couldn't bear to think about it.

One more professional hazard for a P.I. was seeing what happened to families when news like that went public. But Rivers had as big a stake in keeping this secret as the McDaniels did. From the way his representative sounded, the internationally famous jazz musician was less than thrilled about this meeting.

Jake stood, took Deirdre's hand to help her out of her seat. Her fingers were like icicles. He could feel a fine tremor work through her.

She glanced up at him, her eyes big, pleading. "Stay with me when I go in there. I don't want to be alone."

Oh, God. Jake felt a fist close in his chest, humbled that this fiercely independent woman had trusted him enough to ask. He wondered how long it had been since she'd asked anyone for help. Let anyone be there for her to lean on.

"I'll do whatever you need," he assured her, feathering his knuckles across her cheek. Stone groped for something to make her smile. "Just promise once Emma leaves home you won't run off with the band."

Was that sorrow in her eyes? "Those days are over for me."

"Do they have to be?" The question fell out before he could stop it. He hadn't meant to stress her out about that, especially not now. But the question troubled him. He'd seen the way the music had affected her, sensed what it must have cost her to bury her passion, her talent that way.

"Stone, I almost gave up my daughter for my music six years ago," Deirdre exclaimed. "Do you understand that? I'll never forgive myself for being so...so unbelievably selfish."

"So you killed the music inside you, like some kind of a sacrificial lamb?"

"I did what I could to live with myself. I...oh, God. Not now. I can't talk about this now."

Stone swore under his breath. "You're right. I'm way out of line. I just..." He hesitated, not knowing how she'd feel if he said it aloud. Hell with it. "I love you, you know? And I feel like there's this huge part of you I've never even heard. Like it's missing."

"It's too late to get it back. The price was too high." She turned and walked up the aisle. The lobby was emptying the last few guests into the street beyond.

Jake crossed to an usher, gave the man the note Rivers had stuck in the envelope with their complimentary tickets.

The usher escorted them back, through halls growing progressively shabbier, to the chaos of backstage. Roadies were scrambling to take the show down, pack things up so the Spunky Bottoms band could get back on the road for their next gig—in Madison, Wisconsin, a band T-shirt Jake had seen at intermission had said.

The usher paused outside a closed door, knocked respectfully. "Mr. Rivers, sir?" he called. "The party you invited backstage is here."

A muffled voice bade them enter. Stone held the door open for Deirdre, knowing the next half hour would change her life forever.

The room was cramped, with a worn green sofa, a giant makeup mirror surrounded by white lights. Stage makeup, a wooden hairbrush and the blue bow tie worn in the performance were cast off on the shelf beneath the mirror. A bottle of Boodle's gin sat beside an empty glass, a wedge of lime among melting ice cubes.

The man on the stool before the mirror turned toward them, his eyes red, his face falling in soft wrinkles, his thin gray hair looking disordered from the frenzy on the stage.

Deirdre stared into the face of the man, trying to imagine he was her father. He seemed so alien, so strange, tall but too thin, as if the cigarette he was smoking and the booze he'd obviously been drinking had somehow shrunken him. His skin, pallid, unhealthy, as if it rarely saw the sun. But then, Deirdre knew about musicians' hours. Night after night in smoke-filled clubs, or playing for audiences like the one tonight. Rivers seemed like so many other musicians she'd known, brilliant but self-destructive, a creature of the dark who rarely saw sun or fresh air or slept in the same bed for more than a few days at a time while on tour.

She'd been so sure she wanted that life for herself when she'd been Emma's age. Why did this sour-smelling little room make her feel as if she needed to get outside where she could draw a lungful of chill autumn air?

"I thought you decided not to come," Rivers said, barely bothering to look at her as he popped open another button on his sweat-soaked white shirt. The lights on stage could be hot as hell. "I couldn't decide whether to be relieved or ticked off." Rivers laid his cigarette in an overflowing ashtray. "How'd you like the show?"

"It was hard to concentrate," Deirdre confessed. "Seeing you on the stage and wondering if…well, if you really are my father."

Rivers turned toward her, his gaze sweeping her from head to toe. A strange expression flashed across his face, then was gone. He held up splayed hands that coaxed such magic from the saxophone. "Honey, aren't you a little old to be lookin' for a daddy? I know you're too big to be sittin' on my knee."

Deirdre stiffened at the sarcasm. She wasn't sure what she'd expected of this meeting, but she knew this wasn't it.

Rivers drawled, "So why don't we get right down to it and you tell Big Jim what the hell you want?"

"I want to know if you're my father," Deirdre said, her cheeks still burning from Rivers's acid remarks.

Jake took control. "It's very common for people to want to know their birth parents, Mr. Rivers. For one thing, Deirdre has a daughter, and needs your health history for practical reasons. And for another, well, it's natural to want to know where you come from to ground yourself."

"Well, if that's the case I'd hit that door runnin', little girl, 'cause I've got no more roots than a tumbleweed, and when it comes to my health, I count on Jim Beam and Lucky Strike cigarettes instead of doctors." Rivers slurred a laugh, watching Deirdre from beneath hooded lids so intently it made the hairs at the back of her neck prickle. "I'll probably live forever. The devil's scared I'll take over."

"Well, since Ms. McDaniel and I probably will die sometime in the next fifty years, maybe we should just get to the point of this visit," Stone bit out. "Are you willing to field a couple of questions?"

Rivers poured himself another tall gin, his brow darkening. "It's still a free country, at least last time I checked. You can ask anything you want. But that doesn't mean I have to answer it."

Frustration poured through Deirdre, leaving her vulnerable, helpless, at this stranger's mercy. "Then why meet with me at all?"

Rivers pinned her with shrewd eyes. "You went to a hell of a lot of trouble, working this supposed relationship of ours out. Can't blame a man in my position for wantin' to find out exactly why you did it. Now, you're supposedly the daughter of a woman named..." Rivers seemed to forget. He glanced at a piece of paper on the shelf, frowned. "Emmaline McDaniel, is that right?"

"Yes," Deirdre said.

"This private investigator you hired—"

"That would be me," Jake inserted grimly.

"Yes, well, maybe you proved I was in the town you listed, during the time you mapped out. But that doesn't prove anything 'cept I might have passed this girl's mama on the street."

His cavalier tone infuriated Deirdre. "According to my mother's letter you did a hell of a lot more than that."

Rivers laughed. "And you think I should remember her, do you? Have her printed in indelible ink in my mind?" Rivers took a gulp of gin. "Honey, in my line of work I go through women faster than I do packs of cigarettes. I'm not trying to be an insensitive bastard, but thirty-four years is a long time to remember some affair that lasted a few weeks in a town I was just passing through on my way to fame an' fortune."

"My mother remembered you," Deirdre insisted, her stomach leaden with disappointment. "It was obvious my mother loved you. She wasn't the type of woman who would have had a casual affair."

Rivers barked a laugh. "None of them are, darlin', none of them are. It just happens. Music makes 'em crazy."

"Hey," Jake snapped. "You want to show a little respect here? You're talking about her mother."

"I'll talk however I see fit. You're the ones who came

here, poking into my private life." Rivers made a soft sound of dismissal. "You say you want the truth, well here it is. I'm just not a man who can be specific. Had a wife back home and kids of my own back then. Not that they would've stopped me from enjoyin' someone pretty as you. You look like your momma, girl?"

For an instant Deirdre just wanted to run. Flee this smoky, claustrophobic little room and the debauched man inside it. But she'd come too far to turn back now. She dug into her purse, pulled out a worn photograph of her mother holding a two-year-old Cade. "Maybe this will help. It was taken about the time she says you were together."

Rivers took another slug of gin, then lifted the photograph from her hand. He scraped the stool back and climbed to his feet, turned his back to her as he held the photograph to the light.

Did she see his hand tremble just a little? No. She must have imagined it. He turned, running his eyes dismissively over the image one more time. "What she said is possible, I suppose. It's equally possible I never saw her in my life."

"Look closer," Jake ordered, looking grim.

"Won't change a damn thing." Rivers shrugged. "If there was an affair, it was nothin' worth remembering. In the past seventy years I've found not many women are."

Deirdre loathed him. She imagined the Captain in the same position, facing down a strange young woman who might be his daughter. He would have addressed the issue with his usual candor and sense of honor, with a chivalry startling in this day and age.

He would have been worlds different—where Rivers's belly bulged over his belt, Martin McDaniel was still trim.

Where Rivers's eyes looked dulled with alcohol, the Captain's were hawk sharp and alert.

"How about you just spit it out, Ms. McDaniel?" Rivers demanded. "What is it you want from me?"

What did she want from him? Something this man could never give. "I guess I'll have to settle for the truth," she said evenly.

"The truth is this—" Rivers crossed to the window, looked out on the dark Midwestern night "—one of the fringe benefits of singing onstage is that I never go to bed alone unless I want to. And I don't want to very damned often. All the faces run together after a while."

Deirdre felt sick, repulsed, wanted to deny any connection to this man. Yet when he turned back, she saw the shape of her own nose on the man's face, the curve of her little finger matching the one on his hand.

"After going through this information your paid spy gathered, I'll admit, it's possible I made your mother pregnant," Rivers said. "But the hard fact is you're nothin' to me and neither is she. Still and all, I like to keep my life simple. So how about you and I strike a bargain, little girl? I pay you a hundred thousand dollars under the table. One lump sum. In return, you swear I'll never hear from you again."

Deirdre reeled, sickened. "I don't want your money. I don't want anything from you except…"

To feel like I belong, to see where my music comes from, to understand how I came to be and if my mother loved you.

But she couldn't humiliate herself in front of a man like this one. The Captain's craggy face flashed into her mind. Proud. Indomitable. Honorable. Martin McDaniel had raised her better than that, even if he might never forgive her.

Her chin bumped up a notch. "What I need, a man like

you could never give me." She turned and walked out the door, Stone a step behind her. They hurried out of the theater, never once looking back.

She didn't see the jazz musician dig out his wallet, pull a battered photograph from inside it. She didn't see Rivers look at the dark-haired woman and sweet-faced little boy smiling from the image.

Big Jim Rivers buried his face in his hands and wept.

DEIRDRE BARELY NOTICED Jake's hand on her elbow as she burst out the theater door, the cool night air striking her in the face. He drew her around to look at him. She felt his hand curve under her chin, trying to force her to meet his gaze.

"Deirdre, you need to talk about what just happened. Don't shut it up inside."

"Great idea, Stone," she cried, despising herself. "Maybe I'll run over to Cade's when we get home, announce what a gem my birth father is to the whole family. Tell them I must take after the guy, because I'm completely selfish. After all, look what I was willing to put Cade and Finn and Emma and the Captain through."

Jake cut in. "Captain McDaniel isn't completely innocent in this, either, you know. You felt alienated, not good enough—"

"Yeah, that's me. A complete fuck-up. And here, once again, I prove that no one can screw things up better than I can. It's a gift, Jake."

Stone circled her arms with his big hands, gave her a little shake. "You're not responsible for the fact that Big Jim Rivers is an asshole. Or that you were devastated by what you found in that letter."

"The Captain was pretty devastated, too. You should have seen him." She couldn't stop shaking. "All I wanted was for him to walk across the room to me, Jake. I wanted him to hug me. Tell me it didn't matter, you know? I wanted...but it wasn't all about me. He'd just found out his wife had cheated on him, loved another man. That I wasn't his blood daughter."

Jake tried to imagine how he would have felt in Martin McDaniel's place. If he'd just found out Deirdre had been unfaithful, that the daughter he'd never questioned was his own had been conceived by another man. "That would be a hell of a blow to anyone," he said. "Let alone a man like Captain McDaniel."

"I've barely talked to him for weeks. And now...I'm so ashamed. But that doesn't change the hurt between us. But maybe this whole mess will be a relief for him in the end. He finally has an excuse when it comes to me." She dropped her voice low, mimicking the old man's stern voice. "Deirdre makes a mess of things, but at least she's not really mine."

Jake's gaze burned into hers, so full of pain for her she could barely stand to look at him. She started toward the parking garage, wishing she could outrun Stone's voice. But he followed, his long strides easily matching hers.

"You're sure that's what the Captain thinks?" he said. "You can read his mind?"

"I don't have to." Deirdre's voice broke. She wheeled on him, pain stark in her face. "If Emma did the same thing...decided I wasn't enough for her, that she wanted a father she'd never seen...I'd— How would I ever survive it?"

"I don't know how. But you would. You're strong, Deirdre. A survivor."

"That's me, all right. A survivor. Just wall myself off, go through the motions, pretend that everything's just fine."

"You don't have to pretend. Not anymore. I'm here for you, Deirdre. I love you. And so does Emma."

"Oh, yeah. Emma's just crazy about me. But then, I'm the only mother she's got. The Captain got stuck with me."

"Are you sure he sees it that way?" Stone asked, trying to enfold her in his arms. She tore away from him, too raw inside to be touched. She wrapped her arms tight around her middle, storming toward Stone's truck. Jake hit the unlock button on his key ring, and Deirdre wrenched open the door and slid into the seat before he had the chance to open it for her.

Stone rounded the vehicle, climbed into the driver's seat next to her. He put the key in the ignition but didn't start the engine. Deirdre clenched her hands in her lap, not wanting to talk anymore. Just drive... until she could process everything that had happened. Until she could get her emotional shields back up. But why would Jake start cooperating with her now? The man was relentless. Too damned intuitive for his own good. She'd let him see too much, touch places in her soul she should have left buried deep.

"Deirdre, I know you don't want to hear any of this right now."

"But that sure as hell isn't going to keep you from saying it," she flung back.

She heard Stone sigh. "Captain McDaniel is an old man," he reasoned gently. "He's sick and hurting and he thinks you don't want him. What would happen if you went to him first?"

"And said what?" Deirdre choked out.

"I don't know. I wasn't in your house when you were growing up. Just think, Dee. From what you've said I know things weren't perfect between you two."

Deirdre gave a harsh laugh. "Far from it."

"But isn't there some memory you can hang real hope on?"

She tried not to look at him, but she couldn't resist.

Stone pressed her with nothing but his eyes, beautiful storm-gray eyes filled with love for her.

"Isn't there something from the past to help both you and the Captain find your way back to each other?"

"Stone, you don't understand."

"Oh, yes, I do," he said, taking her clenched hand in his. "I know you, Deirdre McDaniel, in ways nobody else ever has. You're a fighter. But you fight fair. And you're damned hard on yourself. I know this will eat inside you like acid, no matter how hard you work to tough it through. And time might be running out. If you don't try to find that common ground with the father who raised you, how are you going to feel once he's gone?"

Anguish tore through her. "Damn you, Stone, I can't…"

"Can't what? Admit you were wrong?" Stone squeezed her hand tight. "Explain to the Captain why you felt you had to do this?"

"I wasn't wrong!" She slammed her other palm against the dashboard. "If he'd made me believe he loved me I never would have searched for a father past my own front door."

Stone's face sobered, his mouth curving, so tender, so full of love. She could see emotions warring inside him. Knew he didn't want to hurt her. But he was more afraid of not telling her the truth.

"And maybe if *he'd* been sure that *you* loved *him*, he would have had the courage to stop you."

Deirdre huddled into her seat, looking small and broken. "Enough, Stone. No more. I can't talk—" Her voice broke. "Just leave me alone."

Stone started the truck, headed out to the highway. Deirdre watched the streetlights flash past, like slides in a carousel. She closed her eyes, almost against her will, as if Jake Stone had unlocked some iron box of memories she kept under lock and key.

Tears burned her eyes, and she heard her father's voice inside her insisting McDaniels never cry. But there had been one time tears had fallen free. One time Martin McDaniel's hand had wiped them tenderly away.

Remember, Stone had charged her. *Remember.*

Her mind flashed to a shallow grave dug beneath the oak tree in the backyard of her childhood home. Spot, wrapped in the jacket to one of her father's old dress uniforms, as the Captain laid him in the ground.

Just fifteen years old, Deirdre's life was already beginning to unravel. Cade beyond her reach, her mother changed, fading like a ghost of the woman she'd been. Deirdre knowing it was all her fault somehow.

She'd clung to Spot even harder, the dog the only warm place in her life still the same. Until he'd gotten so sick she'd had to put him down.

The Captain had taken them both to the vet. She'd held the dog until life slipped away, carried him in her arms all the way home in the Captain's Jeep.

McDaniels don't cry—she'd heard it so many times, a litany in her head. But this one day had been different.

She'd tried so hard to choke back the sobs. But then she'd felt her father's strong arms around her, his voice, funny sounding and thick. He'd told her that sometimes even the bravest soldiers cried when they lost their comrades in arms. That he had cried once in the jungle when his best friend had died, right there next to him. Deirdre and Spot had been fighting the whole world since the day Deirdre brought the mangy mutt into the house, the Captain had told her. And that dog would have died for her in a heartbeat.

Deirdre sobbed inconsolably, clinging to her father for

what had seemed forever until he told her it was time to say goodbye. The Captain lined her up beside the little grave, then stood at attention right beside her as they snapped Spot a sharp salute.

She fell asleep remembering how tired she'd been, exhausted. Cade hundreds of miles away, so he couldn't sit with her all night because she was scared to sleep, the way he had so many times before. But at dawn when her eyes had fluttered open, oh, so briefly, it hadn't been Cade's worried young face she saw. Or her mother's thin, worn-down one. She'd seen the Captain's hawklike face bending over her. Knew for just an instant he'd give anything in his power to breathe life into that dog of hers again.

Jake gently shook her arm, and she woke to see March Winds, a familiar shape in the moonlight. He scooped her in his arms and carried her inside. She was too tired to protest. He carried her past Emma's bedroom, pausing to call softly to the girl.

"Help me get her settled. I don't even know which room is hers." The teenager balked for a moment, then something about her mother's waxen face seemed to shake her out of her pout.

Emma led the way, pulled back the covers on Deirdre's bed. Stone slipped off her shoes and had Emma help divest her of the slim pants. The tuxedo shirt was soft enough for her to sleep in.

He wished he could shuck off his suit coat, kick off his shoes and lie down in the bed with her, gather her close so she could sleep on his chest, so she wouldn't have to be alone. But things were bad enough between her and Emma. And Deirdre had asked in the truck that he leave her alone.

Stone leaned over her, pressing a kiss to her cheek. It still tasted salty, dry tracks from quiet tears.

"What did you do to her?" Emma snapped as they slipped out the door.

Stone looked down at the kid's heart-shaped face, torn by indecision. Deirdre might want privacy to deal with everything she'd learned tonight. On the other hand, if Stone didn't clue Emma in, the kid would probably hammer her about sleeping with him or some such.

"I took her to meet her birth father," he said.

Emma gaped, stunned. "You did? She found him?"

"Yeah. If I'd had any idea what a jerk the man would be, I never would have told her his name."

Emma looked solemn for a long moment, shadows falling over her face, making her look younger somehow, her eyes older. "It wasn't your decision to make," she said. "It was up to Mom. Just like it'll be my choice someday, if I want to meet my real dad."

Stone's gut clenched as he thought what such a quest would mean to Emma McDaniel, the ugliness she'd find at the end of her search. The thought of this innocent young woman stumbling across the story of her conception the way Deirdre had, by accident, sickened Jake.

He looked away from her, trying to conceal his rioting emotions.

"What was his name?" Emma asked.

For an instant horror washed through Stone, and he thought Emma was asking not about Deirdre's secret father, but her own. "What was whose name?" Jake asked, trying to buy time.

"Mom's birth father," Emma said, looking at him so intently he had to turn away.

"He's a jazz musician named Big Jim Rivers. But he wouldn't tell her anything. Just that..." Jake stopped himself. It wasn't as if he could tell this innocent girl what Rivers had said about his revolving sex partners and the fact he didn't even remember Emmaline McDaniel's face. He turned back to Emma. "I guess the only thing that really matters is that he didn't want anything to do with your mom."

"Oh." Emma fretted her lower lip. He could see she was torn between relief and pity.

"Listen, give your mom a break tomorrow, will you? I know things have been rough between the two of you, and she seems tough as nails—but she needs you, Emma. Nobody means more to her than you."

"Then why didn't she listen to me? Leave my family the way I wanted it to be."

"Maybe someday you'll understand." Part of Stone was afraid the kid already did. Deirdre had told him about the old yearbook Emma had been poring through, circling faces that might look like her. Please God, let the kid forget about the whole thing, now that Deirdre's search had turned out to be such a disaster.

But nobody knew better than Jake that it was damned hard to shove something as elusive as curiosity back into a box once you'd set it free.

Jake groped for the right words to make her understand. "Ten years from now when all this stuff between you and your mom settles you're going to have to look back on this. What do you want to feel? That you were right? That you paid your mom back for upsetting the family? Or that you loved her the way she loves you—even when it hurts?"

Emma looked away from him, her cheeks turning red. "I'm not sure."

"It's up to you, kid." Jake looked down into Deirdre's daughter's face. "Just remember you'll have to live with whatever you decide for a very long time." He started to turn, walk out into the night. But Emma caught his arm, stopped him.

"Do you think Mom should, well…be alone? Maybe you should stay with her."

Stone stared at Emma, astonished. "You were mad as hell last time we stayed together."

"It was just…just a shock. She'd never done anything like that before. And it's still hypocritical, you know? Lecturing me like she did, and then…"

Stone stayed quiet, letting the kid piece together what she wanted to say.

"But you know that first time I met you? When I maneuvered you into going to the restaurant with us?"

"Before you figured out that I was ruining your life?"

"Before I knew Mom lied to me. And…whatever. What really matters is why I tricked you in the first place."

"Why was that, Emma?" Stone asked, loving the kid for her courage, her honesty.

"All I've ever wanted was to go to New York, you know? Be onstage. But it wasn't until I got the acceptance letter from my drama school that I realized what that would mean…for Mom, you know?"

"You got your letter?"

"Yeah. A couple of weeks ago."

"Your mom never mentioned it."

"I never told her."

"Why not? She'll be thrilled for you. So proud."

"I know that. She's built her whole life around me in the six years since she came back home. But she's going to be all alone when I go. I guess part of me was hoping that you would, well, fill in the empty space I was going to leave behind."

"I kind of figured it was something like that. Then you realized who I was, what my job was and why your mom had hired me. That changed things, didn't it?"

"Yeah. A lot of things. But…" Emma sucked in a deep

breath. "Maybe you can't help who you love, you know? I'm not as naive as I look. I know guys want sex. Is that all you wanted from Mom?"

"Are you asking me what my intentions are?"

"I guess I am."

"Okay. I'll give it to you straight. I'm in love with your mom. I want to marry her. That honorable enough for you?"

"Whoa. I don't know how I feel about that. I mean, Mom always says be careful what you wish for because it might come true."

"You'll have plenty of time to get used to the idea. She's not sure how she feels about all this, either."

Emma hugged herself, the gesture so much like Deirdre's it made Stone's chest hurt. "Oh, she loves you. Believe me, casual sex isn't my mom's style. You know, she hasn't had a date since we've lived here? And it's not 'cause guys haven't asked her."

"I'm sure that's true."

"If you love her and all that, don't you think you should take care of her better than this? I mean, cutting out on her now when she's all torn up."

"I'm not sure she wants me. And making trouble between the two of you isn't what I had in mind."

"Well, I wouldn't want you jumping her bones or anything, but if you could just hold her..." Emma's eyes misted, wistful. "That's what Drew does when I'm sad."

"You care about Drew a lot, don't you?"

"I love him."

"First love...that's a powerful thing," Jake said, remembering the roller coaster his senior year in high school had been. God, what a ride. The end was rocky, most of them were. But Deirdre's first love hadn't just shuddered to a halt. It had crashed and burned, leaving her scarred forever. Emma's memories of Drew someday would be far sweeter than that.

Stone hugged Emma, his voice soft. "Thank you. For letting me stay."

"You ever hurt her, I'll take you apart a piece at a time," Emma said, dead serious.

I'm not the one who hurt her, little girl, Stone thought, looking down into Deirdre's daughter's eyes. *Please, God, don't ever let Emma find out who did.*

Emma watched Stone turn and go back up the stairs, not sure how she felt. There was so much to sort through, so much to figure out. Her mom in love. Someone besides Emma to take care of her. And only a few more months before New York, leaving Drew behind. He said they'd write letters, talk on the telephone, visit whenever they could. He loved her enough to make it work somehow. Emma believed him.

And yet, to be so far away…from Whitewater, the town she'd hated for so long, from her mom and the twins and Aunt Finn, Uncle Cade and the new baby and the Captain. He was getting older, frail. Someday he wouldn't be there when she came home. But she had to go, had to fly, had to at least reach for her dreams. She was too much a McDaniel to know how not to.

Emma crossed to the window, peered out across the garden, certain she couldn't sleep.

It would be hours still before a light shone in the cabin window. But she knew who'd be the one to turn it on. The Captain, always the first to rise.

She might not know how she felt about her mom yet. But Emma did know this.

She had a promise to keep.

CHAPTER 18

DEIRDRE STIRRED IN BED, fighting monsters she couldn't see. Someone had taken sandpaper to the insides of her eyelids and rasped her throat raw. She came awake in stages, the one thing that anchored her in the groggy chaos was that her fingers curled against something hard, warm, alive. A heartbeat. Jake's.

He was here, in her room, in her bed.

Deirdre's eyes opened to his dark hair spilling across her pillow, the hard angles of his face lined with worry even in sleep. He was still dressed, but his tie and jacket were cast aside, and he'd opened three buttons on his shirt to loosen the collar at his throat. She felt far lighter— her legs free of the slacks she'd had on the night before.

What in the name of heaven had happened?

She raised a shaky hand to her face, felt the puffiness of eyes swollen from crying. The night before flooded back to her in excruciating detail. The interminable concert, the music that spoke to Deirdre's soul, the hopes she'd carried with her as she'd tied her blue silk scarf and climbed into Jake's truck.

But her rosy dreams of the reunion with her birth father had been shattered. She'd never be able to forget Big Jim Rivers's alcohol-reddened eyes, his cynical drawl as he'd dashed all hope that this stranger could somehow make her feel what? Whole? As if she belonged? Explain why she'd felt so disconnected and why there was such strain between Deirdre and her mother?

Your mom was nothing special....

The casual cruelty in Rivers's dismissal cut Deirdre anew. She closed her eyes, Emmaline McDaniel's image haunting her memory. Her mother's fragility, the gentleness in her, as if she was no stronger than the china ladies she'd loved to collect. Exquisite women in bonnets and hoop skirts, their delicate hands stretched out as if reaching for things only Emmaline had been able to understand. Peace. Tenderness. Quiet and serenity.

Qualities the rest of the McDaniel family had lacked.

Her mother, always trying so hard to be good, do everything right in the eyes of the rest of the world. She'd broken her marriage vows, believed she was in love with a man she could share the things she loved with. Her music, her books, her quiet teas and lace-trimmed tablecloths she'd stored away beneath the lid of the hope chest. But that forbidden love had come crashing down on her head, until the only thing left was guilt and shame and a daughter who was a daily reminder of her transgression.

Deirdre stilled, suddenly aware of the weight of Stone's gaze. His lashes so thick they threw shadows on his high cheekbones, his sensual mouth softened, unmistakably tender, his gaze racked with worry.

Alarm shot through Deirdre. Oh, God! Stone here. In her bed. Was she out of her mind? Emma was going to explode.

"What are you doing here?" she asked, bolting upright, clutching her blouse together at the throat. "Emma—"

"Emma asked me to stay."

"She what?" Deirdre gasped, disbelieving.

Jake brushed a stray lock of hair back from his jaw. "She didn't know how to talk to you but she didn't want you to be alone."

Deirdre frowned. "You told her about last night?"

"Yeah."

Shame washed over Deirdre, hot and fierce. "You had no right!"

"I was afraid you might feel that way." Stone slid his big body up until he leaned against Deirdre's headboard. He looked rumpled, pillow lines pressed into his beard-stubbled cheek. If circumstances had been different he'd have been any woman's hottest fantasy. But Deirdre felt as if he'd dragged her behind his car all the way from St. Louis last night.

Her temper sparked, blessedly familiar, centering her after the misery, the sense of helplessness that had tormented her the night before. "But you just blurted the whole sordid story out, even though you knew I wouldn't want you to."

"I had to tell her something." Stone took her hand, held it fast even when she made a halfhearted attempt to pull it away. "You looked like hell, passed out in my truck. I...carried you in. You were so damned exhausted. No wonder, after worrying about that meeting for days."

"But Emma—"

"Emma was in her room when I carried you up. She helped me get you settled in bed, got your shoes off and your slacks."

"She's the child!" Deirdre snapped. "She's not supposed to be taking care of me."

"What she is, Dee, is nearly a woman," Jake said softly, "and she loves you."

"Oh, yeah. She's plain old adored me lately." Deirdre gave a hoarse laugh. "But then, if you told her what a disaster my meeting with my birth father was, it's no wonder she was in such a helpful mood. What's that old adage? To every cloud there is a silver lining. Guess I should focus on the fact that at least one person will be thrilled with the way things turned out. It looks like Emma was right. I tore my family apart for nothing. So I could meet a man like that."

"You couldn't have known things would turn out this way." He feathered his thumb across her knuckles.

Deirdre winced, felt herself curl inward. "I keep thinking of Mom. How humiliated she must have been when Rivers left her. Just…threw her away like that. As if she was nothing. No wonder she couldn't love me the way she loved Cade."

Jake cradled her cheek with his hand, urged her to look at him. She ached from his touch, wondered how she'd survived without it so long, wondered what would happen to her now if she lost it. If she'd shrivel up inside like her mother had done, fading away a breath at a time. No. She was made of sterner stuff. She'd turn into a hard shell, look the same, act the same, but there would be nothing soft left inside.

"Whatever Rivers did to your mother, however he hurt her, Dee, it's not your fault," Jake insisted. "You're not responsible."

She knew in her head that was true. It was her heart that wouldn't believe him. "Want to hear something funny?" she asked, leaning into his warmth.

"What's that?"

"When I was growing up my mom was always saying, 'You're just like your father, Deirdre.' Now I can't help wondering which father she meant." She shuddered. "I keep thinking how I talked about being a musician all the time. It must have sickened her when I started to sing. I made fun of the jazz she was always playing, old love songs about broken hearts. Now I know why she sang them. I wish I could make it up to her. Tell her I didn't understand. I'm sorry. But it's too late. She can't hear me anymore."

Stone drew her into his arms. She laid her cheek against his chest, comforted a little by the rhythm of his heart, so steady, already so familiar. "If Trula were here, you know what she'd say?"

Deirdre managed a halfhearted smile. "Besides 'Jacob, don't you know you're supposed to take your clothes *off* when you go to bed with a lady?'"

Stone chuckled. "Emma's one stipulation for me staying the night was that I wouldn't—and this is a direct quote—jump your bones. I'm trying to abide by the peace treaty I struck with your daughter. She said she'd tear me limb from limb if I hurt you. It was plenty scary, let me tell you. The girl takes after her mother."

Deirdre's heart squeezed, grateful to know that beneath Emma's teenage drama and the strain and hurt Deirdre's search for Jim Rivers had caused, her daughter still loved her. And yet…

"Emma's nothing like me. She's so…open, so eager for life. So sure she'll find something wonderful." Wistfulness tugged in Deirdre's chest. "What if…"

She couldn't put her fears into words, not even with Jake. What if she finds disillusionment, disaster, hard falls instead of bright lights and an audience who loves her?

"She'll get her chance. Her acceptance letter from the drama school came through."

"She never told me," Deirdre said, hurt flooding through her.

"She will." He was so certain, she had to believe him. Had to remember how hurt and confused her little girl had been. Deirdre would find some way to make it up to her.

But that would be between her and Emma. No more secrets and resentment and walling each other out. She'd tell Stone all about it later. But for now, Deirdre reached for a far safer subject. "You were going to pass on one of Trula's gems of wisdom. About my mom and me, and it being too late. What would your grandmother say?"

"It's not so much what she says as it is this crazy thing she does."

"Besides painting things in colors that give sane people migraines?"

"Yeah. Besides that. Sometimes at night, Trula dances for Tony. He used to love it when she danced just for him, and she can't imagine God would mind him taking a peek from heaven now and then. She says she knows when he's watching because she hears him wolf whistling, just like he did the times he saved enough money to buy a front-row ticket to her show in Vegas."

Deirdre imagined feeling so close to someone, loving them so much that even death couldn't break the tie between them. Wondered if she'd still be able to feel Jake's heartbeat as if it were under her own skin fifty years from now.

"What if..." Stone flushed, uncertain. "What if you sang a set of your mom's favorite songs at the reunion next week?"

"You mean instead of my angry feminist fare? It was going to feel pretty weird performing Janis Joplin and Pat Benetar. 'Hit Me with Your Best Shot' is my signature song."

"Maybe it was, but not anymore." Shadows deepened

the love in Jake's eyes. "You're a woman now, with a woman's wisdom and a woman's sorrow and strength. You've lived, Dee. Survived. Hell, you've thrived."

He looked so awed by that, so proud of her. But Deirdre knew her facade was a lie. "You're wrong about that, Jake. For the past six years I've just put one foot in front of the other, that's all. I made a home for Emma. Tried to forget I ever wanted anything else."

"Emma knows that. She wants more for you. She's leaving home soon to start her life. Her only regret is that when she does you'll be alone."

Deirdre knew it was true. She'd seen the worry in her little girl's eyes, the anxious hope when she'd trapped Deirdre and Stone into that first date at Lagos.

Jake cleared his throat. "I told her I'd do my best to change all that."

"What in the world?"

Jake looked defiant, a little bit like he was steeling himself for an explosion. "Your daughter asked what my intentions are concerning you. I told her I love you. I want to marry you."

Deirdre's heart slammed against her ribs, her whole body shaky. "That's insane, Jake. I can't…"

"I'm not asking you for an answer," he asserted stubbornly. "Just give us time, a chance. You're only thirty-three years old, Deirdre. Your life's not over when Emma walks out that door. You've lived for your daughter the past sixteen years. Now don't you think you deserve to live for yourself?"

Did he have any idea how terrifying it was, looking out at the future through his eyes, seeing infinite possibilities. Chances to fail again, to mess up not only her own life, but Jake's and Emma's, as well? To be responsible for someone's happiness? Terror jolted down her spine. "Jake, I—"

He kissed her, his mouth sinfully persuasive, seductive on hers. "Let me give you what Tank and Lucy have," Jake murmured against her cheek, "what Trula and Manoletti had. I never thought that kind of happiness was possible for me. I never believed I'd fall in love this way. I'm a cynical P.I. with secrets I could never tell. But from the moment I met you, you made me want all that happily-ever-after stuff. You belong in my bed, Deirdre, wedged in between me and Ellie May. I want your face to be the first thing I see every morning and your body the last thing I feel every night. I want you to have my babies. Little girls with your attitude and my eyes."

Oh, God, Deirdre thought, stark panic washing over her. She'd just managed to raise Emma, if she could just get the girl through these last months in Whitewater the tearing suspense would be over, her fears that she'd do something wrong, damage her little girl the way she'd been damaged years ago. And yet, the thought of Jake filling her with his child made her ache with emptiness inside. She closed her eyes, picturing him with the Rizzos' tribe of little boys, Jake's smile blazing, his laughter ringing out across the sweep of backyard. "I...I don't know what to say."

Jake peered down into her face, his eyes filled with dreams she wasn't sure she had the courage to share. "Don't say anything until you're ready," he soothed her. "Just think. What would it be like if your life was more like Emma's than you realized, Dee? What if your life is just beginning?"

SHE WAS WEARING A DRESS. If anyone could call this swath of black material by a name so pretentious.

Black satin hugged her curves, a swath of creamy skin bared all the way to the small of her back, a few delicate crisscrossing straps keeping the bodice from falling down. The tops of her breasts and just a hint of cleavage swelled above the deep vee of the neckline, while just beneath the place where the center of her bra would have hit, the designer had cut out a keyhole where a tantalizing flash of forbidden skin peeped out.

Deirdre stared at her reflection in Emma's full-length mirror. What in God's name had possessed her to take her sixteen-year-old daughter shopping for an outfit to wear to the reunion? Deirdre asked herself. They'd gone out for a day's shopping at a mall an hour from Whitewater, celebrating Emma's acceptance into drama school. And Deirdre had hoped to smooth the waters even more between them, capitalize on the latest truce. But she'd had no idea that Jake Stone had created a monster the night he'd confided in Emma the hopes he had for the future.

Emma had latched on to Stone's proposal the way she'd latched on to Deirdre's breast the first time she nursed her, Emma's tiny, little rosebud mouth fastening on with a fierceness that had made Deirdre certain she'd passed to her daughter the strong McDaniel will.

Guilt stirred in Deirdre at the thought, a reminder that she hadn't been able to make herself take Stone's advice, hadn't been able to really *talk* to the Captain at all.

Except, of course, for tentative conversations that meant nothing at all. *How was Montana? Cade said the house at Linden Lane sold last Tuesday. I see you're walking without a cane, you stubborn old son of a gun. But then, I knew you would prove the doomsayers wrong.*

She'd said everything except the one thing that really mattered. And yet, she'd comforted herself the only way she could. Telling herself that maybe she didn't need to say a thing to anyone where her birth father was concerned.

No doubt Emma had blabbed what had happened with Big Jim Rivers. Part of Deirdre couldn't help but be grateful.

Especially the part of her that still had no idea what to say to the people her search had hurt the most.

"Mom, you look so hot!" Emma enthused, driving back the sobering thoughts as she zipped Deirdre up in back. "I barely recognize you!"

"Is that a compliment or a slam? I'm not quite sure."

"A compliment. Definitely." Emma grinned over Deirdre's shoulder, the mirror catching the devilment in Emma's dark eyes. "Jake's jaw is going to hit the floor when he sets eyes on you."

A flutter of anticipation brushed against Deirdre's ribs. She had to admit imagining Jake's reaction was what had made her lay down her cold hard cash for something she doubted she'd ever wear again.

"That's just the effect I was going for. My date looking like a dead fish when we head into the hall. Think how impressed the reunion Nazis will be."

"They'll be green with envy. Especially when you get up onstage and sing," Emma said, wistfully. "I wish I could be there to hear you."

"I'd think you'd be sick of hearing me practice."

"Never. I missed it so much. I'm not dumb, Mom. I know you quit your music because of me. It made me feel so bad. Like I'd stolen it from you."

"I'm the one who stole from you. My time. My attention. I don't think I'll ever forgive myself."

"You'd better, or you're going to have to take it up with me, Mom. Maybe it's time we both got over that whole guilt trip, huh? When I hear you sing, it's like…like listening to secrets from your soul. I guess I'll have to be satisfied watching the tape," Emma said. "Drew's doing all the tech work, the sound and stuff tonight. I made him promise to film your performance and tell me all about it. If only I didn't have to go on this stupid choir trip I'd have made him sneak me in."

Deirdre felt a flash of gratitude that Emma's bus was leaving an hour before the festivities began. Facing the demons of her tumultuous high school years was going to be hard enough for Deirdre. She didn't want Emma to see…

See how she was dreading it, sense that there was something Deirdre was hiding.

Deirdre turned toward Emma to tug one of her daughter's wayward curls. "I'll bet you can con Jake into giving you a blow-by-blow description. You two are getting to be thick as thieves."

"Well, if he's going to be my stepdad and the father of my future siblings…"

"Emma, don't." Deirdre warned more sternly than she'd intended. "Don't count on anything. I still don't know how I feel about…"

"Jake?" Emma filled in, undaunted. "Well, I do. You're crazy in love with him. I figure it's a good thing I'll be out of the house soon. It'll be downright embarrassing, all those yearning glances, him trying to sneak kisses. I mean, really. That last little trip the two of you took into the laundry room? You don't have to close the door to fold socks, Mom."

Deirdre's face flamed. She'd told Jake it was too risky. But he'd been so hungry for her, his eyes black with need. She hadn't been able to resist.

Sneaking away like guilty teenagers, trying to come before they got caught.

The thought was both titillating and terrifying, Deirdre's dread for her daughter still racking her nerves.

"Emma," Deirdre said, suddenly serious, "maybe I haven't been such a great example lately. For you, I mean."

Emma's eyes filled with love, tenderness. "Mom, maybe it's time I clued you in on something. I mean, I owe you, I figure, for coercing you into buying this dress. Drew and I...well, we're not having sex. And we're not going to. At least until we're older."

"But you...at Sullivan's Point..."

"I got dressed in the dark, Mom. That's why I buttoned my shirt wrong. We were just talking and kissing and... well, part of me wanted to do more, but another part of me thought about all the stuff you said and it scared me."

Relief weakened Deirdre's knees. "You mean..."

"Drew and I love each other and I know I want him to be my first. Someday. Not now."

"And this...this is okay with Drew?"

Emma's chin jutted up. "Yeah. He says I'm worth waiting for. However long it takes. How great is that?"

"That's wonderful." Tears burned Deirdre's eyes. "Oh, God. Emma, I've been so scared."

"I know. And I've been a real butthead about it. Letting you believe Drew and I were doing the dirty deed. But you've been acting so psycho about the whole dating thing, it just made me crazy. I felt like I had to fight back just to do normal stuff the rest of the kids were doing. Forgive me?"

"If you forgive me," Deirdre choked.

"No way." Emma raised one brow in Jake-esque fashion. Deirdre knew her daughter had been practicing the gesture in the mirror for dramatic effect. "Not if you make your mascara run. It took me forever to get your makeup just right!"

Deirdre gave a soggy laugh. "Have I mentioned I think you're the most wonderful creature on earth?"

"Yeah, a few jillion times. Can I give you a hint for tonight, Mom? On the romantic front, that is?"

"I can't wait to hear it."

"*Don't* talk about me tonight. Stone's already worshipping at my feet."

"Thanks for the tip."

"One more thing." Emma suddenly sobered. Deirdre felt a frisson of fear.

"Don't let what happened to you in high school ruin tonight. Getting pregnant, I mean. It all turned out great, didn't it? You and me against the world?"

"Oh, Emma." Deirdre touched her daughter's face. "You're so...so amazing. Growing up so fast."

"I am, Mom. Growing up, I mean. Maybe someday you'll even be able to tell me why..." Emma hesitated. "Why you get that haunted look in your eyes. What happened to make you afraid."

"Afraid of what?"

"Afraid to be happy. Afraid to say yes to a man who loves you as much as Jake. I keep hoping that maybe someday you'll trust me."

If only it were that simple. Deirdre's heart twisted.

"Marry him, Mom. You know you're dying to."

Was she? She closed her eyes, imagining a lifetime of Jake Stone in her bed, at her breakfast table, teasing her, fighting with her, making love to her.

It was dangerous to care that much for anybody. To let Jake in to secret, scarred places in her soul, where all her doubts and fears and flaws lived.

But Jake knew it all—the dark of her as well as the light.

Marry him... Emma's plea reverberated through Deirdre, leaving her shaken.

She kissed Emma on the cheek. "I love you," Deirdre whispered, and blessed Jake for ringing the doorbell before she cried.

JAKE CURVED HIS ARM around Deirdre's slim waist, feeling like a jungle cat marking his territory. It was all he could do to keep from glaring at the people crowding the hall, knowing what they did—how they'd made Deirdre's life hell.

But the woman whose bare back was underneath his palm was worlds different from the defiant outsider she'd been in school. She was fire and passion and quicksilver humor, a dazzling blaze in a room of lackluster mannequins trying desperately to recapture their youth.

He'd seen their faces as he'd led Deirdre onto the dance floor. He'd stared deep into her eyes to touch the center of her, the place where she was learning to love him. He'd whispered in her ear, "Dance just for me."

She'd melted against him, holding his gaze like a lifeline. Their bodies did the rest, so in tune with each other by now that the movements of the dance became just another way of making love. People stopped, stared, a circle of onlookers forming around them.

But even with the crowd watching, Deirdre hadn't gone shy on him. She'd clung to the bond between them and let him…let him show her off, keep her safe, make every man in the room wish he was the lucky son of a bitch who held her in his arms.

It was damned near perfect until a skinny redhead in an outdated prom dress called out, "Too bad Adam Farrington isn't here, Deirdre! If only he could see you now! You sure didn't dance like that with him!"

"She was too busy doing other things with him," one of the redhead's friends sniggered.

Jake had felt Deirdre miss a step, squeezed her hand as if force of will could drive the jibe out of her mind.

"You're just jealous," Lucy's neighbor Liz cut in, trying to smooth things over. "Not only does Deirdre date the homecoming king in high school, but her escort tonight is the handsomest man in the room."

Decent save. Stone had to give Workout Barbie credit. He'd been close to breaking Manoletti's first rule of chivalry. Never hit a woman. Of course, jamming a wad of crepe paper into the bitch's mouth would have been listed under "just cause" in any courtroom under the circumstances.

"Don't let them bother you," Deirdre had said, keeping her smile pasted in place. "I quit caring about that kind of catty stuff years ago."

But she shouldn't have had to put up with it at all, Stone thought grimly as they all ate dinner. And he wished the scum who'd left her open to that kind of torment was somewhere within his reach.

Stone gritted his teeth as they milled through the crowd once again. When he thought what the bastard had done to her, all the years of guilt, fear in her cold, lonely bed, killing fury filled Jake's gut.

"Did I step on your toe or something?" Deirdre asked, low. "You look like you're in pain."

Stone tried to force a smile. "You never even came close. Trula would have been proud." But he couldn't deny Deirdre's query had hit a nerve. Pain? Hell yes, he was in pain, every time he thought of Deirdre at Emma's age, pinned underneath the crushing weight of the slime who'd raped her.

"Jake?" She squeezed his hand.

He kissed her to hide the fury in his eyes.

The bandleader, a guy who looked like a bald Bob Dylan, saved Jake's ass by grabbing the microphone.

"And now, the event we've all been waiting for," the musician announced. "The vocal stylings of Whitewater High's class of '88's student voted Most Likely To Be Famous. Our very own bad girl, Deirdre McDaniel."

Stone stiffened and wondered how the Bob Dylan clone would look without his front teeth.

Jake felt a tremor go through Deirdre. She glanced up at him, for reassurance. He brushed a kiss close to her ear and whispered, "Knock 'em dead."

DEIRDRE MOUNTED THE STAIRS to the makeshift stage, her heart trying to beat its way out of her chest. It had been so long since she'd taken that solitary walk, felt the stage lights heat her face, curled her fingers around the microphone and slipped it from its stand.

She'd been so sure it would feel alien, somehow. Like relics from an archeologist's dig, interesting, intriguing, but completely foreign to the woman she was now.

Instead, the sensation floored her. It was just like coming home.

Home, the place she'd found in Jake's arms. Whole, the way she felt when he made love to her. Right after so many things she'd done wrong.

Every eye in the room was on her. She felt the tingle of excitement at the nape of her neck, a power that spread along her nerves, setting her whole body aglow with the anticipation she saw reflected in her audience's eyes.

It was crazy, intoxicating, no wonder she'd been drunk with the sensation she was feeling. No wonder she'd craved more.

But it had cost her so much. Emma's small, distraught features rose in her memory, her little-girl arms clutching so tight about Deirdre's neck she could barely breathe. *For months and months I couldn't find you, Mommy… Where did you go?*

The lights blazed into her eyes, the room beyond dark, people just shadows and shapes. Guilt flooded through her, a sick self-loathing. And for a moment she wasn't sure she could go on. Then she saw Jake move to the front of the crowd, a good three inches taller than anyone near him, his ruggedly handsome face familiar even in shadow, his teeth flashing white in a smile that was for her alone. His confidence in her almost a physical touch, a powerful belief in her that Deirdre could never feel toward herself.

Deirdre swallowed hard, holding on to the love Jake was sending.

"I'd like to open tonight with something a little different from my usual," Deirdre said into the microphone. "A Cole Porter melody my mom used to sing, 'Someone To Watch over Me.' Mom, wherever you are, this one's for you."

Deirdre bowed her head, breathed deep, waiting. The band played its intro and Deirdre reached for the music, indefinable, elusive, something so near her heart she wasn't sure she could still find it.

When her voice rippled out from her throat, Jake's heart filled to bursting with the beauty of it, the ineffable longing, the exquisite loneliness, the silvery thread of hope that made him want to close the space between them, crush her in his arms, promise her he'd love her forever. She didn't have to search for safety anymore. He'd watch over her for the rest of their lives.

A hush fell over the crowd, conversations dying, trailing off until the room was filled with nothing save Deirdre's stunningly beautiful voice.

Her spirit poured out from the lips he'd kissed, her proud, courageous, tenacious-as-hell heart bared for all to see in a way Deirdre would never be able to reveal if it weren't for the shield of her music.

She'd shown them all, Jake thought. The self-righteous bastards. She could walk out of this place with her head held high and all that fire in her eyes. And she would know, for the rest of her life, that here in this room she'd reclaimed what was her own.

Her power. Her strength. Her soul-stealing gift.

As the last notes faded, dead silence fell. Jake saw Deirdre look up, as if shaken from a trance, her eyes full of questions only her audience could answer.

Jake froze, knowing he couldn't be the first to start the applause. It would only mean something if it came from someone who didn't love her, someone with whom the music was the only bond.

After what seemed an eternity, the room exploded, a roar of cheers, a thunder of clapping, a hundred faces filled with amazement.

Jake felt the praise fill her up in places that had been empty for six long years. Saw her skin glow, her eyes sheen over with a pleasure almost as intense as when he made love to her.

His throat ached as he clapped until his palms burned, adding his praise to everyone else's. He might have been jealous if Deirdre hadn't searched him out in the crowd. Her mouth formed silent words, meant for only him and he could barely believe they were real.

Marry me.

Jake staggered back a step, trying to believe it was real.

"Encore!" someone in the crowd roared. Other people taking up the plea.

Deirdre gave a graceful bow, then whispered something to the band. She straightened, spoke into the microphone. "The last song was from my past. This one speaks to my future."

Oh, God. She'd really meant it. She'd be his wife, Stone marveled as Nat King Cole's ballad, "Unforgettable" cut straight to his heart.

He was glad the lights were low so he could blink away tears. His chest felt too small to hold all this—Deirdre's love, her triumph, his awe at the fact that this incredible woman meant to let him slip his wedding ring on her finger.

It was all he could do not to tug her down from the stage and into his arms, carry her back to his house where he could make love to her for the first time knowing she'd be his wife.

But tonight was Deirdre's night. They had all the time in the world.

A crowd of about ten people crossed in front of him, and Jake slid deeper into the crush, glad for his sudden anonymity, time to pull himself together. He heard a rustle of excitement, some late arrival no doubt. He closed his eyes, concentrating to block out any sound but the voice of the woman he loved.

The music carried him away until he felt the intrusive press of a hand on his arm.

"Jake!" the redhead trilled, smiling up with feral innocence. "Here's somebody you just *have* to meet! A real blast from Deirdre's wild past."

Jake turned in irritation, intending to shut the woman down. He found himself staring into a man's face. Curly black hair framed skin that had spent time in a tanning booth. The man had the body of a professional tennis player and a suit that cost more than Jake could earn in a month.

The new arrival offered Jake a hand adorned with a diamond the size of a lemon drop.

"Looks like I made it to the reunion after all," the man said heartily.

"This is Jake Stone," the redhead said.

"I'm sorry, but I don't remember you," the man said looking at Jake with Emma McDaniel's eyes. "I'm Adam Farrington."

Black rage roiled into Jake's gut.

"Dr. Adam Farrington," the redhead exclaimed. "Jake is Deirdre's date."

"Make that her fiancé," Jake growled. He saw a flicker of fear in the man's eyes before Dr. Rapist shuttered it away under cool superiority.

"You're a lucky man, Jake," Farrington said levelly. "Deirdre has a real talent."

"But for what?" the redhead elbowed Farrington slyly. She slanted a glance up at the stage, like a cat sucking down cream. "Now that you're here, Adam, the night is just perfect. I can't wait to tell everyone the best news of all. The medical practice Adam is planning to buy? Why, it's right here in Whitewater! Looks like our homecoming king is coming home to stay."

CHAPTER 19

HATE RAGED WHITE-HOT through Jake's veins, and in that moment he knew what Tank Rizzo had felt when he'd pulled the trigger. He wanted Adam Farrington dead.

Dead.

Before the good doctor could move back to Whitewater. Before Deirdre would have to risk stumbling into him on her way to the grocery store or the bank or Emma's school.

Dead before the innocent young woman Jake loved like his own daughter stumbled across Adam Farrington and found the man staring back at her with eyes the same as hers.

Jake's hands knotted. Damned if he was going to let the prick tear down Deirdre's new confidence, threaten the new joy she found in her body and in Jake's. Adam Farrington could practice medicine in hell for all Jake cared. But the asshole would practice it here in Whitewater over Jake's dead body.

Jake's head pounded as he counted out the number of songs Deirdre had left in the set. It gave Jake time...

To what? Grab the guy by the collar? Break his neck in front of Deirdre's whole senior class?

The bastard deserved it. Let all the prom queens and his swimsuit-model wife hear the truth about the son of a bitch. That he was lower than pond scum. A rapist who'd gotten Deirdre pregnant and left her to bear the shame of it alone.

Farrington deserved to be exposed, Jake reminded himself. Deirdre didn't. But there had to be some other way.

Jake started at the sound of a voice at his shoulder.

"Hey, Mr. Stone. I mean, Jake."

Drew Lawson. He'd told the kid to quit calling him "Mr. Stone." It made him feel like he was eighty.

So damned young, the kid smiled up at Jake as if he was a hero or something.

"I just wanted to thank you for, well, smoothing things out for me with Emma's mom. I can't figure out where I goofed up. Moms usually love me, you know?"

Funny thing about moms who've been date-raped, Stone wanted to say. *They don't trust guys who take their daughters up to make-out central.*

"Yeah, well, keep your nose clean when it comes to Emma, or you'll deal with me."

Drew must've heard the edge of danger in Stone's voice. The boy straightened as if a ramrod had been run up his spine. "Yes, sir. I promise, sir. I want you to know that I really love Emma. I'd die before I let anyone hurt her."

Jake stared at the kid's earnest face. *You'd die before you let anyone hurt her...but there are things worse than death. Living, and knowing, anytime, anyplace, your wife might have to face the animal who brutalized her. Or your stepdaughter might stumble across her father, find out...*

Emma, sweet, bright little Emma had been conceived in a night of violence while her mother screamed....

Stone looked up at Deirdre, knew how much he had to lose. She'd be mad as hell. She might never forgive him for interfering. Stone's fists clenched, remembering the sweetness of the future she'd offered. Deirdre mouthing the words *marry me.*

But what kind of a husband would he be if he let Adam Farrington walk back into her life? If Jake didn't risk losing everything to protect her, he didn't deserve to be called a man.

The kid was babbling something about the music. How he and Emma had conspired to tape Deirdre's voice tonight, send it to clubs around Whitewater, get her some gigs to sing. Emma's thoughtfulness made Jake even more determined to protect the women he loved than before.

"Drew," Jake said, "see that guy over there? The one with the redhead?"

"Yeah."

"Tell him you saw a bunch of kids put a dent in his car."

Confusion wrinkled Drew's brow. "But I don't even know which car is his."

"It won't matter. Guys like that think everybody's drooling over their wheels. Bet I could pick out his ride in about five seconds. In fact, I think I'll head out to the lot right now and prove to myself that I can."

Drew looked at him, the boy quiet, as if sensing dangerous currents just beneath the surface. "Whatever you say, Jake."

"Once you get the guy out the door, get lost, will you?"

Confusion, curiosity sparked in Drew's eyes. But something in Jake's face must have killed off the urge to ask questions.

"Right. Okay, then," Drew agreed.

Jake owed the kid big-time. But with luck Drew would never know the reason why.

Jake took one more moment to look up at Deirdre, drink her in as she poured all of her love for him into her music, memorize the new softness in her beautiful face, sweet possibilities that might never get a chance now to become real. Squaring his shoulders, Jake wove through the crowd, making his way toward the entrance where they'd come in.

Maybe there was no way to protect her from seeing the man who raped her tonight. But once the reunion was over...

You'll never have to see him again, Jake swore, loving her so much it hurt. *I swear to you and Emma, I'll keep your secret safe.*

Jake's eyes glittered like the predator he was. He'd hunted men before. He slipped into the deserted parking lot to wait.

JAKE WAS LEAVING. Slipping out of the hall for a breath of fresh air. Deirdre tried not to mind as the last measures of "Unforgettable" melted into silence.

It seemed so strange, his reaction, since she'd dedicated the song to him. And yet, Jake was as fiercely reluctant about showing his vulnerable side as Deirdre herself was. And she knew full well what it meant to him, the answer she'd given him from the stage.

Marry me.

She gripped the microphone, torn between euphoria and panic, an unnerving sense of impending doom. It wasn't safe to be this happy, a voice whispered inside her. No, she told herself firmly. She was just gun-shy because so many things had gone wrong in the past. Time would change that holding-her-breath kind of feeling, waiting for the ax to fall. Jake's love had taught her to take chances again. She trusted him. He would never let her down.

Her heart leapt, as behind her the band fired up again, the intro leading into her next song. How in God's name was she ever going to get through the rest of this set? She needed to touch Jake. To see the joy in his eyes, to feel the hot anticipation when he pulled her tight against him. Taste the passion he'd resurrected inside her when she'd thought that part of her dead.

She felt her nipples tingle, her breasts suddenly too tender, a liquid heat flowing down to settle in the place Jake had claimed for his own.

How had she ever believed she was frigid? Cold and withered and dead? The music, the dancing—just the brush of Jake's gaze was the most powerful aphrodisiac she could imagine. Left her burning, wide-open with wanting.

She almost missed her cue, fell into the song half a beat too late. She didn't care. Why had it seemed so damned important that she dazzle these people she didn't even know anymore, people who'd shunned her when she'd been at her most vulnerable and alone? She didn't care that they'd once thought she'd be some disembodied voice in their car radios.

Only one thing mattered now.

To get herself into Jake Stone's arms, into his life, into his bed before she wasted another minute worrying about things she couldn't change.

She'd never told him what he needed to hear. Not in words, simple, undeniable, infinitely precious. Words she'd never said to any man before.

I love you.

Her voice broke as her eyes strayed longingly to the door through which Jake had disappeared. She caught a glimpse of someone far too young to be part of her graduating class. Recognized Drew Lawson heading the direction Jake had gone.

An agitated man was rushing out in the boy's wake.

A jolt of something cold plunged to Deirdre's toes. Something about the way the man in the exquisitely tailored suit moved...

Stop imagining things, Deirdre warned herself sharply. *Don't be summoning up old ghosts. Adam wasn't coming tonight, remember? Or you and Jake wouldn't be here.*

She could hear Jake's voice in her head. *Don't give that bastard power over you. Not ever again. We beat it, Dee, all the pain, all your doubts, all the scars that held your loving back from me. You're mine now. Adam Farrington can't hurt you anymore.*

Just one more verse to get through, Deirdre thought, instinct alone keeping her on key. Then she'd tell the band goodbye. They'd have to play without her tonight.

She and Jake had the rest of their lives to begin.

IT WAS ALMOST TOO EASY, Jake thought, as he lounged against Farrington's car. A red Porsche 911 with vanity plates that read HOUSCLL. The good doctor had had some lackey polish it until Stone could have shaved by his reflection. This was going to be just as sweet and easy as he'd imagined.

His gaze fixed on the bank of glass doors marking the entrance, Jake felt a shock of adrenaline as he saw Drew Lawson push his way through them into the night, a taller, broader figure a few steps behind him.

Jake slouched, to disguise his height, counting on the fact that Farrington had just crossed the brightly lit foyer to blur the man's vision long enough to keep the guy from realizing who was laying in wait. Jake's lids slid to half-mast, hooding the danger glittering in his eyes.

His heartbeat slowed, schooled by years of training in martial arts, years as a cop, knowing that calm was far more powerful than frenzy. He didn't want Farrington to see the trap until its teeth were buried in the bastard's neck.

The doctor was so intent on the shape his car was in, Jake needn't have worried. Farrington rushed up, looking as if someone had poured gasoline on his baby.

"What side is the dent on?" Jake heard Farrington ask Drew. "Which way did they run?"

"I don't remember. I just…" Drew stunk at lying.

"See for yourself," Jake growled. Farrington missed a step. But fear for his car outweighed his wariness of Jake. Stupid, stupid man. How the hell did anyone like him get to be a doctor?

Farrington's eyes locked on Jake, but the years of hiding emotions from people he'd been investigating stood Jake in good stead. He schooled his features into bland lines. At least he tried to. Maybe facing down his future wife's rapist with a blank expression was beyond even *his* powers of deception.

"What are you doing out here?" Farrington asked, looking around him—the lighted parking lot and Drew's presence seemed to ease his mind. The arrogance of the man enraged Jake, the guy's certainty that he was too important, too powerful for his ugly past to touch.

"I chased the vandals away," Jake drawled.

Drew was backing toward the door, a line of unease between his brows. "My wife and daughters bought this for my last birthday," Farrington said in a good-ol'-boy kind of tone. Stone half expected the guy to clap him on the back. Farrington would have a hard time performing surgery once Jake ripped off that arm.

Farrington offered his hand. Jake ignored it, all that Zen calm shit be damned.

The doctor flushed under his tan but tried to bluff his way through. "I'm real sentimental about this car."

"Really?" Jake asked as if the guy had just tried to sell him some of his daughters' Girl Scout cookies. "If I'd known that, I probably would've gone into the gym and gotten those punks a couple of baseball bats."

Farrington's jaw dropped open in surprise. He tried to act cool, but Jake could smell the fear in him. The guy walked around the car, and Jake wasn't sure if even Farrington knew for sure the reason why. Was Dr. Rapist looking for the damage, or was he hoping that a few tons of steel and chrome would keep Jake a safe distance away?

"Funny," Farrington mused, even more off balance. "It must be the bad light back here. I...I don't see any damage."

"You don't?" Jake said silkily, rounding the door with a perplexed frown. Jake's gaze skimmed from the gleaming bumper, to the pristine passenger door. "I'm sure it was here a minute ago." Jake's leg flashed out like lightning, his hard heel connecting with the door panel, Farrington's cry of protest drowned out in the heartwarming sound of metal crushing under the force of Jake's kick.

Pain shot up Jake's leg at the impact, but he barely felt it, elation searing through him as the door caved in.

"My God, what the hell's wrong with you?" Farrington roared, his face suffusing with color. "I'll call the cops! Sue you for—"

Jake flashed a tiger's grin. "Oh, yeah. Call 'em now, you piece of scum. I'll even dial the dispatcher for you on my cell."

Farrington started to back away. The stupid fucker didn't even remember there was a concrete wall behind him. "What...what are you? Crazy?"

"Rabbit-assed crazy," Jake said, with fiendish satisfaction. "Just ask them at the station house when they pick up the call. It was a helluva scandal when they threw me off the force for shooting some poor son of a bitch who liked to beat his wife. Of course, that was eight years ago, but that's the kind of exit people tend to remember."

Fear flared in the jerk's eyes as Farrington tried to edge around the car, make a run for the building, but Jake had planned his attack too well. The prick had parked in the concrete L of a retaining wall, so no "regular people" would ding his precious car doors.

"Know what's funny?" Jake asked silkily. "That guy I shot down like the dog he was? I didn't even know him. But he pissed me off so bad that...well, I just lost all control. Imagine the damage I could do to the cowardly son of a bitch who raped the woman I love."

Farrington blanched. "It...it wasn't like that!"

"Wasn't it?"

"I was just a stupid kid. I thought...you know how girls are. Saying no when they really mean yes."

Jake grabbed the guy by the collar, jammed Farrington up against the concrete wall so hard his head smacked against it. The guy groaned. "Deirdre was sixteen years old, you rotten coward. You conned her into thinking you loved her, and then when she said no—hell, what part of *no* didn't you understand?"

"I can see...see you're angry," Farrington choked out.

Yeah, Jake thought grimly. Just you try to reason with the crazy man.

"But you'd better stop. Think. You won't get away with this. That kid who told me to come out here—he'll identify you."

"Abso-fucking-lutely," Stone said, letting the vee between his thumb and first finger press just below Farrington's Adam's apple. A doctor would have to know he was one quick shove away from death. "Drew's a great kid. He'll tell the God's honest truth. I'm counting on it."

Farrington tried to swallow. Stone could feel him sweat.

"It'll be a hell of a party in that courtroom," Stone said, "when I tell the whole town what you did to Deirdre at Sullivan's Point."

"You…you can't prove…a thing!"

"Try me. Oh, they'll put me on the stand and I'll tell the whole goddamned ugly story with your wife sitting in the front row. And then there are those poor daughters of yours. Kids at school are mean as hell once they get their hands on some juicy gossip. But then, you know that, too, don't you, Farrington? You saw just how much mercy the rest of your class showed Deirdre once your baby started growing inside her. But you didn't do a damn thing to stop them from tormenting her."

"Please. Try to understand. She was…was…you don't know her reputation! Everyone in school thought she'd slept with half the senior class!"

"But you found out different, didn't you? She was a virgin when she got in your car that night."

"I…said I was sorry. Offered to pay for an abortion. How could I even be sure the baby was mine? I mean, who knows what other guys followed—"

Stone's fist flashed out, connected with the man's jaw. The guy cried out, blood pouring from his split lip. "Wrong answer, doctor. You think after what you did to her she'd rush out to sleep with anybody else? For years she…" No. Even in Stone's fury he pulled back. "You know how close she came to spending the rest of her life alone? How hard it was for her to trust me enough to say she'd marry me?"

Adam actually looked sick. Was that guilt in the man's eyes or just plain yellow-bellied fear for his own worthless hide?

"Come on, hit me, you cowardly son of a bitch, so I can

beat you to a pulp like you deserve," Jake goaded. "Or do you only brutalize girls half your size who don't have a chance in hell of fighting back?"

"It only happened that one time," Farrington said, his excuse just making Jake madder.

"And that makes it all right? Is that your pathetic story? Did you ever even think about Deirdre and Emma when you were playing house with your wife? When you sent out family pictures with your yearly Christmas cards, did you think about the child who was missing?"

"Of course I thought about her," Farrington admitted, low. "But there was nothing I could do about any of it."

"You never approached Deirdre and offered her some of that money you like to flash around with your big diamonds and fancy cars. Never offered her a dime to support Emma?"

"I…it was difficult. I didn't want to stir things up. I have a family of my own now. I have to protect them—"

"From the truth about who you really are?"

"Who I *was*." Farrington squared his shoulders, met Jake's hate-filled glare. "I'm not that person anymore."

"Tell me another pretty story. You're the news of the reunion, the hometown football hero returning to the scene of the crime. After all you've done to Deirdre, now you're going to move back to Whitewater and remind her every day—*every goddamned day*—of what you did to her? You're going to make her live in fear that her daughter will look into your eyes and see…"

"I didn't even know Deirdre still lived in town," Farrington argued. "She was supposed to head to L.A. or New York. Everybody thought—"

"It's a lot harder to play gigs all over the country when you've got a baby to drag along."

"I…yes. I suppose it would be." Farrington sagged, raised a shaking hand to his mouth.

"You took her innocence," Jake snarled. "Raped her and left her pregnant and alone. You took away her chance for the life she wanted. But damn you, you're not going to take anything more. This is her *home*, you rotten sonofabitch. Her home and Emma's. You're going to drive out of Whitewater tonight and never show your face here again, or I swear, by God, I'll kill you where you stand."

"Jake!"

His name sliced into him like a knife to his heart. He turned.

Deirdre stood there, her face ice-white, her eyes wide with horror, Drew Lawson and half a dozen onlookers a few feet behind.

"Deirdre." Jake's stomach plunged. Devastation racked the face that had glowed with hope up on the stage such a short time before. How much had she heard? Too much. It hollowed out her eyes with despair.

And the rest of the people watching—their faces were stark with shock. The doctor wiped blood from his lip with the back of his hand.

"Want me to call the cops?" Some guy with a pot belly asked, cell phone in hand.

"That's not necessary," Farrington said quietly. "Mr. Stone and I have come to an understanding."

Jake wondered what in hell the guy was going to tell his wife.

Jake took a step toward Deirdre. She shrank back, not letting him touch her. He glanced down, his knuckles red with blood. He'd cut them on Farrington's teeth and hadn't even noticed.

But of all the people clustered around the red car, it was Deirdre who was bleeding the most, deep down, where no one but Jake could see.

"He was going to move back here," he said, trying to

reach through to where he'd cut her. "Don't you see? I couldn't let him do that to you and Emma."

But she backed away, betrayal flooding her eyes, the secret she'd kept for seventeen years stripped naked before Emma's boyfriend and the rest of the stricken crowd.

"Damn it, Dee," Stone said, desperate. "I did it for you."

"No," Deirdre said in a dead voice that chilled him. "You did it for *you*, for your stupid male pride."

"Like hell I did!"

"And now…now Emma…"

"I didn't mean for anyone else to hear." Bile rose in Stone's throat. "I love you! You and Emma. A man has to protect his own."

"Stay…stay away from me," Deirdre choked out. "I never want to see you again!"

"You don't mean that, Deirdre."

"It's over, Jake. I never should have— Oh, God. Why didn't I turn you away? Then Emma would never know…" Deirdre shattered on a sob.

Drew Lawson slipped his arm around her, and Jake feared the kid's support was the only thing keeping Deirdre on her feet.

"Dee?" Lucy's neighbor Liz said softly, her voice filled with self-blame. "If you're worried about… about anyone here saying anything to Emma…we won't." Her eyes filled with empathy. "We all hurt you enough back in school. Didn't we?" Workout Barbie glared at her classmates. *"Didn't we?"*

The others mumbled, faded back between the cars, carrying shame seventeen years old with them. Jake hoped to hell they'd lose plenty of sleep over it tonight. But no guilt on their part would ever absolve Jake of his. Or of the deadly finality he saw in Deirdre's eyes.

She turned away from him and stumbled as Drew took her to his car.

Jake stood, rooted to the spot, trying not to retch. Farrington had raped her body years ago, but Jake realized he'd just done something to wound Deirdre far worse.

He'd betrayed her. Broken her trust. In spite of all the pretty promises, in spite of all the decent intentions, it was only a matter of time now before Emma learned the ugly truth about how she came to be. Because of Jake. Because of what Jake had done.

He remembered Tank Rizzo's face after he'd learned he'd killed another man.

Jake had killed something now himself. Deirdre's belief in the future he'd promised them both.

She'd trusted him, and he'd broken that trust all to hell in this darkened parking lot. And she and Emma would pay. Grief and self-loathing wrenched Jake's heart.

Deirdre would never love him again.

CHAPTER 20

DREW PULLED HIS CAR UP in front of March Winds, the boy's face seeming years younger than before, weighed down with confusion, outrage and empathy because of what he'd heard.

Deirdre knew she should talk to him, but she couldn't squeeze words through her throat, felt as if the tiniest sound would shatter her into a thousand pieces. Oh, God, how could Jake have done that? Betrayed her? Exposed the secret of Emma's birth?

She couldn't shut out the image of the people clustered around the car, their ghastly faces, the way their eyes darted away, as if they couldn't bear to look at her.

"Ma'am," Drew said softly, touching her arm. "You're home."

But home had vanished with Jake's love, with a future far too happy for a woman like Deirdre to share.

Deirdre nodded. Opened the door. She should tell him thank-you. He'd had a shock in that parking lot, too.

But she felt too brittle.

"I...get it now," Drew said, looking at her with pain-filled eyes. "Why you were so...so mad the night Emma sneaked out. I'm sorry...for what that guy did to you. It was horrible, you know?"

Deirdre swallowed hard. "I know."

"I just want you to know that, well, Emma won't hear what happened from me. I swear it. You have to believe me. I wouldn't ever hurt her like that."

The dam was cracking, agony pouring molten red through the breaks. "Drew," Deirdre croaked. "I..."

"I know," he said, and Deirdre knew why Emma loved him, his soulful eyes filled with understanding.

Deirdre had to get out of the car. She stumbled out onto the gravel drive, glad Emma had someone like that to love her, praying her little girl would never have to live through that sweet love's stark betrayal, or have to try to keep breathing when her whole world was breaking apart.

Oh, God, Deirdre thought. She had to get away. Run...where?

A sliver of light flickered in the distance, Cade's cabin window beckoning through the garden. But she'd lost the right to go to them, hadn't she? She'd torn her family apart. Hurt them in ways that might never heal.

But she'd felt hurt like this before, the tearing grief, the feeling that nothing in all the world would ever be right again. She closed her eyes, remembering Spot's melting brown eyes, the day they fluttered closed forever.

This hurt too deep to be alone, washing away everything but her need to feel arms around her, arms that knew how much it cost her to reach out for them when in such pain.

Deirdre dashed her tears away with the back of her hand and ran—past the gazebo where she and Jake had almost made love, through the picket fence that had seemed like barbwire the past months, cutting her off from the one haven she'd been able to count on. Cade and Finn. The Captain and the twins. Her family.

Deirdre ran to where they were waiting.

An hour later she sat, curled into Cade's big leather chair, her fingers clutching a glass of Glenmorangie, the whiskey warming her veins not half so much as the people surrounding her warmed her heart.

Cade looked stricken, his handsome face pale, eyes filled with self-recrimination. "Why didn't you tell me this before?"

The Captain glared at him, his warrior face savage. "Because she knew what you'd do, you hotheaded fool. Providing there was anything left of Farrington when I was done. There wouldn't have been," he said grimly. "I know where to hide the bodies."

"I...I didn't want to tell you how...how stupid I'd been," Deirdre confessed. "I was ashamed. I should have been able to fight him off. But the car seat was so small, and he was so big. I couldn't...couldn't move enough to matter."

Finn's cheeks were wet with tears. "Neither one of you men will have to do anything," she said, arms folded protectively over the child still in her belly. "I'll kill this guy myself. Plead insanity. After all, I'm in hormone hell."

But it was the Captain who crossed to Deirdre, limping on legs still unsteady but growing stronger every day. He signaled to Cade and Finn. They slipped out of the room. Deirdre remembered how she once had dreaded being left alone with her father. She'd always feared they'd lose their tempers, kill each other. But she'd never seen this side of Martin McDaniel before.

He looked so lost, so sad. "I wish I'd been a better father to you, girl," he said. "The kind of man you could tell...

tell everything to. You shouldn't have had to carry this secret alone for all these years."

"It...it doesn't matter anymore. Now you know."

The Captain's craggy face twisted in fury and grief. "Too late to help you. But that's always been the way of it with us, hasn't it, Dee?"

"I don't..."

"Don't be making excuses for me. I've made plenty of my own over the years for why I couldn't be the father you needed me to be. Maybe it's time we both faced up to the truth."

Pain stripped Deirdre's defenses bare. "I wasn't an easy kid to love. I know that now. Mom always said..."

Martin McDaniel's face darkened, harsh with pain he had never let anyone see. "You know why she said that? What made you harder for Emmaline to love? You were like *me*. A real McDaniel, that's what she'd say, rolling her eyes in exhaustion when she didn't know what to do with you."

Martin's face softened, so tender Deirdre's throat burned. "You were such a brave little thing. Not afraid of anything on earth. It used to make me so proud, and then...scared me to death. It's one thing to be father to a son who races into the world head-on at Mach 1. A few broken bones, a bunch of stitches, and he'd come out even tougher than before. But a girl...a daughter..." The Captain's voice broke. "A man's supposed to protect his daughter. All the women he loves. You can't know how it feels in a man's gut when he fails."

Deirdre wept as Jake's haggard face rose in her memory, the anguish in his features, the determination in his eyes.

Farrington was moving back to town. I couldn't let him... didn't mean for anyone else to know...

"Deirdre—" Martin McDaniel scooped up her hand "—when I read that letter you found in the hope chest, all

I saw was how badly I'd failed as a husband. As your father. I thought…it was only right to let you go…find someone maybe better."

"He wasn't better, Daddy." Deirdre confessed. "He was awful."

Her father's mouth set, grim. "Big Jim Rivers will be a hell of a lot more cooperative next time you two chat."

Deirdre's eyes widened. "You knew who he was all the time?"

"Didn't have a clue. Maybe I didn't care enough even to notice that your mother…well, it doesn't matter anymore, does it? She's at peace. As for how I found Rivers, it's simple enough. I made Emma promise to tell me the minute that private eye of yours found the man. She's a good girl, our Emma. Came over right away." Thunder lowered on the Captain's brow. "Told me what Stone said—that your father didn't want you."

Deirdre couldn't look at the Captain, pain a lifetime old slicing through her.

Martin McDaniel's voice broke. "Big Jim Rivers and I had a 'come to Jesus' meeting. I told him I don't give a damn what he did with my wife. But I'll break his goddamn neck if he ever hurts my little girl again. He'll answer every one of your questions now. Real nice and gentlemanlike. That's for sure."

Martin looked away, a little wistful. "He did love your mother, you know. After his fashion. He told that to me. Showed me this old picture he'd carried all these years. But then, I'm sure he'll tell you about all of that for yourself when you go to see him."

"I don't want to see him. Don't want to speak to him ever again. I haven't got any more questions for him. Because…well, after what you just told me, I know every-thing I needed to know."

"What's that, little girl?"

"It was Jake who...who made me remember. Something sweet. Something good. With the two of us. When Spot died. You remember?"

The Captain looked away, his voice gruff. "Damn fool dog. Scared of the neighbor's cat."

"If he were a marine, you always said, they'd have shot him by now."

The Captain shrugged, sheepish. "I suppose I did say that. I didn't mean it, you know."

"I know. You cried when we buried him. You thought I didn't see. When you held me and told me about your friend who died in battle. You said sometimes even the best soldiers cry."

"You were always a good soldier," Martin said. "Too much like me. Scared the hell out of me. What would happen to you when your brother and I weren't around to keep watch? Guess when you fell in the hangar that night and hurt yourself so bad, I knew something was wrong. Not just in your body, but in...in our family. Between your mom and Cade and you and me. She must've felt so guilty, having to face up to what she'd done years ago. And having Cade know."

"Cade thinks that's what killed her," Deirdre confided. "Him knowing the truth."

"Your mother made her own choices. I'll tell that to your brother, too. Maybe now, years later, I understand better why she did what she did. I wasn't the best husband for a woman like Emmaline. She was so gentlelike, fragile, you know? Like a flower. And I was a fighting man with blood on my hands and dark places inside me where I could never let my family go. I wasn't the husband for your mother. And as a father for you, Deirdre, I didn't do any better. Forgive me, honey, for letting you down. And know this one thing. I love you with all my heart. Maybe not the way you needed me to, but the only way I knew how."

Deirdre's tears spilled over. "You've given me more than I needed, Daddy. Telling me tonight…I have a father who wants me."

"You're pure McDaniel, little girl. In *here*." He touched her heart. "You're mine, all right. I never doubted it for a minute, that letter be damned."

Deirdre gently went into her father's arms, mindful of how much thinner he felt, how precarious his balance. To her he still felt like the strongest man in the world.

She closed her eyes, clinging to him, her voice still broken when she whispered.

"What am I going to do, Daddy? What am I going to tell Emma?"

Her father pulled back just a little, fierce eagle eyes peering down into hers. "The truth. Cade and Finn and I…we'll be right here for both of you. But have a little faith in that girl you raised up. Emma's stronger than you think. Takes after me, she does. Pure McDaniel, through and through."

Deirdre nodded, clinging to his wisdom, his strength. Reaching deep into her family to trust.

Her father frowned. "It's what happens *after* you settle this with Emma that I'm more worried about."

Dread tightened in Deirdre's chest. "Why is that?"

"You've got a man who loves you out there somewhere who made a McDaniel-size mistake."

"Jake?" Deirdre shook her head, disbelieving. "After what he did— How could I ever…"

"Forgive him? I don't know. But I'll tell you this, little girl. I don't want you ending up like I did. Filled up with nothing but anger and blame, facing the rest of your life alone. You can have better than I did, sweetheart, if you have the guts to take it."

"Daddy, you don't understand."

"Don't I?" Sadness filled his eyes, and she glimpsed a hundred broken dreams, vulnerabilities she knew he'd never shared. He was drawing them out for her, to show her things words alone could never explain. "You can't take pride to bed, Deirdre," he said softly, cupping her cheek. "It doesn't keep you warm at night or make you laugh or give you babies to fill up the place Emma's going to leave."

"You can't...can't really mean that. Expect me to..."

"Oh, can't I?" Her father caught her chin between his fingers and smiled into her face, his eyes filled with a love she'd never have to question again. "When it comes to you, Deirdre, I believe anything is possible. You're my daughter, after all. And damned if we know when to quit."

EMMA CURLED UP beside Deirdre in the big bed where she'd shared so many childhood secrets, her heart-shaped face pale, her dark eyes brimming with tears. And Deirdre prayed that in telling her about the night Emma was conceived, she'd done the right thing.

"I didn't want you to find out the truth the way I did. From some...letter or some stranger, without me here to explain..."

But how could anyone explain what had happened that night up on Sullivan's Point? All day Sunday, Deirdre had warred with herself, trying to figure out what to do. And in spite of her father's words, his offer of support from him, from Cade, from Finn, Deirdre had known this was one conversation that needed to be between just Emma and her.

"I'm sorry I've been so…so overprotective of you lately. But the thought of you ever going through what I did terrified me so much I went a little crazy."

"A little?" It was a weak joke, and yet it made Deirdre hope. "Maybe I never really asked about my dad because, well, I was scared it was something like this. I saw it in your eyes sometimes when guys came around wanting to date you. The only time that…great big sad wasn't in your face was the past month or so, since Jake."

Jake. Just his name still had the power to hurt Deirdre, infuriate her, fill her with more loneliness than she'd ever imagined. What was she going to do about him? God, she wished she knew. The Captain's voice kept whispering in her ear, making the future so bleak without him. But tonight was about Emma. Deirdre's daughter needed all the strength and understanding her mother could give.

"Emma, I never wanted you to know about any of this," Deirdre said. "I thought I could protect you from…from, I don't know, life. But your grandpa, he helped me to see that sometimes when life knocks you down, you get up stronger, and wiser. And sometimes when you're sure that you've lost everything you ever wanted, you open your eyes and see that…that somewhere in all that ugliness, something beautiful broke through."

"I'm not a baby, Mom," Emma said, looking heartbreakingly young. "You don't have to try to make me feel better."

"I'm not, Emmaline Kate. I swear."

"Did Jake really…well, split the guy's lip?" Emma asked.

"And kicked in his car door," Deirdre tried not to feel even a hint of satisfaction that Jake had. "But it wasn't Jake's right."

"Then whose was it?" Emma asked. "Somebody has to

take care of you. You're always having these delusions of grandeur, thinking you can take care of yourself."

Deirdre pulled back halfheartedly, playing their game of mock outrage. But tonight their old pattern fell flat. She finished it anyway, informing her daughter, "I've done just fine taking care of myself for the past sixteen years, thank you very much."

"No. You haven't." Emma sobered, and for an instant Deirdre saw the ten-year-old waif she'd left behind, a fairy child who'd crashed to earth on a bewildered Cade's doorstep. "You only let *me* love you. Everybody else you held away. Grandpa and Uncle Cade and Aunt Finn. Even them. But Jake...you let him in. It made me feel jealous and mad and then—" Emma faltered, fell silent.

"Then what?" Deirdre urged.

"All of a sudden I knew what you meant about hating Romeo and Juliet."

"What?" Deirdre shook herself, surprised into giving an exasperated laugh. "I can't believe this, Emma, but somehow you managed to bring this whole emotional disaster back around to you standing in the middle of a stage."

"Well, I can't help it. It fits, you know? I mean, before Romeo meets Juliet he's dying of love for some other chick—that Rosalind, whoever the heck she is. And sure, with all the excitement of the masquerade ball and everything, he thinks Juliet's his soul mate."

"Yeah. I remember that much. I read it in the Cliff's Notes."

"Your question is what would have happened to all that star-crossed lover crap if they hadn't died? A month later when Romeo had to take the garbage out of the castle and some pretty milkmaid walked past and blew him a kiss? Well then, I guess we'd get the *real* story."

"Emma, I'm not following this at all."

"Jake would never even see her, Mom. The milkmaid or Rosalind or even Catherine Zeta-Jones if she walked right down Main Street. In Jake's eyes, there's only you."

Deirdre tried to draw a steadying breath. It hurt too much. Pressed too hard on the place Jake had left behind. "Oh, Emma," she said, shaken. "I'm not...after what happened...I don't think I can..."

"Mom, did you ever wonder why he did it?" Emma asked, her eyes big and soft and pleading. "I mean, why Jake went and beat up on that guy?"

Bitterness still welled up in Deirdre's throat. "His pride. He..."

"He knows you, Mom," Emma insisted. "Knows how you are. He'd have to figure if you found out what he'd done, you'd never forgive him."

"I suppose that's true. I hadn't thought of it that way. Somehow that just makes it all the worse."

"Mom, think. He was willing to give up you loving him, to keep you and me safe, the only way he knew how. If that's not real love, what is?"

Deirdre peered down into her daughter's face, knowing Emma was forever changed by what she'd learned tonight, and fearing how that knowledge might haunt her tomorrow.

But even more certain than that was one thing more. Somehow, through all the craziness, all the uncertainty, all of the flat-out mistakes Deirdre had made as a mother when she herself was just a kid, Deirdre had raised one hell of a daughter. Emma was wiser, more together than Deirdre had ever even hoped to be at her daughter's age. Somehow Emma would be able to take what she'd learned tonight and figure things out.

Fear nudged Deirdre. She'd always been a little scared,

thinking of her Emma on her own in a big city like New York. But no matter what happened to Emma's dreams of the stage, Deirdre's little girl was going to be all right.

Deirdre had made certain her baby knew the one thing Deirdre had never been sure of.

Emma knew her mother loved her.

"Now, why don't you get out of here and write a better ending than the one I'm gonna have to perform onstage?" Emma challenged. "I mean really. 'And they all died.' It completely sucks. What's so romantic about that?"

"I...I guess romance was never my strong point. I was more of a...a murder and mayhem, ghosts and deadly Lady MacBeth kind of kid."

"Whoa!" Emma cried. "Don't even be saying that name a few weeks before I step onstage. How many times have I told you, actors are superstitious? We call it *The Scottish Play.*"

"I'm sorry. I forgot."

"Good thing Trula's going to be in the family. She'll straighten you out."

"Don't count on...well, anything," Deirdre cautioned. "I just don't know if Jake and I can...well, fix things."

Deirdre slid out of bed, slipped on her shoes.

"Mom," Emma said as Deirdre glanced toward the door, her hand reaching up to smooth her hair. "Don't even bother with a comb. You look like road kill, but Jake won't care. He'll be so glad to see you. Get out of here, already."

Deirdre turned back to the bed and hugged Emma tight, drank in the feel of her, the smell of her, rejoiced in the solid way love settled into the deepest reaches of her mother-heart.

She cupped her daughter's face in her hands and let her own tears rain down her cheeks, unashamed. "Take this with you, wherever you go. To New York, to the stage, or to a little house with Drew Lawson to love you. Emma, you were the making of me."

Tears trembled in Emma's eyes. She shrugged. Her voice quavered. "Well, Mom. Just don't forget you are a work in progress. I'm expecting Stone to take over from now on."

Deirdre gave a watery laugh and headed for the door.

THE BUNGALOW WAS DARK, but she knew Jake was awake, trying to remember how to live alone. Deirdre pulled out a credit card and fiddled with the lock, thanking God for the one useful talent a boyfriend from her nightclub days had taught her.

She didn't want to risk Jake ignoring the knock on the door. She knew he'd never suspect it was her. He'd been sure she'd stop loving him the instant he smashed his fist into Adam Farrington's face.

The lock gave and Deirdre slipped inside, even Ellie May not realizing anyone had broken in. No wonder the dog had washed out of the police force. She was useless for anything except adoring Jake Stone. Maybe Deirdre and the dog had something in common after all.

Deirdre padded to Stone's bedroom, but he wasn't there. She wandered the house, a dull panic knotting in her throat at the notion that he was gone. Where on God's Earth could he be?

Ellie May nosed her way out of Stone's office, the room where Deirdre had first seen him. And from the mournful expression on the dog's face, Deirdre knew he was nowhere to be found.

Where would he go? Jake, with his heart in pieces and his dreams shards of glass? To Trula's? To the Rizzos'? No, from the start that's how Jake and Deirdre had been alike.

Two loners, too proud to let anyone see where the fault lines lay in their hearts. Too fiercely independent to need anyone… Until they'd dared to need each other.

"I'll find him, Ellie," Deirdre promised, wandering back out into the night.

BY THE TIME SHE RETURNED to March Winds, alone and dejected, the river was shrouded in darkness so deep Deirdre's hands began to shake. She eased her car up the driveway, wondering how she could have been so wrong. She'd gone everywhere she'd thought he might be, but his car hadn't been at any of them. It was as if he'd dropped off the earth.

Maybe she should head back to the bungalow and sit on his steps until he came home from wherever he'd gone to lick the wounds she'd dealt him.

He had to come back home to feed Ellie May.

A bump in the gravel jarred Deirdre. She blinked in surprise, glimpsed a white truck parked in the shadows. She barely remembered to put the van in Park before she leapt out of it.

Was Jake inside the house? Where…

No. She knew in an instant where he'd be. Where the magic lived—where wounded hearts healed. Where love was reborn and vows were spoken from hearts too full for words. And where new lives began. The gazebo Cade had built more out of love than from simple boards and nails.

She ran through the shadowy garden. Her heart leapt as she recognized the lone figure just visible in the gazebo, his silhouette illuminated by the glow of dock lights from the river beyond.

Jake. Hands on hips, head arched back, he stared out into the river's treacherous currents. But Deirdre knew no matter how badly she'd hurt him, jumping in was the last thing on his mind. He had too many other people he had to look out for—Trula and the Rizzos. And God knew how many other people he'd helped over the years, people like Deirdre, desperate for answers only he cared enough to find.

She slowed as she saw him stiffen, knew he'd heard her. His intuition was too keen not to know who she was.

"Jake?" She laid a hand on his shoulder, felt how rigid his muscles were.

He didn't look at her. She moved, where she could see the dock lights spilling down his face, exposing him without mercy. The hard planes and angles of Stone's cheeks were wet with tears.

"You know the first time I saw you here, in this garden?" Stone asked softly, as if he were still a thousand miles beyond her reach. "It was the night Cade and Finn got married."

"You were at March Winds that night?"

"I read about how they were going to have a Civil War–style wedding in the papers. And I just…suddenly I was here, you know? Parked out on the main road, walking through the darkness, watching you. I knew what you thought of me, Deirdre. You'd made that plain enough. And yet…there was something about you I couldn't forget. As if…I already loved you somewhere back in time. I just had to be reminded."

His voice cracked. He braced his hands on the gazebo's white gingerbread trimmed rail, his face so wistful it broke her heart. Jake…on the outside, in the dark, looking at love he thought he could never have because he'd sacrificed any chance of complete honesty when he saved his best friend's wife and children. And, Deirdre thought sadly, because she'd despised him.

"Oh, Jake," she breathed, aching.

"You were all so damned happy that night, setting those little lights off to float down the river."

Deirdre sighed at the memory. Back then she'd felt so alone. With nine months of abandonment to make up to her little girl. Her father and brother fighting their anger toward her. Anger Deirdre knew she'd deserved.

But Cade and the Captain had worked their way through it. Helped her make a good life here in the town she'd once hated.

"Emma said the lights were wishes carried off so they'd come true. Everyone was supposed to make one. But I was too...too scared to make any wishes of my own."

"Want to know what I wished that night?" Jake grated out. "That I could love you. But you hated me then. Probably felt about the same way you do now."

"I don't hate you."

"Yeah, well, you don't love me anymore, either. Hell, I don't blame you. I had no right to do what I did to Farrington." He turned blazing eyes on her. "But I'm glad I did it. You hear me? Glad. I'd do it again to make sure that sonofabitch never gets near you or Emma. But I— God, Deirdre, I just wish I could forget everything I'm going to miss. Emma playing Juliet, and walking her through the garden to marry a man she loves, the way I wanted to marry you. Here, in this gazebo where you claim magic lives. I'm going to miss it all now. Your face when I put my ring on your finger and the way your eyes shine when I'm inside you. And those babies we were gonna have. They're so damned real to me."

"They're real to me, too, Jake. My dad made me see that...and Emma...they made everything we were going to have together so real I had to find you to say...I'm sorry."

It broke her heart that even her tentative apology couldn't make him hope. "I'm sorry, too," Jake said. "I blew it. I know. I can't take it back. I wouldn't if I could. But if I could...could give you back the night he raped you...make love to you the first time, the way it should have been... I'd sell my soul, Dee, for that chance."

Deirdre felt enchantment close around her, so strong in Cade's white gingerbread rails. The power of love in this place, so real. She reached for healing, knew that once again this brave, honorable, infuriating man had shown her the way.

She took his hand in hers, held it to her cheek and looked up into Jake Stone's eyes. "I know everyone at school thinks I'm wild," she said, her cheeks burning with shyness, "but I...want the first time to be special. With a boy who loves me."

Jake frowned in confusion and pain. "Deirdre, don't—"

"Do you, Jake?" she asked, her heart in her eyes. "Love me?"

"Yes. I love you, damn it!" He swore. "I..." Realization dawned in his eyes, disbelief giving way to wonder. A shy, earnest gentleness softened his rugged face. His voice dropped low, so tender Deirdre's heart leapt. "You really...really want me to..."

He touched her face, his eyes smoke, his hand so warm. She nodded shyly against his hand, repeating the words she'd said to him before. "Don't...make me say it."

"I won't...won't hurt you," Jake said thickly. "I promise. I'll stop if you—"

"No. Don't stop. Never stop loving me, Jake. Promise?"

Jake took her in his arms, lowered her gently to the floor of the gazebo. Moonlight danced through the white painted rails, illuminating the riverbank where Emma's wishes had floated free six years before. The sweet night air gleamed with a thousand dreams the gazebo had sheltered for other lovers, as Deirdre and Jake spun new magic of their very own. Jake kissed Deirdre with all of his heart.

He loved her as though it was her first time.

The first night of forever.

EPILOGUE

THE HEAD NURSE of the maternity ward peered at the motley crew invading her waiting room, the myriad of laugh lines in her crinkly face reminding Emma of one of her cousin Amy's little dried apple dolls.

"What is it about you McDaniels that you always have to do the unexpected?" Mrs. Haskins demanded, peering over the top rim of her glasses at Emma and the twins. "Tonight it looks like my maternity ward is being invaded by creatures from the Black Lagoon."

"It's Halloween, Mrs. Haskins," Amy McDaniel explained earnestly.

Her twin, Will's, eight moveable spider legs drooped, a little dejected. "Yeah. We're s'posed to be having a party, with this real cool Frankenstein piñata Uncle Jake hung up in the gazebo. You know, that one where everybody's always kissing in?"

"Like you kissed Lisa Allison?" Amy inquired sweetly. Will howled and slugged his sister, but Amy didn't miss a beat. "Daddy saw it an' said Will had better wait awhile before he kissed anyone else, 'cause there's something about that place that gets people babies. Uncle Jake told Mommy she was right about it being lucky. That's where they got this baby from."

"A new baby. *That's* good, right, Emma?" Amy said, determined to look on the bright side.

"And I was home when it came." Emma glowed with pleasure, knowing that even her beloved drama school wouldn't make up for missing this event. She was a real New Yorker now, from the top of her curls to the tips of her toes, but that didn't change the fact that she was a hundred percent McDaniel, and hated to miss a surprise.

"What *kind* of baby is it?" Will asked. "That's what matters most. S'pose you better tell us what it is, Mrs. Haskins." Emma grinned as he squared his shoulders, looking as if the nurse might just spray him with a giant can of bug spray.

Mrs. Haskins smiled. "It's a girl."

The news swirled through Emma, delighting her almost as much as the reactions of the family around her.

"Aw, cripes!" Will wailed. "Not another girl! I'm drownin' in 'em! Can't we pick a different one?"

Cade scooped his son into his arms and winked at Emma. "Sorry, partner. It doesn't work that way."

"You've got to cherish the ladies," Captain Martin McDaniel warned his grandson. "Looks like you'd better come over to my apartment so I can teach you some manners, young man."

Emma's heart warmed, thinking of the rooms her uncle had built on to the cabin so the Captain could be independent and yet close at hand to raise up all of those grandbabies.

"Yeah," Amy shook her finger under her twin's nose. "And you'd better not be insulting us girls, either, right, Emma? Remember what Daddy said when we got the last girl? That he named her after the strongest woman he ever knew. Maybe she'll beat you up when she grows a little."

"As if!" Will howled. "The Deester can't even walk yet. Let alone punch someone big as me!"

Finn swept in, her two-year-old daughter wriggling in her arms. "We give this child a perfectly lovely name, and what do they call her?" she asked Emma, rolling her eyes. "The Deester. What's wrong with Deirdre Skye?"

"She's a girl. That's what's wrong," Will complained, looking to Emma for sympathy. But for once she forgot comforting her cousin's small woes.

The double doors to the waiting room opened, and Emma's heart leapt as a tousled, exhausted, ecstatic Jake Stone entered the room.

Will looked to his uncle for sympathy. "Uncle Jake, aren't girls nothin' but trouble?"

"Not this little angel," Jake said, and Emma's heart squeezed as she saw how tenderly he cradled his newborn daughter. "She's going to be just like her mama."

"Lock the doors, hide the keys!" Cade laughed.

"Batten down the hatches," the Captain howled.

"Hey, watch it, you two clowns!" Emma elbowed her way between them. "That's my sister!" Emma crossed over to her stepfather, and he held the baby out for her to see.

A miracle. So brand-new. Emma touched her tiny hand in wonder. The baby curled her fingers into a fist, bopped Emma square on the nose.

"Ow!" Emma laughed in protest, pressing her hand to her nose.

"That baby's a McDaniel all right," the Captain predicted with pardonable pride.

"She's a Stone," Trula insisted. "Mix that kind of blood together and you'll get a Thoroughbred, through and through—isn't that right, Emma?"

Emma glowed as Trula hugged her, the grandmother Emma had never had.

"A Thoroughbred or a great idea for a new Stephen King novel," Cade teased. "Deirdre would pick Halloween to have a baby."

"Oh, yeah. That Halloween thing," Jake said. Emma saw him shake his head as if to clear it. "She made me promise to tell Will and Amy she'll buy them all the candy they want as soon as she gets back on her feet."

"Can I see Mom?" Emma asked, glancing toward a small package on one of the waiting room's veneer end tables, the tissue wrapped around it so old and fragile it crumbled at the edges.

"She was asking for you," Jake said, loving Emma every bit as much as the little bundle in his arms.

They slipped into the hospital room, found Deirdre, sitting up in a rocking chair, her face tired, but aglow with a peace still rare in Jake's restless wife. Draped in the robe he'd bought her, her hair a wild tangle, she'd never been more beautiful in Jake's eyes.

"I've got a present for you," Emma said shyly, crossing the room to give her mom a kiss. "I hope you don't mind."

Deirdre smiled up at her oldest child. "Why on earth would I mind, sweetheart?"

"Because I—" Emma made a nervous little face "—I looked inside the hope chest just to see if maybe…there was something there."

Deirdre tried not to show a sudden flutter of unease. "I'm surprised you even thought of it."

"I just…if I had a daughter and knew I was dying like Grandma Emmaline did, knew I'd never see my grandbabies, I would want to leave something behind so that when the time came, they'd know I loved them. Wouldn't you?"

"Yes. I would." Deirdre's eyes misted, touched by Emma's intuition, her love. The knowledge Emma was growing up. Deirdre prayed that whatever Emma's future held, someday her little girl would know happiness as sweet as Deirdre knew right now.

Emma laid the tissue-wrapped bundle in her mother's lap. Deirdre's fingers trembled as she touched the crumpled white bow. "It's silly, I know. But I'm almost scared to open it," Deirdre said softly. "I'm afraid to ruin today."

Emma squeezed her hand. "Don't worry, Mom. I checked it for explosives before I brought it in the hospital."

Deirdre chuckled and untied the bow, folded back the tissue. Her breath caught, folds of hand-crocheted lace and yards of thin white batiste tumbling over her hands. It was a hand-stitched christening gown, Deirdre realized, the garment more exquisite than any Deirdre had ever seen. Emmaline McDaniel's precise stitches made rows of narrow little tucks down the front, the bodice fastened by tiny pearl buttons. The lace was delicate as a fairy's wings. Deirdre ran her fingers over it, reverently, feeling as if she could almost touch her mother's face. Jake picked up the exquisite matching bonnet, his big masculine hand making it look too tiny to be real.

"There's a note, Mom," Emma said. "Tucked inside the bonnet."

Deirdre's heart skipped a beat. She couldn't help but remember the last note she'd found in the cedar chest. Now, almost three years later, she could only bless the day she found it, as she rejoiced in all the love it had so unexpectedly brought into her life. Jake and their new baby, the Captain, all questions shoved aside, and Cade, relieved of the secret burden that had so changed him.

She'd even found her music again thanks to the recording Emma had sent out. Spent two Saturday nights a month singing in clubs while Jake sat at the nearest table, watching her, waiting to sweep her away to find magic again in the gazebo that now sheltered not only Cade and Finn's love story but the most beautiful lines of Deirdre and Jake's, as well. Maybe, Deirdre hoped, just maybe, someday Emma would add a chapter of her own. Deirdre thought of her gentle mother, so romantic, how she would have loved the flower-covered gazebo as much as they all did. Maybe even more.

Deirdre wished Emmaline McDaniel could be right here with them all to see how they'd healed. How they'd grown. The truth Emmaline had feared would destroy her family had made the McDaniel clan stronger.

Deirdre slipped the note from beneath the delicate cloth, ran her fingertips over her mother's sweet lily of the valley stationery.

Dear Deirdre,

I tuck this in your hope chest with a full heart, praying that you will have forgiven me enough to find this by the time you have a baby of your own. Maybe right now you're looking at a new life, have the chance for a new beginning.

I wish with all my heart I could be with you on this happy day, and that maybe the child in your arms would give us both a chance to love each other better. But the doctors say it isn't likely I'll live to see my wild girl all grown-up.

So, I make this for you now, as time slips like the thread through my fingers, and try to think what bits of wisdom I'd whisper in your ear if I was able.

Be just a little selfish. Don't lose yourself as I did. Show your baby how to be a strong woman someday.

Remember never to love anything that can't love you back. Be it a china figurine like the ones you broke as a little girl or a ghost from your past. I spent your whole life, Deirdre, aching for a man I'd given up before you were born. Spent my life grieving for him, holding back love that should have gone to you.

If I had it to do over again, I'd do everything so differently. I'd pack away my foolish wishes for a daughter to share teacups and dolls with and I'd follow you out to the yard, let you show me who you are, not who I planned for you to be.

I loved you with all my heart, but you were out of control, my little girl. A renegade just like your father. In the end, maybe it was your strength that scared me, or chastened me because I had so little of my own.

Be happy, Deirdre. Love boldly. Be true to yourself. I know in the end that you will. Tell your baby, someday, about the grandmother who locked all her own hopes away in a cedar chest by the window, and never took them out where they could breathe.

Hope, scattered like the rainbows in the crystal vase you held up to the sun when you were such a little girl. You dropped the crystal, shattered it, and yet it only made more facets to shine, more hopes to glisten, more rainbows to fill the room. So maybe, even then, you were far wiser than I.

Tears filled Deirdre's eyes. "Emma...thank you for this gift. I might never have looked. She must have been working on it all the time while I was right there in the same house, but I didn't even notice." Deirdre touched the delicate cloth, felt it brush her skin, like her mother's benediction.

"I was so sure she thought I was hopeless," Deirdre confessed. "But somehow, even when I was at my most impossible, she never lost faith that I'd figure life out somehow."

"Isn't that why they call it a hope chest?" Emma asked, sitting gently on the bed.

"I guess it is." Deirdre smiled up at Emma, reached out a hand to Jake. He laid their tiny daughter in her arms.

"So, what are we going to name her?" Jake winked at Emma. "Your mom kept insisting the baby would tell us who she was when she got here."

Deirdre looked from her new daughter's wizened little face to Emma's blooming beauty to Jake. "Her name is Hope," Deirdre said, peering into her husband's eyes. "Because that's what you've given me."